"You'll sigh, you'll cry, and you'll grin yourself silly as this independent and cynical heiress finally gets her duke."
—Virginia Heath, author of *Never Fall for Your Fiancée*

"Fans of Courtney Milan and Scarlett Peckham will enjoy this the Gilded Age Heiresses series opener."
—*Library Journal*

PRAISE FOR *THE DEVIL AND THE HEIRESS*

"A sparkling jewel of a love story, full to the brim with Victorian wit, romance, and heart-stopping heat. Road trips in a carriage and four don't get much sexier than this."
—Mimi Matthews, *USA Today* bestselling author

"Dear Reader: if you love great characters—sexy rakish heroes and strong heroines—and an emotional story set in Victorian England, *The Devil and the Heiress* is the historical romance for you!"
—Terri Brisbin, *USA Today* bestselling author

"St. George's characters are wonderfully nuanced, and their chemistry is all the more enticing for it. It's a pleasure to watch this complex duo navigate their relationship."
—*Publishers Weekly*

"A rich, compelling, and beautifully written romance. St. George brings us the story of Violet Crenshaw, an American heiress with distinctly modern ideas about love and marriage."
—Elizabeth Everett, author of *A Lady's Formula for Love*

"Captivating . . . A delightful romance between a man who learns to be vulnerable and a woman who discovers her strength."
—*Kirkus Reviews*

TITLES BY HARPER ST. GEORGE

The Gilded Age Heiresses

THE HEIRESS GETS A DUKE
THE DEVIL AND THE HEIRESS
THE LADY TEMPTS AN HEIR

The
LADY TEMPTS
AN HEIR

HARPER ST. GEORGE

JOVE
New York

A JOVE BOOK
Published by Berkley
An imprint of Penguin Random House LLC
penguinrandomhouse.com

Copyright © 2022 by Harper Nieh
Excerpt from *The Duchess Takes a Husband* by Harper St. George
copyright © 2022 by Harper Nieh

A JOVE BOOK, BERKLEY, and the BERKLEY & B colophon are
registered trademarks of Penguin Random House LLC.

ISBN: 9780593197240

First Edition: February 2022

Printed in the United States of America
1 3 5 7 9 10 8 6 4 2

Book design by George Towne

To Marsha Sherman

Sometimes you find family when you didn't know you were looking for it. Thank you for always being there for us.

Prologue

❖

It takes two flints to make a fire.
LOUISA MAY ALCOTT

LONDON
MAY 1875

Lady Helena March was inclined to dislike Maxwell Crenshaw without even having met him. There were several reasons for this, but climbing quickly to the top of her list was the fact that he was tardy. A glance at the clock on the mantelpiece revealed him to be a quarter hour later than she would have preferred. They would never catch up to his runaway sister at this rate. As she paced the confines of her drawing room, she considered that she may have to leave without him.

The Crenshaws from New York, excluding the daughters August and Violet, had revealed themselves to be the very worst sort of social climbers. Not only had they touted their extraordinary fortune to make social connections, but they had used their own daughters to further their aspirations. As the heir to the Crenshaw Iron Works fortune,

Maxwell Crenshaw should have been able to stop his parents from serving up his sisters to the impoverished noblemen of London. But from what she could tell, he hadn't, which likely meant that he supported his parents' machinations. Perhaps she *should* leave without him. If he intended to marry Violet to a stranger for a title, then he may very well prove to be a hindrance.

"Mr. Crenshaw." Helena's butler, Huxley, announced the man's arrival from the door of her drawing room.

She whirled from her pacing as a man entered behind him. Maxwell Crenshaw was nothing like she had expected. Tall, at several inches over six feet, broad in the shoulder, and thick in the chest, he should have seemed brutish, or at least unrefined; but he wore the clothes of a gentleman well. The impeccable tailoring of his coat meant that the fine garment hugged his shoulders without pinching or pulling, and it tucked in fashionably at his waist just enough to illustrate his lean frame. He walked into her drawing room with the graceful stride of someone who knew his own size and was comfortable with it. There were no hunched shoulders on this man to minimize the space he filled in her doorway.

None of that was a surprise, really. He was probably one of the wealthiest men she would ever meet. It stood to reason that he would be well turned out. What surprised her was the intensity he carried about him. It was his eyes. Those eyes pinned her in place across the distance, like a falcon sighting a target. Helena had been assessed in the matter of a few seconds, and she had no idea what he had made of her. His face remained impassive. All she knew was that her mouth was dry and nerves rumbled pleasantly in her belly, which was ridiculous. She had stopped allowing men to affect her long ago. She wasn't about to let this one—a man who would use his sisters to further his own ambitions—change that.

"Good morning, Miss . . ." His voice was pleasantly deep

with a rich timbre, his American accent putting a soft edge on the words even as his tone was one of impatience.

"Lady Helena March." Never in her life had she been happier to use her title. "You are late, Mr. Crenshaw." The note she had sent earlier that morning to his parents' rented home on Grosvenor Square had indicated that he should come right away.

An eyebrow arched as he walked farther into the room. "Did we have an engagement I missed? My apologies. Back home we use calling cards and invitations, not cryptic messages left unsigned." He held up the note she had sent him. "I'll have to become accustomed to the way you do things here."

Touché. His censure was probably warranted. Her note had simply read: *Come alone. Leave immediately. 43 Berkeley Square.* She had not dared sign it in case someone aside from the boy she had hired to deliver it had read it. She had even hesitated about adding her house number but had realized having Mr. Crenshaw walking aimlessly around Berkeley Square would have been even more unwise. No one was supposed to know she was in town, but she had needed to see him, so it was a risk she'd had to take.

"Thank you for coming," she said, keeping her voice measured. "I regret that I could not reveal more in my note, but I could hardly take the chance that someone might see it." She doubted very much his parents knew her address on sight.

"Someone? Do you mean my parents?"

It was no use pretending to approve of the Crenshaw couple. While Helena was inclined to believe Maxwell Crenshaw was involved in his parents' scheming, it would be unfair for her to assume so outright. "Yes, I regret to say."

"Lady Helena March, if I recall correctly, you are the one my parents claim accompanied my sister to Bath."

Helena had no true knowledge of what had preceded Violet running away. She had been at her cottage in Somerset when the Crenshaws had written to inform her that they were telling everyone Violet had succumbed to a case of the nerves and accompanied her to Bath. The truth was that Violet had simply left one day, and Helena suspected the girl was fleeing from the marriage to a British noble-man her parents were planning. While she wasn't happy they had used her without her permission, she had returned immediately, and discreetly, to London to help find Violet. She had befriended the Crenshaw girls in the short months she had known them and wanted no harm to come to either of them if she could help it.

"I think we both know that story is contrived. And 'Lady Helena' is sufficient."

His lips thinned into a line of displeasure. "Do you know where Violet is?"

"No, but I have a good idea. If you please, we should get going." She gestured to her travel bag beside the drawing room door. "We can talk on the way." She had made arrangements for them to leave on the next train to Edinburgh, but they needed to get going if they hoped to make it with time to spare.

"We're going together?" The prospect of this seemed to astound him.

"Yes, we have no choice. Huxley has sent for the carriage to be brought round." She had given her butler instructions to send for the carriage as soon as Mr. Crenshaw arrived.

His shoulders squared, and he somehow seemed to stand even taller. "Lady Helena, I don't mean to be rude, but I must insist on you telling me what the hell is going on before I go anywhere with you."

It was in that moment that Helena realized that she was not dealing with an ordinary gentleman, not even an ordinary *American* gentleman. Because while his obstinance should annoy her—and it did—it also made something long dormant inside her stand up and take notice. Something that wanted to rise to the bait of his challenge. Reconciling herself to the fact that they would need to have a discussion about her plans before leaving, she rang for tea and wondered at the risk of an extended amount of time in this man's presence.

Tugging off her gloves, she took a seat on the settee, organizing her thoughts as she pondered the appropriate way to begin. It was only after she had settled herself that she noticed he was still standing there. "Please, have a seat."

Mr. Crenshaw gave her a dubious glance before looking back at the chair next to him. He clearly believed it too insubstantial to support his brawny frame. "A Chippendale original from 1773."

"Impressive," he said without moving.

Stifling an eye roll, she couldn't quite keep the derision from her voice as she said, "I meant that it has held countless men, most of them with conceit considerably larger than your own."

He frowned, his eyebrows pulling together in a stern glower that she found most appealing, as he lowered himself into the chair, which held up beautifully beneath him. Once he was settled, she launched into her theory that Violet had run away because of an overly aggressive suitor, and that she believed he would find his sister in the company of the Earl of Leigh. Their task would be to locate them before the consequences of his sister's actions were irreversible.

"Where would he take her?" Mr. Crenshaw asked.

"To marry her in Scotland, I assume," she answered. "Your family is fairly notorious here, and it would be known they do not consent to the marriage. Perhaps Scotland offers a refuge if the marriage is challenged."

"To Gretna Green? Doesn't that only happen in Gothic novels?"

"No, not Gretna Green. There is a residency requirement now for marriage. He owns property in Scotland, and I assume coin can ease any other restrictions they may encounter."

"How long will it take them to reach Scotland by carriage?" he asked.

"They should be there now."

"Now! Why have you done nothing up till now to stop this?"

The nerve! At the end of her patience—*she* was the one trying to help *him*, after all—she came to her feet. "Your parents were only kind enough to inform me of Violet leaving a few days ago. I wasn't even aware they were using me as her alibi until that time. Had I known earlier, I could have done something. I only returned to London yesterday, and when I called on your mother, she mentioned you would be arriving last night. Forgive me for not trusting her— someone who is highly suspect in her reasoning—with this information. I hoped you would prove vastly more rational."

Despite her anger, her stomach tumbled pleasantly as his brows drew together in another scowl. His face was a granite mask of masculine annoyance. How did such a forbidding expression make him look so irresistible? He was like a stern, scowling Zeus, and she was not at all put off by having that heated passion focused solely on her. She did have to look away, however. Having spent the past five years avoiding any sort of romantic sentiment, she was unprepared for her reaction to him.

"Fine. It is done."

"Good." She made a show of putting on her gloves while waiting for her heart to return to a normal pattern. "Let us leave for King's Cross. I already secured us tickets for Edinburgh, and the train leaves in an hour."

"By all means." He indicated she should precede him out into the corridor.

As she walked, she was absurdly aware of his hulking presence behind her. It was as if he weighted the atmosphere with his burning, angry intensity. The next several days in his company would be interesting, to say the least.

Chapter 1

❦

*Tyranny follows the tyrant. Woe to the man
who leaves behind a shadow that bears his
form.*

VICTOR HUGO

SIX MONTHS LATER

Maxwell Crenshaw had left New York for London three
times this year. The first time had been to save a sister from a marriage she didn't want. The second time had
been to find his other sister, who had run away from a marriage she didn't want. This time he was in London to see his
father, who had been on his deathbed ten days ago when
Max had set off from New York. Thank God the message
that had been waiting for him in Liverpool indicated there
had been substantial improvement in his condition. But it
didn't change the resolution he had come to on the ship. He
planned to convince his parents that it was time to come
home. London had been disastrous for the Crenshaws.

"Max! Thank God you're here." The front door of the
Crenshaws' townhome on Grosvenor Square had barely
closed behind Max and his secretary before Mother came
sailing out of the drawing room, arms outstretched to greet

him. Handing off his hat and gloves to a manservant, he met her halfway. She looked as well put together as usual; her gown was the height of fashion, and diamonds flashed at her wrists and neck. She was pale, however: a sign of her worry.

He held her for a moment longer than necessary, noting how her shoulders trembled. "I came as soon as I could." Since Papa and August had come to London in the spring, Max had assumed control of the American operations of Crenshaw Iron Works. It was a job he had been born and bred to do, having worked alongside his father since he was twelve years of age, but it was very demanding. Thankfully, coming to London twice in the spring had forced him to delegate duties, so he had left the office in the capable hands of a manager.

"I know you did. I'm so happy you're here." Pulling back enough to see his face, she patted his cheek as if he were a child. "Tom." She greeted his secretary. After their pleasantries were exchanged, she instructed the footman to show him to a bedroom.

Taking Max's hand, she tugged him toward the stairs. "How was your voyage?"

"Fine. What have the doctors said?"

"His heart is weak, but you'll have to ask August for the specifics." She waved him off. "She's up with him now. You know me. I can't keep track of those medical terms. The important thing is that he is improving. They believe that with rest he will recover."

"He's been working too hard." It wasn't a question, because they all knew how much the man worked. He was up early every morning and spent the evening at all the social events London had to offer. He wasn't resting like he should. "You both must come home to New York." At least there they maintained a more conventional schedule.

"You'll have to take that up with Papa."

She smiled, but he could sense her reluctance. She didn't want to leave the social acceptance they had found in London. With one daughter married to a duke and another married to an earl, all ballrooms were open to them. Things were different in New York. As new money, the Crenshaws had been excluded from the upper echelons of Society. Mrs. Astor kept her list of the best families in New York, and his family wasn't on it, or they hadn't been before the marriages into nobility.

While this had never bothered anyone but his parents, the allure of acceptance had proven too much for them to resist. And it looked as if it was proving to be their downfall. First, they had sacrificed their daughters, and now Papa's health.

Clenching his jaw to keep from insisting, he held his breath as she pushed open the door to Papa's bedroom. August rose from her seat beside the bed, but his gaze went past her to their father lying back against the pillows. Max's breath caught in his chest at how pale and wan his father looked. The man who was always so in control of the world around him appeared to have lost at least twenty pounds in weight, possibly more. His skin seemed to hang on his cheekbones. For the first time, Max understood how close they had come to losing him, and it left him feeling weak.

"Max." His father's eyes lit up in a way that made the tightness in Max's chest ease the tiniest bit.

"I'm so glad you're here." August closed the leather-bound journal she had been holding and hurried over to hug him.

"Good afternoon, Papa. August."

His sister smiled up at him, but she looked exhausted. Blue tinged the pale skin beneath her eyes, and lines bracketed her mouth where he hadn't noticed any before. She had worked at Crenshaw Iron since she had been old enough to insist upon it. At first Papa had humored her interest in numbers and analysis, but she had proven herself to be more than capable. She had come to London with their parents to help build the European branch of their business, and she had excelled at the task. Max had a sinking suspicion, however, that she was as overworked as Papa, a condition that had likely worsened as she had shouldered their father's workload while he convalesced.

"What are the doctors saying?" Max asked, releasing August and walking over to the bedside to squeeze his father's disturbingly frail shoulder.

Papa gave a low cough. "You know doctors. What do they ever say? Rest, take in fresh air." He shrugged. "I'll be better in a few days."

August's brows drew together in concern. "You will improve, Papa, I have no doubt about it, but it will take weeks to recover from the attacks."

"Attacks? There was more than the one?" Alarm caused Max to speak louder than he meant to.

Mother gave a soft mew of displeasure and left the room, as if the conversation was too much for her. August put a calming hand on his back.

"It was only the one at Farthingtons' soiree," Papa said.

"We were all at a party hosted by the Earl of Farthington when the attack happened," August explained. To her father, she said, "No, the doctors are certain you had another two days later."

Papa waved his hand as if the event wasn't worth mentioning.

Her mouth turned down in displeasure. "We were home, and he was supposed to be resting. But he was drowning in reports and correspondence that he had sent over from the office behind my back. He had another episode."

"It wasn't as severe as the first one," Papa interrupted.

Ignoring him, August went on. "The doctors called it angina pectoris. Essentially, it's pain of the heart caused by periodic loss of oxygen and is a sign of heart disease. They suspect there is an accumulation of fatty tissue compressing the organ."

"I am as healthy as an ox."

"An ox with a heart problem," August shot back but walked over and gave him a kiss on his cheek to soften the words. "I have to go now. Evan sends his regrets for not accompanying me. He had a meeting with his estate manager. We have a dinner to attend, but we'll stop by and check on you on our way home." To Max she said, "We can talk more tonight, but let's have breakfast in the morning to discuss how to proceed."

Max agreed, and she departed, leaving the room feeling eerily still in her wake. The only sounds were the ticking of the clock on the mantel and the chime of the doorbell downstairs. "Healthy as an ox?" Max said, taking a seat in the vacated chair.

One corner of the older man's mouth turned upward, and his eyes seemed to visibly fade. "She worries too much, so I play along."

Max's own heart seemed to stutter in his chest at his father's admission. "Then you did have more chest pain?"

Papa nodded. "A bit, yes. There was another time as well, but I didn't see a need to mention it. What are the doctors going to do? They've prescribed plenty of rest, bone broth to thin the blood, and a tonic." He gestured toward a brown glass bottle with a cork stopper on the nightstand.

What indeed? The energy that had spurred Max onward since he'd received the telegram about Papa's health drained away. Running a hand across the back of his neck to ease the tightness there, he said, "I've arranged to stay several weeks, longer if needed. August and I can see to the office here while you rest. After that, once you're stronger, you and Mother will return to New York with me."

"Leave London?" His face closed in mulish disagreement. "No, I can't see that happening until at least the spring. Perhaps longer. I've been working all summer on plans for India. We already have production underway to lay a thousand miles of track. As a matter of fact, I was hoping to take a trip there before returning to New York."

"A trip to India?" A trip like that could kill him. "Are you out of your mind?"

"Not now, obviously. I had hoped for January, but I concede it might not be the best time, so perhaps in March before it gets too terribly hot. I'll need to see the progress we're making with my own eyes. The railroads will have begun by then. No, don't give me that look; you remind me of your sisters. I will be better then."

"Papa, this is absurd. It is far too early to discuss trips abroad. Besides, you know I don't approve of this India expansion."

"I am aware of your feelings on the matter." Sighing, he added, "I suppose you're right. There are more important matters to discuss now."

Max's stomach churned in warning. "No, you need to rest and recover. Everything else can wait."

"I'm afraid this can't." His father's full mustache twitched in the way that it always did when he had to deliver unpleasant news.

Max sighed and sat back in the chair, stretching his long legs out before him and crossing them at the ankles. The upholstery creaked in protest. At six feet and three inches in bare feet and with a solid frame, protesting furniture was a common problem. There was no escaping what was coming, so he might as well get comfortable. "I believe I know where this is heading, but say it anyway."

"We need to begin thinking about the family legacy." The lines on his face seemed to deepen.

Max had been prepared to suffer through a monologue about the need for him to take the lead in their European venture, which would have effectively taken that role from August. While Papa had been somewhat supportive of her role in the company, he considered it an indulgence and wasn't above taking it away. Max was not prepared for *this*. "The what?"

"The legacy. I would like to have a hand in guiding my grandchildren through the ranks of Crenshaw Iron. I must admit that this . . . spell has given me cause to consider the fact that I may not be immortal as I had once hoped. In fact, I wonder if I will live long enough to see grandchildren through the ranks at all."

Max swallowed against a lump threatening to clog his throat. "Don't speak that way. Violet is with child now and due to deliver in the new year. August could—"

"August has informed me in no uncertain terms that she plans to wait to have children. Besides, her firstborn son will be too busy learning how to be a duke to run Crenshaw Iron. The same goes for Violet's child, and neither of them will be Crenshaws. They won't carry the name, and they'll have responsibilities here."

Max wasn't entirely insensitive to his father's suggestion. All his life he had embraced the Crenshaw legacy, begun by his grandfather, and imagined his own son taking over the reins of the company—though now that August had proven herself so adept, perhaps that mantle could be picked up by a daughter. While he had welcomed the idea, it had always been one that would be realized far into the future. Into his thirties. Not now at the age of twenty-eight when his life was so busy. He had assumed he would have another five years at least before considering the responsibilities of a wife and child.

"Let's talk about this later, Papa. As you said, you will recover."

The older man shook his head, his groomed and oiled hair shining in the lamplight. "We must speak of it now. While I do believe I will recover somewhat, I am not so foolish to believe I will be as good as before. I'm old, Max, but I still know a thing or two about planning for the long run. We must begin laying the foundation now. I want you married by the end of the year."

"Good God, Papa, that's not even two months!"

Papa held up a placating hand. "Yes, I'm aware. I'll settle for an engagement."

Max regarded his father through a narrowed gaze. The man was shrewd when it came to negotiation. He would bargain with the Devil himself to get what he wanted, and Max felt no relief in the knowledge that he was his son. One only had to look at how Papa had negotiated August into accepting her marriage to see that. There would be consequences if Max chose not to agree to his father's terms.

His jaw clenched in anger, he said, "You're trying to manipulate me, to use me like my sisters."

The corner of Papa's mouth quirked upward again. "Aren't you and August always harping on me about equality among the sexes? Well, I have taken your words to heart. A son should marry just as a daughter should."

"I don't know what you have planned, but I will choose my wife. I won't have some brainless pawn served up to me."

"You would never stand for that. I would have nothing less from you. Despite how you might feel about my machinations in the past, I do appreciate the fact that when I'm gone August and Violet will be left in good hands. I have only wanted what is best for them."

Now Max was genuinely bemused. "I don't understand. If you don't have someone in mind, then why—?"

"Oh, I have several young women in mind. Amelia Van der Meer for one." Max was already shaking his head, but Papa continued. "Her father is a good friend and respectable businessman."

"Is she even Violet's age?"

"You mean the Violet who is now married with a child on the way?"

"I won't marry someone so young." He needed a wife he could talk to about his day over dinner, not one who would smile mindlessly at him as she fell over herself to see to his needs. The memory of the one time he had been foolish enough to allow Amelia to corner him at a party sent him to his feet in a state of agitation. Rubbing a hand over the back of his neck, he walked to the pitcher on the bureau across the room and poured himself a glass of water. Miss Van der Meer had all but pawed at him in her bid to keep him to herself.

"I understand," said Papa, but Max rather thought he didn't. "That's why I don't want to suggest anyone. It's not so much who the lucky young woman is as long as you marry soon." There was a brief pause, then he added, "Any woman you choose would need to be respectable, of course. Wealth would be a boon, but not necessary. Did you have anyone in mind?"

Unbidden, an image of Helena came to mind. She was looking at him in disapproval, with a slight smile curving her generous lips, after he had just informed her that she had been wrong. Violet had run away with Christian, and Helena had insisted they go to his Scottish estate to find them. But none of the staff there had heard from the wayward couple. After that, he and Helena had spent several days combing the countryside for his sister before finding her with Christian in a small village outside of York.

Nothing untoward had happened between Max and Helena on the trip; they had both been too worried for Violet's safety to entertain a flirtation, except something *had* happened. The devil if he knew how to describe exactly what. He had become familiar with her every emotion and how each of them reflected on her lovely face. He admired her intelligence and her quick humor, and in the months since, he'd been unable to stop thinking of her.

She wouldn't want to marry him, though. She was settled in London and Somerset, and her family was here. It wasn't as if he knew her well enough to even consider marriage, but he liked what he knew about her. There would be no vapid dinner conversations with her.

No. She was a lady who inhabited a completely different world. He didn't know why his thoughts were even wandering in that direction.

"I do not, because I don't plan to be married anytime soon. This conversation is premature to say the least."

Disappointment crossed Papa's face, but it was gone as easily as it had come. "I thought you might say that."

Taking another drink of water, Max longed for it to be something much stronger. "What are the consequences you've come up with if I don't find a woman to marry?"

Papa sighed. "I don't think we need to delve into consequences. I trust you will do what's right."

He despised this part of his father's character. The man was so ruthless in business that he had forgotten how to not be ruthless when it came to his family. He wanted what he wanted when he wanted it, and he had such faith in his vision being the right one that he manipulated anyone and anything to get it.

Clenching his jaw, Max said, "But there is one. Tell me."

The air was thick with rising antagonism. There was a moment of silence before the man answered. "August has a new project she's excited about. The Prince Albert Dock. She spent all summer on a proposal and is close to securing a deal."

"And it'll be profitable?"

"Oh yes, it's a tidy sum that will help Crenshaw Iron get a firm foothold here in England."

"But?"

"But I'm prepared to block the project if I need to."

"You would stop a project you know is profitable to force me to marry? She would be crushed." It wasn't really a question. It was simply that Max couldn't quite believe the depths to which his father would stoop.

"I think you and I both know that there will be no need for that. Think of it as an incentive. If you make the right choice, all will be well."

Nausea roiled within him. "Right. An incentive." Setting the glass down on the bureau with a hand shaking in fury, Max went for the door. "I'll let you rest."

He tried not to slam the door behind him but wasn't successful. Outside, he paused and drew in a deep breath followed by another. His collar felt suffocating. In one deft motion, he loosened his tie and stood for a time with his fists clenching and unclenching at his sides. The need to hit something had never been so great.

What he wanted to do was to go downstairs, walk out the door, and summon a carriage to take him back to the train station. He could be on an ocean liner tomorrow, headed to New York where he would continue to live his life in peace and run the American branch of Crenshaw Iron as he saw fit. He had been put in charge. It would take a vote by the board to remove him, no matter what his own father might prefer. Max had gained their respect, so he was certain his father's vote wouldn't sway them.

Before he even quite knew what he was doing, he was at the top of the stairs and moving down them. Guilt made it feel like he was walking through mud that sucked at the soles of his boots, but he kept progressing like an automaton. It wasn't until he reached the bottom that he made himself stop. His hand gripped the banister so tight the wood bit into the palm of his hand. He could not leave August to whatever fate their father would give her.

Would she be fine without Crenshaw Iron? Yes. Max had seen her with Evan and knew how happy they were together. Her husband supported her and would happily take her on in the full-time running of his estates and their investments. Her life would be full, and in time she would become accustomed to her new role. But there would always be a part of her spirit that would be crushed by their father's callousness, and she would likely never heal from it. She would always know that he didn't respect her enough to not use her for his own gains. She would always know that she was second in his estimations. And this rift in the family, already begun by their parents trying to marry off their daughters, would be complete, never to be mended again.

"Max!" August's voice rose in pleasant surprise as she stepped out of the drawing room.

Pulled from his thoughts, he still felt as if he were moving through a fog. "I thought you had left," he said. Mother and another woman walked out of the room behind her. It only took a moment for his heart to come to a stuttering halt as he recognized the woman to be Lady Helena.

"Wonderful," Mother said, her pallor and demeanor much more cheerful than it had been when she'd led him to Papa's room. "You won't miss out on greeting Lady Helena."

He had to make himself release the banister and act like a civilized human, even as anger and something dangerous coursed through him. He wasn't prepared to see Helena again, not like this. He had expected it to happen one evening at a dinner or a ball. Not in his parents' home when he had just been fed the most damning ultimatum.

"Lady Helena." He paused to clear the gravel from his throat. "How good to see you again." There was still the slightest hint of venom in his voice. He hoped she wouldn't think it directed at her.

"Mr. Crenshaw." She sank down into a proper curtsy.

God, she was lovely. From the top of her buttery blond hair to the delicate curve of her cheekbones to the tips of her pebbled leather boots, she was polished and proper. The epitome of a lady. When her gaze met his, he was struck anew by the color, a pure cornflower blue.

She raised a brow, and he knew she had detected his tone as well as the livid anger likely visible on his face. "My deepest sympathies on your father's health. I am happy to hear that he is improving."

"Yes, it is a relief." His voice was tight. His mouth went dry, and he couldn't bring himself to say anything more. On the crossing he had imagined their meeting many times. He would compliment her and watch the color rise in her cheeks. He would tell her how he had missed her wit, but in such a way that she wouldn't suspect he had thought about her at night while alone in his bed, or by day as he traveled from one meeting to another.

"I hope you will be staying in London for a time," she was saying.

"Yes, of course he is," his mother said. "We are very much looking forward to the dinner with your parents later this week. Will you be there?"

"Oh yes. It will be lovely to see you all there." Her gaze settled briefly on him before flitting away again when he didn't respond. "I am afraid I have to be going now."

"I'll walk out with you," August said, giving him a strange look. She knew him well enough to suspect something was wrong. He would have to figure out a lie to tell her before she came back later tonight. He refused to wound her with the truth.

Helena looked back at him, and he mumbled a goodbye. Her lips turned down in disappointment, and he realized perhaps it was for the best. He'd be heading back to New York soon.

As the front door closed behind them and Mother hurried past him up the stairs, he had to wonder if she was going to chat with Papa. If they had planned the entire thing. His anger once more returned to the forefront. No, they wouldn't get away with this.

Papa had known Max's weakness and hadn't hesitated to exploit it. He had anticipated that Max's own affection for August and his loyalty to his family would keep him in line. But he had underestimated one thing. Max, in his own way, could be just as ruthless and cunning as their father when it suited him. He was a Crenshaw, after all.

Chapter 2

*Old-fashioned ways which no longer apply
to changed conditions are a snare in which
the feet of women have always become readily entangled.*

JANE ADDAMS

Maxwell Crenshaw had the most divine mouth she had ever seen. Helena had watched it throughout dinner. She told herself it was because he sat across from her and, really, how could one not allow one's gaze to drift to it now and again, but that did not explain why she continued watching it now that dinner was over and the men had rejoined the ladies in the drawing room. His lips were perfectly sculpted, not too thin, not too thick, with the bottom one pleasingly full. When he smiled, they made a perfect bow.

He had only smiled twice tonight, once upon greeting her and once in kindness when Papa had made a tiresome joke at the table. It was the only time he had looked at her outside of conversation the entire evening, and the look had been one of commiseration. She had felt his gaze all the way down to her toes, as if he were saying they were in this together as the only ones who recognized the jest had fallen flat. As if he weren't actually ignoring her at all. Unfortunately, after that one moment of intimacy, he had gone back to his polite aloofness. One would have thought that they hadn't spent time together outside of proper social events.

Perhaps he was maintaining distance to make it seem as if nothing had happened between them. Nothing *had* happened between them. In their days up North, he had been the perfect gentleman, and his concern for Violet had been at the forefront. However, after Violet had been safely found and married, rumors had begun to circulate. No one knew for certain that Helena had accompanied him. She trusted her servants not to betray her whereabouts, but they had been seen together at the train station, and Violet had stayed with her for the week leading up to her wedding.

It was enough for speculation. Never in polite circles, of course, but sometimes people would give them a second look. Gossip never lived long when its object of prey was out of sight, so the talk had died a slow death when he returned to New York. But now that he was back, more than one eyebrow had been raised in their direction at dinner.

"My dear, forgive my impertinence, but if you would like to carry off this charade, then at least pretend to be indifferent to him." This came from Lady Blaylock, who stood next to her, a close friend of Helena's mother.

Helena only realized she was staring at Mr. Crenshaw when the woman spoke. Her face heated as she averted her gaze from the man across the drawing room to Lady Blaylock. They were partially shielded from the other guests by a Japanese screen. Perhaps that was why Helena had allowed herself the indulgence of looking at him. Lady Blaylock, however, continued her perusal of him. If she had a quizzing glass, Helena was sure she would have raised it to her eye.

"There is no charade." Helena smiled serenely.

The older woman giggled and then gave her an indulgent smile. "Fine, I have tried to pull the details from your mother to no avail. She is a terrible gossip, so I suppose if there were some truth to your having run off with that young man, it would have come to light by now."

"You have known me since before I could walk, ma'am. You should know there is no truth to those tales."

"It is precisely because I know you that I question." Lady Blaylock gave her a pointed look. "You are not like your sisters, Helena. You have spirit and follow your own mind."

"My own mind tells me that it would be the height of impropriety to run off with a bachelor." Too bad she didn't always heed her own good sense.

"Yes, I suppose so." Lady Blaylock sounded mildly disappointed as she swiveled her head back to peer at the men across the room. "The young Mr. Crenshaw is charming in a rustic sort of way, isn't he, though? Strapping." Then her head tilted to the side and downward as if she were looking at where his muscled thighs pressed against the fabric of his trousers. "Robust."

Helena bit the inside of her lip to hide her laugh at the woman's enthusiasm. She knew exactly what Lady Blaylock meant. It was that same juxtaposition that had first caught her eye. He held himself like a gentleman, but there was a hint of the untamed about him. Something she couldn't quite specify. He was mannered and stylish, but no matter how he tried, he would never be as polished as his brothers-in-law. And yet, there was an elegance in his ruggedness. He was different but just as refined somehow.

"Quite," she said, hoping to change the subject. She had spent all evening trying to finagle it so that she had Lady Blaylock to herself, and she wasn't about to allow the moment to slip through her fingers. Clearing a throat suddenly gone tight with nerves, she said, "Actually, I've been hoping to take a moment to discuss your pledge to the home."

The London Home for Young Women was a project born from Helena's days volunteering with an orphanage. Many of the children left in the orphanage's care came from women who were unable to keep their children due to the fact that they worked six days a week, and often twelve-hour days or even longer if one counted the fact that they often held multiple jobs. Most of the women had no family to care for the children, and the scarce wages they earned hardly paid for their own needs. The home—once a suitable location was acquired—would be a place of refuge. The women could live there with their children and provide childcare in turns to allow themselves to work. Helena also hoped to provide education for the children and women who wanted it, as well as job training. It was early stages, yet, but fundraising had been going well until recently.

"Yes, of course, darling. I'm glad you brought that up." Lady Blaylock took a short breath and pulled her eyes from the incomparable Mr. Crenshaw, the lines bracketing her mouth deepening. "I am afraid there will be a delay with my funding."

"A delay?" Helena's heart sank. This was not the first time in the past months that a mysterious *delay* had been used as an excuse to not follow through on a pledge to the charity.

"Lower than expected returns or some such excuse. I barely listen to my solicitor when he talks, particularly when the accountant is involved. Suffice it to say that I must defer my contribution until next summer. You know my dear Janie is coming out next Season. I must see to her first."

"First?" Lady Blaylock could not be implying that financing Janie's season depended upon her delaying the contribution. Her second husband had been a very successful financier who had left her quite wealthy after his death.

The woman had the grace to look sheepish. A slight blush tinged the apples of her cheeks. "Well, you have to know how some view this venture."

Helena did know. Many of their beneficiaries were unwed mothers. Some were widows, but most had given birth to their children outside of marriage. Her own father had raised his quiet objection by pointing out that proper Society matrons would not countenance helping fallen women. It bewildered her how giving birth outside of marriage meant they were unworthy of help in the eyes of many, when they were the ones who needed it most. They were the ones shunned by their families and those who would support them otherwise.

Women were doomed to be defined by not only the children they could or could not bear, but the timing and method in which they bore them. Children before marriage and it was ruin and condemnation. None at all and it was pity and scorn. The only acceptable time to have children was after marriage, and even then it better not take too long or the scandal sheets would write about it. Helena had been burned by the gossips when her own marriage had failed to produce children. Helping these women helped her to feel that she was taking back control, at least in this one small way.

Lady Blaylock patted the back of Helena's hand. "I don't agree with them, mind you, but I understand the need for keeping up appearances. I will gladly contribute once my dear Janie has made her match and to Hades with the naysayers."

She chuckled to cover her nervousness, and Helena swallowed as anxiety swirled within her. The woman wouldn't help because she didn't want to risk a smudge on her daughter's coming-out. Thanks to the Earl of Leigh's generosity—he'd sold a smaller estate in Scotland and donated the funds to the charity—they were in a position to purchase a building, but that didn't cover the renovations any building would undoubtedly need to transform it into a home that would house at least fifty women and their children, with an addition of a school and a workroom to teach the women various skills, or the day-to-day operational costs. What had been a robust ledger after his donation was slowly dwindling as more and more people *delayed* their funding. It was looking as if they would have to wait to open the home to the neglect of all the women and children she knew needed help *now.*

The weight of bitter disappointment swelled in her chest. In an attempt she knew smacked of desperation, she said, "But we could maneuver to have it gifted anonymously—"

"Now, darling, I understand you're disappointed and with good reason. Perhaps you could open *next* winter and use the interim to get your own house in order, if you will."

"What do you mean?" Though Helena was quite certain she knew what the impertinent woman meant. Her own mother barely let a week go by without bringing up her lack of a husband.

"Another marriage, darling. My second marriage was the best thing I ever did. Kept me young, and then little Janie came along after I had thought I was done with children." The woman raised a brow and glanced down to Helena's midsection.

"I see you've been talking to Mama." Helena could barely unclench her jaw to mutter the words. Despite herself, she put a shielding hand over her stomach. Ever since her wedding over seven years ago, people had been casting eyes in that direction. First it had been in expectation, but after Arthur's untimely death five years ago, the looks had changed to pity and regret.

"We only want what's best for you, Helena. I happen to agree with your mother. A husband would go a long way to giving your charity an air of respectability. With the right man behind you—"

"Good evening, ladies."

Without her even realizing that he was coming over, the object of their previous scrutiny stood next to her. His voice was as potent as the rest of him. Smooth as an aged whisky, but rich like coffee. Heat emanated from his body, warming her left side. The way he stood next to her blocked her from the rest of the room because the screen was on her other side. It made her feel closed in, but it was a pleasant sensation. She still froze, however, reluctant for some unknown reason to make eye contact.

"Mr. Crenshaw, how is your father?" Lady Blaylock asked.

"Well, thankfully."

As he went on with the health update—one she had heard earlier from Mrs. Crenshaw—Helena allowed herself to take him in. His boots were polished to a high shine, and the tailoring on his trousers was divine, giving the barest hint of the press of muscle against the fabric. His coat sleeves began precisely a quarter inch above the edge of his shirtsleeves, but her gaze caught on his fingers. Strong but elegant as he gently cradled a snifter of brandy.

She was stalling because she didn't want to see cool politeness on his face. Their meeting a few days ago at his parents' house had been anything but what she had hoped. While she had spent a considerable amount of time thinking about him in the ensuing months, he had obviously not felt the same. The way he had looked at her so dispassionately had made her suspect as much. His cool politeness tonight had reinforced her suspicion. It seemed that her memory had exaggerated the attraction on his part.

To look into his eyes up close and not see warmth beyond the merest suggestion of friendship reflected back at her would confirm it. Ordinarily, it wouldn't matter so much, but she felt particularly raw after her conversation with Lady Blaylock.

"It must have been such a shock to hear of his condition," Lady Blaylock said. "And you all the way in New York. I rather hoped that he might come tonight, but alas, I was too optimistic. Your poor mother. I know well her heartache." Without giving him time to respond, the woman launched into a story about her first husband and his heart problems.

Unable to postpone the inevitable any longer, Helena gave him a smile that she hoped conveyed that she was sorry he'd been pulled into one of the woman's long-winded stories. To her immense pleasure, his deep brown eyes shined back at her, intense and with just enough heat to make her breath catch. Some silent message was conveyed in the look, but she didn't understand what it was.

"Thank you, Lady Blaylock," he said when the woman had paused for a breath. "I appreciate your well-wishes."

She gave a demure nod of acknowledgment.

Grateful for the break, Helena wasted no time in speaking. "I trust Mr. Crenshaw will make a full recovery."

His eyes seemed to harden a bit, almost like they had been on the stairs of his parents' home, but his voice was unchanged. Something must have happened with his father, she realized.

"Yes," he said. "He's a little stronger every day."

"Splendid. That is reassuring," the older woman said.

Clearing his throat, he turned fully toward Helena. "Lady Helena, I hoped for an update on your home for women and children. Have you found your location yet?"

"Not yet—"

Helena began her answer, but before she could continue, Lady Blaylock asked, "You know about her charity project?"

"We spoke at length about it in the spring." When he had come to her home to visit Violet was left unsaid. "She asked about real estate, since Crenshaw Iron owns many properties that I manage. I was impressed by her knowledge and ambition, so much so that I made a contribution."

"Thank you again for that." The pledge had come quite by surprise about a month after he had returned to New York. She had written a letter of thanks immediately, though she had wondered at his motives. He hadn't seemed particularly charitable in the time she had known him in London. "Your generosity is very much appreciated."

"You donated to her charity?" Lady Blaylock said the words almost under her breath, in awe. Had she a monocle it would have come out as she looked him up and down again. "How very noble of you."

He grinned at her. "I think anyone who would neglect to contribute to Lady Helena's causes is imprudent. I am certain someone as dignified and judicious as yourself has contributed as well."

Helena had to bite her lip to keep from smiling at his impertinence. He had obviously overheard some of their conversation. Lady Blaylock opened and closed her mouth a few times before she seemed to gather herself and smile. Looking at Helena, she said, "Oh, I do approve of him, Helena." Tapping his arm with her empty snifter, she left them alone.

"What does she mean by that?" he asked, an attractive husk in his lowered voice implying an intimacy that had the muscles low in her midsection clenching.

"Oh . . . I . . . um . . ." She meant to say that the woman was a known matchmaker and to pay her no attention, but as soon as her gaze met his, all words came to a stop. His eyes were alight with knowledge, but he was daring her to put voice to what had been throbbing between them since the very first. She couldn't do it. If she did, she knew with utter certainty that she wouldn't be able to ignore it any longer. "Ignore her."

"I hope I haven't caused any awkwardness. I eavesdropped." Despite his words, he didn't appear the least bit sheepish as he smiled at her.

"You don't hope that at all." Helena smiled back, powerless not to respond.

Their acquaintance had developed into a fragile friendship in the days before he had returned to New York, but there had always been a heated agitation lying beneath the surface. It had sprung from their mutual but unvoiced attraction for each other, mixed with their very different ideas on how Violet's running away and subsequent marriage should be handled. He preferred brute force, while Helena preferred tact and compassion. If he stayed in London for very long, she wasn't at all certain the desire would stay unvoiced. The thought should have scandalized her, but anticipation blotted out her better sense.

"Lady Blaylock is an old friend. She has a high tolerance for plain talk. Unfortunately, she also agrees with my parents," she explained, hoping to guide the conversation to safer territory.

He frowned in question.

"They do not believe my charity to be very morally upstanding as it will benefit women of questionable character, to use their words, which could cause my own reputation to suffer."

"Nonsense. You have a sterling character."

She shrugged, though his assessment pleased her. "There *have* been others who are backing out of their initial enthusiasm for the project."

"Then how are your finances?" he asked in that matter-of-fact way he had, as if he weren't probing beyond the pale.

She found herself answering without even really thinking about it, because she trusted him without actually knowing why. Yes, he was the brother of her friends, and she knew his intentions were good. But it was more. It was the way his brows drew close together and he tilted forward the slightest bit as if it would help him better concentrate on her problem. As if he genuinely cared.

"Not as well as I'd hoped." Gathering herself, she added, "But that's not your concern."

"What if you plan smaller?"

She nodded, having already considered this. "I can, of course. We can find a small house with a small schoolroom and perhaps lease a workshop space. It's not ideal, but it may come to it if I can't find another solution. I simply can't abide the thought of the women we won't be able to help."

"What would it take to make your donors come back? Obviously, they were interested once."

Before she could stop herself, she glanced toward her parents across the room. Lady Blaylock had joined their group. She couldn't help but think that her father's influence, his hesitance to endorse her project, was causing his friends to reconsider. If she could get him on her side again, perhaps they would come back.

Or perhaps it would take marriage. People were reluctant to admit that a woman could be both capable and upstanding in her own right. If her husband would take on a leadership role in the project, even as a figurehead, it would lend the home respectability. No one would have cause to wonder if she was being led astray by fallen women.

She couldn't share any of that with him, however. It was too personal.

"You're awfully curious tonight, Mr. Crenshaw. Careful, or one might think you care about something beyond Crenshaw Iron."

His eyes narrowed a bit, and the corner of his mouth tugged upward in the beginnings of a grin. "Ah, there she is."

His attractiveness easily rose by ten percent when his eyes did that. "Whatever do you mean?"

"That you've been treating me with kid gloves all night, so very polite and dispassionate, when I know very well there is a cauldron of judgment and incisiveness bubbling beneath the surface."

She looked away to hide her smile, but she knew she was unsuccessful. She had missed this, she realized as a soothing warmth grew to replace the anxiety inside her. There was a candor when he spoke that was absent in most of her conversations where polite sentiment and graciousness were valued more than honesty. "Well, you've had a terrible shock. It seemed in poor spirit to be unsympathetic."

"I get enough of that from them, believe me." He indicated the room at large behind them. "I like your candor and sincerity."

There was that tone again, the one that made it seem as if they were the only people in the room. Despite her better sense, her gaze landed on his lips, perfectly framed by his close-cut beard. "I like that about you, too," she said in a tone that mirrored his.

He took in a long and shaky breath. It was the first indication that maybe he didn't have his wits about him after all, that maybe she affected him more than he let on. His eyes revealed a longing that startled her. She couldn't breathe from the intensity. Finally, someone pressed too close, brushing the screen so that it tilted slightly into him. They both reached for it, his hand covering hers on the gilded frame. They paused for a second that stretched on for eternity before she pulled back, leaving him to set it to rights.

"Perhaps it would be best if you concern yourself with your family issues, and I will take care of my own concerns." She couldn't tell if her voice had returned to normal.

"Fair enough." His eyes were shuttered when he turned back to her, leaving her to wonder if she'd imagined the whole exchange.

She pressed on to keep an awkward silence from falling. "Having said that, I *am* glad to see you recovered from the other day." His brows drew together in question, so she explained, "You seemed not yourself when I saw you at your parents' house."

"You're right. I wasn't myself. I'm sorry if I failed to greet you—"

"No, I didn't mean that. I only meant that I was worried about you, and I hope things are better since your father is improving."

His lips parted, as if he meant to speak, but then he put them together again before giving a tip of his head. "I came over to bid you good evening. I have to leave because I have an early morning."

Disappointment tightened her chest. "Yes, of course. Good evening."

After the slightest hesitation, he turned and made his way through the room, leaving without a backward glance. Something was wrong. Perhaps it was the strangeness of the past few moments, but something told her it was more. She didn't know what it was, but she wished his candor extended to confiding in her, even though the last thing she needed was another Crenshaw intrigue to solve.

Chapter 3

❦

Feminists ought to get a good whipping. Were woman to "unsex" themselves by claiming equality with men, they would become the most hateful, heathen and disgusting of beings and would surely perish without male protection.

QUEEN VICTORIA

Helena found her father, Lord Farthington, later that evening. He was conferring with the butler in the drawing room. The other guests had already left, giving her a few precious moments to speak to him while Mama walked Lady Blaylock to the front door.

"Never again, I tell you." Her father's voice was full of irritation.

"I will see to it personally, my lord," Greyson replied with solemnity.

Papa looked up as she entered the room. The butler bowed and took his leave. Both were obviously displeased with her. Greyson would never show it, but there was a certain additional stiffness in his bearing that she had learned over the years meant he was cross. Papa scowled. She had a feeling she knew the topic of their little conference.

"You arranged the menu for tonight's gathering, didn't you, Helena?"

She smiled. "Yes. If you recall, Mama asked for my assistance because she and Penelope had to go out today."

"Then it *was* you who arranged for the serving of oysters?"

"Guilty."

Papa gave a sigh that reeked of disappointment. "You'll have us living in a Dickens novel."

"Oh, Papa, you exaggerate. They were served chilled and on the half shell, not pickled or in a beef pie." He despised being reminded of how there were others less fortunate than they, especially in his own home.

"Any oyster is a bit too close to the rookery for me." He shifted beneath his coat somehow, his throat bobbing as he took a sip of his champagne as if to clean the taste of the word from his palate.

"Times are changing. Many hostesses serve oysters now. They are delicious."

Ordering the shellfish had been meant to irritate him, because she took any opportunity to remind him that there were others in the world outside of their class. If the presence of an oyster would make him take a moment to consider the many poor in London who had lived on oysters and gruel for decades, then she would serve them when she could. He was a renowned speaker in the House of Lords. A man in his position needed to understand the lives that he held in his power.

"Not in my home again, Helena."

"Fine. I didn't come to talk about the appropriateness of oysters on a dinner table." She hesitated, her breath catching in her throat. Now that she planned to confront him, she almost didn't want to hear him say her suspicion was true. "I wanted to ask you about something Lady Blaylock said."

"Yes?" He gave her a pointed look from behind the spectacles perched on the end of his nose.

She licked her lips. Why was this so difficult? She clenched her hands in the folds of her skirt to hide how her palms were sweating. "Donations for the London Home for Young Women have not been promising of late. Have you, perchance, said something to your associates?"

"Only the truth, as you are well aware. It is unseemly for you to associate with such people." She opened her mouth to argue, but he raised a hand. "I am not forbidding you from such a folly. God knows that it would do no good. I am merely stating a fact. Haven't you noticed how many have been willing to support your orphanage but not your home for *those* women?"

"Well, yes, that's why I've come to talk with you." Most of the orphanage's board members had politely refused to collaborate on the new project, even though they had seen the need for it with their own eyes. The few who had joined with her on the endeavor had been largely unsuccessful in sourcing donations from their close friends and family. Not many were willing to be associated with unmarried women having children, not even the men who fathered those children. If not for Leigh's—Christian's, Violet always corrected her when she referred to him more formally—recent generosity, they would not be in the process of searching for a suitable building.

He nodded. "And I've been informed of your trips into St. Giles."

"Papa—"

"That slum is home to all manner of vice and ill character. I do not want you going back there."

"Who told you about that?"

"I know everything that goes on in Parliament. Do you assume that I don't know what goes on with my own children?"

"Sometimes it is necessary. Most of the women are from St. Giles, and we are called upon from time to time to go there. I never go alone."

"I should hope not, but it doesn't change the fact that your behavior with this endeavor is quite too much. If I have shared my concern with close associates, then it is nothing more than what any other father would do when presented with concerns of safety for his daughter."

The only problem was that his influence extended far beyond that of most fathers. His associates wouldn't want to cross him, not when he had the power to refuse favors. She didn't like it, but she had her answer. The donations were dwindling because of him. It was no less than she had suspected, but the knowledge still chaffed. "But I am safe, Papa, and I am not being harmfully influenced by these women. What can I do to convince you of that?"

He sighed. "You could do with a husband, Helena."

"We have had this discussion before, and I have made my feelings on this matter very clear." Marriage had been at the forefront of her parents' thoughts from the day she turned fifteen until the day she was married at nineteen. After her husband's premature death, they had waited a year before subtly bringing up the subject again, though the subtlety had disintegrated in the four years she'd been out of mourning. "I will marry someday." She wouldn't. "But my hands are full with the orphanage and now with the London Home for Young Women." He cleared his throat in obvious displeasure. The silk of her gown seemed to cling to her chest. Tucking a fingertip discreetly into the neckline, she gave the fabric a tug. "I hardly have time to consider a courtship, much less all that would come after."

"That *place*"—he said the word with meaning—"is precisely why we must consider a marriage."

"There is nothing to consider." Her attempt at keeping her voice light was failing. Even she could hear the thread of steel that had made its way into her words.

Papa's face did not change, but something about his demeanor hardened. "A husband would be accountable for you and, if he's sensible, not allow you to go at all. I cannot be responsible for this behavior."

A hot flush rushed to her face. "Of course not. I can be responsible for myself. In fact, my dower has seen to that."

"I am not discussing money with you, of which I believe you are very much aware. I am discussing your safety and the responsibility of a husband to provide that for a wife."

"I have seen to that myself. We have security, Papa, and I have traveled with them the few times I've had to venture into an unsafe area. I am not foolish."

"No, you are not. Of all my daughters, you are least likely to give in to hysterics."

Helena ground her molars. She had two younger sisters, and not one of them had ever given in to a case of hysterics. "Then you understand that whether I have a husband or not—"

"Helena, my dear." He turned fully toward her and took her hands in his. "I am telling you this because I want what is best for you. If you persist in this home for women nonsense, then your reputation will suffer. If your reputation suffers, then you will be even less able to find funding and reputable people to support this charity. You may not want to hear this, but I am your father, and I do know a bit about a few things. Marriage will help you. If you choose the right partner, then your reputation can be upheld . . . somewhat."

A lump of dread settled in the pit of her stomach. "You are saying that I cannot even control my own reputation? That it is dependent upon the man on my arm?" Yes, that was exactly what he meant. She simply needed to hear him say it rather than infer it.

"You know how the world works." He gave her a pitying look.

So that she wouldn't give in to the sudden, unreasonable despair that attempted to overcome her, she said, "And whom would you suggest, Papa? Shall I marry Maxwell, the last remaining Crenshaw, so that the American con-

quest is complete?" It was meant to be sarcastic, a teasing
jab that would once again turn the increasingly serious conversation away from herself. However, something about the
suggestion resonated with her. The memory of his brown
eyes looking at her from across the carriage as a sobbing
Violet sat between them. The way he could so effortlessly
convey compassion, arrogance, and heat all in the same
look.

"Vulgar wealth would not be my first choice, but the
selection is yours to make. Although, I've dealt with the
elder Crenshaw enough as we've developed the railroad
contracts to know that you would not enjoy his influence as
your father-in-law."

Helena understood that the concept of noble blood was
a construct of Society. She did not believe herself to be
above anyone based on their name or station in life, but she
was inclined to agree with his conclusion if not his reasoning. She admired Maxwell Crenshaw, but he was not for
her. There were many reasons for this, among them that he
was American and firmly rooted in his life in New York,
and Papa was right about the elder Mr. Crenshaw.

The fact of the matter was that she would not marry
anyone, no matter how well suited he was to her. Men who
sought marriage, sought children. A family. It was the one
thing that she could not give. Two and a half years of marriage and several very intrusive examinations by physicians
had told her as much. While her parents might want her to
marry, and she herself wasn't completely against the idea in
the depths of her heart, marriage was not in her future. If
she had learned one thing in her years as a daughter of the
aristocracy, it was that her main purpose in life was to bear
children. Heirs made their world go round. She wasn't
about to set herself up for a lifetime of disappointing another husband. One had been enough.

"Then who would you suggest? Hereford is already
taken." She referred to the old duke who had married a

young American heiress only last year to emphasize how distasteful this conversation was.

Papa sighed with impatience. "There are any number of men who would qualify. Lord Verick would be suitable. He was a good friend to Arthur, and I firmly believe the man should be someone of whom he would approve."

So even dead men would have more control over her life than she did. The thought shamed her as soon as it crossed her mind. Arthur had been a good husband to her, despite how they had felt at the end. Squaring her shoulders, she said, "You are Lord Farthington, my father, and a formidable gentleman in Society. Your support would go far toward overcoming all of those obstacles."

"I cannot do that, not when I worry so about you."

"Fine. Then I will make the home a success without your help."

"As you wish." He inclined his head in mock encouragement. "You are your own woman now, as you say."

She whirled and stormed out of the room, faintly aware of Mama and Lady Blaylock calling out their goodbyes as Helena accepted her cape from a footman before hurrying down the front steps to her waiting carriage.

She would figure this out on her own. Somehow.

The London offices of Crenshaw Iron Works were situated in a quaint brick and stucco building in Tyburnia, north of Hyde Park. The building had been purchased over the summer after August had married the Duke of Rothschild, and Papa had been assured of the family's place both in Society and in British commerce. The fashionable district had been chosen because of its proximity to Mayfair where the family had a rented townhome; though Max had overheard his mother gushing to one of her new friends about looking for a permanent residence, so he suspected a move would be forthcoming as soon as Papa recovered.

It wasn't the move that Max disapproved of so much as the reason for it. His parents had developed an apparently insatiable need for acceptance into a society that wasn't theirs, simply to gain entrance into a Manhattan Society that did not want them. This had never set well with him. Even less so now that he had seen the damage to the family that such aspirations had wrought. Both of his sisters had been pushed into marriages they hadn't wanted. While those relationships seemed to have worked out for them, their relationships with their parents had yet to recover. August was still as dutiful as ever when it came to family obligations, but there was a coldness between her and their parents that Max had never seen before. Violet seemed to have taken things worse. She only saw their parents socially and just managed to utter the barest of formalities to them.

Standing to stretch his legs, Max walked to the open door that separated August's modestly sized office from Papa's. Their father's office was paneled in dark wood and brocade wallpaper in tones of gray and darker gray. A plush sofa with wingback chairs flanked the fireplace. Huge maps of London, England, Scotland, India, and the United States took up the wall behind the desk and the wall opposite the windows that looked out onto Connaught Square. Bookshelves and filing cabinets filled the area behind the desk, which itself was a marvel. Made of hand-carved mahogany and walnut, it was quite possibly the largest desk Max had ever seen. Papa's office back in New York was half the size of this one, and the desk easily a mere third. There was a metaphor in the difference somewhere, but he was too damned tired to find it.

The office had been where he spent most of his time working this past week, but every moment at that desk had felt oppressive and troubling in a way that Max couldn't put words to yet.

August walked into her office to find him rubbing his weary eyes with the heels of his hands. "Are you unwell?"

"I haven't been sleeping." He hadn't managed to get a full night of sleep in the week he'd been in London.

"Oh, well, why don't you go home early today? We can reschedule our meeting." Setting the papers in her arms on her desk, she sat down and pulled out a leather-bound journal. "I'm certain I have free time later in the week."

"No." Max sighed and sat back down in the chair across from her. "Best to talk now."

She nodded, but her brow furrowed in concern. "We could talk in Papa's office. It's much more comfortable."

She was right. Her office was little more than a cramped cell stuffed with more papers, contracts, and registers than it could hold comfortably. One solitary window at her back gave the room a watery light. "*You* should be working in his office while he recovers." Like Max, working for the family business was August's passion in life. Luckily, Evan respected that, and the couple had found a way for her to be a duchess and continue her duties at Crenshaw Iron.

"I'm more comfortable here. I don't need a fancy room to make me feel as if I'm getting things accomplished," she said.

"You need a bigger office. You're a high-level manager at Crenshaw Iron. He still treats you like his personal secretary."

"On some level I think he still believes that I am, but we all know the truth. I know that you and Papa clash on many issues in the day-to-day running of the company, but I've learned that it's best to pick the battles I wish to fight very carefully. I don't have any choice but to win them, so I have to save up my ammunition to make certain that I do. If it makes him feel better to have me in the smaller office next to him, then fine. It only helps me keep a better eye on him." She grinned, and he couldn't help but smile at the flash of defiance in her eyes. "Now, I'm certain we have more important issues to discuss than the size of this room."

"Well said, little sister." Leaning forward, he tapped the proposal for the Prince Albert Dock project lying on her desk. "I've been studying your work here. The statistics and projections are all sound. Even the least profitable scenario has a return of ten percent while still introducing the possibility for future contracts. I believe it's a secure investment."

"I hoped you might say that. I've run the numbers five different ways, and even with the depressed markets, I believe we can turn a profit." She pulled out the additional pages from a drawer and set them out in front of him. Each one was a different scenario based on various market prices of ore and carbon. "The variable of course being that we cannot buy at once. We first have to secure a factory, and then we can sign a contract price, but even then our production is bottlenecked. No supplier will sign a contract with terms so loosely categorized. We don't know how much we'll need, because we don't formally have a contract for work. And we have no warehouse space here like we do in New York and Pennsylvania to hold any excess until we can use it."

"What if we could take that variable out of the equation?" he asked.

"How?"

"What about the supplier in Rotherham? Have you considered purchasing it?"

She nodded. "Yes, of course, but the owner refused to sell, and Papa wouldn't agree to a higher price to prompt the sale—a decision I reluctantly agree with."

"Have you considered a solution here in London?" When she frowned, he continued, "I had Tom make some inquiries. Apparently, your solicitor has a contact here who is looking to sell his metalworks, a Sir Phineas Penhurst. It comes with a significant warehouse space. It seems the owner is looking to sell the entire block."

"Where is it?"

"Somewhere between Whitechapel and Limehouse. Close enough to the docks to make it interesting."

"That is interesting. Do you know the details? What's the price per square foot?"

"He was squirrelly on the details, but everything is negotiable. I've arranged a tour this afternoon if you're up for it."

They would need to move fast on the deal. From what Max understood, it would sell quickly, but that wasn't the only reason. If Max could sink enough money into the deal, Papa wouldn't be able to shut everything down when Max refused his ridiculous marriage ultimatum. He wouldn't cost the business millions just to prove a point. Or would he? At one time Max had been very certain of who his parents were, but he wasn't any longer.

"Today?" August was smiling as she shuffled through the papers for her appointment book underneath. "Possibly. Violet is supposed to come by for luncheon."

"Did I hear my name?" As if she had been summoned by the word, their youngest sister swept into the room. She looked radiant. She had always been pretty, but there was a glow of happiness about her now that he'd never seen before. It was the primary reason Max hadn't finished the beating he'd started on Christian when he'd found them together back in the spring. The earl's reputation and the fact that he'd run off with Violet had meant Max hadn't been pleased with their hasty marriage, but seeing her so content had him slowly warming up to Christian.

August quickly explained their plan to tour the factory as Max stood to kiss Violet on the cheek. He had missed her in the months since she had left home, and unlike August, whom he heard from regularly because they worked together, he didn't have the same cause to communicate with her as often. Since he was eight years older, he sometimes forgot that she wasn't the same adorable but irritating little girl who used to follow him around begging for rides on his shoulders.

"You should come with us, if you feel up to it," he said, glancing down at her swollen belly. Her cape was covering all evidence of her pregnancy now, however. "We can eat afterward."

"I'll come, but only if we can eat first. I'm famished, and I'm sure I'll be ready for an early tea after the tour."

August laughed as she shrugged into her coat. "You're always hungry."

"It's true. I don't even care anymore about maintaining a semblance of civility when it comes to food." Violet shrugged, drawing his eye to the sapphire broach she wore. It was the same exact shade as Helena's eyes.

What a strange thought. Violet was the creative one in their family. The one given to sentimental descriptions. Several years ago, he had toured Italy with friends, and upon returning home Violet had asked him about Michelangelo's *David* and how he had felt when he had seen it in the Palazzo della Signoria. He'd replied *good* to her everlasting disappointment. It wasn't that he hadn't *felt* the awe any person experienced when standing before such an example of human exceptionalism; it was that he lacked the skills to verbalize and examine the emotion to the depth she wanted. He still hadn't learned, apparently, because the color on that broach made him feel things he couldn't quite comprehend.

"Do you like it?" she asked, running her finger across the filigree setting. "It's been in Christian's family for a hundred years. He said it was so beautiful he couldn't bear to sell it."

"It looks old," he said, making her roll her eyes at him.

"My driver is waiting." She wrapped her arm around his and led them all out into the corridor. "Cook will have a fine luncheon ready. I'm glad you're coming with us. You can see the house and the restorations I've made, and we can talk about Lady Helena."

August laughed behind them.

"Lady Helena? Is something the matter?" Had something happened in the few days since the dinner at her parents' home?

"No, I meant that we could talk about Lady Helena and *you*. You and Helena."

August pulled abreast of them as they walked down the front steps to the carriage waiting on the road for them. "I'm afraid Violet has it in her head that you and the lady in question might form a special sort of relationship."

There was no way to explain away the sudden jolt of interest that her comment provoked. He paused, letting that information digest as a footman helped both of his sisters into the carriage. Feeling as if his tie had somehow tightened itself around his neck, he followed them into the carriage and gave it a tug to make certain that it hadn't. "To what purpose?" he asked as he settled in across from them. "I'll be returning to New York in a few weeks, and from what I can tell, Lady Helena has a full life here." As he spoke, the seed of an idea began to form, but it was so outrageous he could hardly countenance it.

"Things change, Max. Priorities get rearranged." Violet smiled at him, her brown eyes wide and hopeful.

He sighed as he realized that they would have to see this conversation through before she would be satisfied. "Why are you suddenly so enthusiastic about this?"

"It's not sudden. She's been going on about this for months now. What exactly happened between you and Helena on your trip to Edinburgh?" This was from August, the sister he had assumed to be on his side.

"Nothing. Nothing at all. If you recall, we were too absorbed in saving Violet from the clutches of a fortune-hunting scoundrel to indulge in a flirtation." He looked pointedly at his youngest sister and was gratified to see that she had the grace to blush. It wasn't entirely true, however. There had been some flirting, if one would call it such. It

wasn't the elaborate and vapid flattery that was thrown at
him in ballrooms. It was quieter and deeper. A genuine
admiration had bloomed between them as they had traipsed
across the North to find Violet.

"But afterward there was," Violet insisted. "You came
to visit almost every day the first week we were back in
London and I was her guest. I saw with my own eyes how
you looked at her."

Max was beginning to understand that Violet had all the
subtlety of an omnibus. "I admire her, I'll admit that. She's
beautiful, kind, and intelligent." And he'd spent more than
one frustrated night in bed imagining her beneath him. He
shifted uncomfortably to look out the window as they
passed the park. A group of nannies pushed their young
charges in baby carriages.

"Then you can see a future for the two of you?"

"No, I cannot. I can admire a woman and not entertain
some bizarre notion of spending the rest of my life with
her." No. His imaginings of Helena were much baser in
nature, making this topic with his sisters completely uncomfortable and borderline inappropriate.

"It's hardly bizarre. I know you like her. I saw you talking to her after dinner the other night." Violet was pouting
now. Her bottom lip actually puckered the way it had when
she was ten and he had insisted she was too old to ride on
his shoulders, not that his protesting had done him much
good then . . . like now. "She would make a fine wife."

"A fine wife? You sound like Papa."

That turned her pout into a scowl. "What does that
mean?"

He was sorry he had brought it up, knowing her feelings
of aversion to their parents' opinions at the moment, but
before he could apologize, August explained. "Papa believes that Max should marry very soon to carry on the
family lineage. It seems that his brush with ill health has

made him long to see the Crenshaw Iron Works legacy confirmed."

Max had told August that much but had stopped short of telling her the ultimatum Papa had given him. It had seemed unnecessarily cruel to share it with her.

"Oh." Violet's scowl softened, but she appeared very perplexed. Perhaps she would take his side in this simply to subvert their parents. "Well, that is an imprudent reason. You should consider Lady Helena because she'll make you happy, not because she'll satisfy Papa and his schemes."

That was exactly right. She *would* satisfy Papa and his schemes. He'd probably be overjoyed at the thought of the future generation of Crenshaw Iron descending from a genuine lady. The idea Max had hardly dared to acknowledge grew roots: Lady Helena could buy him time, lots of precious time to thwart Papa at his own game.

Chapter 4

Woman's ability to earn money is better pro-
tection against the tyranny and brutality of
men than her ability to vote.

VICTORIA WOODHULL

"Violet, this is perfect." Helena stepped through the door
of the former priory that Violet had found to potentially house the London Home for Young Women. It was
very obviously a religious relic of another time with its
stone walls, arched windows, and tower. Over the centuries, the building's use had probably changed a dozen
times, but tall stone columns inside and much of the stained
glass remained, allowing in the gray autumn light from the
small courtyard outside. Most recently, the large chapel appeared to have been put to use as some sort of factory. Machinery lined the back wall, and rows of trestle tables were
set up in the middle of the floor.

The small campus was nestled at the end of a narrow
residential street off Commercial Road at the very edge of
Whitechapel where it bled into Limehouse. It included the
chapel, an attached three-story building that had once
housed monks, and the mews in the back. The whole
grounds were surrounded by a wall that was crumbling in

places and would need substantial refurbishment. Helena liked it because it would keep the courtyard as an outdoor space for the children and provide some separation from the street. While the surrounding streets were populated by earnest and hardworking people, there were warrens and dens of criminals lurking deeper into the East End.

"I knew you would like it," Violet said from behind her. Ostler, the manservant Helena had hired to help provide protection at the orphanage, followed them inside and closed the door.

Since her marriage in the spring, Violet had joined the board of the orphanage and had followed Helena's enthusiasm for the London Home for Young Women. Because Christian had donated the money to purchase a building, Helena had thought it only logical that Violet take the lead on the committee to find a location.

"There's already a workshop here and private rooms with a communal kitchen in the attached residential building, and I think perhaps the rooms above the mews could be used for a school," Violet continued. "The owner, Sir Phineas Penhurst, was gracious enough to give me a tour himself yesterday. I knew as soon as I saw it that you just had to come look for yourself."

"Do you know what work was performed here?" Helena ran her gloved fingertips across the edge of what appeared to be a loom and came away with years' worth of dust.

"Sir Phineas said that it had been leased, but it seems that it's been vacant for a while. He mentioned it has been in his family for around two hundred years, and he'd rather it be put to good use."

"Sir Phineas Penhurst . . . I do not believe I've had the pleasure of meeting him." She wondered if he would be amenable to selling it to the charity for less than market value, or if he was in a situation where he needed the funds.

"Nor had I until yesterday. He indicated that he's anxious to be rid of it."

"One can understand why." Helena walked to the other end of the cavernous room, eyeing the cracks in the plaster over the stones as she went. Despite its age, the floor wasn't sloping and the columns appeared to be in good condition. "It needs some refurbishment, but I believe it's structurally sound. Would he be opposed to having an engineer look it over to make certain before we begin negotiations?"

"My solicitor is helping to manage the sale for Sir Phineas. I can ask him."

If the owner would be willing to sell it to the charity for a discount, there may be a chance of opening in the early part of the new year. The floor of the orphanage diverted to the needs of the women her charity would help was already filled to overflowing. This space *was* functional, assuming no structural issues were found. She held firmly to the excitement that was threatening to take flight. There would still be challenges, even if the owner agreed. The main one would be how to manage the monthly expenses with her reduced budget. Unease made the lump she always seemed to carry in her stomach these days grow slightly larger.

Every time she thought of that night, Maxwell Crenshaw came to mind. When she was alone and still, she could make herself remember the warmth of his body as he had stood next to her. She could imagine exactly how far she would have to rise on her toes and tilt her head to kiss him. Entirely inappropriate thoughts, especially now in this priory with his sister at her side.

Whirling her attention back to the space, she once more surveyed the state of the workroom tables. She could already see the women studiously stooped over them as they learned new skills. "Let us take a tour of the rest of the property," she said.

Violet led the way to the other parts of the space. As she had suggested, the rooms above the mews would make perfect schoolrooms. There were even two small apartments that could be used as housing for staff who would live here full-time. The adjacent building that formed the entire north end of the campus was almost completely divided into small rooms, housing for the monks who originally resided here. They would make perfect transitional homes for the women and children who needed them now. The main floor held gathering rooms, which would work well for a nursery area for the smaller children and a social area for the women. There was even a communal kitchen. It was housed in a small building that had obviously been added on later. Unfortunately, it would need to be almost completely refurbished with updated appliances.

There was so much potential here that Helena found herself smiling as the tour concluded, and hope began to take root in her chest no matter how she admonished herself to be sensible. Nothing was decided, and she very well may not be able to afford the property. But it was so perfect for their needs that she couldn't help but hope it would work out.

As the three of them walked out to her waiting carriage, Helena said, "Violet, you have outdone yourself. I don't think I could have found a more perfect solution if I had commissioned a building myself. How did you find it again?"

Violet flushed, a sheepish look coming over her face as she glanced at the tall building to the south, fronting the main road. "August has expressed interest in purchasing the metalworks factory over there. I came with her to view it a few days ago and noticed this place seemed vacant. As you may recall, my sister and I share the same solicitor, Mr. Clark." At Helena's nod, she continued, "I asked him if he knew the owner, and it turns out the same Sir Phineas owns nearly that entire section of street, including the factory."

"How convenient," Helena said, still uncertain why this revelation would cause her friend to appear guilty, but that question was completely forgotten as another possibility came to mind. "Violet . . . do you suppose that August would consider hiring some of our residents if she pur-

chases the factory? We could provide the training they
would need, of course."

August was well-known as a progressive thinker when
it came to women and their roles in the world. While most
factory owners who would hire women relegated them to
roles they deemed suitable for the weaker sex—textile
work, usually—August might actually consider women for
jobs that carried responsibility and better pay.

"That's an excellent suggestion. I am almost certain that
she would."

"This could be the answer we've been looking for. Do
you suppose it would be terribly unseemly if we go directly
to your Mr. Clark and inquire about the building?"

Violet laughed. "I don't know, but it won't be the first time
I've barged in. Let's make a quick stop there and find out."

B loomsbury Orphanage had been in existence in one
form or another for nearly two hundred years. Starting
in an abandoned hovel one lane over from Newgate Prison,
it had been a place to house the cast-off children of the
prisoners. From there the charity had moved to bigger lodg-
ings in Whitechapel, then Clerkenwell, before finally settling into its new home and name in Bloomsbury. Along the
way its patronage had changed hands several times, until it
had come under the very capable stewardship of Helena's
mother-in-law, Lady Sansbury. It was under her influence
that Helena had been inspired to begin volunteering in the
first year of her marriage. After Arthur's death a mere two
and a half years after their wedding, Lady Sansbury had
retreated to the countryside to nurse her grief, while Helena
had found sanctuary in her work at the orphanage. The one
place where she felt that she could make a difference.

Perhaps she had been foolish, or greedy even, to think
that she might foster that initiative and create a charity on
her own. It was looking more and more like the London

Home for Young Women would not materialize soon, at least not any further than the upper floor of the orphanage.

"I don't understand, Charlotte. How does my father have such control over them? How can he make them renege on their promises without regret?" Helena put her elbows on her desk and dropped her head into her hands, giving in to a rare moment of pique. The words on the letters before her swam on the papers. Two more of her father's associates were pulling their pledges. It was all due to poor planning and financial issues on their part—or so they said—but she knew the truth. This was his very unsubtle way of making a very unfortunate point.

Charlotte hurried around the desk and placed a reassuring hand on Helena's shoulder. She was one of the few patronesses of the orphanage who had been willing to follow Helena into this new endeavor. The same one that seemed in danger of faltering before it even got started.

"I know it doesn't look promising, but something will change in our favor. I simply know it will."

"That is a wonderful thought, but . . ." Helena took in a breath to regain control of her despair. Moving the papers to the side, she stared at the columns of numbers on the ledger Charlotte had presented her along with the letters. "What does Mr. Fitzgerald have to say on the matter?"

Charlotte's husband had managed the accounts for the orphanage for over a decade. It was how Helena had met her, and they had become friends in the ensuing years. When the woman didn't answer right away, Helena looked up to see the worry shining in her dark brown eyes. "The projections do not appear to support opening this winter."

Helena followed her well-manicured finger as she flipped the pages, each spread showing a different month and how their coffers would be empty by summer.

"That's it, then. We cannot open."

"Could you perhaps make an appeal to the owner of the property? If we could get him to agree to a delayed payment schedule, it would help. Or would he agree to make the property a donation?"

"Donate the property? That would be asking for so very much."

"It would, but families do it."

"You're right, Charlotte. We could offer to name the building after him. Create a legacy that will be known clear into the next century."

"Yes, appeal to his vanity."

"I think we have no choice but to try it. I haven't received a reply yet to my inquiry from yesterday. Once I do, we shall have a clearer idea of what to expect."

Before Charlotte could answer, one of the young girls from the top floor tapped at the office door.

"Yes, Abigail?"

"I'm sorry to bother you, Lady Helena." She bobbed a curtsy, the cap on her head flapping in her enthusiasm. "Miss Taylor sent me to ask you to come upstairs. She needs help."

"Thank you, Abigail."

The girl curtsied again and ran away, her footsteps echoing in the stairwell as she went upstairs.

"Thank you for bringing these over," Helena said.

Charlotte smiled, her kind eyes crinkling at the corners. "Of course. I shall see you at the upcoming board meeting."

Helena walked her to the front door of the orphanage before making her way through the cheerful whitewashed rooms on the first floor to the stairwell. The orphanage was decorated like a home should be, with art on the walls and inviting furniture throughout. She had tried in her years here to make it feel less like an institution and more like a place of comfort, reasoning that the children would feel more welcomed and supported in such an environment.

That thinking had extended to the residential floors as well. Each child had their own bed and bedding they selected themselves and a framed piece of art to hang above their bed. It wasn't much, but it gave them some autonomy over their surroundings and a sense of belonging.

On the second floor, Helena walked down to the room where the children who were too young for school lived. Mary was one of the young mothers from the top floor who minded the children on days she wasn't needed in the printing shop where she worked three days a week. She assisted Mrs. White, the governess the orphanage employed. Usually, the days went by without incident, so Helena was surprised when she opened the door to complete chaos.

The beds around the periphery of the room had been almost completely stripped of their bedding. Toys were strewn hither and thither about the space. Fabric dolls dangled by their yarn hair from the draperies, and wooden locomotives were being driven along the walls by several pairs of chubby hands.

"Mary, what in heavens . . . ?" Her words dropped off as a pillow came tumbling her way with a small child stuffed inside the casing, laughing as he rolled. "Ho there! We mustn't have an accident." She stooped and helped him from the pillow. Andrew merely giggled, his dark curls bouncing as he ran to join two girls who had found their way into the painting supplies. "Girls, perhaps we should reconsider an art project at the moment."

She hurried over to them and put the lid back on the jar of watercolor that had been filled with water but was only seconds too late to stop the spill of diluted yellow that covered both of their skirts. The boy yelled, "Pretty!" and swiped his hand through the paint and proceeded to smear it on the wall.

"Mary?" She called again as panic began to take over. The girl appeared to be in the middle of three sobbing children all competing to see who could go about it the loudest.

"Lady Helena, I am terribly sorry to interrupt you, but I seem to be at an impasse."

"Where is Mrs. White?" she asked, wiping down the

girls' dresses as best she could with a length of toweling before the damage could spread. There was no stopping Andrew, however, who had continued his finger painting on the wall, leaving a trail of finger marks that went all the way to the other wall.

"Andrew, you must stop that and go clean your hands," Mary ordered to no avail. To Helena she said, "Mrs. White was feeling under the weather this morning, milady. I didn't let you know because I thought I could handle things."

"I wish you would have called for me earlier—"

"No, milady, you don't understand. I didn't call because I need help, though I can see getting the paints out to occupy them was unwise."

Having decided there was no saving the dresses, Helena paused in unfastening Anna's dress. "Why, then?" It was only at that moment that she realized an older boy stood near her, a look of stunned horror on his face as the drama in the room played out. In his hand he held a note. He was clearly a messenger.

"The printer has asked if I can come now. He's had a rather large order for invitations and needs me to get started on them right away."

"Today?" Helena looked around the room in near despair at the implications of being left alone with ten unruly little children. She had always helped out with the older children. The ones who were civilized and eager to learn. She didn't know if she could handle the younger ones.

The older boy came over and shoved the paper under her nose. "Letter from the printer, ma'am."

"Yes, yes. I see."

"You're right, milady," Mary said. "It's not a good day. I'll tell him—"

"No, Mary, you must go. You cannot turn down work that could benefit your future."

She hurried to finish taking the impossibly small dress off Anna followed by the second girl, leaving them in their cotton shifts. By that time, the trio of sobbing children had quieted somewhat.

"Thank you, milady." Mary passed the smallest of her charges over to Helena, who quickly sat with him on her lap so that the other two could lean against her.

"Would you be kind enough to send Mrs. Cavendish up?" Helena asked.

"I'm sorry, milady. All of the smalls are being attended by only one mistress today. Mrs. Cavendish is assisting in one of the other rooms. It seems that whatever ails Mrs. White has taken hold of others."

Wonderful. This would explain why the headmistress hadn't been at her desk this morning when Helena had come in. Charlotte had been her first meeting of the day, so she hadn't yet had time to do a proper walk of the home as she normally did.

"I hope it's nothing serious. Would you have Kathleen from the kitchen come up to clean the wall before the paint sets in?"

"Of course, milady." Mary gave a quick curtsy and hurried out of the room.

Helena spared a moment of envious contemplation in the direction of the door, before a crash drew her back to the circumstances at hand. "Oh, Andrew." He grinned in triumph as red and blue paint ran in rivers of color around him on the floor. The children with the locomotives squealed in glee as they hurried over and wasted no time in dipping their hands into the paint.

Thus, Maxwell Crenshaw found her in the midst of giving the children baths when he arrived approximately a half hour later.

Chapter 5

❧

It appears that ordinary men take wives because possession is not possible without marriage.

THOMAS HARDY

Max was momentarily dumbstruck by the sight before him. There was no other way to describe how his mouth became dry and every word in his head died a silent death. The doorman, a Mr. Ostler, had been reluctant to show Max to where Helena was working upstairs, but he'd relented readily enough when Max had given his name. Now he knew why as he stood in the corridor watching her gently scrub the child in the bath. She really had been indisposed.

Several strands of golden hair had escaped the confines of her hairpins, and her sleeves were pushed up to her elbows. He had never seen her so disheveled. She had always been the quintessential English lady: hair appropriately restrained by the astute hands of a lady's maid, clothing impeccably maintained and styled without a single wrinkle or unwanted crease, and a voice always within the acceptable range of moderate but benign interest.

This was not the woman he knew, while at the same time being more of the woman he wanted to know. What a contradition she was. She was earthy and real, and he found himself taking a step closer without even realizing it.

"Lady Helena?"

Her eyes widened when she looked up at him through the open door, and her mouth dropped open. It was the most ungraceful expression he had ever seen her make, and that was including the angry way she had scowled at him on the train back to London when he had lectured Violet about running off with scoundrels. He imagined how she would look tousled after sex, after she had come apart in his arms, and he had to force the vision away as heat swept up his body. That wasn't why he was here. His plan, if she agreed, might call for them to pretend to be engaged, but he would not be entitled to the benefits of her charms.

The chubby fist of the child splashed the water in enthusiasm, sending a deluge down her apron front, which brought her out of her momentary stupor. Blowing a strand of hair off her face, she said, "What a pleasant surprise to see you here, Mr. Crenshaw." Her tone was the epitome of a polite lady, but her eyes showed her displeasure.

"The gentleman was insistent, milady," Ostler explained. He gave Mr. Crenshaw a glance filled with censure. Max knew that he should make his apologies, or feel some sort of remorse, but he couldn't bring himself to regret anything that had brought him to this moment in this corridor watching her wash a child in the bathing room.

She raised a brow at him and said, "Thank you, Ostler." The man gave a short bow and left them. Turning her full attention back to the child, she picked her up and wrapped her in toweling as she handed her off to a harried-looking maid who took her charge off into another room.

"In you go, Emily." The last child of the group, a young girl who appeared to be two or three years at most, eyed the water with distrust but bravely stepped into the tub. She had a swatch of blue paint on her cheek, likely the reason for the morning bath.

"I can see I've come at a bad time, but I confess I am glad to be here."

"I cannot imagine why." Her face heated, a pleasant flush rising from her neck to settle in the apples of her cheeks. She was probably embarrassed, another reason he should feel poorly about barging in, but he couldn't summon the emotion.

"Because it's good to see you this way." Now that Ostler was gone he walked closer and leaned a shoulder against the doorjamb. "You are always so well put together and polished." Seeing her like this sent a strange rush of possessive energy rising up within him. What a sight she would be coming undone for him.

She opened her mouth to say something but then seemed to think better of it as she hurried through the child's bath. Finally, she said, "I cannot imagine what you find so amusing about that." Her voice held a crisp note that he imagined was her attempting to inject some properness into the situation.

Amusing? Well, he *was* smiling, he realized. "I wouldn't use the term *amusing*." There was a momentary silence between them, broken only by the splashes of the child in the water. "Enchanting, perhaps."

She glanced up at him. Her blue gaze fixed on his. The whole situation became even curiouser as she again seemed to be at a loss for words. The English lady who always had a rejoinder at the ready was silent. He could get accustomed to using flirting and compliments to fluster her.

She tried very diligently to not look at him as she gently rinsed the girl's fine dark hair, careful not to get water in her eyes. "Perhaps you could assist me?" She indicated the last bit of toweling draped on a hook. He leaned forward to take hold of it and held it out for her. When she took it, her fingers brushed his, drawing the dangerous energy that coursed through his body to the place of the simple contact. A delicious tingle began in his palm.

"Up you go," she said to Emily as she pulled the rubber stopper from the tub and picked the girl up, wrapping her in the toweling. The child's chubby hands clung to her shoulders. To him, she said, "Is there a reason you called?" A current of cool detachment infused her voice. That more than her blush or anything else told him how he affected her far more than she wanted to acknowledge.

The thought pleased him immensely, though he didn't really know why. So what if there was mutual attraction between them? It couldn't lead to anything. She was hardly going to indulge him in a tryst. She probably wasn't even going to indulge him in the betrothal plot.

"I happened to be nearby and thought I would call. Violet and August are always going on about the good work you do here. I wanted to see it for myself." He stepped back to allow her passage into the corridor. As she walked past him, the pleasant smell of lilies teased his nose, making him want to stay close enough to her to get more of her scent.

"You've come to check the wisdom of your donation?" she asked.

"No, I never doubted the funds would be used appropriately under your stewardship. However, I admit that I didn't think to find you so personally involved in the care of the children."

She turned to face him with only inches between them. He took a deep breath of her. "I teach classes to the older children, but I don't typically have reason to be so participatory in the daily care of our younger children. We are shorthanded today."

They stood for a moment in the narrow space. Something happened inside him, something that stopped time and the litany of words in his head, until there was only her.

"Ah," he managed. It was all he could say with her scent around them and the heat from her body warming his front.

What if he kissed her impossibly soft and pink lips just once before returning to New York? What if he held her lush body against his, fitting her curves to his harder angles? Would it be enough to assuage his curiosity, or would it whet his appetite for more of her? He knew it would be the latter. Every new piece of her he was able to grasp hold of only made him want more.

"Lady Helena?" The child's voice was plaintive and soft. She was so young the name came out a bit like *Wady Hewena*. Her soft hand touched Helena's cheek. "I'm hungry."

Max blinked and took a step away from her. This was foolish. She was so rigid and proper, he doubted she would be inclined to indulge their attraction for one night only. Unfortunately, that's all they could have. His life was Crenshaw Iron. Even if she could be persuaded to move to New York, he was too busy to give a wife and eventual children the attention they deserved.

"Yes, it is nearing luncheon." Released from the spell, Helena moved to the door of the room the maid had disappeared into earlier. The faint din of children could be heard from within. "I apologize, but I cannot give you a tour of the premises today."

"Of course. I understand. I shouldn't have dropped by unexpectedly."

"It's no trouble. Any other day . . ." Her voice drifted off as she opened the door and stared at the disorder before her. Half the children were naked, while the other half were in their underthings, except for the one the poor maid was dutifully dressing as he wriggled and squirmed and generally did his best to thwart her efforts. Some of the children were running in circles, trailing bedding behind them.

"Apologies, milady." The young maid glanced up from her charge. "They do not seem to take instruction well." Clearly, taking care of the younger children did not fall under the girl's normal duties.

For her part, Helena appeared faintly horrified. This was out of the realm of her normal duties as well. The possessiveness from earlier reared its head, awakened by seeing this vulnerability that so few ever saw. Some deeply buried part of him liked seeing her armor of polite indifference falling away, almost as much as he relished witnessing how she was able to rally herself.

"Go help Cook prepare their trays." She spoke kindly to the girl. "I think it would be best if they dine in their room today."

Finished dressing the boy, the young maid rose to her feet and gave a quick curtsy before rushing out of the room. Turning to Max, Helena said, "As I was saying, I'm afraid there isn't any time to continue our chat."

"No, I suppose not. There *was* something I had hoped to discuss."

They both noticed the sudden silence in the room at the same time. Helena whirled to see the children staring at them with wide eyes.

"Who's that?" one of them asked.

"Children, this is Mr. Crenshaw. He's come to say hello."

Taking his cue, he said, "Hello. I was passing on the street below and heard such a commotion that I decided to come in and offer my assistance to the dear Lady Helena."

A couple of them giggled, but most continued to stare at him. "Aside from Ostler, who generally stays downstairs, they haven't had cause to interact with very many men," she explained. "I suspect your deep voice and size have rendered you an interesting specimen."

"Have they?" He couldn't resist teasing her, having noted the way her own gaze had taken in his height as she had knelt at the tub.

The hint of flirtation in his voice had her looking back at him until one of the girls asked, "Why does he talk like that?"

"Because I come from a land of giants." Smiling, he strode past Helena into the room. Jeremy, a good friend of his from his university days, had three boys already, all born in the span of three years. Max had had a little bit of practice entertaining them. "Who here likes a good story?"

"I do," answered two of the older-looking boys. The others continued to stare with wide owl eyes.

"Excellent," he answered before glancing over his shoulder at Helena's stunned expression. "I could keep them occupied while you finish dressing them, if you'd like?"

She nodded, slowly at first as if she couldn't believe what was happening. Gathering herself, she said, "Yes, thank you," and hurried to the wardrobe to begin dressing Emily.

Sitting on the end of one of the narrow beds, he asked, "Who here has heard the story of a fellow named Jack and his magic beans? He visits a land of giants, where I'm from."

For the next quarter hour, he kept them entertained as she pulled children over one at a time to dress them. She snickered when he affected a terrible and exaggerated English accent for the part of Jack. She smiled when he stomped around the room as if he were a giant when the story called for it. Despite himself, he was trying to charm *her* as much as keep the children occupied. Winning her approval gave him a rush of elation that was quickly becoming addictive.

Finally, the children were all dressed, and the maid and a woman who appeared to be the cook came in a few moments later carrying trays of apple slices, toasted bread, and cheese. He stayed to help, enjoying his time with her. It made him think of the reason for his visit. Would she agree to a pretend betrothal?

He couldn't answer that any more than he could stop himself from imagining what might happen if the facade of a relationship faded away, if she really did become his wife and the mother of his children. Perish the thought. Two weeks ago he had been assured of his status as a bachelor for at least several more years, and now he was ready to make her his wife. Perhaps *ready* was an exaggeration, but it didn't strike him as an unpleasant thought.

The next half hour was busy as the children ate and were rounded up for yet another story—this time Helena read one to them—before putting them to bed for their naps. He stepped into the corridor as she went around the room tucking them in one by one.

After a moment she stepped out, closing the door softly behind her. "Thank you again for your help," she whispered, walking toward the stairs.

"I enjoyed it."

"Yes, I thought you did. You have children in your life?"

Holding his hand out to indicate that she should proceed him down the narrow staircase, he said, "A close friend has young boys. I've become something of an adopted uncle."

"You'll do well with your own children someday."

He gave a soft laugh. "I hope so. I'm looking forward to the challenge one day, which brings me to the reason for my visit."

She paused on the stairs, her voice only half-teasing as she asked, "You're here because you're in need of an orphan?"

"Not precisely, no. Would there be somewhere we could talk . . . privately?" Now that the time to ask her was here, he felt his tie getting uncomfortably tight, and a prickle of sweat broke out on the back of his neck. He'd had years to overcome his nerves in business negotiations, but this was something different.

Her brow rose in curiosity. "My office." Turning, she led him down the stairs, and he followed, breathing in her scent like someone who had been starved for sex for too long. Even as he thought it, he knew his fascination was with her and not sex. Not *only* sex.

A few moments later she was closing the door, gesturing to the chair before her desk. Her office was small, but uncluttered and polished like her. Everything had its place and its use: a chest of drawers held a tea set on top of it, and he was certain the drawers held important papers; a stand in the corner held her coat; a small stove was there for warmth; and a low row of built-in cabinetry sat below the double windows no doubt containing more papers. The walls held bucolic and brightly colored works of art, lending the room a sunny atmosphere that reminded him of her home. It was a comfortable place that made one feel cozy and at home just by stepping inside it.

He waited politely for her to circle around and take her own seat before sitting. His throat was dry again, and he had to swallow several times before finding his voice. "I won't quibble. I've already taken up far too much of your time."

"It's no trouble at all, Mr. Crenshaw. You were actually very helpful. Please don't worry yourself, but I am intrigued." The smile she gave him seemed genuine. He couldn't help but stare at the imperfection of her two front teeth on top; they were slightly longer and out of alignment with the others, but the flaw only made her more real, more appealing somehow. "The last time we spoke like this your parents were forcing your sister to wed, and we were plotting to go find her and save her reputation. I'm confident that whatever it is this time cannot be that terrible."

His stomach dropped at the reminder of the low opinion she must have of his family. His parents. What right did he have to ask her for this massive favor?

Something of his thoughts must have shown on his face, because she said, "Oh no."

He took in a breath, her sweet scent touching him again, making the nerves in his stomach dance. Best to get this over with so they could both go about their day as if this morning had never happened. "I find myself in need of a temporary fiancée, and I hoped you would agree to the task."

Chapter 6

❦

*I dare not show you where I am vulnerable,
lest . . . you should transfix me at once.*

CHARLOTTE BRONTË

Helena stared at the man across the desk from her. His deep brown eyes looked as earnest as ever with the slightest tinge of misery, and her heart ached a little at the sight while a thousand butterfly wings flickered in her stomach. His request had caught her completely by surprise. In fact, she was certain that she had misheard. When she was taken aback, she reverted to the training of her youth, to be proper in all ways, even in the most improper of circumstances.

"Are you asking me to marry you, Mr. Crenshaw?" Her voice was as even and tempered as if she had asked about the weather, while her heart pounded in her chest.

He wasn't asking her to marry him. Of course he wasn't. He had said *temporary*, which by its very nature seemed to mean the engagement would not reach its usual end, so why did it feel as if he were serious and this were real?

"More specifically, to become engaged, but only for a little while."

"I-I don't . . . I'm afraid I don't understand." Her body felt heated, and she had to struggle to stay seated and not get up and pace about the room.

"No, I suppose I haven't explained it. Let me start from the beginning." He sat back, his long legs stretching out before him.

She noted the way the fine wool of his trousers pressed against his thighs, something she hadn't been able to unsee after that dinner and Lady Blaylock's perusal. What did he do to get the thigh muscles of a laborer? Did he labor in his factories? She thought of an engraving she had once seen of the *Farnese Hercules*. Would his legs resemble those of the statue, all hard sinew and intriguing indentations where muscle met muscle? Forcing herself to look back up at his face, she realized his lips were moving and he was talking and she had missed the beginning.

"Leopards cannot change their spots, and neither can my father."

"Your father?" Yes, this request had to be because of his father. To clarify, she asked, "He wants you married?"

His brow rose slightly at her inattention. "His brush with ill health has him recommitted to seeing *all* of his children settled, myself included." He looked toward the window, the tendon in his jaw clenching and unclenching as he appeared to struggle with what he wanted to say. "He wants me married and producing children as quickly as possible. He wants to be assured that the Crenshaw legacy is kept intact and on track before he . . ."

Before he died. "But he is recovering, yes? He hasn't taken a turn for the worse?" she asked in rising alarm.

"No, no, he hasn't. He appears to be recovering under the good care of his doctors. I believe the scare was enough to galvanize him into action, as it were, to have an heir after me."

For some unfathomable reason, a pit seemed to open up

in her stomach. Her heart was merely seconds away from falling into it. "I suppose you Americans aren't that different after all."

The corner of his mouth ticked up in a grim estimation of a smile. "No."

"But this isn't what you want?"

"No." He paused. "Well, yes, I do want a wife. I do want children. The Crenshaw legacy is important to me. I wish to have children to carry it on long after I'm gone."

The words were not unexpected or careless, but they carried sharp edges just the same. Edges pointed enough to make them prick her as they landed. There was no future for them even without his wish for children. It was stupid that an ache rose in her throat, but it was there just the same. She swallowed and stared at the folded newspaper on her desk until the ache eased enough for her to find her voice again. "Then I don't understand the problem. You're approaching thirty. Isn't it time you consider his wishes and settle down with a family?"

A deep groove appeared between his brows. "Eventually, yes, but not now and not at his whim. As you've mentioned in the past, Crenshaw Iron takes up much of my life. I don't have the time to devote to a family right now."

"I'm afraid you won't find a sympathetic audience with me. I had this conversation with my parents at sixteen, seventeen, and again at eighteen years of age when I was betrothed. You've had at least a decade longer to enjoy not being married, and look at your sisters."

His scowl deepened. "You're saying that I should relent?"

"No, not precisely. I don't condone forced marriage, as you know." That seemed to placate him, and he relaxed. "Though I do understand you are busy, people of our station in life have to marry. It is the law, probably." She smiled.

"Our station?" His brow ticked upward again. "Are you

saying that I am your equal, Lady Helena?" He put a particular drawl on her title that she found very pleasing.

"Of course not, but near enough." She teased him, hoping to lighten her own troubled feelings.

"And you're not married." He gave her a pointed look.

Not because her parents hadn't tried to pack her off again. "A perquisite of widowhood."

He blinked, looking chastened. "I'm sorry. That was unforgivable."

Waving off his apology, she asked, "Has he picked a bride who is wholly unsuitable?"

"He hasn't chosen one. I'm to pick my own bride by the end of the year."

The marriage wasn't set, then. Relief swamped her, but she wouldn't allow herself to examine why. He stood in agitation and walked over to look out the window. The street was fairly busy with midday traffic, but he seemed lost in his own head rather than taking in the scene.

"You have been bidden to marry, but you get to choose your own bride. That's more consideration than your poor sisters were given."

He whirled; hot anger tightened his features and made something deep inside her clench in response. "You know that I was against what they did to my sisters. I came over here twice to try and stop it."

"And yet they are both married now." What in the devil was wrong with her? Why was she needling him this way? She only knew that she liked the wave of fury that drifted over his features, turning his eyes hot and dark, and making his body tighten as he closed in on her. She stood to meet him, feeling her heart beat in every extremity. It didn't beat with fear but with exhilaration as he came to a stop a mere foot away from her.

"Are you saying that I should have done more? That this is my penance?"

What *was* she saying? This was madness, and yet, she couldn't stop.

"Perhaps. Women have been sacrificed for centuries at the whims of wealthy men. It's only fair that a few men fall as well." The passion of his response was surprisingly addictive. When every interaction she ever had was restrained and veiled in refinement, he gave her something true. Real pieces of himself that she could hoard away.

His jaw clenched. She had the strangest urge to run her fingertips along his close-cropped beard to see if it was as soft as it looked. "Then you won't help me?"

"I didn't say that." Somehow, she managed not to sound breathless, even though she could barely draw air because every time she did his scent made a fresh surge of excitement flicker in her belly. He smelled spicy and warm and clean. "I merely meant to demonstrate your place of privilege."

He stared at her, his gaze taking in every imperfection in her face, leaving the echo of a sensation everywhere it touched. Even the density of his form seemed to weight the air around her. "I'll concede you've made a fair point," he said, the tension leaving his jaw. "You'll forgive me if I attempt to thwart my fate."

"And you want me to help you do it?"

He gave a single nod, not bothering to step back to keep a respectable distance between them. She didn't mind.

"Why don't you want to marry now, Mr. Crenshaw? You're the right age; you've mentioned a desire for children."

"I'd like to take my time and find the right woman. I want a union of mutual respect and affection, someone who can be a true partner to me instead of an ornament at my table and on my arm. An equal. I'm prepared to wait for such a woman."

She parted her lips to respond, but no words were forthcoming. Perhaps she was losing her grasp on reality, but the position of his wife suddenly seemed very appealing.

He did not seem to notice. "I need your promise not to share with anyone what I'm about to tell you. It could hurt someone whom we both care deeply about."

He spoke so emphatically that she had to agree. "I promise."

He nodded again and leaned back against the edge of her desk, bringing him to nearly eye level with her. His thigh pressed against her skirt. "Papa knows he stands no chance of getting me to agree to a hasty marriage, so he's upped the ante. While he's been working on that ill-advised Indian railroad plan, August has been working on a special project. She's obtained permission and the promise of funding to become a major contractor on the Prince Albert Dock. Papa has decided that if I don't cooperate, he'll pull resources from her so that she can't follow through with the project."

It seemed so cruel and unfair that Helena brought a hand to her chest. "But that will crush her. Not only will it crush her, she'll be a laughingstock. You know how many doubt her abilities as it is because she's a woman. This will prove them all right, at least in their eyes."

"I know. It's why we can't tell her, but I've come up with a plan. As it stands now, the project isn't due to start until the spring. Papa believes that he can bring me to heel before then, which is why he's insisted on a betrothal announcement by the end of the year. He wants me married soon after. To stop him, we need to accelerate the timeline of the project." He spoke fervently but with a calm that said he knew exactly what he was doing. His confidence set her at ease. She understood why people listened to him. "If she can begin production by the first of the year, then when I don't marry, it will be too late for Papa to pull his support. The investors will have bought in, and there will be too many contracts at stake because the work will already have started."

"This is why you need a temporary engagement?"

He nodded, his eyes lighting up with intrigue. "We can start a courtship over the next several weeks while I'm still in London. By Christmas we announce our engagement, privately to the family. I believe that will be enough to placate him. We can take our time setting a date and then drift apart over the ensuing months. It'll all be perfectly believable, because I'll be in New York, and you'll be here. Once August has things up and running smoothly, we call off the wedding."

She was so caught up in the idea of starting a courtship with him that it took her a few moments to process the rest of what he said, so she walked toward the windows to take some time. It was an ingenious plan, really. She would have been impressed if she wasn't so worried about what the courtship might do to her. She wasn't a debutante. She had been courted by men before her marriage. There were men now who had subtly made their interest known to her. It wasn't the courtship that bothered her. It was that *he* would be the man doing the courting. It was the extended time with him. Maxwell Crenshaw was like no other man she had ever met. No, that wasn't right. On the surface, he wasn't that different. No, that wasn't right, either.

There were bound to be other men like him somewhere in the world, but she hadn't met them. No one she had met was as unpolished and yet refined as he was. No one else wore the demeanor of a gentleman like a second skin, hinting at the existence of a wilder, more visceral man underneath. No one else made her feel when she was so determined not to feel.

As if he was afraid she would reject the proposition out of hand, he shifted behind her and said, "I know that there could be ramifications of our calling off the engagement. You can be the one to end things. We'll come up with some suitable reason, and if need be, I am prepared to come here and face public degradation to beg for your hand. It will be a harrowing scene where you can outright refuse. Hopefully, that will keep your reputation intact."

The smile in his voice had her turning to face him. "You would do that? You would come here and humiliate yourself in front of all of London to protect your sister from finding out the awful thing your father is prepared to do?"

"My penance." His lips curved in a smile, all evidence of his earlier anger evaporated. His eyes were back to being earnest and deep, but there was the look of a predator about him now. A man on the verge of getting something he wanted. That clench deep within her happened again.

"I don't know if we can convince them of the ruse. Everyone knows that I have sworn off marriage for now."

"We can," he said with a cool confidence that would have been annoying had she not liked it so much, especially when his hot gaze landed on her lips.

They went dry, and she licked them before her fingers found their way to a strand of hair that had escaped the pins earlier. They were having this conversation, and she hadn't even had a chance to tidy herself. "I'll have to consider my reputation. If it reflects badly on the charity . . ."

"I don't want to overstep, but I heard enough of your conversation with Lady Blaylock after dinner the other night to know that your home for young women is in jeopardy. I don't know if she's correct in her assessment, but I will be happy to help you find out."

"What do you mean?"

"If we're courting, and then engaged, let's see if the donations come back. I will do my utmost to show my support for the venture and encourage others to do so as well. If we have to extend our engagement, say until you have the building secured and operations funded, then we extend it. Spring, summer, it doesn't matter to me." He shrugged.

He seemed so reasonable and agreeable about the whole

thing that she wanted to say yes. The fact that she very much wanted to know what it would be like to be courted by him shouldn't figure into the matter. She would be doing this to help her friend. If it also helped her charity, then wonderful. If it *also* assuaged her curiosity, then so much the better.

But what if she couldn't withstand the full charm of Maxwell Crenshaw without losing herself?

"I would like some time to think about it before giving you my answer."

He stared at her for so long that she thought he meant to offer an argument, but then he gave a curt nod. "I suppose it's only reasonable. I've given you a shock."

"It's not every day that one is given such an interesting proposal."

He grinned and pushed himself up from her desk so that she had to look up at him. "It's beyond me why you're still available for such an interesting proposal. Are Englishmen really so blind?"

That sounded like a compliment. She didn't know how to manage compliments from him, because she was certain he wasn't the type to toss them out casually. When he spoke them, they meant *something*. But what? He was leaving soon. There was no possible outcome of a flirtation between them that would lead to any sort of satisfying conclusion.

No, he had to be saying it to soften her toward him. "I'm disappointed. I didn't think you were the type of man who would toss out sweet words simply to sway me. Do you not trust your skills as a negotiator?"

"I trust them wholeheartedly, Lady Helena. Enough to know that I'll be hearing from you soon." His grin stayed on his face as he gave a tilt of his head at the door to tell her goodbye.

From the window she watched him dash down the steps out front, practically skipping in his confidence. As he greeted his driver, her gaze took in the breadth of his shoulders and the strength of his hand on the carriage door.

She had already made her decision, and they both knew it. All that was left was for her to shore her defenses against the whirlwind courtship that was coming. She wasn't entirely confident that she could do it . . . or that she even wanted to try.

Chapter 7

Virtue can only flourish amongst equals.
MARY WOLLSTONECRAFT

My dear Mr. Crenshaw,

A ball is being given in honor of the birthday of His Grace,
the Duke of Hereford, four days hence. It is certain to be
well worth your efforts to attend.

Yours very sincerely,
Lady Helena March

Madam,

Save your waltzes for me.

Yours,
Maxwell Crenshaw

Helena had not been this anxious and excited at a ball
since her coming-out season. This was partially due
to her state of dress, or lack of dress, as it were, but mostly
because of Mr. Crenshaw. *Maxwell.* She should try to remember that after tonight she would refer to him by his
given name, because she planned to accept his proposal.
Tonight, they would dance and flirt and do all the things
that a couple in the beginning stages of a courtship should
do. It would be a deception, but her body didn't seem to

know that. The palms of her hands tingled with the expectation of touching him as they danced. Her heart seemed to
beat faster whenever she caught sight of a tall, dark-haired
man. He hadn't arrived yet, and the anticipation of tonight
had her seeing him in every man over six feet.

"Helena, dear." Mama's harsh whisper caught her ear as
the woman approached. She wore a modest but stylish
gown in burgundy with similarly dyed feathers in her elab-
orately pinned hair. She was one of those attractive people
who would look elegant no matter what they wore. It was
as if she had somehow managed to arrange the silver
streaks in her hair to frame her face and perfectly highlight
the brown tresses. People milled around them, significantly
slowing her progress as she was forced to greet them all as
she passed. Helena was accustomed to this. Her mother had
been quite popular before Helena's birth, and time had not
changed a thing.

Helena waited patiently. Having arrived on the arm of
her brother a mere half hour ago, she had yet to see her
parents. It was only after they came together in the midst of
the crowd that she noticed the admonition burning in her
mother's eyes. "Good evening, Mama. You look lovely."
Her mother's gaze took in her gown surreptitiously.

"Helena . . . dear," she repeated, leaning forward so that
no one would overhear. "Have you entirely forgotten your
improver?" The last word was said so quietly Helena might
not have known what she meant had she not been anticipating this very conversation.

Helena laughed. "I have done no such thing, Mama. You
know the new style doesn't call for an improver."

Her gown was a striking combination of black and
white. The white bodice was cut into a deep V in the front
and back and fell just off her shoulders. There was a second
layer of black silk trimming the bodice that gave the provocative effect that the white gown revealed the top edging
of her black underclothing, not that she would ever wear

such a color under her clothes. The cuirasse-style bodice extended down over her hips in a shape that was almost formfitting. From there, the short skirt and a series of underskirts alternated the black and white pattern all the way down to the floor. The various layers were gathered up in the back and secured just beneath her bottom to create a lovely draping effect across the front. This meant that the gown did not need a dress improver, and the various layers created a graceful fall of black and white silk that trailed on the floor behind her.

"I disapprove of this." Mama sniffed her displeasure.

"I'm hardly the only one wearing the new style. Don't you remember August—" She stopped talking when her mother closed her eyes for a moment. It was probably wrong to remind her that August had been one of the first to wear the look back in the spring. Many of the older women considered it an indecent display of hips, and almost all of them also considered the Americans indecent in a variety of other ways. The truth was that while most of the women present still wore a bustle, several had adopted the new Continental style.

"Yes, I recall."

Helena smiled. It would be in poor form to tell her mother that her small rebellion had been in part because of their subtle marriage pressure. At twenty-six she felt old, and a pretty and provocative gown made her feel young and attractive again. Instead, she said, "You might try it next year. The fall of silk would look attractive on your figure."

Her mother pursed her lips, but Helena could tell the compliment had soothed her ruffled feathers. However, she had been reluctant to give up her crinoline and could not understand why the current fashion was moving toward a more natural silhouette.

"The colors of your gown are remarkable," Mama said to soften her earlier censure. "Mature but daring, which suits you very well."

"Thank you."

"You could do with more bodice. You must take care of how much of your bosom you display."

Helena fought to keep her eyes from rolling. Her mother was fine boned and with a small frame. Helena, however, had inherited her larger frame from her father's side of the family, and as a result, her shoulders had always been broader than she wanted and her breasts larger than was fashionable. Smile intact, she said, "I'm certain there is a more appropriate place for this conversation."

"You're quite right, dear." Mama patted her hand and glanced over toward where a group of men stood talking with Papa. "I've already spoken with Lord Tilbury and Sir Stratton, and both have indicated an eagerness to dance with you tonight. Please make certain you save them both dances. Stratton has recently inherited, if you recall, so perhaps a waltz for him."

"I can find my own dance partners."

"I know that, but I want to make certain we don't leave anyone out. I know that Stratton isn't the most exciting—"

"Mama, he's almost sixty years old."

"And what does that matter? He's fit and an excellent sportsman."

Helena could feel her jaw clenching, but she fought the urge and retained her smile. "I trust you spoke with Papa?" He must have told Mama about their conversation after dinner last week, which had put her into a matchmaking mentality. Not that the idea of matrimony was ever far from her mind; it was only not typically this aggressive.

"I have, but that's neither here nor there. Stratton would be an excellent match for you. You would be very comfortable with him."

"I *am* very comfortable now." Between her moderate income, the townhome, and the cottage in Somerset, she would be able to live the rest of her life in modest luxury. She had no need for more than that.

Mama smiled and waved at an acquaintance across the room. "Do not forget your objective, Helena."

"And what is my objective?"

"Your home for young women. Stratton seems inclined to indulge you in the endeavor, and his reputation is above reproach."

"Have you talked with him about my charity?"

"Well, no, not specifically, but he favors you very much." She gave Helena a knowing look. "With a little finesse, you could have him agreeing to anything."

Before Helena could answer, Lord and Lady Stampford greeted them. Was this truly how she was supposed to plan the rest of her life? Find a man who would lend his financial support to her causes in exchange for her hand in marriage?

Hand in marriage. No, it was more like her body in his bed. Despite her best efforts, her face flamed at the idea. It felt as if they all walked around using euphemisms because the real words were so unpalatable.

A murmur rose through the crowded ballroom as the Duke and Duchess of Hereford made their way in from the receiving line.

"Ah, the American." Lady Stampford's high voice was hard to miss as she practically sneered the word.

The American was how they all seemed to refer to Camille, Hereford's wife. She had married Hereford about a year ago and had been regarded with various versions of condescension ever since. Everyone knew that he had only married the pretty girl for her wealth, and instead of looking upon Camille with kindness and pity, they all regarded her as a shallow social climber. The censure had eased a bit since the arrival of the Crenshaw heiresses in the spring, but poor Camille still bore the brunt of being an outsider worse than they. She lacked parents who were attempting to expand the scope of their business, which had, at least to a small degree, softened the sharp tongues that would wag about the Crenshaw heiresses otherwise. Camille had been cast to the wolves, all alone to face the wrath of London Society with her parents back in New York.

She was only around twenty, and Hereford was nearing sixty himself. She stared straight ahead as they walked in, her chin up a notch higher than it should be as she faced down the scrutiny of the guests. Everyone fell silent as she accepted a glass of champagne and asked them all to raise their own glasses in a toast to her husband. He didn't bother to look at his wife once, not even as she spoke, all but praising his virility and youthfulness. He stood next to her, surveying the crowd like a king finally receiving his due.

Helena had to look away as unreasonable fury rose within her. After concerning herself with August's and Violet's marriage predicaments earlier this year, and now facing her own albeit minor pressure to remarry, she held a newfound sympathy for Camille. Women were like expensive ornaments to men such as Hereford. They were there to brighten the space around them, to be interesting to look upon, to stroke their sense of pride, to give of themselves so that men could take and take, filling up all the holes and dark places within themselves with women's light because they lacked their own. What would become of the poor girl when she could no longer fulfill that role for him? She would be relegated to the country to wither away in an old house until she died of boredom. If she was lucky, he would go first, and she would be free.

"She has no shame," Lady Stampford whispered.

But there was no mention of Hereford's indignity. Camille wouldn't be here if not for his need for her money.

Mama shook her head, but Helena couldn't hear her reply. Her mother was never unduly harsh with someone, but even she disapproved of Camille. She only seemed to tolerate August and Violet because she had no choice. Over the course of the year, the Crenshaws had slowly dug their financial talons into the British upper crust, and while many might resent them, they were too dependent upon them to act on their feelings.

It only made what she was planning with Maxwell seem that much more provocative.

A large hand on her lower back caused a lovely ribbon of warmth to drift through her belly in recognition as a soft, deep voice whispered near her ear, "Apologies for arriving late."

Maxwell was grinning down at her, the corners of his eyes crinkling attractively. The gaslight caught the flecks of amber in his deep brown eyes, making them appear warmer than usual. A thrill of pleasure shot through her stomach. "Good evening, Mr. Crenshaw . . ." She swallowed then remembered herself. "Maxwell."

His smile broadened, and he leaned in again. "Helena."

His hot breath touched her ear, sending a delicious shiver across her skin. She very much felt like a debutante caught in the intoxicating excitement of her first infatuation. He was handsome and charming, and for one night she wanted to allow herself to forget that this was a ploy. For tonight she wanted to pretend that he was wholly suitable for her.

"No apologies needed. The dancing hasn't started yet."

Her mother glanced back at her. When she saw Maxwell, she smiled and nodded in greeting, but her gaze caught Helena's before she turned back around. It held a warning that Helena understood. Something must have changed between them. Something that could be seen by those around them, because Mama was warning her away from him.

He shifted beside her, his thigh brushing the silk of her skirt, and she realized that was why. He stood entirely too close to her. He had dropped his hand from her back, but it rested at his side dangerously close to hers. She could feel the heat of his arm near hers. She smiled as she pretended to listen to Camille while soaking in Maxwell's presence. A curious sensation on the back of her neck as if someone were watching her had her turning her head to see Violet and Christian near the entrance. Violet smiled at her in silent greeting, but her gaze immediately caught on her brother's tall frame beside Helena, and a question crossed her lovely features.

Did his sisters know about the plan? Probably not, because Maxwell had implicitly said that no one could know the whole truth. They would have to tell Violet and August something, Helena decided. It wouldn't be fair to make them think the relationship was real.

Camille finished her prepared words to a round of "Hear! Hear!" which brought Helena back to what was happening. Everyone took a drink from their glasses. A footman appeared by magic to offer Maxwell champagne, meaning he must have come directly to her instead of wandering around. That pleased her immensely.

"To us," she whispered, holding her glass aloft again.

"You're officially accepting?"

She nodded in silent acknowledgment.

He smiled behind his glass before tipping it to his lips. "I'm beginning to think you're going to enjoy this too much. Your life was sorely lacking in intrigue."

"That hasn't been true since you Crenshaws came to London."

He laughed, drawing her mother's disapproving eye. "We do have a certain quality." Winking at Helena, he turned his attention to Hereford, who was now thanking everyone for coming.

Hereford spoke again for several minutes, but Helena only heard every few words. She was too busy trying to deconstruct Maxwell's smell. A soft cloud of his scent surrounded her, not too intrusive, only enough to have her wanting to lean in closer to get more of it. There was the pleasant, clean scent of citrus, possibly lemon, which quickly gave way to a deeper woodsy fragrance, perhaps vetiver, but underneath that was something stronger and warm with an almost smoky depth. What was it?

"Shall we dance and begin this ruse publicly?" He shifted and offered his arm to her.

It was only then that she realized the opening strains of the waltz "Tales from the Vienna Woods" had started. She accepted his arm as her mother turned, momentarily blocking their path to the dance floor, where couples were already beginning to take their places.

"Good evening, Mr. Crenshaw." To Helena, she said, "Say hello to Sir Stratton, darling."

Helena hadn't noticed that at some point during the speeches the man had taken a position at Mama's far side. "Hello, Sir Stratton. How are you?"

He opened his mouth to answer, but before he could, Maxwell said, "Good evening to you both. I'm afraid that Lady Helena has promised me her waltzes this evening." That was all he said before politely bowing his head and ushering her through the crowd. They had no doubt left both Mama and poor Sir Stratton behind in openmouthed shock, but Helena couldn't bring herself to look behind her and check.

"That was poor of you," she said when he gently took her champagne glass from her hand and put it on the tray of a waiting footman. Then he pulled her into his arms as they joined the other couples.

"I imagine it's nothing less than your lot expect from a Crenshaw." There was a slight edge in his voice that caught her by surprise. The fact that he would lump her in with the others hurt her far more deeply than it should have.

She waited until they had completed a partial turn around the room so they were on the far side of the dance floor where there was less of an audience. "My lot?"

"Aristocrats. The men and women who naively believe themselves to be above others because they happened to have been born in a manor house."

"Do you think that I believe myself to—?" She paused because a couple drifted a bit close, and there was no need for anyone to hear them arguing. Not if they were hoping to be convincing in their ploy. "To be above you in status?"

His brow arched, but otherwise his features stayed calm and composed. "How could you not?"

"Are you implying that you yourself were not born in luxurious surroundings? If gossip can be believed, your annual income far exceeds even that of Evan's with his newly inherited gold mine."

"And yet we both know that income does not a gentleman make."

"Apparently not." She couldn't believe how quickly her anger had taken hold of her. One moment she was anticipating the dance with him, and the next she was ready to storm from the room.

He glanced away, though his feet kept perfect time to the music. She could see the muscle working in his jaw as he got a handle on his own anger. After a moment, he appeared contrite as he said, "I don't know what . . . I shouldn't have lumped you in with them."

"No, you shouldn't have. Need I remind you that the entire reason this deception is going to work is because of my *elevated status?*"

His expression softened a bit. "Point taken. I do appreciate your assistance."

She sniffed and glanced toward the crowd as he led her along in the dance. He really was a good dancer. He didn't exude grace, but he managed the steps easily without making it seem as if his large frame were weighting his every move. "I should hope so."

"Truth be told . . ." He paused, prompting her to look at him in time to see an unlikely pink tinting his face and ears. He was embarrassed. She nearly stumbled at the realization and only recovered because of his strong hand at her back. "I didn't like the way your mother looked at me. Like I wasn't good enough to dance with you."

"She looks at everyone that way."

"Not that Stratton fellow." He looked down at her again, meeting her eyes, and for the first time ever she saw the hint of vulnerability in their depths. It was actually very charming. Before she could comment on it, he hurried on. "That doesn't matter, though. It was no reason to take my irritation out on you."

Speechless for the moment, she gave a small shake of her head. He was jealous of Sir Stratton. The knowledge made her unreasonably happy.

"You *would* make a lovely couple, however," he added.

She missed a beat and managed to step on his foot. Glaring up at him, she opened her mouth to reply but paused when she saw how he was watching her. His eyes had narrowed slightly, drawing his brows into the beginnings of that furrow she so enjoyed, but the corner of his mouth tugged upward. "You're baiting me."

His expression didn't change as he led them into a turn. When it was finished, he said, "Perhaps."

"Why?"

He somehow managed to shrug while keeping his perfect form. "Because I like how you become exceedingly proper when you take offense to something. You're adorable."

Adorable. She hadn't been adorable in at least two decades, and even then, no one had called her that. "I am an adult woman. That is hardly an appropriate—" She broke off when she realized he was still amusing himself at her expense. They went through two more turns as she attempted to calm herself. What reason did she have for allowing herself to get upset about his teasing, when she herself had done the same thing at the orphanage? There was something when they were together that led to this sort of immature chiding.

"This is precisely why this isn't going to work."

"Why?" His hand was on her back slightly lower than necessary. It had been there ever since he had helped to right her and hadn't moved back to its appropriate position. It wasn't completely improper; it was simply that she kept focusing on it.

"No one will believe that we're in love when they see us constantly arguing with each other."

His gaze became thoughtful as he watched her. The dance continued, but she could feel his scrutiny through every turn and step. Finally, he said, "I don't believe the idea is to make them think we're in love." When her brow rose in question, he tilted his head slightly toward her to be heard over the music, but so he wouldn't have to raise his voice very much. "That wouldn't work."

"Then what is the point of this charade?"

He gave her a slight grin, but there was something dark and devilish in his eyes now. "I've always thought lust is the more powerful emotion, and it gets mistaken for love far too often."

"Lust?" She repeated the word stupidly, because she couldn't understand what he meant. The woman next to them glanced over her shoulder at them, and Helena blushed, only then realizing that she'd been too shocked to lower her voice.

"Unfulfilled desire can cause men to do forceful but ridiculous things. No, we don't have time to convince them we're in love. We only need to make them believe that I want you beyond reason."

She swallowed thickly as every word she had ever thought died a slow death in her head. It was a good thing the music was dying away, because she probably couldn't have continued to waltz.

Maxwell bowed over her hand and placed a chaste kiss to the back. "Meet me in the conservatory at midnight."

She watched him walk away, unable to talk or even move. The couples passed around her as they traded partners and prepared for the next dance. She had never once met a man in secret at a ball. It seemed only fitting that Maxwell Crenshaw would be the first.

Chapter 8

For a few seconds they looked silently into each other's eyes, and the distant and impossible suddenly became near, possible, and inevitable.

LEO TOLSTOY

The conservatory was a modestly sized space at a far corner of the house that overlooked the garden. It existed on both the ground and first floors with a spiral staircase adjoining the two. A small receiving room separated it from the ballroom, making it a quiet but not scandalous place for Max and Helena to meet. Or so he had thought. As Max roamed the narrow aisles formed by specially built shelving, he realized the room easily contained double the recommended allotment of plants for the space. The aisles were wide enough to traverse without issue; the problem was that the greenery rose all the way up to the glass ceiling. The effect was that no one could see who lingered in the aisle on either side of them, while potted trees, shrubbery, and ferns stood sentinel at the ends of the rows, their full leaves and branches working as shelter.

"Mr. Crenshaw."

Max turned from his study of the unsuitability of the conservatory to see Helena approach. Her gown shimmered as she walked, the gaslight emphasizing the way the fabric clung to her hips, making them appear full and lush. He couldn't stop his gaze from resting on the creamy swell of her breasts that spilled over the bodice. She really was quite breathtaking. He'd known this all along, obviously, having spent considerable time in her company, but there was something about the way that gown fit her so perfectly that had him unable to look away. He'd never seen her wear anything so seductive.

A trio of older ladies had beaten him to the otherwise deserted conservatory. They had smiled at him pleasantly enough when he had entered the room moments earlier but had since cast dubious glances his way as if he might try to pounce on them as they perused the roses. The three watched them curiously as Helena walked up to him, their stares drawing him from his stupor.

"Helena," he said, rediscovering his voice.

She smiled up at him, her white teeth gently tugging her bottom lip. "Have you called a meeting to discuss strategy?"

Casting the older women a fleeting look, he offered Helena his arm and led her to the other side of the room, which had a wall of windows overlooking the garden. She offered the ladies a greeting as they walked.

"Yes, but I didn't realize this place might be inappropriate for our purposes. I wanted somewhere quiet, but not scandalous."

She laughed. "I guess you haven't heard of Lady Russell's obsession with botany. They call this her Petit Garden of Eden."

"I'd heard, but I suppose I underestimated her enthusiasm." Everyone who had dinner with Hereford and his sister had been subjected to at least one long discussion of her conservatory here in London, which she had taken over after her mother's death and kept as a shrine to the late dowager. If one were very unlucky, they were treated to a second, even lengthier discussion about her larger conservatory at her country estate.

"Now, Mr. Crenshaw, you should know to never underestimate a lady." She teased him as she reached out to touch one of the lilies housed on this side of the room.

"I would never underestimate *you*."

She smiled at that, and he had to drag his gaze away from her lips. They were the pink of rose petals. He wondered if they would feel as soft and supple as them, too. Now that they were far enough away from the women, he paused and said, "I want to apologize for earlier. I know you're not like them. It was unfair of me to lash out at you in my frustration."

She appeared thoughtful as she looked up at him. "I wouldn't say that I'm completely unlike them, but thank you."

He took in a breath, feeling like the oxygen had been sucked out of the room. Standing here with her felt different than all the other times he had been near her. Maybe it was because they were so much closer now to acknowledging the unspoken heat that lay between them. "I wanted to make certain that we are on the same page, as it were. That you realize what we're undertaking."

She glanced behind them toward where the trio had only recently disappeared down another aisle. Gently pressing her hand to his arm, she guided them down their own aisle. "Oh yes, I understand completely." Lowering her voice, she continued, "Flirting, courtship, betrothal. Then I get to break your heart in a humiliating display of backpedaling. Well, humiliating for you."

She gave a soft laugh, and he couldn't help but smile at her. She really was adorable in a sensual sort of way. "Good. I'm glad we understand each other, and you're anticipating my future set-down with relish. Now that you've had time to think things over, are there any additional rules you would like to put in place?"

"Additional rules? Have we come up with any?"

"Only the unspoken one . . . that I won't leave you compromised beyond repair." He loved how her cheeks flushed at that one as she quickly glanced away at a potted plant that he couldn't identify.

"Ah, that one. Yes, it is an important one." She leaned forward, bringing a long strand of leaves to her nose, which wrinkled slightly at the unpleasant smell.

"Any others?" he prompted.

"Perhaps one. I'd like to not break the hearts of your sisters, particularly Violet. I suspect that she may be of a mind to play matchmaker."

Residual dread settled in his stomach at the memory of being trapped with Violet in the carriage as she joyfully arranged his romance with Helena. "I fear you're right, but I don't know how to tell them without giving too much away."

"Do they know *anything*?"

He quite liked the look of concern that crossed her face. In the gaslight, her eyes appeared deep pools of touching apprehension. Clearing his throat against a sudden huskiness, he said, "I have told them of Papa's demand, but not his ultimatum."

"Good." She nodded, and the spell she was weaving was broken. "That should be sufficient. We can tell them that we've conceived of the idea to placate your father, and my donors, and leave out the rest about August."

"That might be enough, though I think August might suspect there's something more to the scheme."

"Can you put her off?"

"I believe so. With pressing business concerns at home, I'm only here in London for a little longer. I can certainly string her along until I leave for New York."

"And then?" She arched a perfectly formed brow.

"She can't very well force the truth out of me with an ocean between us, though I know she will try with her sternly worded letters and telegrams."

Helena laughed. It was both husky and light, a full-throated sound that made his blood thicken in an awakening of carnality. He really needed to not be alone with her in public.

"She would try." Then soberly, but with a gentle curve of her lips, she said, "I admire your friendship with your sisters."

"In what way? Do you not share a friendship with your siblings?" He'd never thought about her family before beyond her parents, whom he'd met, and a few fleeting jealous thoughts cast toward her dead husband. Thoughts of which he was not proud.

"No, not as such. We are family who gather for holidays and special occasions. Do not misunderstand. I care for them, but we don't have your ease."

"And you don't enjoy spending time with them when it's not required of you."

She grinned, lowering her head a bit in sheepish discomfiture. "No. You probably think poorly of me that I would admit to such a thing."

"Not at all. I feel the same way about your family."

"Blackguard!" Her eyes widened in mock outrage, but the smile stayed on her lips.

He laughed, enjoying this ease between them, rare as it was. "We should get back soon, but before we do, are there any other concerns or rules you'd like to discuss?"

"No, I trust that we'll both behave as adults. Obviously, we can't do something embarrassing or untoward that would make any reasonable person call off a courtship."

"Obviously." He nodded, slowly leading her farther down the row. Her hand felt comfortable on his arm, as if it were natural for it to rest there. "Do you expect any resistance from your parents?"

She kept walking but went still in every other way. It was enough to let him know that he had hit upon a sore spot.

"Helena?" He stopped and faced her.

"Oh, nothing I cannot handle." She looked at everything but him, bringing a lily to her nose to smell.

"What is it?"

She shook her head and gently took another lily in hand, its soft white petals resting over her fingers. "Nothing."

He sighed in exasperation. "Helena, we cannot begin a charade without being honest with each other."

"Who says I'm not being honest?" Twin lines appeared between her brows as she frowned at him.

"My grandfather was a coal miner, and so was his father. God knows how much further back they go. I am well aware that a man like Lord Farthington would not choose a man like me as his son-in-law if he could help it, so tell me if he has said anything."

Her frown only deepened. "I thought your grandfather was the one who began Crenshaw Iron?"

"He did. He grew up in the coal mines of Pennsylvania but ran away to New York City at the age of fourteen."

The gaslight caught the blue of her eyes again, making them shimmer like sapphires. "And then what happened?" she asked, leaning closer to him in genuine curiosity.

He took in a shallow breath at the heady intoxication of having her interest solely on him. "He bought a small boat—some say he stole it, but that point has been disputed. Then he began ferrying businessmen across the river and into the city. He did that for a few years and found a regular customer, Werner. Mr. Werner took a liking to him and brought him on as a jack-of-all-trades. He'd drive his carriage, carry messages, anything that needed doing. After a while, my grandfather ran the enterprise that imported coal into the city. He was given a stake in the company and soon was involved in all the coal being distributed in New York. When Mr. Werner died, he inherited a large sum, enough to open up the ironworks. I suppose you can imagine the rest."

"It's fascinating how one man can change the fortunes of generations to come in one lifetime."

"You sound as if you approve of him?"

"I don't know him, but I admire his ambition."

"How very American-sounding of you."

She smiled. "Ambition isn't only American."

"I suppose not, but I thought you English didn't like it. That you thought a man should accept his ration in life and dare not ask for more." Why did he persist in this baiting of her? He couldn't seem to stop himself.

"My lot, you mean?" she asked, referencing his statement from earlier.

He should feel repentant about that, but riling her was too addictive. "Come on, Helena, you can't think I'm completely off the mark here. You all but admitted your father doesn't like me."

"Yes, fine, I admit that you would not be his first choice. I suppose it's no secret."

"Did you tell him that I was interested in courting you?" She shook her head. "Not yet."

"Perhaps we've been hasty, Helena. I don't want to make things more difficult for you. If your father feels that way, then this plan may not work for you at all. I don't want to give him even more reason to not support your endeavor."

Her eyes went wide in shock. "No!" Then more calmly, she rested her gloved hand on his arm. "No, I don't believe he'll react badly. You would be my second husband." The way her voice caressed the word had a prickling sensation starting at the base of his spine. "I married into a titled family the first time. I can hold my own counsel for my second. He understands the need for a suitable financier for the charity. He is a practical man, after all. He might not have chosen you, but he wouldn't put a stop to our marriage. Besides, I would not mind inciting his irritation, at any rate. Far too many people give him exactly what he wants."

"Then he could be persuaded to accept our courtship." He didn't know why, but this relieved him. Yes, it would make things difficult if he had to call this plan off and think of something else, but that's not why his knees felt weak. The truth was that he wanted to play this game with her. He resisted the urge to examine that too closely, not at all certain he'd like what he discovered.

"Yes, I believe so, and I admit to some delight in thwarting his wishes for Sir Stratton. He's Mama's plan to be precise, but she never does anything without Papa's approval."

"Good. Then we should begin."

"Haven't we already?"

"It sounds as if we're about to have visitors." A group of both men and women could be heard laughing and talking as they made their way toward the entrance of the conservatory. "We should appear as if we're in the midst of a flirtation."

"You've smiled more in the last several minutes than you have in the entire time I've known you. I believe we're well on our way."

She was right. Life for him had become one long series of tasks to complete as he managed both his family and Crenshaw Iron. He enjoyed the thrill of it and the satisfaction he got from the work. However, being with her tonight felt good in a different way. The pleasure of her company was for him alone. Turning toward her fully, he put a hand on the window at her back. He stepped forward until her skirts brushed the front of his trousers. Sucking in a deep breath, he almost felt dizzy with her scent. The prickling at the base of his spine had been joined by a familiar and pleasant heaviness farther down as blood filled his cock. His hand found her cheek before he knew what he was doing. Her lips parted in surprise, but he didn't think she found the stroke unpleasant. She tilted slightly into his touch. Leaning closer, he lowered his voice even more. "I want to be clear that we do not have to do anything with which you aren't comfortable. It's not necessary to kiss, but we do need it to appear that we have."

"To make it seem as if you want me beyond reason." She quoted his earlier comment.

"Yes." The word came out as a breath.

The tip of her tongue came out to touch her lip, leaving a moist trail that shimmered in the light. He wanted to kiss it, to taste her.

"How will you ever convince them of that?" she whispered.

He couldn't tell if she was being serious or not. Didn't she know how attractive she was? "You have to be kidding. You're the most desirable woman I've—"

She rose up on her toes, closing the distance between them so that her soft mouth pressed against his. He nearly gasped at the sudden craving that jolted through him. It was fierce and so immediate that he had to force a gentleness he didn't feel as he kissed her back. Jesus, she tasted like champagne and berries. She was so soft and pliant that he imagined how it would feel to sink into her heat, to hold her still against him as he—

She pulled away, her breath coming in a rush. She looked stunned, as if she hadn't expected to do that. A hand went to her chest as the other came up to steady herself against the window. He stepped back to allow her space.

"Maxwell . . . I . . . I didn't—" She closed her mouth as the newcomers wandered over to the windows.

The group gave them a cursory glance before continuing their rather loud conversation at the end of the aisle. Without saying another word, she hurried around him and exited at the other end. He could hear her heels on the stone tiled floor as she made her way down the next aisle and left the conservatory. He was almost glad for her hasty departure so that he could deal with his own visceral reaction to her. To lose hold of himself in public like that was not something that happened to him. He felt as if he were in over his head for the first time in his life.

Chapter 9

❖

I think people really marry far too much; it is such a lottery after all, and for a poor woman a very doubtful happiness.

QUEEN VICTORIA

Thank you so much for coming on short notice, dear." Helena met Violet in the entrance hall of her town-home. Huxley closed the door behind her friend and accepted her coat.

Violet smiled, nearly bursting with joy from the looks of her as she tugged off her gloves and handed them over to the butler. "Thank you for inviting us. I hope you don't mind that I'm a few minutes early, but I hoped to beat Max and August so we could chat."

The sheer happiness all but exuding from Violet's pores was the exact reason Helena had invited Violet, August, and Maxwell over for tea today. She didn't want his sisters to get the wrong idea about the state of her and their brother's relationship and be hurt. Inviting them all for tea so they could explain had seemed the best way to handle things, even though the last thing she wanted was to see Maxwell so soon after that kiss last night.

She still didn't understand what had possessed her to kiss him.

Taking her friend's hands and giving them a loving squeeze, she noted the ink stains on some of her fingers. Jumping on this topic to delay the inevitable, she asked, "How is your manuscript coming along?" Violet was a writer who would soon have her first work serialized in a publication based in America.

"Good, but slow. I'm a little anxious about how my work will be received come January, which is playing havoc with my creativity. That's to be expected I suppose, but that's not what I wanted to talk to you about."

Helena sighed inwardly as she led her friend to the drawing room. Perhaps it would be best just to blurt out the fact that her relationship with Maxwell was a fabrication. "I'm afraid that I know why you want to chat, and I have to confess that it isn't at all what you hope."

Violet gave her a puzzled look at they stepped into the drawing room. "You mean you haven't heard back yet from Sir Phineas?"

Helena's mind went blank for a moment as she had been taken entirely off guard. She had been certain that Violet meant to ask about their display last night, that she might have even heard about their ill-advised kiss. The conservatory hadn't been exactly private. Fumbling her words to start, she managed to say, "You mean the building? The priory?"

"Yes, of course that's what I mean." Then Violet smiled knowingly and wagged her eyebrows. "What did you think I meant?"

Helena laughed despite herself. "You know very well that I thought you were going to ask about your brother and last night."

"I do want to ask, but since you invited the three of us today, I can only assume you mean to address it with everyone present."

"Right you are. Best to discuss that once everyone is here." Helena crossed to the settee and indicated that Violet should join her. When they were both settled, she said, "Unfortunately, I do not have very promising news. Sir Phineas doesn't seem to be inclined to make any sort of immediate determination regarding the property."

"What did he say?"

"His letter was short. He merely conveyed his thanks in my contacting him. He says that he will look over the proposal that I sent, and he is currently entertaining several offers."

"Several offers? Oh no, this will not do." Violet rose and began pacing. "That sort of interest will drive the price higher."

Helena sighed. That was precisely her fear. Multiple parties could only mean that they would all eventually end up bidding against one another. She could not waste the charity's limited resources by expending them on the purchase price alone, not with the refurbishments needed, which meant it was very likely that they would lose the priory. "Yes, I'm afraid you're correct. I sent a letter in reply all but begging for a chance to meet him in person and plead our case. Obviously, I haven't heard back yet, but I'll let you know the moment I do."

"I hope he will at least hear you out. I'll have Christian contact him as well. He mentioned that he had met Sir Phineas some years ago and offered to speak to him. Perhaps with Christian's support, he can be persuaded to acquiesce."

"Thank you, Violet. That would be most helpful." She didn't hold out much hope of it swaying the gentleman, however.

Violet nodded. "You know how much this charity is coming to mean to me. I could do nothing less."

The sound of the front door opening had Helena on her feet again. Butterflies swirled in her belly as she heard

Maxwell's deep voice. A moment later, he and August appeared in the doorway. Helena was reminded of the first time she had seen him in that very spot, and all of her impressions from that day came back—his impressive height and breadth, the force of his sheer presence—only now she knew what it was like to feel his lips on hers.

His gaze met hers, and the power of it nearly sent her sinking back down to the settee. The intensity and the way it drifted quickly down to her mouth before he looked at Violet was the only acknowledgment from him that the kiss had happened. If a simple kiss that hadn't even been particularly long or deep could do this to her, what would making love to him be like? She admonished herself as soon as the thought crossed her mind, but it was far too late to stop the heat rising in her face.

"August." She forced herself to greet them in turn. "Mr. Crenshaw. It's so good of you both to come on short notice."

"I must say that my insatiable curiosity would have had me here sooner if your note hadn't specified four o'clock," August said.

Mrs. Huxley walked in with a tea tray followed a moment later by Huxley, who carried another tray laden with sandwiches, small cakes, and petits fours. They all settled themselves as Helena poured the tea. It wasn't until the servants left them alone that Helena took a sip of hers and cleared her throat, trying and failing to dissolve the lump that had grown there. Why was it so difficult to come forward with what they were doing?

She didn't know, but Maxwell seemed to understand her reticence, because he gave her an almost imperceptible nod from his chair opposite her. Shifting toward his sisters on the settee, he said, "I'm certain you both noticed that Lady Helena and I danced a few waltzes last night."

"Is that what they're calling kissing in the conservatory now?" Violet muttered from behind her cup.

Maxwell's eyes narrowed at his sister in displeasure, his

brows coming together in that fierce scowl that was absurdly attractive, and a bolt of desire shot right through Helena. Her lips parted in a gasp that she managed to silence at the last moment, as heat roiled inside her, turning her molten. She shifted, drawing Maxwell's smoldering attention, which did nothing for the heady dose of lust she was battling.

"We . . . um . . . that is to say we spoke in the conservatory, but nothing happened, whatever you may have heard." She could not admit to kissing him. She had barely managed to admit it to herself; she would not discuss it in front of his sisters.

Maxwell stared at her, and for one terrifying moment she thought he meant to betray their secret, but he lowered his eyes, and she breathed a sigh of relief when he said, "Lady Helena and I have decided to pretend a flirtation."

"Pretend?" August piped up. Apparently, even she had thought it had been real last night.

But could Helena blame her for the mistake? She herself had got so caught up in the game that she had kissed him. It was mortifying! She had to do a better job at keeping her attraction to him under control. He wanted children, children she could not give him, *and* he lived in New York. This would not do at all.

"Yes," Maxwell saved her by answering. "Papa wants me involved with someone by the end of the year, and it seems expedient to let him believe that Lady Helena and I have developed a relationship."

"But why?" August shook her head. "Why must he be led to believe anything? He wants you married, but you are your own man, Max. He'd hardly be able to force a marriage on you."

"That is true, but he could make things unpleasant if he believes I'm not proceeding down that path. We never thought he and Mother would force both of you into marriage, but here we are. With his health as precarious as it is,

I believe it is better, easier, to play along for a while until he recovers."

August pursed her lips in thought, and Helena could almost hear the gears churning in her head as she tried to poke holes in her brother's logic. She was too inquisitive for this sort of subterfuge, but they could not come out and tell her of the awful ultimatum her father had delivered.

"This seems extreme," Violet said into the silence. "To what extent will this go on?"

Maxwell cleared his throat. "Well, before I leave for New York, I'll propose, and Helena will accept. Once Papa is better, likely by spring, we'll call the whole thing off."

Neither of the sisters appeared convinced.

"Let me see if I understand this," August said. "You'll court Helena, and convince all of her friends and family that you are in love, and then you'll call it off in a few months?"

Put like that, she did make it sound radical.

The moment Maxwell opened his mouth to reply, Helena took over, positive that if given half the chance he would explain his theory of *want* versus *love* and she would be a puddle of mortified jelly by the time he finished. "Yes, that is what your brother means, but that isn't precisely the whole story. You see—and Violet might have already explained to you—the London Home for Young Women is in trouble. My father, bless him, has made it known that he doesn't entirely approve of the endeavor and some . . . well, several . . . *most*"—she winced at the truth of the word—"of our donors have decided that now is not the time to give to such a cause. It is my belief that with a strong male figure at my side lending his support, my father will come around and his friends will come with him."

"I'm certain I could persuade a few donors on my own, as well," Max added, his voice firm and deliberate.

The proof of his support settled within her like hot chocolate on a cold winter morning. She did her best not to savor it, but that was impossible.

"Do you really believe that your father will come around so easily?" August asked, raising a skeptical brow.

"Papa has been after me to entertain the idea of another marriage for a while now. I do believe this will help. There's also the issue of it being somewhat unsavory for a single woman to support women who some believe have questionable moral character. Mr. . . . um, Maxwell will serve as a buffer temporarily. Once things are up and running, and we call off the arrangement, it will be too late because everyone will see how well the charity is working."

The room was silent for a moment too long. Sweat prickled the back of her neck. Taking a linen napkin from the table, she discreetly patted her mouth. She felt as if she were under interrogation and losing the battle with the truth, though she couldn't understand why. Everything she had just said was entirely accurate. No one had to know that she had secretly, at some point, developed an interest in Maxwell that went beyond the rules of their ploy. Not even twenty-four hours later and she was already on the edge of failing.

"I suppose that makes sense." August picked up a biscuit and took a bite as she continued to turn the issue over in her mind.

Violet looked pensive, but also a bit sad. "I know it was no secret that I wanted you two to . . . well, you know . . . but for some reason this makes it seem even less likely to happen."

"It was never going to happen, Violet." Maxwell's voice was flat, making him sound bored.

Helena tried not to let his words hurt her, but they did. "It simply doesn't make sense, dear. We live in two separate worlds." Maxwell straightened a bit, prompting Helena to add, "He wouldn't want to move to London, and I'm afraid

I'm in no position to leave," lest there be some mistake in what worlds she meant.

"That brings up an interesting point," August said. "What of your father, Helena? I know that you want him to come around with your charity, but I daresay Lord Farthington will not want Maxwell as a son-in-law. I'm certain he'd want a titled noble for you. This could all backfire if he can't be persuaded."

"I have made it known that if I do marry again, I will choose my own husband. He has had years to come to terms with this, and I would never select a titled gentleman." They all seemed to look at her in question about this, so she hurried onward so she wouldn't have to answer them. "I don't anticipate a problem."

The conversation continued for some time after. August or Violet would volley questions, and she or Max would answer them. By the time Helena walked the sisters to the door later, she was convinced that they might actually be able to pull this off. It was only when the door closed behind them and she turned to see Maxwell waiting for her in the doorway of the drawing room that her earlier doubts began to resurface.

Huxley quietly removed himself from the entry hall as she walked toward Maxwell.

He watched her intently the whole way. His gaze sweeping over her features and lingering on her mouth before coming back up to her eyes. "It was right to tell them," he said when she came to a stop before him. "Thank you for suggesting it."

"I'm glad we were able to convince them without having to tell the whole thing. If August ever suspected . . ." She drifted off, unable to finish that.

He gave her a nod of understanding. "You really do care for them, don't you?"

"Yes, they're almost like my own sisters." Only that was too close to the trick they were playing, and it reminded her of how she had behaved last night. Her entire body felt as if it were flushing in humiliation, though her face burned the brightest. "I want to apologize for last night. I shouldn't have . . ." But she couldn't bring herself to say the word. To acknowledge the kiss out loud seemed to be a sort of sacrilege.

"Don't, Helena. You have nothing to apologize for." And just that quickly his eyes seemed to darken as they settled on her mouth briefly. "I liked it." There was no hint of a smile on his lips or in his gaze as it met hers. The fire that always burned beneath the surface of their exchanges began to crackle, making itself known. It felt as if an electric current had come to life, buzzing between and around them.

"You liked it, too." There was that hint of a smile around his lips.

She opened her mouth to refute the statement even though it was true. Her first instinct always seemed to be to counter him, but what if she didn't? What if she acknowledged the heat between them? Then he might kiss her.

She shouldn't kiss him again. It would be foolish in the extreme, but already she wanted to feel his mouth on hers, and this time she wanted to touch her tongue to his, to taste him, to know what it was like to have some small part of him inside her.

Huxley cleared his throat from where he stood near the base of the stairs, and she realized she had been leaning toward Maxwell. The butler had returned with Maxwell's coat and held it ready for him to slip it on. Maxwell didn't seem very affected by her lapse in decorum. He moved around her and allowed Huxley to help him into the coat. How had she been thinking of kisses while Huxley was so near?

"Will you be available for the theater tomorrow evening?" His voice was bland and formal.

She had to fight to find her voice. "Yes, that would be lovely."

He gave a nod of acknowledgment. "Good afternoon, Helena." And with that, he left, but not before she caught the wicked gleam in his eyes as he turned away.

This was all part of the plan, she told herself. There was no reason to look forward to seeing him tomorrow or to even be particularly concerned about what she would wear. But she was too busy cataloging her wardrobe in her mind to listen to good sense.

Chapter 10

❦

There is only one thing in the world worse than being talked about, and that is not being talked about.

OSCAR WILDE

Max had seen Helena twice over the course of the next week. They were never completely alone on those outings. August and Evan had accompanied them to a dinner, while Violet and Christian had attended the ballet with them. They had been seen together enough times to start people talking about them.

Even he had seen a few of the mentions in the papers. Mother had helped this along in her unadulterated joy at their supposed mutual interest. Just this morning she had spent a considerable amount of time at breakfast delighting over how often their names were mentioned together in various gossip sheets. One brave speculator had even wondered if there might be a wedding announcement in time for Christmas—a conjecture that was so on the mark Max wondered if they had overplayed their hand. Perhaps they should take a break for a week to whet the appetites of the gossipmongers.

Yet tonight, sitting next to Helena in the music room of

his parents' rented townhome, he realized that he only had a few weeks to spend in London, and he didn't want to waste one away from her. He enjoyed the way she would verbally spar with him. It wasn't excessive, but enough to give him a glimpse at the passion lurking beneath her placid surface. Enough to make him fixate on their kiss at the ball. Though it had barely been a kiss, it had been enough to make him want it again, to want a deeper taste of her. As the music swirled in the air around them, he couldn't pay attention to it because he was filled with her.

The scent of lilies wafted over to him when she politely clapped at the end of each song. A wisp of hair had come loose from her otherwise impeccable chignon. The golden curl touched the soft skin where her neck met her shoulder. He could imagine how silky it would feel if he took it between his thumb and forefinger. Would she like it if he gave it a tug? Was she the type to enjoy a bit of rough play, or would she prefer touches that were soft and sensual?

Helena glanced over at him, catching him watching her. Her brow rose and the corner of her mouth tilted upward, as if she knew his thoughts. Rough, he realized. The passion he suspected lurked within her would crave a little wildness mixed in with the tenderness. He shifted with the tightening deep in his groin. Her smile tried to widen, but she bit the inside of her lip to stifle it. He nearly groaned as an ember smoldered inside him, brought to life by her attention.

The soprano hit a high note, drawing his attention to the front of the room where she stood next to the piano and accompanist. Mother had planned this evening of musical entertainment as a way to slowly ease Papa back into their social life now that his doctors had consented to allow him to leave his bed for a couple hours per day. Close friends of the family, including Helena's parents, had been invited for the performance with a light supper to follow. The aria was beautiful, but Max could hardly concentrate enough to listen.

He kept going back to that afternoon in her home. He was certain that Helena would have kissed him again right there in the middle of her house if Huxley hadn't interrupted them. The memory of the way she had looked at him had stayed with him all week, coming back to him during the odd moments he had alone with his thoughts. It was always accompanied by his resolve to kiss her properly before he left for New York. He'd promised her that he wouldn't do anything untoward in this counterfeit courtship, but he'd already plotted a hundred different ways to get her alone. And each one ended with them doing a hell of a lot more than kissing.

He glanced over at her again, only to meet eyes with his mother. She sat on Helena's other side, leaning back slightly to watch him with speculation running rampant across her face. He gave her a harsh glare, subtly indicating that she should mind her own business. Her bottom lip pushed out in an exaggerated pout, but she did as he bid her and faced forward. Lord Farthington sat in stony profile farther down the row, the fact that he *hadn't* looked over nearly as obvious as his mother's attention. The man had to have heard about their outings this week. Max wondered if he would let his feelings about them be known tonight. Max had already concluded that he'd find another way if their courtship would make things more difficult for her charity.

A few minutes later the music came to an end, and everyone applauded while rising to stand. A pair of servants dressed in formal black and white opened the French doors that led to the adjoining room.

"Let us adjourn to the drawing room to enjoy refreshment," Mother announced, as she accepted Papa's arm. His father's weight had yet to return to normal, but his color was good and his tread steady. Max resolved to escort him to his room in a quarter of an hour. The older man had already been downstairs for well over his allotted time.

As Max followed Helena down the row of chairs, he took in the nip of her waist, which flowed into the sensual flare of her hips. His hands were large, and he imagined they might almost meet if he held her about her waist as he pulled her back toward him. He would nudge against her soft bottom, which would be lush and firm, as he found his way to her. She'd be ready when he notched within her, wet and—she reached the end of the row and turned to take his arm.

Smiling up at him, she said, "I cannot decide if your heated glances are part of the ploy or real."

He nearly stumbled over his own feet at her boldness. He loved that he never knew what she would say. Quickly finding his step, he noted the playful glint in her beautiful blue eyes. "Can't they be both?"

Her cheeks colored prettily. "For someone else perhaps." Facing forward, she added, "But you are Maxwell Crenshaw. Your passions are Crenshaw Iron and saving your sisters when needed."

"You make me sound like an automaton." He kept his voice light, but something about the remark hit him in the gut. It was true that his entire life had been about work, but that was only because running an enterprise like Crenshaw Iron demanded that sort of diligence. "But never fear, I do pursue my own interests outside of my family."

"And what would those be?" she asked smoothly. "Accountancy and risk evaluation?"

"Horseflesh. I enjoy riding and caring for horses." He owned several prized Thoroughbreds that he rode weekly in Central Park and in the summers at the family's cottage in Newport.

By this time, they had reached the drawing room. She released his arm to accept a glass of champagne from a footman. He took one as well, but mainly to cover his disappointment at not having her touching him anymore. As he did, he was almost certain that she took in his legs. Her gaze settled in the general area of his thighs before moving up to his backside, except the fall of his coat would have obscured her view.

"That explains much," she said, bringing the glass to her lips. Her eyes were filled with mischief.

A gentleman would have let the comment pass, but he couldn't. He also didn't claim to be a gentleman. "What does it explain?"

She blushed, having not been prepared for his challenge. "Only that your . . ." She hesitated over the next word before resolve settled over her features and she started again. "Your build is stronger than one might presume given your occupation."

Heat coiled like a wound spring in his stomach. "You've been looking."

Somehow her face reddened even more. She looked across the room, and without meeting his eyes, she said, "Perhaps."

"Tease," he whispered.

She grinned and gave a barely perceptible shrug as a couple walked by, exchanging greetings with them. When they had passed, he said in a low voice, "Before we're interrupted, I wanted to tell you that I have good news." He'd been waiting all evening to share it with her, though he didn't know why it had seemed so important to tell her. Perhaps it was that she was a part of his strategy to help his sister, his accomplice.

"Oh?"

"It hasn't been announced yet, but the company signed the contracts for the dock proposal. The first step of helping August in her new endeavor is underway."

"Maxwell, that's wonderful!" She truly meant it. Her eyes illuminated with joy, though she kept her voice soft. "August must be ecstatic."

"She is." Just watching her face as she shared in his sister's joy made him smile.

"Could I congratulate her tomorrow? Would she be upset that I know?"

"No, I think she'd like you to know, but don't mention it to anyone else. Papa doesn't know yet." He glanced to where his father sat across the room. A footman presented him with a tray of hors d'oeuvres.

"I won't. We should raise a glass to her success." She held up her champagne, compelling him to follow suit. After she clinked her coupe to his, she took a swallow. He couldn't help but watch her lips press against the glass, remembering that all-too-brief kiss and wondering when they would repeat it, because he knew that it would happen.

"The contract stipulates that we have sixty days to find an appropriate site, but we've already located prime real estate, nearly a whole city block. It's big enough to house a factory, warehouse, foundry, even a small residence building for employees."

"Will you be signing the contract for the property soon?"

"Not yet. It appears there is interest from other buyers, but I'm not concerned. I'm willing to pay almost any price to secure it." Sir Phineas was being reticent with the details, but it seemed there might be interest from another party in the portion of the property that contained the priory.

Her gaze narrowed. "The benefits of being a Crenshaw. Money can buy you everything you want."

As he was trying to decide how to reply to the sardonic comment, one of his parents' new acquaintances greeted them. He had met the older woman earlier, but for the life of him he couldn't remember her name. It hardly mattered because she was clearly here to talk to Helena. She turned to her and began a conversation about the health of Helena's mother-in-law, Lady Sansbury.

Helena inclined her head as she listened. He couldn't stop his gaze from following the graceful column of her neck, pausing briefly on the slight dip between the fragile-looking clavicle bones pressing against the silk of her skin, to fall to the lovely swell of her breasts above her gown. Tonight, she wore a deep, rich plum color that emphasized the pale creaminess of her skin and made the blue of her eyes even deeper. Ever since the night of the ball, she had resorted to wearing more revealing gowns. He loved them all on her and had spent the last week attempting to convince himself that she did not wear them for his benefit. She was a lady in every sense of the word, which meant that she put a great deal of thought into how she presented herself. Every gesture along with every stitch of clothing was for a purpose. He had concluded that she wore them to signal that she was available for courtship, thus helping their ruse.

Had she dressed for her husband in that way? Guilt clawed its way up the back of his throat, so he took another swig of champagne, hoping to drown it. Max had no right to wonder about him, but he was curious about the man who had been able to call himself her husband. The man who had held the singular privilege of sharing her bed. Had she cared for him? Had he known, *really known*, the woman he called wife, or had their marriage been shallow like many Society marriages?

The questions made a hollow open in Max's chest that he preferred not to think about too much. He was leaving for New York soon, so none of those answers really mattered. Excusing himself, he went to his father, who was sitting in an overstuffed chair holding court on the far side of the room. It took some cajoling and a bit of scowling, but ten minutes later they were making their way up the stairs.

"Millie tells me that you've seen Lady Helena several times this week," his father said, referring to Max's mother.

"Has she?" Max was intentionally noncommittal. He walked a razor's edge of plausibility: too agreeable and their relationship would seem suspiciously convenient; too obstinate and it would seem forced.

"Are you considering her?" Papa's voice was calm and difficult to read, but his breathing was labored.

"Considering, yes. I haven't made a decision." Max grimaced inwardly at the difficulty his father seemed to have navigating the stairs. They were almost to the top, and he held on to Max's arm with more force than when they had started.

"I'm surprised."

Max paused at the top of the stairs to give his father a moment to catch his breath. "Why? She's attractive, reasonably wealthy, from a respectable family."

"No, no, you misunderstand. She's entirely suitable; it isn't that. It's . . . well . . . to be honest, you didn't seem to get on well back in the spring."

Damn. He'd hoped his parents had been too blinded by their triumph in adding another nobleman to the family to have noticed that. "I wouldn't say that. She was instrumental in finding Violet. I very much appreciated her assistance. Besides, when did you ever see us together?"

"The wedding breakfast. I admit that I watched you both, hoping to see interest there." At Max's questioning look, he added, "You'd spent considerable time alone together traveling North. A father can hope."

Max stifled a curse. Apparently, even his plan to thwart his father's wishes was playing into the man's hopes. This was what he'd wanted, but galling nonetheless. "Let's get you to bed," he said, leading his father toward his room whether he wanted to go or not.

"What has changed?" His father persisted in his questioning.

"Nothing has changed. I was interested in Helena before. How could I not be? She's beautiful and intelligent. The coldness you saw was on her part."

Papa was quiet as they made their way into the room. A fire blazed in the hearth, making the bedroom almost too hot. Gibbs, his father's valet, stepped forward, but Papa held up his hand to ask for another moment as he sat gingerly on the side of the bed.

"It came from her." Papa mulled this over before he nodded. "What happened to change her mind?"

Max stood looking down at his father. He could say that he'd written letters to her. That he'd charmed her. That he'd won her over with his wit and grace. Even if those were all true, Papa wouldn't believe them. There was only one thing the man respected, and though a lump formed in Max's stomach, he said it. "I donated to her charity."

"You clever boy." A smile of pride twisted the older man's lips. "They always say that blood will tell, but they're all wrong. It's money. It doesn't even take all that much to show a person's true nature."

Max refrained from agreeing as his stomach churned, souring on his father's satisfaction. This was the man who raised him. This was the man who taught him all he knew about the world. This was the man who had agreed it was best for Max to spend his summers working in the heat of their factories so that he would understand the challenges their workers faced. When once Max would have agreed with almost everything he said, now they were falling more and more out of step. The past year had Max questioning everything he thought he knew about his family, his business, and their legacy.

"I have to get back downstairs." He turned without another word.

"If you'd like a bit of alone time with the fair lady, you have my blessing."

Max closed the door harder than necessary, a common occurrence these days as nausea roiled through him. His earlier base thoughts about her came back to haunt him, shaming him in how they so completely aligned with his father's words. She deserved more than to be a convenient answer to his father's demented schemes. She deserved more than to be even momentarily allied with his family, who would only use her for their purposes. She deserved more than him. A sudden need to protect her came over him.

He walked down the stairs with a newfound purpose—to save her from the folly of their plan. It wasn't too late. He would find her, release her from their agreement, and apologize for ever trying to bring her into this chaos that had become his family. With the plan for the building almost certain to move ahead, they were almost at the point where Papa couldn't stop it if he wanted to.

Only, when he got downstairs, he couldn't find her. The party had trickled out like spilled tinsel, taking up parts of the music room, the drawing room, another sitting room, and the dining room. The accompanist played Chopin's "Nocturne in E Minor," and the music floated around the house, lending the evening an air of romance. Voices hummed in low conversations.

"Louise!" His mother laughed at something her friend had said. Her voice came from the dining room, so he headed in that direction, in case Helena had made her regrets and left. As he approached, Mother stood in profile just within the open door, a small circle of three women surrounding her. "Not so loud," she was saying. "Nothing is decided yet. You know it's all rumor."

Lady Louise Ashcroft, a close friend of his mother's, said, "Yes, I'm well aware of that, but we all know there is a little truth in every rumor." The woman's voice was as devilish as his mother's. Max bristled, certain they were talking about him and Helena.

"I cannot confirm it, but neither can I deny it," his mother said, setting off a round of tittering.

Lady Ashcroft touched his mother's shoulder with the tip of her fan. "Be careful there. We all know the lady in question to be virtuous, but that business with the fallen women is rather undesirable. None of us can understand what she's thinking."

His mother murmured something too low for him to

overhear, but he paused in his approach, anxious to know where this was going.

"Your daughters are married, but what of your grand-children?" Lady Ashcroft's voice was insistent. "If they marry, you will have to worry about the influence of *those* women on the children. I don't care what anyone says. Immorality is a stain that cannot be washed away with a new beginning."

A woman he couldn't see murmured in agreement, adding, "I believe her heart is in the right place, but those women will always be wicked. There is no saving them."

Lady Ashcroft nodded vehemently. "I agree completely. Unfortunately, the stain can spread. If she's not careful, it will take her over as well."

Rage propelled him into action before he had a chance to even acknowledge it, much less quell its existence. Four sets of eyes widened at the sight of him. "Lady Helena is the most compassionate person I have ever had the pleasure of knowing. Who are you"—he had been glaring at Lady Ashcroft, who stood with her mouth agape, but now turned his attention to take in the rest of the group, including his own mother—"*any* of you, to question her integrity? She has gone to great length to offer aid to people the world has left behind. At great risk to her person, and apparently her character, she has done what none of us would lift a finger to do. How dare you, her *friends*, disparage her?"

Everything was silent when he finished. Even the piano from the music room had gone quiet in the seconds it took the musician to transition to another piece. As the full weight of what he had done came over him, Max found the wherewithal to take notice of the room. Lord Farthington stood at the sideboard, pausing in the act of placing a pastry on the small plate in his hand. His expression was unreadable. While Max did not regret a single word he said, he did regret that Helena's father had heard it all. He knew the man wouldn't completely approve of welcoming an untitled man into his family, but he would approve of a vulgar display of temper even less.

Still, there was nothing to do but meet the man's gaze head-on. Max stood by the sentiments of his speech, and he would not be cowed. Helena deserved better than these careless, entitled people sneering at her.

"Maxwell." Helena's calm voice cut through the silence like a warm knife through butter. She stood at the door at the far end of the room. The apples of her cheeks were lit from within. How much of it all had she heard? "Would you be so kind as to accompany me to the . . ." She faltered slightly, leading him to conclude that she had heard enough. "The library? Violet left a book for me there, but I can't seem to find it." Without waiting for a reply, and with every eye in the room focused on her, she gracefully departed with her chin perfectly parallel with the ground.

"Excuse me," he said, inclining his head as if he hadn't just handed the Society matrons their heads on a platter.

Chapter 11

You were made perfectly to be loved, and surely I have loved you, in the idea of you, my whole life long.

ELIZABETH BARRETT BROWNING

Max followed Helena to the back of the house, uncertain of her destination. The only library in the town house was his father's study upstairs. He was left to follow the combined sounds of the swishing of her skirts and her heels on the carpets to find her. He caught a glimpse of plum fabric as she turned into the small morning room that looked out over the garden. His mother frequently had her coffee in this room, and Violet had used it for writing. It wasn't a library, but it did hold a bookcase stocked with books.

Conscious of how everyone at the party would be aware they had disappeared together, he kept the door open when he entered behind her. A lamp burned in the far corner, having been lit to invite private conversation if someone needed to step away from the rest of the guests. It cast a pale yellow light over one side of the room while leaving the other in shadow. The effect created a false sense of privacy, as if they were the only ones in the house. His skin felt tighter, too small for his body, as every nerve ending came alive.

She whirled around to face him. Her eyes were bright, but he couldn't tell if she was angry or not. Into the silence, he said, "I won't apologize for what I said."

"I am not asking you to apologize." She simply stared at him, searching his face.

He relaxed slightly. "Then I don't understand . . ." His voice trailed off as light shimmered in her eyes, coalescing into twin swelling teardrops that wavered on her lower lashes, threatening to fall.

She blinked rapidly, turning away with a sound of frustration as she tried to hide the tears from him. He went to take a step forward, but his muscles seemed to freeze, momentarily paralyzed by the sight of her distress. "Helena," he whispered.

"No, it's fine. I'm fine." She held a hand out behind her to ward him off. The sight of her gloved fingers, long and slim, had him reaching out. The urge to touch her was too great. She gasped when he took her hand in his and looked back at the touch.

He was also entranced by the sight. Her hand was smaller than his, but it somehow fit perfectly tucked against his palm.

"I've upset you," he said. She looked stricken, the lines of her face taut.

"No." But it was a lie and they both knew it. Pressing her lips together for a moment, she said, "Well, yes, but not for the reason you think."

Forcing a bit of levity, he said, "Then you're not upset that Lady Ashcroft despises me?"

The hint of a smile tugged the corner of her lips. Her eyes were still brighter than normal, but there was no imminent threat of tears. She faced him again but had yet to pull her hand back. "No one has ever come to my defense as you did."

"I find that difficult to believe."

She gave a small shake of her head, and her grasp on his hand tightened. His body took it as an invitation, and he stepped closer, slowly narrowing the space between them. His eyes glued to their hands. "Believe it. To be fair, I don't have a long history of rebellion. Not like August. I had my Season like any other girl, and by the end I was betrothed to a man known to my family for years and beloved by them. I was never obstinate because there wasn't a need."

He barely heard her last sentence because he was stuck on the preceding one. "And was he beloved by you?" He had no right to ask her, but here he was overstepping for no reason other than his selfish need to know more about her.

She paused for a long time, drawing his gaze. He should call the question back, but he didn't. Finally, she said, "Yes, I loved him." There was a sadness in her eyes that tugged at his heart. "It was after his death that I began to question myself. I had spent my entire life doing everything that I thought I was supposed to do, but to what purpose? There I was still a widow before my time. My family urged me to remarry as soon as it was acceptable. I'm ashamed to admit that I didn't understand until then that my only purpose in life was to be a wife and produce children . . . at least according to my family . . . to the world."

"But that's not your only purpose," he said, his voice stronger than he intended.

"I know. It took me a while, but I know now. Being a wife and mother would be wonderful things, but they're not the *only* things that matter to me."

"You care about the orphans and the women under your protection."

She nodded, smiling up at him. "Yes, I feel that I've finally found a place where I can make a real difference. These women become pregnant and often are almost immediately abandoned by the men responsible. All life is supposed to be sacred, but from the moment the life inside them begins to show, they are ostracized. Most of them lose their jobs, and sometimes their homes, because of it. They give birth in squalor. You wouldn't believe some of the places I've seen."

He probably wouldn't. His life took him to the industrial parts of the city, to pubs and bars, and occasionally to the home of one of his workers, but never to the places she referenced. He knew that she had actually gone there herself. When she could have sent Ostler or some other person in her employ, she had gone herself to see with her own eyes these people she wanted to help. His admiration for her, already high, soared.

"Why do you do that to yourself?"

"Because if I don't, who will?" Shaking her head as if to clear it, she looked down at their still-clasped hands. "But that's neither here nor there. I only meant to thank you. No one has ever deigned to support me publicly."

"Helena." His voice rasped against his throat. With his other hand, he touched her chin, resting it between his thumb and forefinger. She looked up at him, her eyes almost shy now that she had revealed so much to him. "I admire you more than you know. I will always champion you."

She smiled again, and his thumb traced over the silk of her skin, touching the tiny little indentation at the bottom of her chin that was only barely visible. Then it moved upward, daring to touch the soft fullness of her bottom lip. She didn't move. Her eyes darkened, dilating with passion, as he slowly lowered his mouth to hers. He paused mere inches away, letting their breaths mingle, breathing her into him.

Jesus, he wanted this woman more than he had ever wanted before. His body ached with it. Every part of him felt tight, needy, desperate for her touch. His breath shook as he exhaled, trying to stop himself from devouring her. She made a soft sound of want in the back of her throat, and he was undone by it. His mouth touched hers, and she responded to his kiss, her lips parting, letting him inside to taste her like he wanted.

She was hot and soft, her tongue bold as it touched his, taking what she wanted as much as she gave. Somehow they had moved across the room. His back came up against the wall, pushing a painting askew. His hands moved up and down her back, flattening her against him as best he could with the layers of clothing between them. He'd have given anything to have her naked and beneath him. *Anything.*

"Helena?" Her mother's voice cracked through the air like a shot. They managed to jump apart a mere second before the woman stepped into the room. "There you are, darling." An eyebrow shot up as she looked them over, and an expression of bored disappointment settled on her face. It had to be painfully obvious that they had been kissing. "Mr. Crenshaw, lovely to see you again." To Helena, "We must be going. Your father has called for the carriage."

"Yes, I am ready." Her voice was calm, having no doubt learned the trick at the skirts of the woman who had judged him and found him lacking.

"Oh. Did you find your book?" Lady Farthington raised that all-knowing eyebrow again.

"We did," he said a bit too fast, grabbing a book that rested facedown on the shelf beside him. "Here." He presented it to Helena with possibly a bit more ceremony than the moment called for.

"Thank you, Maxwell." She plucked it deftly from his hand and smoothed back that single strand of hair that had escaped from its knot. Something about the movement was telling. She was so accustomed to projecting an outward calm that she did it without even noticing. "Shall we, Mama?" she asked, avoiding looking at him.

"What book did Lady Leigh leave for you?" her mother asked, clearly enjoying herself.

Helena's brows drew together as she glanced down,

holding the book up. "*North and South* by Elizabeth Gaskell."

"How appropriate." The words floated behind Lady Farthington as she wafted off, already tired of her game.

Helena gave him a conspirative smile as she followed her mother. The implication of that look hit him right in the gut, like an arrow with an invisible string that was tied to her. They were together, alone in their collusion against the world. It might be a fragile intimacy drawn by circumstance, but he felt closer to her than he had anyone ever before.

He stayed where he was long after she left, the back of his head and his palms pressed to the wall behind him. It took him that long to regain his equilibrium. He knew without question that holding her so briefly, kissing her, wouldn't be enough. Before he left for New York, he had to have her.

As the carriage pulled away from the Crenshaws' townhome, Helena kept her gaze out the window. Her lips still throbbed from Maxwell's kiss, and the skin on the lower part of her face tingled pleasantly from the rasp of his beard. She had never kissed a bearded man before. To be fair, aside from a couple of stolen pecks in her first Season, she had never kissed a man other than her husband. Arthur had still been relatively young at twenty and two when they married. He'd always been clean-shaven and reserved with her. His kisses had been shy and quiet.

Maxwell was whatever the opposite of that was. Impatient. Fiery. Wild. The imprint of his hands still warmed her back, as if his touch had burned through the layers of her clothing and corset. She couldn't deny anymore that she was interested in exploring whatever this was between them. When they touched, it was as if the twin mantles of restraint and composure that she shielded herself with fell away, shredded by him. But she didn't miss them when they were gone. To the contrary, she felt that she was herself without them for the first time in . . . well, ever.

As a woman who had spent the last five years of her life trying to find out who she was on her own without a man in her life, she didn't know what to think about that. What did it mean that he so casually and brutally tore her shrouds to threads? More importantly, what did it mean that she liked it?

"Haven't you already read *North and South*, darling?" Mama's knowing voice floated through the darkness of the carriage, penetrating it in a way the small carriage light had been unable to do.

If there had been any doubts about her knowing what Helena and Maxwell had been doing, her tone extinguished them. Helena clutched the leather-bound book in her lap, avoiding looking at her mother, who sat on the bench next to her. "It's an annotated copy." The lie came so easily that she should have been ashamed, but her only concern at the moment was getting out of this carriage with her parents. Why had she agreed to ride over with them? At least Berkeley Square was only a few streets away.

"How kind of the young Mr. Crenshaw to help you find it."

Helena contemplated jumping from the moving vehicle but disregarded the idea because such recklessness might have rightfully been interpreted as hysterical. Since avoidance wasn't a tactic she could use right now, she decided to face the dragon head-on, as it were. "Is there something you wish to say, Mama?"

Her father shifted on the seat across from them, drawing their attention in the silence. Shadows played over his face, making him appear rigid and forbidding, which wasn't that much different from how he appeared in full daylight. Only this time she could read his expression even less. Mama quietly gripped her hand in encouragement.

"Is it to be Maxwell Crenshaw, then?" he asked in that forthright way he had.

With every fiber of her being she wanted to say no to avoid what was coming, but she knew that she had been doing that her whole life. Giving a little bit to save trouble had caused her to lose tiny pieces of herself along the way, pieces that she hadn't missed at first, until they had chipped away at her core. She had only begun to gather them up over the last several years. It would be too risky to drop even one. It might make them all come tumbling down.

"Yes," she said. The one word had a silent echo that beat through her in a thumping bass.

Papa sighed. "And what of Verick? I sent a letter, asking him to Claremont Hall for our Christmas gathering."

"I shall look forward to seeing him."

Lord Verick had been one of Arthur's closest friends. He had been one of the only ones who had continued to visit with him throughout his sickness from cancer and right up to his final days. For that, she loved him dearly, but she had never seriously contemplated Papa's suggestion, nor had she realized that he'd been earnest about a marriage between them when he'd mentioned him as a possible suitor.

"You will not consider him?"

"No, Papa, we would not suit."

"But Maxwell Crenshaw suits you?"

He did. He suited her very much. Not for marriage, obviously, but in the other ways a man could suit a woman. She was glad for the low light as a blush stained her cheeks. She'd been doing that a lot lately.

"He suits me very well," she managed as her mouth went dry.

"All right."

That was it? "All right?" she asked.

"It's your life, Helena. You're a widow, a woman grown. Your mistakes are yours to make now." He tilted his head down to stare at her over the top of his eyeglasses, a sure sign that he was being thoughtful with his words.

This did not sound like the father she knew. That man

walked around certain that he knew what was best for everyone around him, even a stranger on the street. But then, he hadn't actually agreed with her, had he? He was simply content to watch this all bubble over like a kettle that had been set to boil too long. Then he could proudly boast that he'd been right.

Because she wasn't at all certain of him, she said, "You won't *do* anything, will you?"

"*Do anything?* What would you have me do?" With raised brows, he looked at her as if she'd sprouted a horn.

"I only mean that you won't make trouble. You won't tell your friends horrible things about the London Home for Young Women?"

"Helena! What do you take me for? My own daughter believes I plot to thwart her."

"Farthington, dramatics are tiresome. You would plot against God himself if he set a task against you," her mother said, giving her hand another squeeze.

He huffed. "Nevertheless, I bear no ill will for that place beyond the fact that my daughter associates with those beneath her. You have done as I asked. You found a man who seems intent on supporting you, and despite what I may think of the Crenshaw elders, Maxwell Crenshaw seems to be an upstanding man." He inclined his head and added, "Do what you will."

"Thank you, Papa, I appreciate that and am glad to hear it. I have found a building, and it would be a shame if it were snatched out from under me before I even had a chance to bid."

He huffed again, this time looking out the window, indicating he was finished with the conversation.

"Bid?" Mama asked. "Are there others interested?"

"I believe so, but I have arranged a meeting with the owner," Helena explained as the carriage rolled to a stop in front of her house. "I hope to plead my case before him."

"And this owner knows what you intend for this building?"

"Yes, the basic idea, at any rate."

Mama raised a skeptical brow. "Good luck, darling."

The door opened, and her parents' groom helped her out.

"See her to the door," Papa instructed him. To Helena, he said, "You really must see your home properly staffed. Huxley is well past his retirement."

"Good evening, Papa. Mama," she replied, hurrying to her door.

"Helena," Mama called out. "We'll speak more about the gentleman soon." Then for good measure, she added, "Tomorrow!"

Helena waved, already dreading that conversation. But then Huxley opened the door for her, and once inside her own home, thoughts of what had happened with Maxwell came flooding back to her. With them came the feeling of his hands on her, and his tongue in her mouth. She was smiling as she sailed up the stairs, already wondering when she'd find a way to kiss him again.

Chapter 12

❧

In the tragedies and triumphs of human experience, each mortal stands alone.

ELIZABETH CADY STANTON

The next evening, Max found himself at Montague Club, the club owned by Christian and his half brother, Jacob Thorne. Evan had owned voting shares but had given up most of them after inheriting his mining interests in Montana. Unlike White's and Brooks's, which catered to an exclusive class of aristocrats, Montague was the home to the second sons, bastards, and cousins of those nobles along with a few of the distinguished merchant class. Anyone was welcome, even women, as long as they could pay the expensive membership fee and abide by the rules. Being of that class himself, Max had found it only natural to eschew White's in favor of Montague. Not to mention the fact that he wanted to support his brothers-in-law, particularly after the rocky beginnings of their entrance into the Crenshaw family.

The club was also known for its world-class bareknuckle brawls, and Max intended to watch a few while in London. Apparently, that meant learning the basics of the sport, since here he stood as a boy pulled a length of cotton batting tight around Max's hand. It nearly cut off his circulation as he weaved it through Max's fingers and made another circle of his knuckles, encasing almost his entire hand with the white cloth.

"I'd prefer to be able to feel my hands," Max teased.

The boy, who couldn't have been more than twelve, scrunched his nose. "It'll loosen as you work, guv'nor."

Max nodded, and the boy continued until he tied off the end a moment later. Flexing his hands to test the wraps, Max took in the gymnasium. It was around three times the size of the modest gymnasium at his club in Manhattan, which was outfitted with steel bars mounted to the walls, dumbbells, and parallel bars. Montague Club operated at an entirely different level.

The club itself was a grand mansion, and the gymnasium was a converted ballroom. A large chandelier glittered above them with hundreds of crystals to reflect the light. The walls were plastered with gold brocade paper. A large fighting ring was roped off in one corner of the room with benches for spectators. The rest of the space was littered with machines and apparatuses to work every major muscle group. For the arms, there was a slatted climbing wall, an area for dumbbells fixed with various weights, and a standing machine with straps connected to sandbags for lifting. A couple of other machines were similar to that one but meant for working the legs. There was also a machine built on an incline fitted with a simple cable and pulley system that somehow worked the abdominal area. He had yet to figure out how that one worked.

"Ready?" Christian clapped him on the back, having been similarly outfitted with hand wraps. Unlike Max, who still wore his shirtsleeves, he had stripped down to his trousers and boots. Both Christian and Evan participated in brawling matches from time to time.

"I didn't realize you employed children," Max said,

glancing over at the boy who was winding the leftover batting into a ball. Crenshaw Iron had once exploited child labor, but he had put a stop to it years ago.

"We don't typically. He's one of Lady Helena's orphans. Kept getting himself into scraps and running away. She asked if we could employ him here to give him a purpose. So far the arrangement has worked out nicely. He still goes to the orphanage for his weekly lessons."

Helena. Of course. It seemed he couldn't escape her. Not that he wanted to, though she was partially responsible for his being here tonight. Over dinner with Christian and Jacob, Max had shared his frustrations about his father's demands, only telling them what he had told August and Violet. No one except Helena needed to know the depths to which his father would stoop. Because of his frustrations, Christian had suggested they go to the gymnasium and hit something, and Max had agreed even though he hadn't been entirely certain what that would involve.

He glanced down at the fabric binding his hands and flexed his fists to test the hold. They gave slightly but were still uncomfortably tight. "I've never done anything like this before."

"Fighting?" Christian asked.

Max nodded. "My last fight was at Princeton."

"You'll like it. Promise." He grinned, his limp only slightly noticeable as he led Max over to an area where bags of sand hung suspended from the ceiling. He demonstrated in a few moves how Max should hold himself as he hit the bag repeatedly. "Use your legs and swing with your hips." He demonstrated again in a slower motion. "You try."

Max took up position and landed a hook square in the middle of the sandbag, sending it jolting backward, vibrating as if it had been struck with electricity. It felt good, so he did it again with his left fist.

"That's it. Keep it up until your arms feel like they're filled with jelly."

Putting his head down, Max leaned into a series of blows against the unfortunate sandbag. In the weeks he had been in London, he had come to realize a couple of very important things. The first was that his father irritated him. No real surprise there. The second was that it had been over a month since he'd last had sex, and riding every morning in Hyde Park wasn't giving him the physical outlet he needed. Unfortunately, the only woman he wanted was Helena, and that wasn't likely to happen anytime soon. So here he was, attempting to work out his frustrations in another way.

The room faded to the background as he stared at the X marked in chalk on the bag. It diminished a little more with each strike of his fists until finally it was gone and he was left with the satisfying thump of his fist hitting burlap and sand.

"Crenshaw."

His head whipped up to see Jacob Thorne standing not very far away with Christian at his side. They seemed to have been watching him for some time. How long had he been punching? Now that he'd stopped, he realized he was covered in a layer of sweat and his shirt clung to his back.

Thorne smiled, a flash of white as he tilted his head toward the door. "You have a visitor."

No one was at the door, which meant the visitor must be waiting somewhere. His first thought was Helena, but that would be too improper for her. The club had a reputation for having secret rooms that catered to very particular desires. God, the very idea of meeting her in one of those rooms had the hair on his arms standing on end in anticipation. Who even knew he was here? "Who is it?"

As if he was pausing for dramatic effect, Thorne waited a beat before saying, "The honorable Lord Farthington requests that you join him in the lounge."

"Farthington?"

Christian grinned. "You can't court his daughter and not expect him to find you."

"No, I suppose not." Only he hadn't thought the man would seek him out so soon. "Damn. I didn't come dressed to meet him."

"Go have your shower bath. We'll find something for you to wear," Christian said.

A quarter of an hour later, Max was in the club's sleek lounge area in borrowed shirtsleeves and his own coat to face Helena's father. The lounge consisted of two rather expansive rooms with an open door between them. Dark wood paneling and gas lighting fixtures set at intervals along the wall gave the space an intimate feel meant to foster conversation. This was further enhanced by groupings of plush leather chairs arranged around low tables at each of the several fireplaces.

Lord Farthington wasn't difficult to spot. He sat in a chair near the fire looking over a newspaper like any other man enjoying a moment of solitude in his club; the only difference was that Farthington seemed unable to relax. His back was as straight as a board, his chin perfectly parallel to the floor. A similar posture to his daughter. The thought almost made Max smile, but it wasn't quite enough to overcome his anxiety at having to face the man.

The whole room appeared to be aware of what was happening. Though it was only half-filled with patrons, they all seemed to watch as Max passed, their eyes going automatically to Farthington and back again.

"Lord Farthington. Good to see you." Max took the chair across from him.

The older man took his time folding the paper and removed the cigar from his mouth. "Crenshaw." The few times Max had met him socially, he had been difficult to read, but he seemed to be attempting to keep a stoic face even more tonight. As a well-known member of Parliament, Farthington was renowned for being particularly sharp, and Papa had confirmed that to Max through his dealings with him as the railroad contracts were being negotiated.

"I didn't know you were a member." Max kept his voice measured and hoped it wouldn't carry. The groups in the room were far enough removed that their conversation shouldn't be overheard, though several men glanced their way surreptitiously.

"White's is my club. I came here to see you."

"I thought so." Max kept still under the man's narrowed inspection. He was accustomed to dealing with irate stakeholders and adversaries; this was no different.

"What are your plans for Helena?"

He hadn't been prepared for the man to come out with it. In his experience, men like him preferred to hem and haw, saying things without actually saying them to maintain plausible deniability. Thankfully, a footman approached with a tray bearing a single tumbler of scotch, giving Max a few precious moments to collect his thoughts.

"Thank you," he murmured to the man, who gave a short bow and silently walked away. He was impressed that someone had obviously remembered the drink he'd had after dinner and sent over a fresh one. Lightly resting it on his knee after savoring a sip, he said to Farthington, "Right now we're simply enjoying each other's company."

"And then what will you be doing?"

"That will be decided when the time comes."

The older man's expression didn't change, but he let out a light huff of air. "Don't you think you should deign to speak to me before continuing this courtship?"

"Forgive me, my lord, but Helena is a grown woman. A widow. I was led to believe that she controls her own concerns."

Her father took a slow puff of his cigar, letting the smoke escape in a slow wisp. "So she does, but a courtship is a different matter. She is still my daughter, still a part of my family, and she always will be. Make no mistake that if this courtship progresses and I disapprove, then it will go no further."

A fresh wave of anger and frustration came over him. It wouldn't do to antagonize the man, because they *would* eventually need his blessing. If the courtship were real, then it might not matter so much, but it wasn't, and the smoother this went the better for everyone. Still, he couldn't let the comment pass. Perhaps it was because he was fresh from the fight for both August's and Violet's future, but he was angry on Helena's behalf. "You don't own your daughter."

"I do not." He looked as if he were disgusted by the very suggestion that he might. "I do, however, own her trust, her esteem, and her loyalty. She won't go against my wishes, not when they're to the betterment of the family."

Max took another drink of the scotch, forcing himself to not challenge the man. "Are you saying you disapprove?"

Farthington picked up his own drink, which appeared to be brandy, and took a swallow. "It should come as no surprise that you were not my first choice . . . until last night."

Awareness of the profundity of that statement moved through his body like a physical sensation. His skin prickled, and he found himself sitting up straighter. "Last night?"

"Helena is a strange woman. I care for her deeply, but she has never been like my other daughters. She has . . . sensitivities, as you are aware."

"Sensitivities? You mean her charities?"

Farthington nodded. "She wants to save every unfortunate she finds, doesn't matter that it never helps."

"Well, it sometimes helps."

"About a year before she was married, she read an article about an entire family who had nearly frozen to death in the January cold because they slept with their windows open. The theory at the time was that one could be asphyxiated slowly overnight due to lack of oxygen. The idea became exaggerated as it spread to the masses to the point where an entire slum in Manchester slept with window sashes open in the dead of winter. This unfortunate family lost two young children because of it. She wanted to save the poor from themselves, so she printed pamphlets and hired a physician with her allowance to hold lectures about the dangers of the cold. Only it happened again the next year, different family, same result.

"The point is that the poor will always be such, whether it's due to unfortunate decisions, chance, education, character; there is no changing their ways."

"You speak as if they are different than you or I."

"Aren't they?" He leaned forward to tap the ash off the end of his cigar into a crystal dish before settling back and eyeing Max with meaning. "You've only to look at your family to see that, to see how far you have come. Providence may select a few, but most remain as they are."

Max bristled, his jaw tightening. "It's hardly providence, and what do you know of my family?"

"I know your grandfather had coal in his blood. I know that *his* father was a petty criminal who was jailed for larceny and died penniless."

The man had done his research. "I don't understand your point."

"I'm saying that out of the masses that earn their living in the coal mines of Western Pennsylvania, how many change their fate?" It was a rhetorical question, so he quickly went on. "Your family is different, whether you want to believe it. Fate intervened on your behalf."

"It was hard work and more than a little conniving on my grandfather's part."

Farthington shrugged. "Call it what you will, most of the poor won't change their circumstances when given the chance. However, I did not come here to discuss your opinions on the poor, though now that I think of it, it's good that you don't agree with me. If you did, you would soon find Helena tiresome."

Max opened his mouth to argue, but the man continued. "I was impressed with you last night, young Maxwell. You defended her when most men I know would have left the women to their tongue wagging without interfering. Or at least backed down once they saw me present. You did neither. You stood up for her."

"I couldn't have done less, nor could any other man worth her time. Misguided as you think she may be, she has made a difference in the lives of those around her. There is a boy who works in this very club instead of living on the streets, because of her aid. He has a mind, a soul. He could be an Augustus Crenshaw, or he could make a scientific discovery, or simply be there to help another person in need when the time comes."

The man looked him up and down. "You sound like Helena."

"The world would be a better place if more of us did, my lord." The gibe landed neatly. Max saw the pinched look come over Farthington's face as he realized he'd just been insulted.

"I disagree with you," the man began, "but as we've already established, I haven't come here to quibble with you. I've come to tell you that I will allow this courtship to continue, pending your attendance at Claremont Hall in a fortnight. We have a small gathering of friends there every year for a celebration before Christmas. Your parents are already planning to attend. I sincerely hope that your plans will accommodate a visit."

Max was speechless for a moment. Never had he imagined it would be so easy to gain her father's cooperation. His common roots and wealth would provide a nearly overwhelming barrier. He had assumed the most they would obtain was Farthington's grudging tolerance. Then, he would be immensely relieved when they called off the wedding, possibly thinking his disapproval had been instrumental in the decision.

To say this was unexpected was an understatement. To say that Max felt unreasonably happy was not.

Their courtship wasn't real. He shouldn't feel as if everything he had ever wanted was within his grasp, because it wasn't. Helena wasn't his no matter that her father approved. This was all for show, and he had no idea why he was having such trouble remembering that. Heat diffused through his chest, and he struggled to take in a breath.

Helena's life was here in England. She would never agree to give it up to come with him to New York, no matter that he could now imagine her there with him. Reality brought his joy back down to a more reasonable level.

"Thank you, my lord. I'm certain that I can arrange my schedule so that I can attend. I'd already planned to stay through Christmas."

"Good. I'll have my secretary send over the details."

"Of course," Max answered, following Farthington to his feet.

"I must be going now." Farthington turned but twisted back to face him after taking a step. "I don't want to regret this, Crenshaw. Helena *must* have someone willing to indulge her sensibilities."

"I'll look after her properly. I have great affection and admiration for your daughter."

Farthington nodded in acceptance and left him there pondering how true those words really were.

H elena rose to her feet when Huxley announced Maxwell at her drawing room door. She hadn't seen him since their kiss the night before last, approximately forty-one and a half hours ago—not that she'd been counting them. He filled the doorway almost entirely, and the way he stood there as if uncertain of his reception made her think back to their very first meeting. He had affected her even then, though she wouldn't have admitted it for a million pounds.

"Maxwell. How unexpected."

He seemed grim, his eyes withdrawn from her somehow. A warning flickered in her belly. "My apologies for stopping by unannounced. I meant to send a note. I was home visiting with Papa, and it seemed more expedient to call on you personally."

"Please do not apologize. I am happy to see you." Nervous, but happy. Why did she feel as if butterflies were at war with one another in her stomach? Smoothing a hand down her skirt, she said, "Won't you come in? Would you like tea?"

"No, thank you. I have to be leaving shortly." He walked into the room slowly, hesitantly. He'd given his hat and gloves to Huxley, so he obviously intended to stay for a few minutes. She couldn't figure out why he was acting so strange, unless he was as anxious about their kiss as she was.

Huxley backed out of the room, leaving the door open as was proper. Still, a pleasant tingling moved over her skin at being somewhat alone with him. She sat back down on the settee, moving the piles of papers spread out there to the table before her. She had been preparing for the arrival of the women who served on the board of the London Home for Young Women. They were going to help her get ready for her meeting with Sir Phineas at the end of the week to discuss the purchase.

"Please have a seat." He surprised her by sitting next to her on the settee, making her realize how small the piece of furniture actually was. When he turned toward her, his knees almost touched hers. "Is something wrong?"

He paused, taking in a breath. She couldn't help but watch his mouth, remembering how soft his lips had been on hers. "Your father visited me last night."

"Oh dear God." She covered her mouth with her hands as soon as the words were out. She could well imagine what he had said to Maxwell. No wonder he was aloof and with-drawn this afternoon. "I am sorry. Was he unspeakably rude? He had no right to—"

He reached out and took her hand, making her realize that she'd been gesturing excessively with it. "No, Helena, it's fine. I can't deny that it was a bit tense. We clearly do not see eye to eye on many issues. However, it went much better than I expected. If you can believe it, he tentatively gave his blessing on our courtship."

No, she could not believe it. Her father was stodgy and old-fashioned, and he had plainly said that he did not ap-preciate *vulgar wealth*. "I don't, actually."

He flashed a grin. "He invited me to a party at Clare-mont Hall. Apparently, it's an annual tradition."

She couldn't have been more shocked had he told her he had first-hand knowledge of the sea monster in Loch Ness. "I cannot believe it. How? Why?" At his expression of mock insult, she laughed. "I am glad of it, of course I am. I simply can hardly fathom it."

"Perhaps we've given the old man too little credit. He cares for you deeply, Helena." He squeezed her hand and then let it go. She drew it back to her lap, feeling unreason-ably bereft at the loss of his touch. "He appreciated the way I took your side against those people saying horrible things about your charity. He believes that you need a strong man willing to challenge such opinions, and he believes I could be that man."

"Oh . . . that's rather unexpected." Her father was a cold man at the best of times, never revealing his true feelings on anything, if he even had feelings. She was touched to learn that his affection for her outweighed his abhorrence of Maxwell not being titled or even a proper gentleman.

The hint of a grin lingered about his mouth. "He's right, you know. I can and will stand up to them for you."

The way his gaze swept her face made a blush steal over her, which was ridiculous. She was a widow, not a debutante in her first Season. Still, she glanced down at the pale green and gold embroidery of the settee. "I do appreciate you doing that. It isn't my intention that you feel the need to intervene every time someone says something careless."

"But I want to."

"Thank you."

His eyes met hers, and it was almost like a physical touch. He meant what he said, and she felt the same sense of belonging she had felt the night of the music performance. It was the both of them together against all the rest. That was a feeling she hadn't had in a very long time, since before Arthur had died. Unfortunately, their relationship by the end had changed from what it had once been. He had retreated from her, justifiably wounded and upset by their inability to have a child. Ever since, there had been a sense of loneliness about her, lurking around the edges of her life. Even filling her time with the orphanage, the new venture, and friends hadn't made it go away completely.

Because she couldn't allow her thoughts to drift to those old memories, she asked, "Will you be able to come to Claremont Hall? Won't it mean changing your plans? I thought you meant to return home to New York by then."

"My mother has already intervened and begged that I stay through Christmas. I've arranged my schedule to accommodate her, so there's no harm done."

"All right. It will be good to see you there." There was no accounting for the sheer excitement she felt at the prospect.

"I thought . . . if you agree . . ." He glanced away in a rare moment of uncertainty. A feeling she couldn't quite describe came over her that this man who was so confident and assertive would feel out of his element around her. "I'll bring a betrothal ring and give it to you there before I leave. Unless you think it's too much. I can always send one to you later, if you'd rather have that part of the courtship take place over mail."

Her heart began pounding so fast that she had to consciously catch her breath. This wasn't real. None of this would lead to them getting married, so why was the very idea of a betrothal ring so thrilling? "You do not have to go to such trouble. I don't think a ring will make this any more or less real to your father."

"No, perhaps not, but it doesn't seem proper that you wouldn't have one. If this were real—" He abruptly stopped talking, glancing out the window into the garden. Golden sunlight touched his features, and his strong nose stood out in profile. Possibly it was too strong, but she loved it. No, not love. She appreciated it and the way it enhanced his masculine beauty. It made her think of him as a beautiful Roman statue. Clearing his throat, he seemed all business again as he faced her. "If this were real, you would have one."

"But it's not." She felt the need to say the words out loud to remind them as her gaze held his.

"No." After a moment's pause, he shifted and came to his feet. She followed, disappointed that he was leaving so soon and things seemed stiff and awkward between them. "I have to get back to the office. There's a rather important meeting I must prepare for."

"Of course." He hadn't said one word about that kiss the other night, and she couldn't help but feel dejected because of it. He didn't even seem particularly affected by it, certainly not as affected as she was.

He started to walk toward the door but paused. "About this not being real . . . I think now that we have your father on our side—somewhat—we probably don't need to be seen about town as often. There's already talk of us, and that's really all we needed. I'll send you trinkets, flowers, but as long as the house party goes as hoped for, we don't need to carry off the ruse so dramatically anymore. Why give ourselves more opportunities to fail?"

"Are you sure? Won't that seem suspicious?" Sadness rose within her most unreasonably, and it was quickly followed by a dose of desperation. She despised it. None of this had been real. So he had kissed her? They were adults. Adults kissed and it didn't mean anything sometimes. *She* had never kissed without meaning, but apparently he did.

Dear God! She had never kissed without meaning. What had it meant to her then, and why was that question so difficult to face? She should be rejoicing that this would be over soon. She couldn't give him what he wanted. This had to end at some point. Better to be over now before her feelings for him deepened.

"I think it will be fine as long as the house party goes as planned."

The chime of the doorbell sounded through the house. "That will be the first of the board members arriving. We're having a meeting today to discuss the property. Violet will be here if you'd like to stay and say hello."

"No, I won't keep you." He sounded happy and relieved. "I have my own meeting to prepare for."

She walked with him to the door, the mild feeling of dejection growing more intense with each step. Huxley was taking the cape of Charlotte, the first board member to arrive. After cursory introductions, during which the woman gave her a knowing look, Maxwell said, "Goodbye, Helena," and tipped his hat as he hurried down her front steps to his waiting carriage.

She couldn't help but think that goodbye had sounded particularly formal and final, and after it she felt bereft in a way she hadn't in years. He was telling her that what had passed between them meant nothing. She already knew that. Right?

Before she could contemplate the question, another carriage pulled up, and Lady Betringham alighted. Helena knew that she must push all thoughts of Maxwell Crenshaw to the side. The rest of the afternoon would be taken up with figuring out how to convince Sir Phineas to grant his family's property to her charity. But she couldn't do it.

Despite the fact that her drawing room was filled with the women on the board, she felt lonely. Alone. She hadn't felt so alone since Arthur's illness. It was ridiculous to think that it was because of Maxwell's rejection, and yet she knew that it was. He hadn't even rejected her. They'd had an arrangement, a business deal. A simple kiss wouldn't change that.

Chapter 13

Nature has given woman the same powers, and subjected her to the same earth, breathes the same air, subsists on the same food, physical, moral, mental and spiritual. She has, therefore, an equal right with man, in all efforts to obtain and maintain a perfect existence.

FREDERICK DOUGLASS

Good evening, Lady Helena. How good of you to come." Sir Phineas greeted her in the expansive foyer of his fashionable Bloomsbury home with a customary bow. She positively vibrated with nerves now that the night to convince him to let her purchase the priory had finally come.

"Sir Phineas." She gave a curtsy, having just handed off her cape to his butler. Rain dripped across the floor as the man carried it to the coat stand in the corner. "Thank you for arranging this meeting."

"My only regret is that it has to be on such a rainy night," he replied.

"It's no bother. The ride over was fine."

All this time she had been imagining Sir Phineas as a doddering old gentleman, but he stood before her a strapping man who appeared to be no older than thirty-five. He wasn't handsome in the conventional sense, and not like Maxwell, but his broad features and thick brown hair held a certain charm, as did his eyes. They were that indiscriminate color between blue and green and filled with an intelligence that she immediately respected.

But her heart fell a little bit despite how likable he was. He was too young. At his age, he wasn't liable to care very much about his legacy and that of his family name. She had come armed with arguments that might appeal to an older man entering the sunset of his days with an eye to what he'd leave behind when he was gone. She didn't know if that line of reasoning would have the same effect on someone younger.

"I hope you can forgive me for taking so long in making up my mind," he said. "The priory has been in my family for almost two centuries, and while I suppose it's not very valuable in the grand scheme of things, it holds sentimental value to me."

"Perfectly understandable. I believe that places hold on to our memories for us and develop a sort of essence of their own because of it. Parting with a property can be like letting go of a family member."

He grinned, revealing a very attractive smile. "Well said, Lady Helena. Could I offer you refreshment before dinner?" He indicated a drawing room off the foyer. "We shall dine momentarily, but we're waiting for one other guest."

"Oh yes. Brandy, thank you." Strange. None of their correspondence had mentioned another guest.

He nodded and waited for her to lead the way into the drawing room. The decoration here matched the dark wood and red wallpaper in the entry hall. It was all very somber with every surface cluttered with an antique or trinket from faraway travels. She took a deep breath, willing herself to calm, as he poured a drink for her. She examined a glass case displaying butterflies of all colors. A twinge of pity wafted through her at the way they had been splayed out with pins, but it took her mind off the nerves threatening to run rampant through her.

Tonight would decide whether the home could move forward as planned or if she would be left scrambling to find somewhere else. After days and days of optimistic planning, convincing him suddenly seemed like a colossal task. She hoped she was up for it and didn't let everyone down.

"Thank you," she said when he presented the brandy to her. "I was unaware there would be another guest for dinner."

"Yes, unfortunately, I have been called away to Norfolk. I leave in the morning." She recalled a pair of trunks stacked near the front door. "There's no need for concern. It's simply a small matter on my estate there, but rest assured that I've arranged it so that whatever is decided tonight can proceed in my absence." Inviting her to sit, he took the chair opposite her. "As I explained in my note, there is another party interested in the property. With the time constraint, I thought it prudent to have you both here tonight to present your plans."

She kept her smile in place, while inwardly she cringed. The other person would likely have the funds to go higher than her offer, making this much more difficult.

The doorbell rang before she could answer, its knell echoing into the depths of the house.

"It appears that our other guest has arrived. Excuse me, Lady Helena."

She watched him retreat to the entryway, already preparing herself for battle. The board had emphasized offering to name the tenant hall after him. She would lead with that. A man such as him would like the idea that a building would stand in London bearing his name long after he was gone, despite his age . . . she hoped. Penhurst Hall had a nice ring to it. She'd even go so far as to offer the Penhurst Home for Young Women if that's what it took.

Murmurs from the entrance hall reached her as the men's voices came closer. She rose to her feet. Being caught sitting seemed as if it would put her at a disadvantage.

"—scotch or brandy?" Sir Phineas's voice preceded him into the room.

"Scotch, thank you." The American voice sent cold water gushing through her veins.

In the space of a heartbeat, she thought back to the night of her last kiss with Maxwell. He had been excited because he'd seemed confident that he would close the deal on the new building for August's venture. *It appears there is interest from other buyers, but I'm not concerned. I'm willing to pay almost any price to secure it.*

He had meant *this. She* was the other buyer.

He had meant *her* priory!

The moment he walked through the door, her body felt his presence like a substantial weight that changed the pressure in the room. She grew at least a degree warmer, and her entire body bristled in both warning and pleasure. It had been a few days since his visit to her home, and she missed him, but never had she thought their next meeting would be this one. "You."

His head swung around toward her. The very second he saw her, his eyes narrowed in that attractive way of his, the furrow deepening between his brows. His eyes grew so dark they were nearly black. Her stomach seemed to tumble over itself at the sight. This was the heat and interest absent from their last meeting. Then, he had been armed with his shield of forced indifference. But not now. Her presence had caught him off guard, and he couldn't hide it.

"Helena?" Max's voice struck through the stuffiness of the room.

Sir Phineas's head whipped around to look at her in surprise and then back at Maxwell.

When she was unable to find her voice, Maxwell filled the silence. "I wasn't expecting to see you here."

"You know each other?" Sir Phineas asked, sounding rather pleased with himself.

Her scalp prickled in warning, getting the message a

little too late about what was obviously happening here. Ignoring Sir Phineas, she asked Maxwell, "You're interested in the priory? That's the building you want for August?"

"The whole section of street actually."

"Yes," Sir Phineas interjected, apparently not one to be left out of a conversation. "I own the priory and the warehouse space surrounding it, though it's not really fair to refer to it as a simple priory now, is it? It's been a factory—a part of a proper industrial compound—for decades."

She supposed he was right. Helena and the board had been too narrowly focused on how to make the priory and attached residence hall into a suitable home and schooling facility to really appreciate how it played a larger part in the compound of industrial space surrounding it.

This was terrible! If Maxwell Crenshaw wanted *her* priory, then he would get it. He had the money to do whatever he wanted.

The benefits of being a Crenshaw. Money can buy you everything you want.

Those words had come from her own mouth because they were true. The Crenshaws had bought themselves a right proper place in society. They had purchased both a duke *and* an earl, spending well over a million dollars to accomplish the task—the fact that they had both ended up being love matches was neither here nor there at the moment. The important thing was that Maxwell would buy this building right out from under her if she let him.

But she couldn't allow that to happen. With the next beat of her heart, another thought struck her. Perhaps he would let her have it. He hadn't known all along that he was bidding against her. He understood how important this was to making the London Home for Young Women a reality. It could only be crammed into the top floor of the orphanage for so long, particularly with the list of names she had needing a warm place to live for the winter. Now that he understood, perhaps he would go find another facility that would be just as suitable.

She knew that she needed to speak, to say something—*anything*—but her tongue felt as if it was stuck to the roof of her mouth. Thankfully, the butler walked in as soon as Sir Phineas delivered the scotch to Maxwell. "Sir Phineas, dinner is ready."

"Perfect timing. Shall we?" He gestured to them both, and the butler led them to the dining room.

Maxwell waited for her, moving into step beside her as she walked by him, following the butler. He held himself stiffly, as if he, too, were still in shock. Sir Phineas chattered behind them, but for the life of her she couldn't pay attention to him with Maxwell's looming presence next to her. Her entire right side felt warm.

The dining room was like the rest of the house with its dark wood paneling and furniture. Only here the wallpaper started halfway up the wall and was a rich brown instead of red. A beautiful chandelier lit the room, filled with beeswax candles instead of being a gas fixture. Candelabras were set at each end of the table. The candlelight lent the space an even more intimate feel than the rest of the house.

"Sir Phineas? A moment please?" the butler asked as soon as they entered the room.

"If you please." Sir Phineas indicated the table and that he would be back in a moment, and they were suddenly left alone.

Helena was too focused on Maxwell to care. He assumed the position of host with no footman present and held her chair out for her. His face was like stone. She wished she knew what he was thinking. "Thank you," she said as she sat.

He leaned down as he pushed her chair in. "What are you doing here?" he asked in a low voice, as his breath tickled her ear. His tone was harsh with a soft, serrated edge that might have hinted at desperation. She couldn't be certain without seeing his eyes. It didn't matter. She knew then that he would not give up the priory to her.

"The same thing you're doing here," she answered, taking in an inadvertent inhale of his scent. It made everything inside her light up in excitement, even though it was most inappropriate given the situation.

"You know that August needs this."

She stared at him aghast as he walked around the table to take the chair across from her. "How was I supposed to know that the priory I found was a part of your industrial compound? Violet only mentioned that you were interested in a nearby metalworks."

His jaw still seemed tight as he sat, but he inclined his head. "Very well. You're right. You couldn't have known, because we never went into specifics. Now that you do know, will you do the right thing and leave off?"

"The right thing?" Impotent anger rose inside her so fast that she almost raised her voice. She had never raised her voice to anyone. Taking a deep breath, she let it out slowly and then said, "Me? You should leave off. I need the priory and the residence for the families who will go cold this winter without it."

"Dammit, Helena." His hand on the table clenched into a fist, and his stern expression leveled on her.

They always seemed to quarrel to a small degree, and she enjoyed riling him. That was the only way to explain the satisfaction that wound through her at the physical evidence of her effect on him now. He was like a lion, powerful and magnificent in his ire, but she never felt afraid of him. She never felt that his bite would wound her. Even when real anger was involved, their spats were playacting. God help her, she wanted to be his plaything.

The thought shocked her, stealing the breath right from her lungs. Had she no shame? This is the same man who had practically booted her from his life the moment he'd got what he wanted. She hadn't heard another word from him since his visit earlier in the week to tell her that now things were settled and they needn't bother with being seen together.

"Damn yourself!" The words burst out of her as soon as she could get her breath back. His eyes widened in surprise. "You with your infinite funding, you can purchase any building you want. Why should I be the one to give up the home that so many people need so desperately?"

"I cannot purchase any building I want. Like anyone else, I am bound—" He broke off as the door swung open and Sir Phineas returned, leading a footman. Maxwell's furrowed brow indicated that the conversation was far from over.

"My apologies for that," Sir Phineas said. "There was a minor mishap in the kitchen, but all is well." Taking his seat at the head of the table, he didn't seem to notice the tension between his guests as the butler hurried to pour sherry for them.

"No apologies necessary, Sir Phineas," she said. The footman set a bowl of turtle soup before her. "It was good to chat with Mr. Crenshaw in your absence." At least she knew where they both stood now.

"What a marvelous coincidence that you two have met. How long have you known each other? It can't be very long. You've only just come to town, haven't you, Mr. Crenshaw?" Apparently, the man did not pay attention to the scandal sheets or he would have read all about their courtship.

"We met in the spring. I . . ." Maxwell hesitated, and Helena disguised a smile at his discomfort by bringing a spoonful of soup to her mouth. Their history was somewhat complicated if one didn't want to explain the entire fiasco of Violet running away from an arranged marriage. "I was here in June for my sister's marriage to Lord Leigh."

"Ah yes, I read about their marriage in the papers. A belated congratulations to your sister and her husband." If he had read about the accompanying scandal, he was too kind to say.

Maxwell nodded, but then his gaze held hers and she had trouble looking away. "I met Helena then. She had befriended my sisters."

He insisted on using her first name without her title. Did that mean he would reveal their supposed courtship?

"What brings you back to London? Is it solely Crenshaw Iron Works?" Sir Phineas asked.

"My father fell ill." When the man was quick to offer his condolences, Maxwell added, "But he's improving. I've had to lend a hand to my sister who has been running things while he recovers."

Sir Phineas's eyebrow rose at the mention of August, but to his credit, he didn't comment. "Then you have been busy. I understand now your need for haste. You probably want to get this settled before returning home."

Maxwell relaxed visibly. "Yes, that is my hope. We're keeping our father as calm as possible, and—laws being as they are for married women—the company would prefer my father or I sign the purchase contracts."

One of the best reasons to remain a widow. Helena was able to sign for herself without a man's approval. Knowing this, why was she feeling so irritated with Maxwell's coolness toward her? She didn't understand it. That frustration combined with her earlier irritation made her say, "You might as well know, Sir Phineas, that Maxwell and I have been . . . we've begun a courtship of sorts." Adding *of sorts* was as close to the truth as she could get. She mainly confessed to their relationship to see how Maxwell would react, but she also felt that it would be unfair to not reveal it, especially since it was well-documented in the papers. If Sir Phineas read about it later and they hadn't confessed now, he might feel misled.

Maxwell paused in the act of bringing his spoon to his

lips. The furrow between his brows deepened, and she ignored the little thrill that flickered through her belly.

"Is that so? Why, this night is proving to be very interesting. And you never knew that you were both hoping to obtain the same property?" asked Sir Phineas.

"No." Maxwell's voice was strong and firm.

She smiled in an attempt to keep her composure and regain the upper hand. No one could win a battle if they gave in to their emotions. "Perhaps in hindsight we should have been more forthcoming when we spoke."

The mild accusation landed if one could judge by Maxwell's scowl. "I didn't realize you would be so interested in the minutiae of Crenshaw Iron." His voice was pleasant but blade sharp.

"Fair point. We can't all possess fanatical fixations with industry. Some of us wish to actually improve lives for those less fortunate." It was a bit of a low blow, even she could admit, but before she could feel bad about it, he spoke.

"Industrial endeavors improve lives for all of society by providing jobs and trade," Maxwell said, his tone sharpening by a degree.

"Oh, I agree that industry *can* improve lives, but the reality is that those improvements only trickle down to a chosen few and the rest are cast away, used and discarded to end up in the depths of St. Giles and every other rookery present in every industrial city."

The table shook when Maxwell shifted, as if he'd accidentally kicked a table leg. The sherry trembled in their glasses, and the porcelain clinked. His eyes were as fierce as she had ever seen them as he fixed them on her. A lion forced to hold back his fury. What would it be like if he was ever able to unleash all that passion on her? A blush accompanied the thought, sending her attention back to her bowl of soup.

A tiny voice in the back of her mind that sounded suspiciously like her mother berating her said, *"A lady does not think such wicked thoughts, Helena. Baser impulses are the purview of men. True ladies learn to overcome them."*

This wasn't the first time she had wondered if she wasn't a true lady, despite her birth. The last time had been as recently as the night of their last kiss when she had been alone in her bed wondering what it would be like if Maxwell was there with her. Her hand had found its way beneath her nightdress, but she'd been unable to find the relief she sought.

Her face flamed as she stared down at her food. What inappropriate thoughts for such an important dinner. Thankfully, Sir Phineas came to her rescue.

"Er . . . That's a very astute observation, Lady Helena," he said, clearly having trouble finding his way through their tense exchange. "Tell us more about your charity, if you will. I have been fascinated by what I have learned, but I'd like to hear more about it from you."

She couldn't stop herself from glancing toward Maxwell. He'd paused with his spoon partially raised to his mouth as if the sight of her blush had stunned him. The furrow on his forehead was gone as he stared at her. Dear God, it was almost as if he could read her thoughts. Jerking her gaze back to Sir Phineas, she raised her napkin to her mouth to buy herself an extra moment to gather herself.

"Sir Phineas, I'd be delighted to elaborate."

Helena kept up the bulk of the conversation throughout the meal. No one mentioned the industrial compound through the fish course or the main course of roast pork with potatoes and brussels sprouts. The talk was filled with the history of the orphanage and the thousands of people who had grown up within its walls. Maxwell contributed nominally. He'd gone back to glowering at her as he ate.

After the orphanage, she launched into the need the London Home for Young Women was currently filling. Thankfully, Sir Phineas seemed interested, asking all the

appropriate questions that allowed her to discuss her vision
for the future, and how many more women and children she
hoped to be able to help. By the time the conversation
turned back to Crenshaw Iron when the dessert course was
served, Helena felt better about her chances of securing the
property, until the conversation took a slight detour,
prompted by Sir Phineas's endless questions.

"As you mentioned earlier, industry can be very benefi-
cial to a local economy. Can you elaborate on that as it re-
lates to Crenshaw Iron Works?" the man asked.

"Certainly," Maxwell answered. Was it her imagination
or was there a taunting glint in his eye? "We employ two
thousand people across New York and Pennsylvania. That's
not to mention the people we employ across the railways.
Our wages are fair, creating economies that support three
different municipalities." He looked at her as he said this,
none too subtly letting her know how Crenshaw Iron had
improved those lives. When she raised a brow, he turned his
attention back to Sir Phineas. "Our endeavor here in England is young yet, but we have plans to hire over a hundred
workers in the new year, and the contract work given to
several other companies will provide jobs for even more."

"And how necessary is the industrial compound to at-
taining that goal?" Sir Phineas asked, genuinely interested,
if the way he leaned forward was any indication.

She sat quietly as Maxwell went into detail about how
the property would be used to fulfill their recently acquired
contracts to participate in the building of the Prince Albert
Dock. Her heart sank farther down into her stomach with
each word. What he said made sense. Crenshaw Iron would
provide jobs for men who needed them, but it would not
help the women and children who needed a place to stay
the winter, who desperately needed skills training and education to improve their future prospects.

As the conversation progressed, she could see Sir

Phineas becoming more interested. Maxwell was a good speaker and engaging conversationalist. He understood his business and could explain it in terms that someone outside of the industry could comprehend. He made it sound as if Crenshaw Iron would be all but saving St. Giles.

She knew that she was on the losing end of the arrangement when Sir Phineas sat back, Madeira in hand, and asked, "Could we not come to some arrangement where you could both benefit?"

Maxwell had won him over. She bit the inside of her lip to keep it from trembling. "How so?"

"Well, couldn't you divide the property?"

"I don't see how," Maxwell said, sitting back as a footman cleared their dessert dishes away.

"Crenshaw Iron could control the warehouses, and Lady Helena's charity the priory grounds," Sir Phineas said.

Could they? Perhaps if she could keep the priory, but she would need every bit of the campus around it. Before Helena could get too excited about the suggestion, Maxwell said, "Crenshaw Iron needs the residence on the grounds for the workers, and the factory there can work as a foundry. We've plans to modify the machines."

Sir Phineas frowned and asked Helena, "Could you do with a smaller share of the residence?"

"And have the women and children housed along with working men? No," Helena said. "Besides, we need the space. We have a list of fifty women and children who can move in as soon as it's ready. I have no doubt that by the end of winter we'll have a hundred more. There won't be room for all of them if we have to share with his workers."

Maxwell's brows drew together. "She's right. It will never work. You'll have to choose."

"Unless someone withdraws," she said, sitting back and crossing her arms over her chest. Her meaning was clear. "Then, yes, Sir Phineas will have to choose."

"I don't see why either one of us would want to with-draw," Maxwell said.

"Because *one* of us can find somewhere else easily."

"It's not easy to find warehouse space, factory space, all within a distance that makes production cost-effective."

"Well, neither is it easy to pluck one hundred and fifty women and children from the only homes they have ever known and move them to a completely different city. In fact, most would balk at such a plan and refuse to leave. Then we'd be right back where we started with women and children living in reprehensible circumstances."

"They will be better for it if they are moved," he said.

"The point is to help them, not to save them, Mr. Crenshaw. You can't simply pick someone up, shake them off, and say, 'Here, go do this or that.' It doesn't work that way. Our mission is to assist them by providing access to housing and safety. We then give them the tools they can utilize to make their lives manageable going forward. They are not pawns or nameless beneficiaries of charity. They come to us for help and we build their trust in us, and only then can we provide them opportunities for education and training."

"Yes, but my plan will provide necessary jobs."

"Right, it will, and that is all very good. But how many of those jobs will be for women? How many women are employed across your factories, Mr. Crenshaw?"

"That isn't fair," he said.

"No, it's not fair, but neither is it fair that these women have no system of support. That is why it is so important that people who can help, people like the good Sir Phineas here, be allowed to offer aid when they can. Employing more men will not help the women and children in my care."

His jaw was tense, and silence spread throughout the room. "You know that August needs this property," he finally said through gritted teeth. "You know what's at stake for her."

"Now *that* isn't fair."

How could he stoop so low? Was she supposed to put the lives of the women and children in her care aside to aid his sister?

"None of this is fair, Helena. I believe we've established that. The fact is that August will be crushed beyond what is fair if you impede this purchase."

Guilt tore through her in a terrible wave, causing her stomach to churn in protest and her throat to tighten.

Rushing to her feet, she said, "This has been a lovely evening, Sir Phineas. I appreciate meeting you."

Both men hurried to their feet. Maxwell grimaced as if struck silent by the shock of his own words, so that Sir Phineas spoke first. "Must you leave already, Lady Helena?"

"I'm terribly sorry, but I have said all that I can on the matter. Please consider how badly the London Home for Young Women needs this."

She waited only a moment to lock eyes with Maxwell; his gaze was already filling with regret, but it was too late. Whirling, she hurried to the front hall, grabbing her cape before the butler could offer it to her. He barely managed to open the front door before she got there. Rain fell still, but she didn't let it stop her from hastening toward where her carriage waited down the street.

"Helena!" Maxwell's voice followed her down the front steps, but she did not dare look back. "Wait!"

Her driver was caught unaware and fumbled with the umbrella as he hurried toward her.

"There's no need," she said, waving off his attempt. "Please get me home as quickly as possible."

"Yes, milady," he said, opening the carriage door and helping her inside.

She had completely and utterly failed at her task and ruined the whole night. How would she ever face the women and children who needed her? How would she face the board? She blinked back the tears that welled in her eyes, but the ache in her throat still lingered.

The fact that Maxwell had contributed to her loss made her feel the sting all the more. It was like a knife twisting in the wound. What did this mean for them?

Chapter 14

❖

Genuine learning has ever been said to give polish to man; why then should it not bestow added charm on women?

EMMA WILLARD

An hour later, Helena sat in her drawing room attempting to read. She'd been on the same page for almost a quarter of an hour, but at least it was something. It kept her from sulking. Sort of. Her mind kept going over the disastrous evening, churning over it as if to relive it would help to change what had happened, no matter how she tried to pay attention to the words on the page. Finally, she closed the book with a huff and stared at the fire crackling in the hearth.

After she had come home, she had changed out of her wet clothes and into her nightdress and dressing gown. Then she had sent the Huxleys to bed. There was no need for them to stay up and keep her company. Only now that she was alone, she rather wished she had taken up Mrs. Huxley on her offer to play a round of cards. Doing something would be better than sitting here and stewing. Despite how badly she felt about the lost opportunity for the charity, she couldn't deny that some of her moroseness was because she felt that she had lost Maxwell, too. Not that she had ever had him.

Groaning in frustration and residual anger at him, she walked to the hearth and used the fire poker to move a log around, sending sparks skittering. She had been terribly rude to him. He hadn't been fair himself, but that didn't excuse her own reaction. She'd probably have to jot down a note to send over to him tomorrow. He'd reply back in clipped prose. Then she wouldn't see him again until he made an appearance at Claremont Hall. She would still need to carry out the charade. She might have lost the priory, but she still needed her father on her side to maintain their funding and find a new building. She and Maxwell would continue their little performance for their families, and then he would leave. This was exactly how their little drama was meant to play out, so why did she feel so bereft and lonely?

It was because she felt abandoned by him. All this time she had felt that he understood her, that he would support her, only to have her worst fears about him confirmed. He had turned his back on her the moment he had needed to in order to further his own ends. But that wasn't completely fair. He was doing this for August, not his own personal interest. And yet, she felt that August would be on her side in this. Guilt, anger, and heartache twisted into such a tight knot in her stomach that she couldn't tell one thread from the other.

A tapping at her window made her think the rain had picked up, but then it happened again. Her heart leapt into her throat as she looked up to see a man standing outside the window. The small halo of light given off by the sconce on the wall illuminated his large size, and something about the set of his shoulders made her think it was Maxwell. He took his hat off, and a gasp tore from her chest as her suspicion was confirmed.

Maxwell Crenshaw stood outside her window in the dead of night! What on earth could he want?

It took a moment for her mind to catch up with what was

happening. She stood there in shock as he motioned to the door that opened to the garden. It was the same door he had come in and out of back in June when Violet had been staying with her. After coming home from Yorkshire, Violet hadn't wanted to go home to her parents. Helena had invited her to stay here while Maxwell and Mr. Crenshaw negotiated the marriage arrangements with Christian. Maxwell had come nearly every day to visit and give them updates on how the negotiations were faring. Because they didn't want to advertise to all of London that Violet was here, he had come in and out through the mews, using the garden exit and that door.

She nodded and held her hand up for patience. She could not chance one of the servants seeing them, so she hurried to lock the door that led to the rest of the house. Only then did she open the leaded-glass door to the garden. A blast of cold air had her pulling her dressing gown tighter around her.

"Can I come in?" he asked, rain dripping off his hair.

For a moment, Max believed that she would close the door, that she had opened it for him only so that she could slam it shut. He couldn't entirely blame her. Dinner had not gone well.

Her face grew taut, and he was certain she was about to say no, but then she stepped back to give him space.

He hurried in past her, and she closed the door and turned the latch behind him. Unexpectedly, her hands gripped the shoulders of his outer coat and she helped him to shrug out of it. He was cold, but he'd warm up a lot faster without the coat, which was nearly soaked through.

"You're drenched. You didn't walk here, did you? You could catch your death in this weather." She sounded annoyed and irritated, while at the same time pushing him toward the fireplace.

Good. He was annoyed and irritated, too. After the carriage had dropped him at his parents' house, he'd been unable to find a moment of peace. Instead of going to bed, he had walked here, and he was starting to realize how impulsive the act had been. "You ran away. I had to come find you."

Setting his hat and gloves on the mantelpiece, he held his hands up to the flame, savoring the warmth as she looked for somewhere to put his coat that wouldn't ruin her furniture. She was in her nightclothes, an eventuality that he hadn't considered when he'd first set out to see her. He shouldn't look, but he couldn't help but watch her from the corner of his eyes as she hurried around the room. The nightdress and dressing gown ensemble was white flannel, thick to guard against the cold night. There was absolutely nothing provocative about them, except for the fact that she was wearing them. Except for the fact that they clung to her body, the skirts swishing about her legs. He could plainly see the swell of her breasts, the outline of her hips, and the curve of her buttocks. Worse, he knew that she was naked beneath her clothes. He would find nothing but warm, soft skin if he reached beneath them.

He took a deep breath and stared at the flames, lust and leftover fury burning him up from the inside as a coil of longing began to twist and tighten in his belly. No one could make him as simultaneously frustrated and aroused as she could.

Finally deciding on the chair at the little desk he had seen her use to write letters and where a stack of newspapers were kept, she pulled it toward the fireplace and draped his coat over it so that it could at least begin to dry in the few minutes he would be here.

"I left because you were being a brute." Her voice was low but laced with steel. Now that her initial shock was wearing off, he could see her anger returning. Her defenses were up again. She crossed her arms over her chest, and he tried not to look, but he couldn't help but watch as the flannel pulled against the curves of her hips.

"A brute? You all but attacked me, because I am committed to doing what is best for August and Crenshaw Iron."

She rolled her eyes, and aggravation simmered through his veins. "You are hiding behind your sister instead of addressing the very good points I brought up at dinner. The fact of the matter is that without that building, people will suffer."

He turned toward her before he could rein in his emotions. "No, the fact of the matter is that you could find another building if you wanted. It may not be there, and it may be outside London, but there are other options. There are always other options."

"The world doesn't operate in your narrow scope of reality, Mr. Crenshaw."

He bristled at that. He liked it when she called him Maxwell instead of injecting this artificial formality between them. Nothing had ever been formal and proper between them. "So we are back to *Mr. Crenshaw* again. I thought when you said it over dinner it was because you were angry."

"I was angry. I am still angry, because you don't seem to even care to try to understand. These women and children won't come to us if they think our only goal is to cart them off to another part of England. London is their home, and they have every right to it, just like any other Londoner. The objective is to change from within, to improve their lives by improving their homes, not pulling them away from everything they've ever known."

He closed his eyes and took in a deep breath. This was getting them nowhere, and she was partially right. He didn't understand, because they had never talked about her plans beyond their surface. When he opened his eyes, she was breathing just as hard as he was, her breasts rising and falling. She had braided her hair for bed, and it had fallen over her shoulder, making her look attainable somehow, as if she were not the cool and detached Lady Helena March but the much more touchable Helena.

"You're right in that I don't understand everything you're doing, and I am sorry for charging in like this," he began, forcing his voice to stay calm. "I went home fully expecting to pay a call tomorrow, but I couldn't let this wait."

"You walked from your parents' house in the rain to tell me I am being unreasonable?"

"Well, I didn't want to rouse the driver to do it," he said, sarcasm dripping from his voice. "Besides, I couldn't let him drop me off out front, not at this hour, and if he left me at the mews, that would look even worse."

She stared at him in bewilderment, as if she was unable to decide if he were telling the truth or jesting. Her lips were parted, and he wanted to drag her into his arms and kiss her. It was a wildly inappropriate thought, but even so, excitement swirled in his stomach and he clenched his teeth to keep from acting on the impulse as he forced his gaze anywhere but on her.

"You're unbelievable," she said. "What if I had been in bed?"

There was a subtle shift in her tone when she asked. He couldn't put his finger on it, but she wasn't angry anymore. Not like before. This was softer. His eyebrow quirked upward as he glanced toward her, as if half-afraid of what he'd see. There was a glint of wickedness in her eyes. The same one that came to life in their previous sparring sessions. She was playing with him. His blood thickened in response, making his body feel heavy and languid, half-aroused already.

"Yes, I thought of that. Thankfully, I saw your lamp on." He indicated the sconce on the wall.

"What if all had been dark?"

He shrugged, his feet taking the smallest step toward her. "I thought I might throw pebbles at your window."

"Do you even know which one is my bedroom window?"

"Not yet."

She shivered, the movement subtle enough that he might not have seen it had he not been watching her closely. Her eyes darkened, the pupils growing larger in arousal. God, he wanted her. That need frightened him. After a decade of indulging himself in only the most casual of sexual experiences, he felt that this could be something deeper.

"I didn't come here to argue," he said, realizing he needed to get to his reason for visiting so late. Perhaps Montague would still be open, and he could go there afterward to work off his excess energy. "I told Sir Phineas that I want you to have the priory."

"What?" Her body drew back as if her disbelief had propelled her into motion.

"Helena, both of our projects will benefit many people. I . . ." He paused and took in a breath. He'd been taught all his life that being vulnerable in any way was an undesirable thing. But she deserved to know that she had changed his mind. "Despite how it seems, I heard what you said; your argument was sound. I couldn't live with myself knowing that those women and children were without a home when I could have done something to stop it."

"What about your contracts . . . and the . . ." She looked as if she could hardly think straight. Her body was almost trembling with nervous energy. A smile tugged at his lips to see her on the verge of coming undone, but he was wise enough to quell the urge. "And the industrial compound . . . August? What about August and the dock?"

He took a step toward her and gently took hold of her shoulders. "After you left, I stayed and talked with Sir Phineas. We discussed his suggestion . . . the benefits of Crenshaw Iron taking over the rest of the compound with the priory going to your home. He seemed to truly want that scenario to work out."

"Because you talked him into it?" A line of disappointment formed between her brows.

"No, because *you* talked him into it. When he made the suggestion at dinner, that's what he wanted. He wanted you to have the priory all along."

"To *have* it?"

"Yes, he wants to grant it to your charity. I believe he'd been intending to sell it to you, but he quite liked your suggestion of naming the hall Penhurst. You have an admirer in him." The pang Max had felt every time that tender gleam came into Sir Phineas's eye when he would look at her at dinner was not jealousy. He didn't quite know what it was, but jealousy would be foolish.

She smiled, a slow, tremulous thing that made her bottom lip quiver. "I don't believe you." But she did. He could see the wonder coming over her face.

"Believe me. You'll probably be hearing from Sir Phineas in the morning."

Almost immediately, her brow furrowed again. "But what about August?"

He shook his head. "I'm not certain. We still have time before I leave to figure out a plan. I have committed to purchasing the rest of the compound. The warehouses in that location will be invaluable, but it's not enough. We'll have to scour the area for someplace that will house the workers. Someplace suitable, and we still need the foundry."

"You could hire the women at the home."

He laughed but stopped just as quickly when he realized she was serious. Still, he felt the need to ask, "You're not serious?"

"And why not? Do you think the women are only suitable for positions as seamstresses or going into service?" Anger lit her face again.

He'd had enough similar discussions with his sisters to know that he was on fragile ground. "Not precisely, no."

"Women are as capable as men. It would only take training."

"A lot of training. It would be nearly unsurmountable."

Now her hands were on her hips, loosening his grasp, and her dressing gown had almost become undone. The flannel nightgown pulled taut across her breasts, revealing their size. They would be more than a handful. He closed his hands into fists because he could imagine the weight of them already. He needed to get out of here. She might desire him, but she would not welcome him into her bed, into *her*. Even just imagining it had a wave of lust crashing through him.

"Are you saying that you are bringing in skilled workers?" she asked. "Men who are already familiar with working at a foundry? I thought your plan was to hire men from the area around the property?"

The woman was exasperating. "I am saying that there are machines they'll need to learn."

"Then we can train them."

"But women aren't strong enough—"

"It's a foundry. There are metal castings, correct?" At his nod, she hurried on. "And you'll be making small pieces, parts for the dock and tools?"

He nodded. "I suppose, yes. But some of these jobs are highly skilled positions. We'll likely have to hire pattern-makers and hand molders."

"Is every job so highly skilled?"

"Well . . . no. Machine molders and coremakers can be trained within a few months."

She smiled in triumph. "Then we could train the women to do those jobs, if they want."

August had opened his eyes to the fact that women could fulfill the same roles as men in business. She had a head for numbers and was capable of working harder and longer than most men he knew. He simply had never considered women might also fulfill roles that were labor intensive. That they might work machinery or toil in the heat and tumult of a factory floor.

"I'm willing to discuss the option," he said after a moment.

She frowned, her brows drawing together as if she couldn't decide whether to argue more or not. He couldn't help but chuckle at the befuddled expression on her face. She was frustrated, but she also realized she had won a sizable concession.

"You are exasperating," she finally said.

"Me? Have we ever had a conversation that wasn't an argument?"

"That's precisely my point. You, Mr. Crenshaw, are a shrew."

He laughed out loud. "*I'm* a shrew?"

She raised her chin in self-righteous indignation.

It was a step too far. "The truth is that you like to provoke me." He grinned at the startled look that came over her beautiful features, confirming what he had merely suspected. She enjoyed stoking the heat between them as much as he did.

Chapter 15

The demand for equal rights in every vocation of life is just and fair; but, after all, the most vital right is the right to love and be loved.

EMMA GOLDMAN

Helena should have felt mortified that Maxwell had found her out. He knew that she intentionally provoked him. If that glint in his eye was any indication, he realized that she got a secret thrill from it. And if she was honest with herself, she was a little embarrassed. However, he was walking toward her with that predatory look in his eyes that sometimes accompanied his stern glower, and butterflies were swarming in her stomach, and she could only think that even as she backed away from him she very much wanted him to catch her.

"Admit it," he said, an all-knowing smile curving his lips, mixing with his furrowed brow in a way that had her stomach dropping in anticipation. Her back came up against the wall, but he kept coming, raising his arm to press it to the wall above her head, which allowed him to lean over her a bit so she had to look up at him. "You intentionally bait me. You like getting a rise out of me for your own pleasure."

"Why would I admit to something so ridiculous?" Even

she could hear the catch in her voice and how heavily she breathed.

His face relaxed, the glare melting away as his body settled close to hers. Not touching, but almost. Close enough that when she took a deep breath in, the tips of her breasts grazed the lapels of his frock coat, sending shock waves through her.

"Because you want me to kiss you and I won't until you admit it."

She opened her mouth to deny it, the residual effects of her earlier anger and disappointment in him tangled with her relief, gratitude, and desire, so that she couldn't tell one from the other. She couldn't think. So instead, for once in her life, she decided to only feel, to let her body guide her tongue. What would it hurt just this once?

"I like when you scowl at me. I like how handsome you are when your brow furrows . . ." Hardly understanding what she was doing, she raised her hand up. His eyes narrowed in on it, making that wonderful glower reappear. They might have both stopped breathing as she brought her hand to his face, letting the tips of her fingers touch his furrowed brow and the line etched between his eyebrows. "Here. And how intensely you look at me."

His eyes were dark and in shadow, so she couldn't really see them, but she could feel them boring into hers. She could also feel the weight of his gaze when it shifted down to her mouth. She licked her lips in anticipation, but he didn't move any closer, prompting her to take a deep breath, swaying just the tiniest bit closer to him so that her breasts grazed his chest again. Delightful sparks of yearning shot through her.

"Ask me to kiss you." His voice was low and harsh, almost a growl.

"You said you would if I admitted it, and I did."

He grinned, his flash of teeth white in the dark. "I want to hear you say it."

Indignation was swift to take over. He was asking too much. Rising up onto her toes, she simultaneously wrapped her arms around him to pull him down to her. Their mouths met in a heated exchange, quarreling in a way that went beyond words. The wet heat of his tongue invaded her, taking what he wanted without apology. Not that he had anything to apologize for. She wanted everything he would give to her and wanted to give whatever he would take.

The thought shocked her into immobility. *Whatever* he would take?

Yes.

"Helena?" Her name came out as a rough groan as he kissed a path to her ear, nipping the tender lobe before trailing openmouthed kisses down her neck.

She couldn't form words, and her body—true to her earlier conviction—took over, her fingers gripping his hair and holding his mouth to her. He bit the place where her neck met her shoulder, making her yelp before she could stop herself.

He was smirking as he pulled back enough to see her face. "You like rough play."

She blushed and glanced toward the mantelpiece next to them, anywhere but look at him. Did she? She didn't know, but she couldn't deny the thrill that had shot through her at the pleasure-pain of the bite. Her only sexual experiences had been with Arthur, and while her memories of that time were mostly pleasurable, he had never used his teeth. He had never kissed her like this, standing against a wall and tasting her as if he couldn't get enough.

"Shh . . . don't be embarrassed." Maxwell's voice was soft and uneven against her ear as he rubbed his bearded face gently against her. She closed her eyes and savored the prickling pleasure that radiated from where he touched her. "I can give you what you want."

"I want you," she whispered without opening her eyes.

Neither of them moved for a moment as the idea settled

between them. Then he shifted slowly, taking hold of her plait and winding it around his hand as he tilted her head back. The slight pull on her overly sensitive nerve endings was nearly ecstasy. Her heart pounded as she stared up into his shadowed face.

He swallowed thickly, his Adam's apple moving down and then up. He lowered his mouth until it closed over hers. This kiss was infinitely gentler, his lips stroking over hers in a slow back-and-forth until she tightened her fingers in his hair and pulled him down for more. He groaned deep in his throat and let his other hand roam down her body. She gasped against his mouth when his palm closed over her breast. He made another low sound, squeezing as if he were testing out the weight and feel of her before dragging his thumb across the tip. Pleasure rushed from her nipple to deep in her core. Releasing her hair, he tugged at the knot on her dressing gown, dragging it open so only the layer of her nightdress separated his hands from her skin. She stifled embarrassment at the sight of her rigid nipples clearly outlined beneath the fabric.

She wasn't supposed to be this deeply in the throes of arousal. Not here in her drawing room where she served tea once a week to her friends and where her own parents visited with her. But any flare of shame faded as he unhurriedly lowered his head to her breast. She hardly dared breathe as she watched him part his lips. When he dragged his teeth over her nipple in a teasing rhythm that culminated in him biting her, she nearly splintered apart at the bliss.

"Maxwell." She gasped his name over and over, unable to form any words beyond the one responsible for what was happening to her. In answer, he sucked at her, and she arched into him to get closer to the heat of his mouth.

Thank God he knew what she wanted. He grabbed her hips, his hands sliding down to fill themselves with her bottom as he squeezed and caressed her, making the molten heat between her legs intensify. Just that quickly it no longer mattered that they were in her drawing room. All that mattered was that she knew she had locked the door, so they wouldn't be disturbed. Tomorrow would be soon enough to face the consequences of her want. Being with him might not be wise, but she'd be bloody well damned if she would let that stop her.

She wrapped her arms around his shoulders at the same time he lifted her against him, settling his hips into the cradle of hers as his mouth took hers again. He was hard and solid along her front but even more so where he pressed intimately between her thighs. She flexed her hips, grinding herself against him as he took her mouth, his need almost brutal in its intensity, but she didn't care that her lips might be bruised tomorrow. Something about the idea made it more exciting, ratcheting up her arousal by another degree.

Her hands moved between them, trying and failing to feel more of him. There were too many clothes. She pushed at his frock coat, and his hips anchored her between him and the wall as he let go of her to let the coat drop to the floor, followed by his waistcoat. Instead of holding her again, he jerked at the tail of her nightdress, tugging it upward. She nearly jumped out of her own skin when his bare palms touched her legs, and then her buttocks. She sighed in gratification as he squeezed the globes, opening her up to the press of his erection.

"My God, Helena, you feel as good as I knew you would." His face looked like that of a man in pain, his features taut and hardened with need. To tease them both, he moved his hips, thrusting them against her as if he were moving inside her except the coarse wool of his trousers was in the way.

She cried out as the solid ridge of him dragged over her swollen clitoris. "Maxwell, I need your touch."

He gave a soft laugh and took her mouth again. She thought he meant to tease her more, but he granted her request instead. Levering an arm around her hips to support her, his other hand found its way between them. He pinched her swollen flesh to the point of pain, making her squeal in a sharp sound that he swallowed with his kiss. Almost immediately after, he soothed the rough touch with soft, gentle circles of his thumb.

Pleasure wound tight in her belly with each stroke to the point she couldn't keep up with his kissing anymore. She closed her eyes, lost to the magic of his touch. When he pushed one thick finger inside her, her body gripped at him, eager for all that he would give her. She cried out softly as he filled her with another, then bit at his shoulder to keep other cries from falling out of her. Someone would come check on her if she didn't stop the sounds, but she couldn't seem to control herself as he thrust his fingers in and out of her, and her hips moved of their own volition, riding him with abandon. Before she even knew it was upon her, an orgasm shattered through her, sending shards of pleasure ricocheting inside her. She held on to him like a lifeline as the remnants moved through her in delicious waves until the tremors finally subsided.

Maxwell pressed a kiss to her temple and gently withdrew his fingers. "Better?" he whispered as she slowly came back to herself and tried to catch her breath. She could still feel her heartbeat in every extremity as he smoothly let her go and tugged her nightdress back into place.

"No," she whispered, tightening her grip on his shoulders.

"I've waited so long for that," he whispered back, dragging his lips across her cheekbone. But she could already sense him withdrawing, as if they could ever get back to normal after this.

"Maxwell." She didn't like the plaintive note in her voice, but neither could she stop it. "Don't go."

A breath of laughter rushed past her ear, and a twinge of

anger rose from the ashes of her recent pleasure. Her hand traveled from his shoulder, down his chest, across the flat and hard plains of his stomach, to the magnificently rigid length of erect maleness in his trousers. She palmed him, savoring the thick breadth of him. Her body went weak all over again as she imagined him inside her.

"I want you inside me."

He stilled in what she could only assume was shock, even though it didn't make sense. What had he thought they were doing? To encourage him, she squeezed him as good as she was able with the layer of wool between them.

He took in a shuddering breath as he pressed his forehead to hers. "We can't, Helena." She pressed harder with her palm, working up and down his length from root to tip in an imitation of a massage. He let out another shaky breath. "I didn't bring a sheath."

She vaguely knew that he meant a rubber sheath, though Arthur had never worn one with her. "We do not need one."

He let out a soft groan as his hips moved in rhythm to her stroking and he trembled against her. "We do. I don't trust myself to withdraw . . . not with you."

She flushed with pleasure at that. To think that he wanted her so badly that he might lose control. Her aching body grasped at emptiness, needing him to fill her. She knew that she was wet enough he could slide in with relative ease. It was as if the earlier climax had only roused her appetite for more of him.

"You won't have to. I . . . I can't . . . It's not . . ." He couldn't get her with child, but to tell him that would lead to more questions that she didn't want to answer. Not now.

"You're not at that point in your cycle?"

She nodded her agreement, anything to get him inside her. "Yes, that's right."

He drew back and looked down at her, tilting her chin up with his fingers. "You're certain?" He looked at her with such fierce tenderness that she nearly melted into a puddle of need right there.

She nodded again.

"Is the door locked?" he asked, and she could tell he was close to capitulating.

"Yes, Maxwell." Before he could say anything, she grabbed at his trousers, seeking to unfasten them, but he brushed her rather ineffective hands out of the way.

"Undress," he said in a no-nonsense tone that had her shrugging out of her dressing gown before she could think.

Grabbing his frock coat, she spread it on the rug before the hearth and gripped the hem of her nightdress, hesitating before pulling it over her head. She'd never been completely naked before a man and certainly not in her drawing room. Her husband had only made love to her in bed. Not once had they ever done the act anywhere else. Sometimes she was naked, but it was always under the covers with very little light.

"Off." His voice was unsympathetic in his demand. She looked up to see him looming over her, his brow furrowed with an almost painful need.

Biting her bottom lip for something to ground her in the moment, she slowly tugged up the nightdress. She didn't even feel the cool air or the heat from the fire. Every part of her was focused on him and the heat coming from within her in throbbing waves of desire. After tugging it off over her head, she dropped it beside her and settled back to lie on his coat. The silk lining felt decadent against her naked skin, and his scent rose up around her.

His gaze roamed over her in unabashed appreciation. "You're so damned beautiful."

She flushed in happiness. "Let me see you." She didn't know who this woman was making such demands, but she spoke with confidence and desire thickening her voice.

He grinned and let go of the fall of his trousers. His erection stood strong and thick, rising up to his navel with a gentle curve. It was an impressive sight, and larger than she had realized. The ache between her thighs became nearly unbearable, and she shifted to relieve it somehow. But she didn't need to relieve it. He would do that. All those nights she had lain in bed imagining him, touching herself and wanting it to be him, and now he was here.

She raised her arms and he came to her, moving over her as he whispered her name. She spread her thighs and he settled between them, taking her mouth in a desperate kiss. He found her almost immediately, the head of his manhood hot and thick as it slipped inside, testing her, stretching her. She whimpered in disappointment when he withdrew, but he was back before she could complain, easing his way in. Finally, confident in her ability to take all of him, he filled her in one deep thrust that had them both groaning at the pleasure.

It was a tight fit, but the most perfect thing she had ever felt in her life. When he moved to withdraw only to fill her up again, she became aware of the scratch of his trousers against the tender inside of her thigh, and the thickness of his shirtsleeves keeping her from him. But somehow the separation only made her want him that much more. There was something profoundly erotic about him being clothed while she was nude and lying beneath him as he used her for his pleasure.

"Max," she gasped as he thrust into her hard, moving her a short distance across the rug.

"Too much?" he whispered.

"Not enough."

He let out a huff of mirth as he settled over her in a rhythm that was satisfyingly deep and hard. His breath came out in a rush with each thrust. She loved how he sounded, haggard and coarse, his breath more uneven as he drew closer to his own climax. She held him against her as if afraid to let him go, one hand tangled in his hair while the other gripped his buttock. Each time he filled her, stretching her, her passage grasped at him as pleasure tightened in her belly, winding higher and higher with each thrust. All too soon, the pressure inside her built to a crescendo, exploding through her in waves.

He groaned as he felt her come apart, and his hips moved in short, jerking movements. "Helena," he whispered. Finally, his release was torn from him in soft, guttural sounds that escaped his throat as he fell over her. His hips still moving in reflex until he settled on top of her. She tightened her arms and legs around him, loving the weight of him and already realizing that she didn't want to give him up.

He shifted after a few moments, but her body still existed in the ethereal afterglow of lovemaking, pleasure still pulsing through her in languid and uneven waves that kept her immobile for fear of stopping them. Propping himself up on an elbow, he grinned down at her like the arrogant man she knew him to be. She couldn't bring herself to mind right now, not after he had earned his gloating.

But his voice wasn't full of conceit when he spoke. It was there in a much smaller amount, edged out by wonder and the sheer bliss she was experiencing. "You called me Max."

She giggled at the observation, staring up at him in the waning firelight. Someone should put another log on if they planned to stay here for much longer. "Did I? I'm certain I did no such thing."

He laughed and leaned down to press a kiss on her shoulder. The act was so filled with unexpected affection that her heart ached. "You did, and I prefer to be called that from now on."

"Never. What would everyone think?" She let out a squeal that she managed to cut short when he nipped at the underside of her breast.

"That we're lovers," he growled playfully, and sucked

her nipple. She took his head between her hands, but he stopped and looked up at her. "The truth."

He took her nipple again, and pleasure throbbed through her, rekindling the ache where he had so recently been. She closed her eyes as it beat through her, only to open them again when the door shook.

"Milady?" It rattled again as Mrs. Huxley tried to turn the latch, which was quickly followed by a knock.

Maxwell flew to his feet, adjusting his trousers. She couldn't help the pang of disappointment she felt. "Mrs. Huxley?" she called out to buy some time as she cast about for her nightclothes, suddenly lost in her own drawing room.

He grabbed her nightdress and helped tug it over her head. As she pulled it into place, he came up behind her and helped her into the dressing gown. Still having no idea how she would explain the locked door to the woman—the door had never been locked as long as she could remember—Helena hurried across the room.

"Hello." As greetings went, it left a little to be desired. Helena peeked out, hardly daring to open the door any wider lest she reveal that Maxwell was with her.

Mrs. Huxley stood there perplexed, her mouth opening and closing twice before she said, "Are you quite well, milady?"

She must look a fright. Belatedly remembering that Maxwell's hands had been in her hair, she attempted to smooth it down. "I think I must have fallen asleep." Her sheepish smile didn't have to be forced.

The older woman gave a hesitant nod. "What happened to the door? It was stuck."

"Oh, was it?" Helena made an exaggerated face as she visually examined the latching mechanism. "Seems to be working now. There was a draft, so I closed the door to keep the warm air inside. I cannot imagine how it got itself stuck." The lies came to her so easily, she almost felt ashamed.

Seemingly convinced, Mrs. Huxley visibly relaxed and nodded. "Why don't you take yourself to bed now? It's late and you've had a difficult evening."

If only the woman knew the half of it! "Yes, that's a good thought. I think I'll do that."

"Good. I'll tend the fire for you."

When Mrs. Huxley moved to enter, Helena felt real fear overtake her for the first time. If Maxwell were found, they wouldn't understand. The Huxleys were traditional sorts, and they had worshipped Arthur. She glanced over her shoulder to see an empty room. Maxwell was gone.

She was frozen in shock as Mrs. Huxley moved past her and began setting the room to rights. She raised an eyebrow at the writing chair being out of place but moved it back and went to put out the fire. Helena hurried forward, certain that something of what they had done would be visible, but the woman carried on, completely unaware that just moments before, her mistress had been entangled with her lover in the very spot she occupied.

Helena herself was amazed to see no evidence. Maxwell was gone, almost as if he'd never been there. She might question his presence if her body didn't still bear signs of his possession. Patches of skin still smarted from the scrape of his beard, she could still feel his teeth marks on her shoulder, and her body ached pleasantly where he'd been inside her. It was almost unthinkable that he could have gone so easily.

She rushed to the door leading out to the garden, but she couldn't see him if he was still out there. Discreetly turning the lock, she pressed her hands to the cold glass, hoping for some sign that he was waiting for Mrs. Huxley to leave. There wasn't one.

Chapter 16

There is nothing like a dream to create the future.

Victor Hugo

Max checked his watch again. Half after twelve and she wasn't here yet. He was starting to worry that she wouldn't show. The note he'd sent over that morning via messenger—*Come alone. Leave at noon. Penhurst Priory. P.S. Best to bring Ostler*—had been reminiscent of the first note she had sent him, the one that had led him to her drawing room and their first meeting. He'd thought she'd appreciate the inherent humor, but now he realized that she might have wanted something softer and more romantic after last night.

He was not very good with romance. In fairness, he'd not ever had to be. He had never seriously courted a woman before, so all of his affairs had been just that, temporary and casual. There had been flirtations with daughters of family friends, but he'd quickly learned to discern which women were intent on serious pursuits and which were frivolous. He'd opted to only pursue the lighthearted ones, because even at a young age he'd understood that his position as heir to the Crenshaw fortune brought out the worst in many. He had vowed early on to only marry a woman whom he could respect, who wanted more from him than his various bank accounts.

Helena was happy with her life as a widow and didn't want to marry him at all, so she should have fit nicely in the temporary and casual category, but nothing about them felt nonchalant. No matter how he tried, he could not relegate their sex to mere play. It had felt deeper and more profound than anything ever had. His only regret was that her maid had interrupted them, so he'd had to leave rather than face the risk of her getting caught with him. It meant that today he was uncertain and lost, feelings he despised more than any others. He ordered his life around certainties, but without knowing how she felt about them—about *him*—he was out of his element.

"Sir? Mr. Crenshaw?"

Max only realized he'd been staring at his watch when his assistant's voice cut through his thoughts. "Tom?"

The man gaped at him with a perplexed expression before nodding toward the road. Max's heart stopped before he even saw Helena alighting from her carriage with the assistance of her hired man, Ostler. Unable to contain his happy grin, he hurried over the soggy ground to greet her. Thankfully, the rain had stopped soon after he returned home.

"Helena." He raised his hand in greeting, quietly pleased with how she glanced up at him, flushed a bit, and then spent an inordinate amount of time staring down at the path she trod as she crossed the cobblestones to meet him. "You came."

Raising her chin as she stopped before him, she said, "With a note such as yours, how could I not?" Her eyes sparkled with humor, so he was assured she wasn't angry with him, but he couldn't tell beyond that how she felt about last night. She was too good at hiding behind the polite mask she had perfected years ago. One might think her cold, but only if one were too stupid to see the fire shining in her eyes.

"My thoughts exactly." He took in a breath, nearly struck dumb by how beautiful she looked today. She wore black from head to toe, no doubt because of the inevitable mud and mess left by the rain, but it made the pink in her cheeks stand out more against the paleness of her face. There was a radiance about her that he knew he had put there. Pride and satisfaction at how he had made her come apart last night roared inside him. Realizing he was staring, he cleared his throat and said, "Last night—"

"Why have you brought me here?" she asked before he could finish, her voice mild.

Disappointment tightened his chest, but he understood this wasn't the time or place. Dozens of carpenters and masons moved around them, and then there were Tom and Ostler, who hovered a few yards away on either side of them. Their seconds at this strange duel to see who could be the most proper. "I assume Sir Phineas came to see you this morning before leaving town?"

She nodded. "He stopped by briefly, yes, and left the name of the man handling the donation of the property."

"Good. I've asked you here because I want to discuss the improvements on the priory, or foundry rather." He walked in that direction, and she fell into step beside him.

"You've given more thought to my request about employing the women?" There was the edge of a challenge in her voice.

"I agree to your terms, but I'll leave it up to you and August to work out the details." He had gone to visit August early this morning to let her know what had been decided with the priory. Of course, she had demanded to come with him. With time being so short, they had to get working on the improvements right away. He glanced across the courtyard to where his sister was currently en-

gaged in an exchange with a mason and crew hired to repair the stone wall. She didn't like whatever the man was
telling her, if the way she was scowling at him was any
indication.

Helena followed his gaze as they walked toward the
priory. "The unfortunate fellow doesn't seem to know who
he's dealing with, does he?" Wry amusement filled her
voice.

He laughed but all the while wondered why this felt so
strange. It was as if they were playacting at being amused
and content with each other. Part of it was the facade she
used socially—the same one it was so gratifying to see
come tumbling down last night—but part of it was his own
uncertainty with how to proceed after what had happened.
It seemed impossible that the world could continue on as
before, and yet, here they were.

She let out an undignified gasp as they turned the far
corner outside the priory. Nearly the entire wall had been
torn down by an army of men who had been working since
sunup. With the wall gone there was a gaping hole in the
end of the building.

"What have you done?" she asked.

"August and I have decided that we need to expand ca-
pacity, which means we'll have to expand the building for
the new machinery. Don't worry," he added when she continued to stand there and gape. "The wall will be rebuilt in
a few weeks."

Her eyes were wide as she slowly looked from the wall,
as if only realizing the scope of the work being carried out
around them. Much of the wall surrounding the courtyard
had already been torn down, and the sounds of at least
twenty hammers banging rang throughout the area.

"How have you accomplished so much already? Did you
not sleep?"

Pride made his chest swell the slightest bit at the awe
and respect in her tone. "I couldn't sleep much last night."

He glanced at her, noticing the pleasing flush that colored her face. "So I was up before the sun paying exorbitant sums to gather as many men as possible to begin the work."

She finally met his eyes again. "I can see I have much to learn about running an efficient operation."

"Unless you have your own crew ready, it might be easier and faster to have these men handle the renovations of your residence hall. My foreman, Mr. Wilson, can walk you through and you can discuss your needs." He raised his arm and gestured for the man to come over.

"That would be lovely, thank you."

Max tried not to think of the polite distance between them as he made the introductions. He tried not to think of how she sounded when she came, or how damned good she had felt when he'd been inside her. But he couldn't help watching her as she walked toward the residence hall with Mr. Wilson in tow, her eyes already alight with the ideas she had for the space.

"Mr. Crenshaw?" Tom stood nearby, holding up a roll of parchment. "The plans for the factory have been delivered."

"Right." Max needed to get back to work. That required his focus now, because everything had to be in working order before he left so that Papa couldn't step in and take it all away from August.

Helena found him about an hour later, a happy and hopeful smile on her face. Ostler hung back a way, and Mr. Wilson appeared to be occupied talking with a group of his men. "Thank you for arranging this, Maxwell. It's all so much more than I expected."

"Do you think you'll be able to have the rooms ready soon?"

"The residence is in better condition than the foundry and won't need extensive renovation. Mr. Wilson seems to think we can begin bringing in the women and children in a month, or two at most."

"Good." They both stood there for a moment as words

failed them. Every time he looked at her he saw her gasping her pleasure beneath him. Was it the same for her? "I can't tell you how pleased I am that everything has worked out this way."

"Thank you." She colored prettily. "I should go. I came straight here after Sir Phineas's visit, so I haven't had a chance to send a note to the board members to let them know of our good fortune."

"I'll walk you to your carriage."

She nodded and they walked side by side in silence. There were several feet between them, but she might have been pressed against him for how aware of her he was. He waved her driver off and opened the door for her himself because he had to know what she was feeling and thinking. If she hated him for leaving.

When she moved to climb in, he whispered, "Helena. About last night, I left because I didn't want your maid to find us, but if I did something . . . if I hurt you—"

"No." She appeared to be reaching for the door, but she touched his hand instead where it rested on the inside strap. Concern was etched on her features as she moved her hand to his chest. It was the lightest of touches, but it felt as if she held magic in her fingertips. Heat moved from the small points of contact to swirl through him. "You haven't done anything wrong. Last night was astonishing."

Her eyes were filled with wonderment, and a tender smile curved her lips. They confused him even more. "Then why—?"

She swallowed thickly, the hint of a sheen coating her eyes. "I think we should leave it to the one night, however."

Despite his resolve to remain impassive, he covered her hand with his, flattening her palm against his chest. She took in a shuddering breath in response. "Helena, I know that isn't what you want." It couldn't be. Not after what had passed between them last night. It had felt deeper and more profound than any sexual experience of his life. There had been a connection between them that he knew he hadn't imagined.

"Perhaps not, but it's what I need. What would be the point of continuing anyway? We both know it has to end sometime."

It wasn't until sheer disappointment crested through him that he understood a part of him had thought that maybe this *would* lead to the next step, to something more. That she was perfect for him and this could open the door for them to explore that. It would mean she would eventually come to New York with him, but that didn't seem like an unscalable barrier. Or so he had begun to think at some point between last night and now.

"Does it have to?" He drew her hand to his lips, gratified that she didn't try to pull away. Instead, she watched him, her lips parted as he pressed a kiss to her fingers, the supple leather of her gloves cool to the touch.

"Don't be ridiculous," she said, infusing her voice with that cool distance he was growing to dread. "I refuse to move to New York. You won't stay in London. We should take last night as the gift it was."

The more she spoke the more he realized he disliked everything she had to say. "It was more than a pleasant way to pass an hour, if that's what you're trying to say. There is something here, and it's worth exploring."

She swallowed again, her eyes going wide in a sort of naivete. "I think perhaps it meant more to you—"

"For Christ's sake, Helena, you're a terrible actress." He closed his eyes and released her hand. He couldn't force things with her if she didn't want them. Of course he couldn't. Could he? Visions of pleasuring her until she admitted how she felt about them swam through his head. "The least you can do is give me honesty." When he opened his eyes, relief poured over him to see the cool veneer gone from her face.

"Fine," she said, her eyes wide in genuine bemusement

now. "Until last night I never completely understood what I was missing. Now that I do, I'm afraid that I won't be able to go back to how I was before."

She paused, but he didn't utter a sound, stunned by her admission and afraid that the slightest murmur would make her disinclined to continue.

Eventually, she said, "I was lonely. I know how to be lonely. I don't know how to get closer to you and then go back to that lonely place when you're gone."

"Then come with me."

"What? You're asking me to come to New York with you after an hour together alone in my drawing room?"

He smiled. The offer *had* come out without any conscious thought on his part. "Of course not, not yet, that would be ridiculous." And it would likely scare her off. But he could imagine just that scenario. She could come home with him after Christmas. They would rarely leave their stateroom on the crossing, and everyone would know what they were doing, but it wouldn't matter. Then he'd take her to his home in Gramercy Park, and they would make a life together. "I'm asking you to indulge what we've found. *For now.* We can figure out the rest later."

She was shaking her head before he'd even finished. "No, it's best to leave things as they are."

"You're serious?"

She nodded.

"The best night of sex either of us has ever had, and you're willing to resign it to one night?"

She blushed and looked past his shoulder, presumably to check if Ostler had heard the outburst. "It's for the best, yes."

"I disagree with this." He was forced to step back as she turned to ascend into the carriage.

"I know," she called back.

"You still want me."

"I know." This time she grinned down at him from the safety of the carriage.

It was all he could do not to climb in there with her and remind her how good they were together. He might not have won the fight if Ostler hadn't opened the door on the other side and climbed in, his considerable bulk straining the springs of the carriage.

"I can make you change your mind," he said.

She grinned again, but she didn't refute him.

Chapter 17

A loving heart was better and stronger than wisdom.

CHARLES DICKENS

FIVE DAYS LATER
THE CRENSHAW TOWNHOME, GROSVENOR SQUARE

The series of telegrams Max had received earlier in the week from his manager in New York had only marginally prepared him for the contents of the letter before him. The packet had been delivered moments ago by special messenger. Max had torn into it at the bottom of the stairs before returning to his father's study upstairs. The packet included a detailed letter from David Merchant, the man overseeing operations at Crenshaw Iron in Max's absence, and a copy of the list of demands from their factory employees that had arrived in the Manhattan office last week.

Discontent had been brewing—with depressed wages and rising costs, how could it not?—but this meant things were coming to a head much sooner than expected. The board had anticipated no movement in the direction of organizing until at least the summer. This list of demands, which included a fifty percent increase in wages, would be impossible to meet.

Fucking hell.

He slowly dropped into his chair, rereading every line. David was competent and seemed confident in his ability to hold the men at bay until the new year. The last board meeting had ended with a resolution to award a special compensation for the Christmas season. Max would send a telegram in the morning authorizing the disbursement. It would soothe things for a bit, but he'd have to return home earlier than he'd planned. If things didn't go well, he needed to be in New York to handle them.

"What do you have there?"

Max clenched the papers in his hands, wrinkling them as he looked up to see his father coming into the room. He was dressed in his customary suit of clothes, as if he were ready to meet acquaintances. "That is hardly any of your concern. What are you doing out of bed?"

"The doctor has finished his examination. I thought I would take some refreshment before returning to bed. I heard some rumbling from a servant about a messenger and came to see for myself."

Max cursed inwardly. The damned servants here were too loyal to his father for the man's own good. They had been sneaking in visitors and sending telegrams on Papa's behalf the entire time he was supposed to be not working. It was likely because August had insisted on compensating them with higher wages due to the fact that their appointments here were temporary. Since she had moved out, they all but worshipped him to keep his good favor. It also helped that the Crenshaws were now connected to a duke and an earl.

"What has the doctor concluded?" Max asked, ignoring the comment about the messenger. Max had worked from Papa's study all afternoon to be on hand when his doctor came by for his examination.

"Is that Crenshaw Iron business?" Papa asked, leaning forward to study the papers.

"Nothing to concern yourself with." Max tried to shove them into a drawer, but the bottom sheet fell free, catching a drift of air to land near his father on the desk.

The older man swooped it up before Max could grab it. The lines in his face deepened as he scanned the words from the first page of David's letter. "They're threatening to form a labor union?"

So much for keeping his father's intellectual strain to a minimum as the doctor had advised. "Only if these demands aren't met." He held the sheet with the list tighter, unwilling to add to his father's distress.

"What are their demands?"

"Will you not do as your well-respected doctor has advised and allow me and August to deal with Crenshaw Iron for now?"

"Give me their demands." Papa held out his hand.

Max sighed and handed over the entire contents of the packet. There was no point in dragging this out any more than necessary. Now that the man knew something was amiss, he'd not rest until he found out, even if it meant telegramming New York.

Adjusting his reading glasses, Papa sat back in his chair to better examine the documents. He grunted in disapproval a few times, his brow furrowing in concern. Finally, he said, "This is preposterous."

"The requests are a bit steep. The amount they want in wage increases alone is enough to bankrupt the factory, but—"

"There is no *but*. This list is extortion. Railroad growth isn't what it was. We're in the midst of what they are calling the Great Depression. If we gave in to these demands, we'd *all* be bankrupt and living in the street. Don't they understand that?"

"No, I don't think they do," Max said, keeping his voice calm. "The depression has made everyone desperate. We've cut wages by a total of twenty percent since the Panic of

'73, meanwhile food and housing have continued to rise," Max said.

"This is asking for twenty percent above what they were earning *before* the Panic. Do they not understand that if we are earning less, then they, too, have to earn less? I cannot control the price of housing or bread."

Max took in a breath, having had variations of this conversation with his father for years before the Panic set in. "We *can* control the cost of housing to an extent. It's why we have begun to acquire apartment houses in the city and row houses in smaller towns." Even though his father had voted against that move, Max had convinced the board to try it in Pittsburgh and Middletown to much success. "Our resources are considerable when pooled together, allowing us to provide this for them at a lower cost."

"You sound as if you're taking their side."

"There are no sides, Papa. There is only the best way forward. God knows we can't afford to increase wages by fifty percent. But it's not unreasonable for them to expect a living wage when they are being asked to work just as hard as before. If they are assured of having homes and food, then we will all be able to weather this storm."

Papa shrugged. "There are no assurances in life. Banks have collapsed, and the price of steel increases. We can't pay them what we don't have, not if we intend to keep our profit margins stable. They can't expect us to provide comfort"—he glanced down and read from the list—"food, medical care, death benefits. Our responsibility to them ends with their wages."

"If that's the case, then we've done a poor job keeping up our end of the responsibility."

"We live in a market society." Papa shrugged again and leaned forward to place the papers on the desk. "The costs of goods inflate and deflate to reflect that; the same goes for wages. It's absurd that they expect them to stay constant in a world where everything changes."

"Then why must we insist that profit margins stabilize? We could afford to cut into them briefly until the economy recovers."

"And what if it doesn't? What if we slowly eat away at ourselves until there's nothing left. How will it help the workers if we have no factories, no enterprise left? It's cannibalization, and it won't help anyone in the long run, not the workers and certainly not us."

"I said *briefly*. Besides, this is why August and I have been pushing so hard for auxiliary investments. They would allow us to diversify our assets, so we can help avoid these scenarios. The markets have an inevitable ebb and flow; diversifying can help keep our income stable. It's why the dock is such an important opportunity. We cannot solely rely on railroads."

Papa shrugged. "I have relented to the dock, have I not?"

Max couldn't stop the glower that came over his face. "Ostensibly, as long as I do what you want."

The man smiled a sly grin that Max found more irritating with age. "Have you not found favor with our good Helena?"

"It would appear so." He was reluctant to discuss her with his father. His feelings for her and their arrangement were so complex that he didn't yet understand them himself. There was no way he could adequately talk about them with Papa.

"When do you plan to ask her to marry you?"

Max felt seedy and irrationally angry to be forced into the ruse he had concocted. His parents should have no part of what went on between him and Helena, but his father's demand had made it so. Also, Max didn't like the reminder that he, too, was capable of intrigue and subterfuge to further his own agenda. "The house party."

"She'd be a fool to turn you down."

"She won't." He could guarantee it, but he didn't say that, because he actually didn't know where they stood anymore.

Five days had passed since Max had last talked to Helena. Every day he sent her a small token of his regard. One day it was a bouquet of lilies procured from a hothouse on the outskirts of London. On another day, a book from Hatchards. Today it had been one of the new stylographic pens that Violet raved about. They were all gifts ostensibly expected by Society and meant to reinforce their courtship, but to Max they had become small demonstrations of his growing affection. If only she would accept them as such.

Each one had received a short and prompt thank-you written on embossed cardstock in reply.

Not wanting to linger on the subject of his upcoming betrothal, Max said, "Unfortunately, it appears I won't be able to stay through Christmas. I have to get back home to New York, which means I need to settle things here so that I can leave in a week or so." Thank God everything had been arranged with Sir Phineas.

"What about Farthington's house party and Lady Helena?" Papa's eyes narrowed.

"Naturally, I'll still go. I'll bring my trunks so that I can leave from there a few days early."

Papa nodded in agreement. "Yes, unfortunately, I agree that's best. This rebellion needs to be squashed, with force if necessary."

"I'll handle it as I see fit."

"You have the police involved if needed. We cannot allow a strike. I'll telegram Tilden and have him authorize the National Guard—"

"I will deal with it, Papa." Max rose to his feet, his voice rising slightly along with him. "Not you. You are to heal and concentrate your efforts here. You left me in charge for a reason. Do not telegram Tilden."

"I left you in charge because I trusted you to deal with things."

"Then you must let me."

"Then you'll force down this so-called strike, this attempt to organize against you in the very factory your own grandfather built from nothing?"

"It's not a strike yet. I will do everything in my power to make certain it's not elevated to such a crisis, but if it comes to it, I will defend our interests."

Papa nodded and rose, much steadier on his feet after weeks of recovery than he had been when Max first arrived in London. "Good, make certain that you do. I'll see you downstairs for dinner."

Max let out a breath the moment his father left. It had become more apparent with every passing year how differently they each saw the direction of Crenshaw Iron. His father was a dictator who wanted to smite out any hint of insurrection at its first appearance. Max didn't believe that an organization could survive for very long in the shadow of one man. An organization by its very definition became a sum of its parts with no one person able to claim sole responsibility for its success or failure.

Walking to the small bureau near the window, he poured himself a scotch and looked out at the gaslights lining the street as he took several calming breaths. Twilight was descending. He took a sip, savoring the smoky bite of the liquid as he swallowed. As often happened in his quiet moments, thoughts of Helena intruded. He could still feel the press of her soft body against him, and the sense of peace that came over him when he had her in his arms. If she were here now with a proper place in his life, she would spar with him over how to proceed with the threat facing Crenshaw Iron. She'd challenge him with the different way she considered things.

It was maddening that she was only a few streets over. The house party was in three days, which meant they had barely a week together.

Why was she so resolved to deny what was between them?

He walked over to the desk and picked up one of her cards from the stack on the corner. They were cream colored and preprinted with her name on one side in an elegant typeface. On the other side she had perfunctorily written *Thank you* and signed her name. He should consider himself lucky that she hadn't sent the gifts back, but she was as committed to this ruse as he was, so perhaps that was why she kept them. It stung that she could so readily cast aside what they had found together.

The one thing he was understanding with more certainty every day was that he didn't simply want another night or two with her. He wanted her and everything that came with her. He'd realized before that she was perfect for him, but after that night with her . . . There seemed to be no good reason why they shouldn't make this courtship real. She could come to New York as his wife. There were people there who could use her help. She had admitted herself that she was lonely here. Her life was full, but it obviously wasn't fulfilling. Not if she was lonesome. If they were together, then she would never be alone again. She'd spend her nights in his bed and her days any way she wished.

His wife. Once an idea that had seemed very far removed from where he was, now it felt right. He wanted Helena to be his wife.

M ax was on his way to Helena's townhome almost before he realized he meant to go. It wasn't the dinner hour yet, but it was outside regular calling hours. His visit wouldn't be completely outside the realm of acceptable etiquette, not that he gave a damn about that except for how it would impact her reputation. But it was too early still to sneak in through her drawing room door, and he had to see her.

Huxley appeared startled when he opened the door to find Max standing there. "Mr. Crenshaw?"

"Is Lady Helena at home?" When there was a pause, Max added, "I understand this is highly irregular."

"Apologies, sir, your attendance wasn't expected."

It was a strange statement, but he stepped back and allowed Max to enter. As soon as he was within the house, he could hear Helena's voice along with several others coming from the room that faced the street. The door was closed, so he couldn't make out what she was saying. Max had only ever seen the drawing room at the back of the house and had no idea what the front room was. He did, however, have the distinct feeling that he was interrupting. That perhaps he shouldn't have been so quick to barge into her home.

"Huxley, I—" It was too late. The man was already swinging the door open.

The room was larger than her intimate drawing room and more formal. While decorated in the same apple greens, creams, and golds as the rest of her home, the gold won out here as the principal color. This was primarily accomplished with the gilded carving in the paneling on the walls and which encircled the edges of the ceiling. The massive mantelpiece was white but gilded with a whimsical display of gold leaves along the top, mirroring the flowers and leaves inscribed along the panels on the wall. Despite the abundance of gold, it was tastefully done so as not to be overpowering, with the delicate pieces of rosewood furniture upholstered in pale greens and creams placed strategically throughout the room. There were two groupings of settees and chairs with a round table covered in a tablecloth and set with a decadent spread of cakes, sandwiches, and pastries. Every available seat in the room was occupied by a woman, including both of his sisters. Every seat except for the one Helena had likely vacated.

Helena stood at the head of the room near the fireplace. She looked as surprised as he felt. She wore a two-piece walking dress in the new elongated-waist style that exhibited her shapely hips so well. It was a deep, rich blue that somehow perfectly matched her eyes and set off the pale beauty of her hair. She was so gorgeous that he lost his breath.

"Mr. Crenshaw! What a pleasant surprise. Helena, you didn't tell us he was expected." This was said by Lady Blaylock, a woman he vaguely remembered to be a lifelong friend of Helena's mother, the one who had pulled her funding for Helena's charity. She sat on one of the settees with another woman he didn't recognize.

For a long and increasingly awkward moment, neither he nor Helena spoke. He hadn't been expected, and it would be the height of impropriety to come visit after calling hours with so many guests aware of it.

"I wasn't certain that I could come," he finally hedged, having no idea what he walked into.

Regaining her composure, Helena gave him a strained smile as she walked over to greet him. "I am happy you're here." Despite the barely thwarted faux pas, there did seem to be a genuine glimmer of happiness in her eyes. "Sir Phineas was kind enough to invite some of his friends here to listen to me speak about the home we're building."

Max whipped his head in the direction she indicated. There Sir Phineas sat at the table laden with treats, cup of tea in hand and a broad smile on his face. Max had somehow missed him the first time. He seemed pleased to see Max, setting his tea down and standing to greet him. "You're just in time," the man said, retaking his seat. "Helena was about to go over her plans for the London Home."

"Everyone, I would like to present Mr. Maxwell Crenshaw, a very dear friend," she said to the room at large.

He greeted everyone, aware of a murmuring that was sweeping through the space.

"You could take my seat," she said, indicating the vacant chair next to Sir Phineas.

Of course she had been sitting next to Sir Phineas. A hollow pang of jealousy churned deep within him, but he managed to ignore it as he sat down. A young maid appeared from nowhere and set a cup and saucer on the table before him. She wasn't the typical footman he had come to expect at such gatherings, and he couldn't help but smile at his sister's influence. Violet had famously staffed her own

London home with maids hired from Helena's charity, much to the scandal of all the old-fashioned types who believed that only men should serve guests in drawing rooms and dinner tables. Or perhaps it was Helena who had influenced his sister. Max had only ever seen the Huxleys when he'd come over, which made him realize that he didn't know as much about Helena as he wanted.

Over the course of the next hour, Helena spoke about her ideas for the London Home for Young Women. Guests would interrupt to ask questions or for clarification, and the discussion would veer into a tangent until Helena skillfully brought it back on track. Sir Phineas asked the occasional question, but mostly he watched her with clear admiration and nodded along. Near the end, all the nodding made Max suspicious that the man had heard this all before.

When she took off the covering that had been draped over an as yet unnoticed stand to reveal a black-on-white drawing of the finished London Home for Young Women, Max knew that his suspicion had been correct. Unprompted, Sir Phineas stood and walked up to help her display a second page, which was an interior drawing. A hum of approval resounded in the room as Helena's vision was brought to temporary, corporeal life on those papers.

After the man sat back down a few moments later, Max whispered, "Have you heard all of this before?"

Sir Phineas leaned over. "I proposed this idea over correspondence, and we arranged this meeting two days ago when I returned to London to prepare. I have an adequate hand, so I came up with a few drawings based on Lady Helena's discussions with Mr. Wilson." His gaze, full of admiration, was almost immediately lured back to Helena. "She's marvelous, isn't she?"

August heard the comment from where she sat in the next group and glanced over at Max with a brow raised, as if to note that he had competition.

Max ground his molars but managed to nod in agreement. Sir Phineas could claim he was *only* helping her all he wanted, but there was no denying the expression on his face when he looked at her. If she were Max's actual fiancée, he would have set the man straight. As it stood now he was left seething in his unreasonable jealousy, perfectly aware that it was an unwanted emotion, but unable to stop it.

When Helena's portion of the talk was finished, she traded places with Sir Phineas, who stood before them all and gave a short speech about how impressed he was with her initiative before thanking them for coming. He seemed to have kind words and offered praise to the great works each woman present had accomplished from an advice columnist to a woman who sat on the board of a museum. The women, all middle-aged aside from Helena and his sisters, affluent, and simpering in their enthusiasm for the man, applauded politely and thanked him for arranging the meeting.

Inside, Max felt himself splitting in two. He was happy about the opportunity the man was presenting Helena but seething in envy that he had not been able to present the same advantage for her. The whole point of their masquerade was so that he, as her approving betrothed, could attract this sort of approval from potential donors, and now it turned out she didn't need him at all. What was he supposed to do with that? She had already told him in no uncertain terms that one night with her was all he would have, and now she didn't even need this.

He rose and paid his respects to each woman as befitted his place as her suitor and assumed fiancé. Yes, he was proud of the work Lady Helena was doing. Yes, she was tireless in her efforts. No, he had not assisted her in preparing for her presentation. Yes, she was wonderful.

After an endless round of goodbyes, the door finally closed on Sir Phineas and his sisters, the last of the guests to leave. Despite the jealousy roiling inside him, Max could only smile at her as she returned to him in the room. "You did well, Helena."

She was practically glowing, her face flushed with joy and excitement, as she came up and grabbed his hands. "We did, didn't we? I already have two meetings arranged for after the house party."

There was no mistaking that the *we* referred to her and Sir Phineas. "Wonderful news. I bet you'll hear from more of them in the coming days."

Mrs. Huxley and the maid hurried into the room to clean it but paused when they noticed him. Still in a daze of pleasure from her triumph, Helena kept hold of his hand as she led him from the room and into her drawing room. One of the bouquets of lilies he had sent her was set on the mantel. His eyes were drawn to the rug before the hearth where he had been inside her not even a week ago. His cock stirred in fond tribute to the act that he very much wanted to repeat. She didn't seem to notice the direction of his thoughts as she guided him to the settee. The moment she sat she released his hand. It automatically curled into a fist as if to hold on to her heat.

When she finished recounting some of the words of encouragement from the women, he said, "I never knew you had such a well thought-out plan."

She smiled at him but cocked her head to the side in question. Her lips parted slightly, the bottom looking as soft as he remembered. "Whyever not? You heard me tell Sir Phineas over dinner. Did you think I had spent the last year simply not planning?"

"No . . ." But his voice trailed off, because he realized he hadn't actually given it much thought. "I suppose at dinner I was too concerned with my own objectives to listen."

Her grin flattened, but she nodded. "I know. Crenshaw Iron is a burden, but you bear it well. I understand how consuming it can be."

In the face of her immense compassion, he understood very clearly what he had failed to even consider before. He was willing to make her his wife based on superficial standards that she herself had rejected. She fit his life so well that he had never actually considered how well he might or might not fit hers. He had seen taking her to New York with him as a minor inconvenience for her that she could easily overcome, never fully understanding how she would not want to be uprooted by someone who might only have a vague, passing interest in her life.

Now he knew why she hadn't invited him to this. She had likely and reasonably assumed that he'd either be uninterested or too busy to come. He was left with one damning conclusion: he had been a terrible fiancé.

"Helena, I greatly admire the work you've done with the orphanage and the women and children you've taken under your wing. I don't know that I've adequately expressed that to you."

She smiled. "Thank you." But she couldn't hold his gaze because she looked down at where their hands rested, close together but not touching.

"I want to know more about what you do."

Her smile fled completely as her brows came together. "Why?"

"Because I've just realized that there is very much I do not understand. Have dinner with me tomorrow? You can tell me more."

She stared at him, her gaze scanning his face as a tender sort of realization began to dawn. Her eyes, so filled with joy earlier, were now filled with wariness. "There's no need for you to understand more."

Bridging the inches between them, he covered her hand with his. "The work you're doing is commendable and important. I can offer my experience, if you think it will help. Crenshaw Iron has built several apartment homes that I've overseen."

A hesitant smile returned, and she squeezed his hand. "I appreciate your offer, but I don't think it's a good idea."

"What isn't?" he asked.

"Us spending more time together than necessary. It will only lead to heartache."

Aware that pushing her on this issue would only result in her holding him further away, he said, "If we only have tonight, then why don't you show me the drawings Sir Phineas did for you? I didn't get a very good look at them."

"You came over here unannounced to ask to see Sir Phineas's drawings?" She raised a skeptical brow, and her lips curved in a teasing smile.

"I came because . . . I received some harsh news from New York."

"Oh no—"

"Business," he quickly clarified. "The workers are making demands. Nothing you should worry about, but I . . ." He didn't know how to say that he wanted the comfort she brought him, so he simply said, "I needed to see you. My father and I disagree on so much these days with the business and family, I think I . . . needed to be with someone who would understand me."

"He believes you shouldn't give in?"

He nodded. "I think we must negotiate."

"Max . . ." She reached up and stroked a lock of hair off his forehead. The barest hint of her fingertips touched his skin, so he closed his eyes to savor it. "I'm sorry you have to bear so much alone."

"It's not terrible, usually." Her eyes were so full of understanding that he wanted to pull her onto his lap and lose himself in kissing her. Touching her made everything else fall away. Made it bearable.

"How are you . . . ?"

When her voice trailed off, he prompted, "How am I what?"

She looked down as if suddenly too shy to meet his gaze. "It's none of my concern, and you don't have to answer, but I . . . I cannot help wondering how you are so different from your parents."

He let out a long breath. "I wish I knew. Believe me when I say I've asked myself the same thing many times."

She traced his features with her gaze, studying him in a way that he found immensely appealing. "You care for the people who work for you. I don't think one could say the same for your father."

The truth of that made an ache develop in his chest. "No, I suppose not. It wasn't always that way . . . or maybe it was and I only refused to see it. My grandfather, Augustus, required that my summers and any free time during the year be spent on the factory floors, the railroad yards, and the mines we owned. From the age of twelve I worked what amounted to months every year next to the men whose fate would one day be in my hands. I learned to understand them because I slept in the shacks they were meant to call home, and I ate the provisions they were given. I suppose it gave me perspective."

"Did your grandfather not require the same of his own son?"

He shook his head. "Grandpa didn't earn his first million until my father was almost grown. From what I understand, he spent most of his time traveling for work and building his empire. He wasn't home very much to raise his children."

She nodded in understanding. "Perhaps your grandfather hoped to rectify his mistakes with you."

Max had never thought of it in that way before. He'd been so busy learning the company and analyzing all the many ways to improve it that he hadn't ever closely considered the inner workings of his family. "Come to think of it, he was the one to suggest Papa give August a chance to prove herself."

"He sounds like a very wise man. That must be where you get it from." Her eyes widened as if the ease between them had taken her by surprise and she'd said too much. He nearly groaned. If she would only give them a chance, she would have to admit that they were perfect together. Before he could figure out how to say that, she squeezed his hand and rose. "I'll go get the drawings." Then she hurried off to the other room to retrieve them.

Something inside him had shifted in the space of the single conversation. He didn't know how to describe it except that before, he'd been certain of himself. Now, everything inside him trembled a bit. Not quite whole until she returned, smiling in pride mixed with the slightest bit of vulnerability as she presented her work to him. He couldn't tell her about returning to New York early now, not when it would mar her joy. He'd tell her at Claremont Hall.

Chapter 18

❧

He said true things, but called them by wrong names.

ELIZABETH BARRETT BROWNING

THREE DAYS LATER
CLAREMONT HALL
SURREY, ENGLAND

The guest list for the small annual gathering Helena's parents held at Claremont Hall had grown considerably this year. Usually, the party consisted of Papa's younger brother and his family, Mama's widowed sister Lady Isabelle Fawly, Arthur's parents, Lady Blaylock along with whichever of her children could accompany her, and Sir Henry—a childhood friend of Papa's—and his wife. It occasionally included whichever members of Parliament Papa was hoping to influence that year. This year it had swelled to include the entirety of the Crenshaw family, the Duke and Duchess of Hereford, along with the duke's ever-present sister, Lady Isabelle Fawly, and Lord Verick, whom Papa had invited earlier as a potential suitor for her.

Everyone except for Max and his parents were here already. Helena had arrived yesterday along with August and Violet and their husbands. They had spent the afternoon collecting sprigs and holly clippings. Today most of the women were assembled in the conservatory at long tables to make wreaths and boughs to adorn the doors and mantelpieces of the estate.

Helena pulled twine through the spruce needles arranged artfully before her, tying them sprig by sprig to the circular wire frame to make a wreath. She wasn't feeling very inspired, mainly due to her lack of concentration. Every sound from outside had her jumping, her neck craning as she looked out the window hoping to see a carriage coming up the drive.

August giggled softly beside her as Helena did it yet again only to see one of the groundsmen leading a wagon from the stables. "Their train arrived a little while ago if it's on schedule. He should be here soon."

There was no need to define who she meant. "I'm not concerned."

No, she was anxious and excited, butterflies flapping in her stomach like mad to see him again. The past few days apart had only seemed to whet her appetite for the sight of him. She constantly struggled with her decision to keep him at arm's length when being with him felt so good. Part of her wanted to say damn the consequences and spend as much time alone with him as she could; part of her wanted to protect her already fragile heart at all costs.

Camille also giggled from across the table where she worked next to Violet on one end of a bough, her knowing glance drifting from August to Helena. "Has he actually proposed yet?"

Lady Sansbury, Arthur's mother, glanced up in irritation at all the laughter from a table the older women were gathered around. She had become even more severe since his death.

"No, not yet." Helena shifted, uncomfortable with openly discussing the ruse they were pulling over on Society.

"You're very lucky, you know," Camille said, keeping her voice low so that it wouldn't travel past their small group. "Every girl in Manhattan wants him for herself."

Helena wasn't surprised. He was handsome, wealthy, thoughtful, and kind, the type of husband anyone would want.

Violet made a face. "Not *every* girl."

"*Every* girl." Camille nodded with confidence. "Amelia would give her right hand to have him."

"Amelia? No." Violet's tone made it sound like a vast betrayal.

August laughed and explained to Helena, "Amelia is a friend of Violet's and Camille's. She practically grew up in our home."

"And she doesn't want to marry Max," Violet said.

"I'm afraid I agree with Camille's assessment on the matter," August intervened. "If you'd have seen her at my wedding party in New York, you'd know. She had eyes only for Max, and even asked him to dance."

Camille smiled wistfully. "She always liked him. Truthfully, I did, too. Why do you think I arranged to be over whenever he came home from Princeton on breaks?"

"Et tu, Camille?" Violet shook her head. "This is the same boy who put lizards in our shoes."

"I'm not certain if you noticed, Violet, but your brother is not a boy any longer." Appreciation for the man he had become was evident in Camille's voice.

Helena wondered if the woman really was holding on to a tender for him. How horrible it must be to imagine yourself with someone like Max, only to end up with someone cold like Hereford. Not for the first time, Helena considered that she might regret letting Max slip through her fingers, but then she reminded herself that it would be selfish to keep him when she couldn't give him what he wanted.

Violet sighed. "I suppose not. Well, if he must be married, then you are the best choice to put up with him, Helena." Violet winked at her as she went back to arranging her end of the bough.

Camille giggled. "He'll propose before he leaves. I just know it."

Helena shrugged. "I thought he might wait until Christmas."

Camille stopped her arranging and looked up at her. "But he'll be in New York for Christmas. No, he'll definitely do it properly before he leaves."

Helena's fingers faltered in tying off the twine, a sprig of needles slipping from the wreath. "He'll be in New York for Christmas?"

"Oh dear, hadn't you heard?" August asked, abandoning her own wreath. "He's been called back to New York early. There's been a threat of a strike in one of the factories. He's leaving Saturday."

They only had three days together. "He didn't tell me." He had mentioned the workers' demands, but she hadn't thought he'd leave early.

Why hadn't he told her?

"I'm sure it's because we've all been so busy," August said, patting her shoulder before returning back to her wreath.

"Yes, I'm sure it is." But Helena knew the truth. She had been successful in pushing him away. After their heartfelt talk in her drawing room several days ago, he had simply thought it wouldn't matter to her. Her heart ached even as she knew that she had made the right decision.

The crunching of gravel had her looking up to see the carriage that had been sent to retrieve Max and his parents from the train station approaching. Excitement leaped to life in her belly.

"They're here," Violet announced, and it seemed like every eye in the room turned toward Helena.

"Let's go meet them." August squeezed her hand and then untied her apron.

Helena did the same and smoothed a hand over her gown. Mama led their small group to the entrance hall where Max and his parents were already stepping inside. Her breath caught at the mere sight of him. He wore a charcoal frock coat that stretched impressively across his shoulders. Her body clenched as she remembered how it had felt to hold on to those shoulders as he'd lifted and pressed her against the wall.

He turned from greeting her father and paused when he saw her. It only lasted a moment, but she felt the perusal of his gaze from the roots of her hair all the way down to her toes. He smiled, walking across the short space to greet her. "Helena."

"Max." She didn't embrace him as she wanted—that wouldn't be appropriate for many reasons; instead, she gave a quick and abbreviated curtsy.

He reached out and gently took her hand, bringing her fingers to his mouth. Her lips were jealous as she watched.

"How was the train?" She reluctantly drew her hand back as Violet and August walked up.

"Good," but that was all he managed to say before Mrs. Crenshaw moved in, embracing both of her daughters in turn.

Helena's own mother took over, directing a small army of footmen as they descended to deal with the Crenshaws' luggage. Helena noted the two trunks—steamer trunks— directed to the bachelor's hall, and the tightening around her heart throbbed a little.

"You're in time for tea," Mama said. "Helena, please go collect our other guests and bring them to the drawing room."

Helena nodded and turned, hurrying away as if she were out to do her mother's bidding. In reality, she was trying to outrun the ache that had lodged in her throat. She couldn't understand why it hurt so much to know they had so little time left when all along she had been preparing herself for his departure.

None of this was real. So why did it *feel* real?

Because Helena's mother enjoyed entertaining so much, afternoon tea effortlessly gave way to dinner, which melded into dessert and drinks in the drawing room with hardly a difference between the three. The atmosphere for the Christmastime house party was always so relaxed and informal that it was the one event with her parents that Helena looked forward to all year. As a little girl, she'd been able to participate in this in a way that children had been forbidden from other activities, and the magic of that had not faded as she had aged.

They had reached the part of the evening where the group had traveled from the drawing room to the gaming room, a large chamber made dark by heavy mahogany paneling on the walls and burgundy carpets. It was typically a domain reserved for men, which showed in the heads of elk, deer, and boar mounted around the room. The mantelpiece boasted large ivory tusks, one of Papa's most prized possessions from his youth. A billiard table took up the center of the room, while several gaming tables were set up at each corner. Tonight, the women had been allowed inside.

Helena sat at one of these tables losing badly at whist. She couldn't concentrate because she kept watching in growing jealousy as her younger sister Penelope, Camille, and Lady Blaylock took turns flirting with Max as they played at his table. It was social, perfectly acceptable flirting, but she kept noticing how he grinned and how his strong hands easily manipulated the cards and wondering why she had ever thought they couldn't have another night together. Then she remembered that it was *because* of that attractive smile and those strong hands that she had best stay away. She didn't think she was brave enough to take having him again and letting him go. She'd likely do something stupid and end up heartbroken.

For that matter, the longer she stayed here in this room increased her chance of doing something unwise. Twice between rounds she had moved to go to him, and twice she had restrained herself. With a brandy warming her blood and reminding her how alive being with him had made her feel, she knew she had best leave now before she wasn't able to stop herself a third time. When the current round ended, she made her excuses and left for her bedroom.

The gaming room opened onto what had at one time been a great room in the original structure bestowed on their family by Henry VIII. It had been renovated multiple times throughout the centuries, so that now a row of windows looked out over the gardens on one side, leaving the space brighter during the day even though it still boasted a stone floor and wood-paneled walls. Gas lamps lit the hall at night, a medieval effect that she liked very much. She was halfway down the wide hall when the gaming room door clicked open and closed behind her. The excited swirling in her stomach told her who had followed her before she heard him say her name.

She turned as he passed below a wall sconce, the light from the flames licking over his features in flattering adoration. His deep brown eyes were as fathomless as ever, homing in on her with the weight of the immense emotion she imagined this man was capable of feeling if he ever let himself go.

"Max."

He kept walking until there was only a foot of space between them. His size nearly blocked out the light, making her press a hand against the wall to hold herself steady. "I hoped to talk with you tonight, but there never seemed to be a moment when I could get away."

She smiled. "You do seem to have your admirers."

"As do you." His smile was in his voice, as was a hint of jealousy.

"Why did you not tell me you were leaving for New York sooner than planned?" The question was out before she could think of a more tactful way to ask. It had been waiting there on her tongue for him all night.

He was silent for a moment, and though she couldn't see his face very well now, she felt his study of her. It prickled over her cheek and settled on her mouth. Would one more kiss be acceptable? Would she still be able to walk away?

"You were happy, and I didn't want to make you not happy." It was a simple answer and one that made her breath catch in her throat.

"But we have so little time now."

"Yes . . ."

She closed her eyes. He probably thought she was a feebleminded fool. She was rather starting to think that herself when it came to him.

"I brought this for you."

He reached into his coat pocket and shifted so that he no longer blocked the light. The yellow glow filtered down between them, revealing a small velvet pouch. She gasped at the beauty of the ring he pulled out of it. It was a rose-cut sapphire set in gold with smaller diamonds surrounding it.

"Beautiful," she whispered in awe.

"I wasn't sure which stone you would prefer, and then I saw this one and it matched your eyes. I knew I'd found the one."

She looked from the ring to him, certain that she would never hear a more perfect reason for selecting a piece of jewelry in her life. "You didn't need to get me one."

He shook his head, his brows coming together in a way that made her gaze revert to the ring lest she follow her own impulsive instinct and kiss him. "We already discussed this. I want you to have it. You can do whatever you like with it after."

After. After she had no modicum of a claim to him. After, when he would find a proper wife for himself who could give him the children he wanted.

"Keep it or sell it and put the proceeds to your charity. It's yours to do with what you want."

"But I'm already benefiting from our arrangement. You saw the interest at the meeting."

"Which Sir Phineas organized." There was a bitter tinge of jealousy in his voice that she quite liked.

"Yes, he arranged it, but only after he knew about us." She probably should have admitted that part earlier.

He cocked his head to the side as he studied her, prompting her to continue. "He stopped by the next morning, after our dinner, and we began talking about my plans. I may have told him that we were already secretly betrothed. It helped him to feel more confident lending his support. He also had another good laugh about our miscommunication."

"That bastard." But he was smiling, his teeth flashing in the dim light. "I hate to admit this, but I was afraid I hadn't helped you at all."

"Well, you did, so why don't you keep the ring? You can give it to—" Her throat closed up before she could finish.

His brows drew together again, and he said, "There's no one else I want to give a ring to."

That didn't help the lump in her throat at all, so she wasn't able to say anything as he gently took her hand and pushed the ring onto her finger. It fit perfectly. His thumb traced around the gold band, sending pleasant sparks up her arm so that she was afraid to breathe in fear that they'd stop. She couldn't look away from how he caressed her and how pretty the ring looked on her finger. Somehow, they'd drawn even closer without her realizing it. His coat brushed her arm with each intake of his breath, his exhale sending warm air past her temple. If only this were real.

"Helena," he whispered.

Before she could stop herself, she leaned up, clasping his hand as she kissed him. He groaned in the back of his throat, and the sound vibrated inside her, sending need and desire flooding through her veins.

A high-pitched screech sent them dashing apart. Mrs. Crenshaw stood at the open door of the gaming room, a hand over her mouth to quell the sound. Light illuminated the entrance of the room, highlighting the color on her cheeks and the sheer joy on her face.

"Maxwell!" She hurried forward with murmurs of surprise and curiosity spilling from the room behind her. "Does this mean what I think it means?" she asked as she approached.

Max moved inward, putting his arm around Helena in a move that almost seemed protective. "Helena has agreed to be my wife." He said it so matter-of-factly that she almost believed him. Thankfully, his mother did believe him.

"Oh, this is wonderful!" Mrs. Crenshaw closed the distance and pulled Helena into her arms, overcome with excitement. "So wonderful. Welcome to the family." She cupped Helena's face in a maternal gesture before turning to her son and embracing him.

Overwhelming guilt almost moved Helena to protest, but then Max's hand settled on her lower back, and he gave her a nod of encouragement. "Thank you, Mrs. Crenshaw," she mumbled.

"Oh fee! Call me Millie, or perhaps one day you might prefer Mother."

Helena was too stunned to answer, and by the time she recovered, other guests were trickling from the room and joining in the congratulations. Her parents followed, Papa looking as if he had expected the proposal all along. Smiling in rare approval, he ordered champagne brought up from the basement. She was thankful Lord and Lady Sansbury had retired for the evening before the gaming started. While she was certain gossip and her mother had prepared them for this eventuality, it would have seemed cruel to put on this part of the farce with them present.

The rest of the night passed in celebrations and toasts to their long and happy future together. Helena stood beside Max the entire time, not certain if this was how it felt to have her heart break all over again or if it was the guilt making her melancholy. It wasn't until Mr. Crenshaw stood up after having been relegated to an overstuffed chair for much of the evening that she figured out which.

Glass of champagne in hand, he said, "I would like to formally welcome Lady Helena into our family." He looked at her, and she gave a smile and an uncomfortable nod of acceptance, then he turned to the room at large. "We came to your great country not even a year ago with no real expectations, but in that time you have welcomed us, entertained us," looking at Papa, he added, "offered us industry," then gazing at his sons-in-law, he said, "given us two of your best sons so that they could become our sons. So that they could help carry on the legacy left to us by my father, Augustus Crenshaw, may his soul rest in peace. And now you have given to us one of your finest daughters. An angel among women who only seeks to make the world a better place than she found it. Her courage and compassion are admirable, and I can think of no finer woman to welcome into our family." To Max, he said, "May God bless you with strong children to carry on the legacy of Crenshaw Iron Works."

It was definitely heartbreak.

Chapter 19

❧

*I'm not going to act the lady among you, for
fear I should starve.*

EMILY BRONTË

The next morning Helena seemed to be avoiding him
and Max didn't know what the hell to do about it. At
first her evasion was innocuous. After breakfast, she gathered her four nieces and nephews along with her sisters,
Violet and Camille, and set about decorating every door,
window, and mantelpiece with the greenery that had been
collected and arranged before his arrival. Instead of joining, he and August sat ensconced in the study with their
father, Lord Farthington, and Hereford discussing how
Max should handle the threat of a strike back home. Max
had no idea what Hereford lent the conversation aside from
condescension since he owned not one factory, nor did he
run any sort of business operation aside from the small fortune Camille had brought to their marriage. That didn't
stop the man from passing ill-advised judgment on Max.

Max would have much rather joined Helena, because he
had already telegrammed New York with his plans to negotiate, and he would not resort to his father's heavy-handedness

if it could be avoided. Also, as the hours ticked by on the clock, he was disturbingly aware of how very little time he had with her. He wasn't such a fool that he thought in the short days left to him he could convince her to marry him, but he had hoped to quietly press his case by building on what was already between them.

In the late afternoon, when he and August had managed to escape the study, Helena had been nowhere to be found. It was only after tracking down his mother that he had been told she had taken the group sledding in the hills beyond the estate. That was a sight he very much wanted to see, but he was halfway to the stable when they came back, the happy squeals of the children preceding them around the bend in the drive. Since there was only a light snow on the ground, most of the children were covered in a fair bit of mud when they came into sight. Helena was smiling and laughing with Penelope and Camille, despite the mud visible on the hem of her skirts.

The other women fell away as he walked up to the group, leaving him to talk to Helena. "I had hoped to join in the sledding."

She smiled, but it was lacking any real warmth. "You didn't miss very much. Unfortunately, there was hardly any sledding to be had. I knew before we left there wasn't enough snow for proper sledding, but I allowed myself to be tempted by the children."

The rumble of wagon wheels drew his attention to the path behind her as a groom drove the vehicle laden with sleds and paraphernalia. In that time, she walked around him toward the house. He hurried to catch up with her, falling into step beside her. "I'd like a few minutes of your time today to talk."

Smile in place like a shield, she shook her head. "Perhaps after dinner? I'm such an absolute mess right now that I'm afraid I'll miss tea. I'm due belowstairs later to help Mrs. Harding with the menu."

He paused, taken aback by her renewed coolness toward him. He thought they had worked past this, and then that kiss last night . . . He didn't know what to think of her. Before he could say anything, she continued walking. "After dinner, then," he called after her.

She waved but didn't look back. That's when he knew for certain that she was avoiding him on purpose.

He could only explain his behavior later in the evening as a combination of both angry frustration with his father and despair that he was losing Helena.

Dinner was the same as the night before, a relaxed and lighthearted affair. Instead of the typical long table, there were several large round tables in the room, and guests were encouraged to sit where they wanted. It wasn't something Max would have expected from the usually formal Lord and Lady Farthington, but he gathered it was a tradition started long ago and no one had the impudence to change it. Instead of being escorted into dinner, the women led the way and the men followed, taking seats where they were available. It didn't escape his notice that Helena had positioned herself at a table without additional chairs. Therefore, he found himself seated next to his sisters and brothers-in-law. No one but him seemed to think this was odd.

He participated in the conversations around him to a reasonable degree, neither too talkative nor sullen. Afterward, he remembered that he had spoken to Evan and Christian about Britain's recent purchase of a share of the Suez Canal, but he could not recall the particulars of the conversation. He existed at the table, there but not present, barely eating, preferring to sip his scotch instead as he stole glances at Helena and the ring on her finger.

After dinner, the women left, and Farthington, Papa, Hereford, and Helena's brother, Viscount Rivendale, joined him, Evan, and Christian at their table. Christian handed him one of the cigarettes he favored but rarely indulged.

Max could taste the sweet and bitter tobacco on his tongue, but it existed as somehow separate from himself. He wanted to go find Helena for their talk, except Farthington seemed determined to keep up their discussion from earlier about the potential strike.

"Your problem here in England, Farthington, is that you allowed your workers to organize," said Papa. "We are doing everything possible in Congress to stop that from happening in America. Nothing good comes of it, as you've well seen."

Before Farthington could answer that, Max said, "You're lying to yourself if you believe your lobbying will stop progress."

Papa looked over, anger lining his brow. "Progress? If we allow our own workers to dictate to us how to operate our company, then all will be lost. That is hardly progress in my book."

"Indeed," Farthington put in. "These unions were approved with the expectation that they would benefit both employers and employees, and yet we've seen time and time again that they eat into profits that could be put to better use in improvements and advancements."

"Improvements and advancements?" Max kept his voice steady, but he wasn't inclined to sit through a repeat discussion so similar to the one from this afternoon. "Don't you mean profits that could be better put to use lining your pockets?"

Farthington raised a brow and glanced at Papa. "That's not what I said. These workers claim they want safety but in the same breath demand higher wages. They would run our factories to bankruptcy if we gave in to all of their demands."

"They want to work in relative safety and earn a living wage. Those two shouldn't be mutually exclusive," Max said.

"Philosophy is all well and good, Max, but as leaders in

industry, we ultimately decide what is best," Papa said. "You squash that rebellion with force, and mark my words, we won't have trouble for years to come."

"I will *not* use force unless force is used against us, and even then only in defense." His voice rose a bit with that, prompting Evan to put a hand on his shoulder. "Where would we find more men willing to work for us if we brutalize those who do?"

"Canada," Papa supplied.

"Get rid of the lot of them," Hereford said. "Men who are not grateful for what you give them will forever want more."

Farthington shrugged. "Bring them in young, trained by your own hand."

"While children often work twelve-hour days in the factories here, we do not and will not employ children."

"Our factories employ workers who are over the age of twelve, many of them earning wages their families need, and the workday is limited to ten hours in most cases." Turning his attention back to Papa, Farthington added, "Your son has much to learn about British factories."

Papa raised his hand for peace before Max could reply. "Be that as it may, we were discussing our own troubles, Max, of which there are many."

"Yes, and as we decided, I have been put in charge of Crenshaw Iron in America, and I will decide how to proceed. The board has trust in me, even if you do not." Ever aware that Papa had yet to make a full recovery, he tempered his voice, but he was angry at having to defend himself again, and it showed in his tone.

"Hear! Hear!" Evan raised his glass of claret in a bid to redirect the conversation. "While we may disagree on many things, we can all agree that Maxwell has done well for Crenshaw Iron. He's navigated the uncertain waters of falling markets and rising costs with ease."

"Hear! Hear!" Christian was quick to join in.

"Hear! Hear!" Lord Farthington said, raising his own glass. Fixing his gaze on Max, he added, "I may not agree with your methods, but I admire a man who knows how to take control."

The praise was unexpected and didn't set well with Max, but he accepted it anyway and let another sip of scotch roll down his tongue. It was only his third, but he was starting to feel the effects after not having eaten much at dinner.

"Agreed." This came from Hereford. "Besides, the real issue is how we will handle these nasty little disputes when they arise in India."

"India?" While Papa was leading the charge on the railroad expansion to the subcontinent and had worked closely with Farthington to procure contracts through Parliament, as far as Max knew, Hereford had nothing to do with it.

Papa cleared his throat and set his glass down, watching it thoughtfully as he twirled the stem between his fingers. "Hereford has decided to come on as an investor."

"Is that right?" Max asked, suspicion clouding his words. "How does August feel about a new investor?"

"I haven't told her, but it hardly matters. She's not in charge of this particular project," Papa said.

"Do you have a voting interest?" Max asked.

Hereford nodded in reply. "Obviously."

"You should have told her," Max said to Papa.

"I agree." Evan joined in, his voice firm with outrage on his wife's behalf. "She has devoted too much time and energy to Crenshaw Iron to be left out."

Papa shrugged. "Her time has been spent on her dock project, lately. I've taken over this one, and I will continue to run it as I see fit. Besides, we disagree on the India expansion and have finally decided that this is the way to solve it. She runs her project, and I run mine."

"What specific disagreement are you referring to?" Neither Max nor August thought the company should expand into India, but it seemed Papa was speaking of a recent fallout.

"Compensation," Farthington supplied. "Your father and I have discussed the issue at length and come to an agreement on how to treat the workers fairly. Hereford agrees."

Hereford nodded again. Papa held his jaw tight, a sure sign that Max wouldn't like what was coming next.

To Farthington, Max said, "I thought your role was simply to help get the contracts through Parliament."

"Your father values my advice." There was a note of warning in Farthington's voice, as if he was saying that Max should value it as well.

Papa broke the tension by laying out the compensation issue. It was in range with what some other railroads were paying, but below the average. It also did not include any additional compensation for accidental death or medical care arising from working twelve- and fourteen-hour days for the men building the railway.

"This compensation is obscenely one-sided," Max said.

Papa frowned. "It is not. They are being paid the same as others."

"They will be paid but *not* fairly. *Not* with a wage that is livable, *not* with a wage that will allow them to support their families, but they will take it because they have no choice. You"—he indicated the entire table—"you hold these people's lives and livelihoods in your hands and you talk about them as if they are mere baubles for your enjoyment without regard for the effects of your actions. It's made all the worse because you think nothing of taking from them, all the while you despair over what they might take from you. You with your silver cutlery and your aged claret and your heirloom jewelry, you refuse to consider how all of these things are given to you by the men, women, and children you exploit.

"It won't cost very much to see that they are compensated fairly for their work, because you will see it returned to you in the very goods you sell them. Isn't that how economies are supposed to work? Isn't it supposed to be a cycle instead of a vacuum that only works one way?"

"That is quite enough!" Papa pushed back from the table, but he didn't stand.

"Gentlemen, perhaps we should take a moment to gather ourselves," Evan said, but Max barely heard him.

"Papa, you go on and on for hours about the legacy of Crenshaw Iron Works. Have you even considered once what that legacy will be? How do you fail to see that this is not the sort of legacy we should be concerned about leaving behind? In a hundred years we will all be gone, but the effects of our decisions will still be here in the families we reduce to poverty."

He rose and tossed the linen napkin that had been on his lap down on the table. His chocolate tart was left untouched. "That's not the legacy I want."

Grabbing the bottle of scotch, he left the table, ignoring the murmurs of disapproval behind him. Farthington called out, but Max did not stop; he kept walking until he was outside the dining room in the dimly lit hall. His gaze was automatically pulled to the sconce across the way where he had kissed Helena last night. The memory sent a terrible wave of sadness in to meld with his anger.

He shouldn't have yelled at Papa and Farthington, he knew, but he didn't regret it. He would, however, regret whatever happened if he went to find Helena in his volatile mood. No, it would be best to drink himself to the bottom of the bottle and wait until tomorrow to see her. With that in the forefront of his mind, he turned toward the unexplored depths of the house.

Helena put a hand to her mouth to cover any sound that might slip out. She had been coming to find Max in the dining room, to see if he was ready for their talk. The raised voices had stopped her at the door of the adjoining salon where she had listened to the argument unfold. It wasn't until she heard a door close that she realized Max must have left. Voices were raised in outrage at the table with Evan attempting to keep the peace and losing that battle, but Helena couldn't concern herself with the aftermath. She needed to find Max.

Hurrying from the room, she made her way to the hall, but he wasn't there. The only sounds were the muffled voices within the dining room. Panic seized her, because she needed to find him before he disappeared into his bedroom, to tell him how brave he was and that she agreed with his every word. He probably felt all alone now, and while she could not be with him in the way that he wanted, she could support him.

But she didn't find a sign of him along the way to the bachelor's hall. She passed a maid who claimed not to have seen him and gave her a surprised look. It didn't matter. She would knock on his door; it wasn't completely out of bounds of propriety since everyone believed they were to be married. She simply wouldn't enter when he answered. Only her knock on his door went unanswered. Thankfully, the door was unlocked, but the room was empty when she peeked inside.

Damn. Where was he?

She spent the next half hour wandering the halls and varied rooms of the sprawling estate, hoping that someone had seen him. None of the servants she passed had. Finally, she stepped into the darkened room at the back of the house. It was a rarely used parlor that held all the outdated furniture her mother had decided she didn't want in the more fashionable rooms of the estate. She almost judged it empty and turned to leave, but a movement near the window caught her eye. Moonlight caught the glass of a bottle.

"Max?"

A shadow materialized in the darkness, and as she walked closer, she could tell that Max was seated in an overstuffed chair, legs stretched out in front of him as he gazed out the window and drank what she suspected to be scotch straight out of the bottle. He had turned his head at the sound of her voice.

"I've been looking for you," she said as she approached.

"Turn around and leave." His voice sounded gravelly, like the scotch had left scratches on the way down. She shivered inside at the effect.

"I came to find you earlier because we had agreed to talk. I was standing in the salon when I heard what you said to your father. I wanted you to know how brave I think you are and how proud I am of you for saying those things."

He went back to staring out the window and leaned forward to set the bottle on the floor next to the chair leg. It was only half-empty, but she didn't know how full it had been when he started.

"What does it matter?" he finally asked into the silence. "They'll continue to be unrepentant asses, and you will continue to push me away. Perhaps you believe yourself too good for me after all."

"That's not true, at least for me. I don't believe that."

"No? Then what else am I to think?"

He sat back with a sigh, his hands folding together over his stomach. It was only then that she took notice of the fact that he had discarded his coat and sat in the cold of the room in only his shirtsleeves, waistcoat, and trousers. The shirtsleeves had been rolled up at some point to reveal a bit of his forearms. They were strong, wrapped with muscle, but in that way he had of turning brawn into grace. He looked so dejected that her heart clenched. Slowly walking forward, she knelt down next to his chair.

He was right. What else was he to think? She hadn't been completely open with him about her reason for rejecting him, and she regretted that now when it was obvious her silence on the matter was adversely affecting him.

"That has nothing to do with why I believe we won't suit."

His head didn't move, but he was watching her through the slits his eyes had become. She could feel the weight of his perusal. It reminded her of the majestic lion she always imagined him to be, and how she was playing with a particularly dangerous version of him now.

Dangerous because he was infinitely more appealing to her in his volatility, because it let her see how truly vulnerable he could be with her. A thrill of decadent longing unfurled in her stomach. She would never stop wanting him.

Swallowing thickly, she said, "It's past time for us to talk about that. I need to tell y—"

"Leave me, Helena." His voice was so calm that it raised the hairs on her arm in warning. "I have plenty of uses for your mouth tonight, but talking isn't one of them."

She froze in place as blood pounded through her veins in lurid anticipation. His words tugged her toward him more effectively than any physical touch could have.

"Max, you should understand—"

"Go."

She swallowed again, feeling like she was leaning into a precipice. Actually leaving him in the room alone never crossed her mind. Her place was with him. Being with him in this moment felt more right than anything ever had in her entire life.

"Yes," she whispered.

He didn't move, but his entire body seemed to jerk with the force of that word. His eyes glittered with some dark emotion that made her heart beat madly in her chest. She felt as if she had just offered herself up to the vengeful wrath of an angel. He moved so fast that she didn't have time to react as his fingers buried themselves in her hair, cupping her head as he gently drew her head back. Suddenly, she was breathing so fast it felt like she'd been running. He brought his face so close to hers that she could see the pain and despair reflected in the depths of his eyes.

"Don't tease me." He dragged his mouth along her jaw

but stopped short of taking her lips. "I want to taste every inch of you," he whispered. "I want to spend an entire night inside you, just once before I leave you."

"Yes," she whispered again, because she had missed him, and she knew his leaving would hurt her so badly she didn't know if she could recover. The heartache would be hell, but the depth of the pain wouldn't change if they had this night. She needed this memory.

She needed him.

Chapter 20

If I loved you less, I might be able to talk about it more.

JANE AUSTEN

Helena stood and held out her hand. Max stared at it as if afraid it might disappear altogether if he moved too fast, before he looked up at her.

"Helena?" he whispered.

Her breath hitched at the way it sent everything shattering inside her.

"I won't take you on the floor again." His brow raised to emphasize his next words. "If we're to do this, I demand a bed and the entire night."

She nodded. "Yes, I want that, too." She hadn't known how much until just now. Until the thought of not making it upstairs with him left her nearly devastated.

He moved slowly, with uncertainty, likely believing she would take this away, but she couldn't. Whatever tomorrow might bring, she needed this night with him. As soon as his hand touched hers, she closed her fingers around his and helped pull him up. He followed her to the door on legs that were much steadier than she had thought they would be.

Once there, she paused to look out and make sure no servants were around, and he came up behind her, his other hand at her waist and his lips in her hair. She smiled as she leaned back into him for a minute, savoring the solid warmth of his body.

"We can't do this out there." She tilted her head toward the door and the world beyond it.

"Why?" He took her lips in a deep kiss that left her head swimming. Then she was pinned against the wall as he leaned over her. "They all assume we're fucking. We're getting married, and I'm leaving for home soon. Why wouldn't we be kissing in doorways?"

The words sent a shiver of longing through her even as they emphasized how much alcohol he had likely consumed. "You're drunk. I wonder if I'm taking advantage of you."

He laughed, his fingertips brushing across her neck as he moved to bury his hand in her hair again. "I'm only drunk because I couldn't have you. Besides, I haven't had that much to drink."

He took her hand, and her breath caught again when she realized his intent as he guided it down to press against his impressive erection. Molten desire pooled between her legs when she stroked the hard length of him, prompting her to abruptly let him go. She couldn't do what needed to be done if she was half-witted from wanting him, though it might be a smidge too late on that score.

"Listen to me." She took his face between her hands. "We can't be seen going upstairs together. Everyone might *think* that we're sleeping together, but they don't *know,* and we need to keep it that way." Her reputation would depend upon it when their betrothal eventually came to an end. "I'm going to leave first, and then you go to your room in a few minutes."

"My room?" He was poised to argue, but she kept talking.

"Yes, your room. Let Howard help put your clothes away," she said, referring to the servant her father had assigned him since he didn't travel with a valet. "Go through your evening ablutions as if nothing is out of the ordinary."

"I think he'll damned well notice that I'm about to rupture the confines of my trousers," he said sardonically.

She laughed despite herself. "I'll come get you when it's safe."

"How?" He scowled in that way she loved, and she couldn't resist running her fingertips over his brow.

"Trust me."

He tried to keep hold of her waist, but she hurried away before he could answer.

Max paced around his room feeling very much like a caged tiger he had once seen at a traveling circus. He'd sobered significantly in the half hour he'd been in his room, becoming more convinced with every passing moment that Helena had sent him here to cool down. It was no less than he deserved for how he had talked to her, as if she were not a real-life lady with a capital *L*. He didn't think of her that way, though. He simply thought of her as *his*, no matter how presumptuous and premature that may be. He was more certain of that now than he had ever been, even after what he had said to her father, knowing her father might very well ask him to leave a day early. He simply wanted to belong to her in the same way. He already did.

If she didn't send for him soon, he'd—

A scraping sound had him turning toward the far corner of the bedroom. The wall panel shifted, revealing for the first time that there was a minuscule separation between it and the rest of the wall. As he watched, it further separated itself from the wall as it was pushed open. Helena stood framed in the makeshift doorway holding a single candle and wearing nothing but slippers and a dressing gown made of sapphire-colored silk. It was belted at her waist, but a deep V showed enough of her chest and cleavage to be assured there was not a stitch of clothing underneath, and her nipples pressed against the thin material.

"I told you I'd come." She grinned.

He smiled back, unable to do anything less whenever she smiled at him. "What is this?" He walked over, half in shock that she was here but curious at the existence of a secret passageway.

"An old passageway for servants. It's from back in the days when they would use this accessway instead of the main corridors. All of the bedrooms back up to it along this stretch of the house."

He couldn't stop smiling as he peeked inside to see that it was dark and completely enclosed. "I've never seen a real secret passageway."

"Then follow me."

He felt like a freshman sneaking out of his dormitory again as he stepped into the passageway behind her. The corridor was large enough that he could walk through unimpeded, but not so wide that he could walk beside her. She took his hand, and he put his other one on her hip, unable to keep himself from touching her. The silk glided smoothly over her skin as he moved his hand up to her breast to test his theory. Only a thin layer of silk kept him from her. Her breath hitched at the touch.

"Did you tell your maid that you wanted to sleep nude tonight?"

She giggled even as she shushed him. "No, I took off my nightdress after she left," she whispered, her breath ending on a quick exhale as he toyed with the tender bit of swollen flesh.

When she stopped a moment later, he bumped into the back of her. "Here," she whispered, pushing open the panel that led to her room. It was far closer than he thought it would be.

"My room is only on the next corridor over, but you access it from a different set of stairs."

He followed her inside. It was lit by a single lamp burning on the bedside table and the fire in the hearth. The room was decorated tastefully in frilly white and pale blue, clearly the selections of a young woman. "Is this your childhood bedroom?"

She nodded.

"It's conveniently close to my bedroom."

She flushed. "I might have had you placed in one of the eastern-facing rooms on the bachelor's hall for a reason."

He laughed. Her room wouldn't have had access to the western-facing ones. "You planned this?" he asked, walking closer to her.

She had placed the extinguished candle on the table next to the lamp, so she stood there looking uncertain and alone, her hands knotting in the folds of her dressing gown. "Not precisely. I think I wanted you close to me without really understanding why. But now that I think about it, I believe this was inevitable."

"Helena." The very act of saying her name soothed him somehow. Her eyes widened slightly as he approached her and took her face between his palms. Her pupils were dilated, making her eyes seem so deep and bottomless he wanted to dive into her and never come up for air. He kissed her with reverence, hoping to make up for his ruthlessness earlier. Yet the moment their mouths touched it lit a torch to the heat that constantly smoldered between them, until soon the kiss burned out of control and he was all but devouring her against the wall.

She pushed at his chest, and he pulled back thinking she had changed her mind, but she was trying to push his dressing gown off his shoulders. He helped her, untying the belt to let it drop to the floor in a heap.

"I want to see all of you tonight," she said.

Her words burned through him like a wildfire.

"All right." His hands went to the waist of the drawers he wore as she slipped out of her own dressing gown and crawled into the curtained bed, each lush curve put on display as the light flickered over them lovingly. He was still in that position when she turned back to him, having been rendered immobile by the sight of her. Her pink-tipped breasts rose and fell with each of her breaths. "My God, you're beautiful."

She smiled, not looking nearly as lost now as she slipped her legs beneath the covers, hiding the glimpse he'd had of dark gold curls between her legs, and settled back against the pillows. Stepping out of his slippers, he pushed his drawers down and watched as her gaze greedily soaked in the sight of him. Her eyes widened as he took his erection in hand and squeezed slightly to alleviate the pressure. He'd wanted her too long.

She didn't protest when he pulled the blanket down so he could see her.

"You're even more beautiful than I remembered." That night in her drawing room had been hasty and impulsive. Tonight he planned to take his time with her.

She watched with parted lips as he climbed up from the foot of the bed, letting his tongue and his lips taste her on the way up. He had one goal in mind as he moved up her body and pressed a kiss to the nest of curls at the apex of her thighs. He'd bet anything that her husband had never kissed her there. He paused, breathing in the scent of her desire for him. "I said I wanted to taste every inch of you."

Her eyes widened even more if that was possible. "There?" she whispered, too shocked to say anything else.

"Has no one ever kissed you between your pretty thighs, Helena?"

"No." She visibly swallowed, but then a smile hovered around the corners of her mouth. "Max, no." She bit her lip as she contemplated what he wanted, as if she'd never before considered it.

He grinned at how scandalized and intrigued she looked, the threads of her ladylike demeanor fraying. He pressed a soft kiss to her left thigh and then her right, nipping her softly in encouragement. In response she spread her legs a little. He ran the tip of his index finger down the slit that was revealed to him, playing in the slick heat of her need, and drawing it up to ease his way as he circled her clitoris. "I want to lick you and suck you until you come, but you have to tell me that's what you want first."

Her eyes widened as did the space between her thighs. Half in shock, half out of her mind with need, she nodded. "Yes, please, yes."

He groaned in satisfaction as he settled between her thighs and licked at her with the tip of his tongue. He'd been prepared to go home never having this closeness with her again, but here she was making his every wish come true. She cried out, her fingers tightening almost painfully in his hair to hold him to her as he sucked her swollen clitoris into his mouth. Satisfaction crashed over him in waves at the way she writhed beneath him, drunk on the combined power of tasting her desire for him and knowing that no man had ever had her this way.

When her hips moved of their own accord to the rhythm of his tongue, he tenderly pushed a finger inside her. Her body grasped at him, and he pressed a second one in to join the first, curling them upward to find that rough bit of flesh that made her body jolt when he rubbed it.

The sound of his name on her lips filled his ears, and he didn't care if anyone heard her. She was his and he was hers and he wanted everyone to know it. It wasn't long before her cries reached a more frantic pitch, and then she was coming, her sweet passage clasping at his fingers as she trembled.

Only after she came down did he place a kiss on her stomach and remove himself from her by degrees as he slid off the bed.

"Max." Her plaintive voice followed him to his discarded dressing gown where he retrieved the tin of rubber sheaths he'd brought with him. His hands shook as he opened it and drew one out, letting the tin fall to the floor in his impatience. Fitting it on, he turned back to her, and she held her arms out to him, her eyes wide in the same desperate excitement that had him shaking with need.

He crawled over her and took a pink nipple into his mouth. After laving it with sufficient attention, he moved to the other one. By the time he was finished, she writhed beneath him, holding him against her as if afraid he might change his mind.

"Jesus, Helena," he whispered as he settled between her thighs.

He'd hardly dared to imagine he might have her again. As he looked down at her, *I love you* was on the tip of his tongue, but he didn't say it because she wasn't ready to hear it for reasons he couldn't fathom. Reaching between them, he reverently caressed her with his thumb, eliciting a gasp of pleasure, before guiding his cock to her and pressing inside. He groaned at the sheer bliss of the tight heat surrounding him. White stars exploded behind his eyelids as he gave a thrust of his hips to fully seat himself within her. When he opened his eyes, she stared up at him with such a look of awe and affection on her face that he knew he'd remember it forever.

"Max." Her breath caught as she reverently touched his face, her thumb sweeping over his brow in that way he was coming to like so much before cupping his cheek. "I . . ."

He kissed her palm. It might have been the scotch flowing through his veins, but he would have sworn she almost said she loved him. "Shh . . . let me love you," he whispered when a sheen of unshed tears brightened her eyes. He didn't know if he meant sex or what would happen afterward. It didn't matter, because all his focus was on her. On showing her how he felt about her. Tomorrow fell away and it was just them. Now.

He moved within her, slowly at first, drawing soft sighs from her lips, but as with everything between them, the heat quickly burned out of control. His fingers laced with hers, holding her hands captive and pressed in the sheets above her head as he thrust into her over and over. The way she said his name on a gasp as she tightened her legs around his hips added fuel to the fire within him, building their desire into a firestorm of need, until nothing existed but her tight grip around his cock, the salt of her skin on his tongue, and her sweet cries of pleasure in his ears. Finally, she trembled around him, the frenzied and tight clenching of her body nearly sending him over the edge as she came apart in his arms. He held back, letting her writhe on him as she came, waiting for her to come down. Only then did he follow her over, need twisting and coiling inside him until it erupted, and he poured everything he was into her.

Chapter 21

*Even in my dreams, I never imagined that I
should find so much love on earth.*

PRINCE ALBERT

Max left her and moved to the edge of the bed, presumably to dispose of the sheath. Helena couldn't see anything beyond his wide shoulders. She wanted to pull him back to her, but she felt weak and disoriented, her body still quivering in the aftereffects of their lovemaking. Sex had been a pleasurable experience before, in the early days of her marriage, but it had never held this intensity that somehow managed to succeed in separating her soul from her body. If he left her as quickly as he had the first time, she didn't know how she would make it. She honestly felt that she might never be whole again.

When he left the bed completely, she heard a sound of disappointment escape her, and she managed to push herself up a little in dismay, but she settled when he stopped at the washstand. Gathering up the cloth hanging from the wrought iron rod off the side, he wet it and proceeded to wash himself. She was aware in some remote corner of her mind that she should look away and give him a modicum of privacy, but she couldn't make herself obey. Her eyes were greedy for the sight of him. The flex of his buttocks as he walked. The way he moved the cloth over every ridge and sinew before finding his semi-erect manhood, washing himself.

"Max," she whispered as he doused the cloth in the water again, fearful he meant to dress and leave now. But the smile hovering around his lips and the obvious intent in his eyes when he looked at her settled her worries. She didn't recognize this needful creature she became with him.

Wringing out the cloth, he brought it back to bed with him. Her breath lodged in her throat at how he effortlessly seemed to draw all the air from the bed, overwhelming it with his mere presence and making it feel smaller than it actually was. After turning down the lamp and untying the bed curtains so they swished closed, cocooning them in their own world, he leaned over her, kissing her ear and her neck as the hand with the cloth found its way between her thighs. She gasped at the lukewarm wetness as he washed her inner thighs and then that part of her that still felt achy and swollen with need.

He tossed the cloth away to land on the floor near the end of the bed and teased her with his fingers. She closed her eyes when his mouth found her nipple and desire flamed into an all-encompassing need that blotted out everything else but him. His scent, his touch, the sounds he made in the back of his throat when she reacted the way he wanted. Quicker than she would have imagined possible, she was trembling around his fingers, her body splintering into a million different pieces as he played her with the skill of a seasoned musician.

As she came down, he gathered her into his arms and threw a leg over hers, anchoring her within the shelter of his embrace as she found herself again. She pressed her nose into the soft cave of his neck, breathing him in and knowing that he would be a part of her forever. What existed between them was too precious and rare to ever go away.

She knew that, and yet overwhelming guilt accompanied the thought. She should have told him the truth about herself the very moment she had suspected this obsession between them was more than mere attraction. Even tonight she had let her desire for him suppress her better sense, somehow convincing herself that once more wouldn't change anything.

In a way it wouldn't. She'd felt connected to him from the beginning, and nothing would change that. But in a much more harmful way, she had probably made him believe that this could lead to something more. That wasn't right of her.

"Max, we need to talk."

When he didn't answer right away, she lifted her head to peer down at him. It was very dark in their little nest, but his light snore confirmed what she had begun to suspect. He was asleep.

"Max, there are things we need to discuss."

Taking hold of his shoulder, she shook it lightly and then with more vigor when he didn't react. His response was to grab her in his arms and hold her more firmly against his chest. His leg tightened around her until she was held against him like a child's prized blanket. Even though she knew it was the scotch making him sleep so deeply, his arms really weren't an objectionable place to be. She felt warm and secure, wanted in a way she hadn't felt in such a long time, perhaps ever. Perhaps it would be better to talk in the morning anyway without the fog of alcohol to dull her words for him. She snuggled into his embrace and savored the feeling of being held by him.

She awoke much later in the night. His hot breath was in her ear and his teeth were at her neck, biting in a way that sent shivers of longing pulsing through her. His hands were everywhere and had to have been for some time to make her body light up with such a throbbing and violent need.

"Max." Her fingers searched behind her, finding the firm globe of his bottom as she pressed her hips back into him, searching and then delighting in the push of his erection against the small of her back. But that was not where she wanted him.

"Tell me you need me." His voice was a trembling growl that vibrated across her already raw nerve endings.

"My God, yes. I need you inside me."

His breath rushed past her ear. "You're such a good girl, Helena. You do everything I ask of you." He plucked at her nipple before rolling it between his thumb and forefinger.

She had no idea why his words intensified her need, but they did. "Please, Max." She canted her hips, hoping to find him.

And then he was there, his hard length buried inside her to the hilt from behind. He withdrew only to fill her again, sending her plummeting headlong into insensibility as he took her hard and fast. Even though he was behind her, she felt him all around her. He caged her with his body, his fingers finding every responsive part of her as he pushed her over the edge, tumbling down into an abyss of pleasure mixed with possession. She fell back to sleep with tremors still quaking through her body, but his arms were around her keeping her whole.

The next time she awoke it was to bright sunlight catching a break in the bed curtain to fall across her face. She squinted and turned her head away from the beam, snuggling into the warmth at her side. Max automatically tightened his hold and buried his face in her hair. She loved this waking up to him. The coarse hair on his legs rasped pleasantly across her skin as he moved, stretching as he slowly came awake. The spice of his body mingled with their sex surrounded her, lulling her into a languor that made it difficult to come fully awake. She wanted to float here in this stupor, very nearly drunk on their sated pleasure and the heat from his body.

But the unmistakable sound of a door closing down the corridor brought her fully awake. The maid would be here soon to relight the fire and would find them. Had she locked the door last night? She thought so, but even if she had, the locked door would raise suspicion. Bloody hell! She sat up as she remembered Max's door was unlocked. She'd been too caught up in the sight of him half-naked to remind him to lock it. If they found him gone, his bed not even mussed, and then her door locked, everyone would know. He would have little choice in things from here on out and would be forced to marry her for real.

The enormity of her selfishness nearly made her double over in shame. Because she had wanted another night with him, he could be forced into a childless fate that would have him hating her eventually. How could she have been so greedy? For both of their sakes, she had to get him out of her bed and back to his room quickly.

The languid smile on his lips when she looked down at him had her shame intensifying. "Come here." His voice was hoarse with sleep as he attempted to pull her back to him, but she was already moving, donning her dressing gown as she got out of bed.

"Alice is down the corridor. She'll be here any moment to light the fire." Helena moved quickly to set the bed curtains to rights—she never slept with them closed. A quick glance at the state of the bedclothes had her hurrying around to tuck them back in beneath the mattress. It would only take one look for anyone to hazard a guess about what had taken place within the bed last night.

"Max, please," she urged when he didn't seem in any particular hurry to leave her bed. "You must leave."

"You're panicking." The contented look of bliss had yet to leave his eyes as he moved, but only so far as to sit on the edge of the bed.

"Of course I'm panicking! We overslept. You shouldn't have slept here at all."

He grinned a grin of pure male satisfaction. "As I recall, I fell asleep inside you after you—"

She covered his mouth with her fingers. "Don't say such things in the light of day."

Kissing her fingertips, he asked, "Is that a rule they have here in England? Because in America we—"

She pressed her palm to his lips, and her stomach tumbled in dread as another door closed. This one was much closer. "Please, you have to go."

It was either the desperation in her voice or on her face; one of them had him getting to his feet. She bent down to search for his dressing gown, which was partially beneath the bed. "You have to be back in your room before they discover you gone. I can't remember if Alice lights the fires on the bachelor's hall or if it's someone else. It may already be—"

Her lungs seized as she saw the two rubber sheaths they had used during the night lying on the floor. Max had tied off the ends, but they lay there, stark indictments of the night before. Tossing the dressing gown at him, she grasped one of the sheaths by the tie, intent on disposing of it in the bin, but she stopped when she reached the empty receptacle by her desk. The sheath would lie there easily seen when the maid who cleaned her room emptied it. She reached for a sheet of parchment to wrap around it but changed her mind when she imagined the paper coming undone to expose it when it was being transferred to the larger receptacle the maid carried with her.

What if someone rifled through her trash and found it? Servants sometimes did that, and the scandal sheets would be paying good money for gossip now that their betrothal was official. If she were at home, she wouldn't worry, but the staff was larger at Claremont Hall, which meant at least a few of them were less loyal. She couldn't throw it out.

Max was standing, shrugging into his dressing gown when she turned and spotted the fire. It had mostly gone out during the night, but the coals glowed. Burning it would get rid of all the evidence.

"No, don't—" Max's warning came too late as she pitched it over the top of the brocaded silk and rosewood fire screen.

As soon as it settled into the coals, curling wisps of black smoke rose up, and almost immediately the room was filled with a terrible smell. Perhaps most infuriating of all, the sheath sat there stubbornly refusing to go away as it sputtered and released more black fumes. Helena grabbed the fire tongs and plucked it out.

"Jesus! Throw it out the window," he said and rushed to open the sash.

In grateful alarm, she kept her eyes on the thing, which was still belching black smoke as she hurried over and tossed it out the window, very nearly throwing the tongs out as well, but Max covered her hand with his as she brought the tool back down between them. They both looked out, watching as the sheath sizzled and smoldered in the layer of snow accumulated against the house far below. His smile was so broad when he looked at her that she said, "Don't you dare laugh at me."

"I wouldn't." But his smile didn't leave as he closed the sash.

It was only then that she felt the cold morning air and held the folds of her dressing gown tighter around herself. The sides of his own dressing gown flapped around him as he faced her, completely unconcerned with his nakedness. She couldn't help but appreciate his broad chest, flat stomach, and the sight of his penis and bollocks nested in chestnut-colored curls in the full light of day. He was an impressive sight even mostly flaccid as he was at the moment.

And he knew it. There wasn't a shred of self-consciousness

on his face when his gaze met hers. "I can dispose of them. I have a small linen satchel that will hold them until I reach the train station tomorrow."

"Why didn't you say so?"

He did laugh then. "You didn't give me the chance. You panicked." His smile faded as he walked over to her and took her gently by the shoulders. The first trace of self-consciousness graced his eyes when he asked, "Do you regret last night?"

Perhaps if she could say yes, then it would make things easier and lessen her guilt, but she couldn't regret a moment with him. "How could I? I loved every moment of it."

Relief and satisfaction warred for dominance on his features and he pulled her against him. She allowed herself a moment of respite to luxuriate in how good he felt, before tugging away and moving back to set the bed to rights. "You have to go. They can't know."

"Okay." He nodded and walked over to retrieve the other sheath, which he pocketed before stepping into his slippers and picking up his drawers. "Helena . . ." There was a question in his voice as he stopped at the panel leading to the hidden passage.

The uncertainty tugged at her heart, and she hurried over to embrace him again and kiss him quickly on the lips. "We must talk. Later this morning, after breakfast?" she asked.

A smile tugged at the corner of his mouth, and he ran a loving hand over her hair. "You should know, if you're worried about Alice knowing what we did last night, that she only needs to look at you to see everything."

That male satisfaction was back, burning in his eyes as he kissed her hard and then disappeared through the panel. She hurried to the looking glass on her dressing table and saw what he meant. Her hair was a mess of tangles and waves as if a man had spent the night with his hands buried within it, her neck and the portion of her chest exposed by the dressing gown was pink and chafed as if a man's beard had abraded the tender skin, and a suspicious-looking bruise graced the tendon where her neck met her shoulder, but most telling were her eyes. Her eyes were alight as if lit from within by a secret only she possessed. She looked like a madwoman, half-wild with all the pleasure that had been poured into her last night.

She should feel aghast, but she could only smile at the woman staring back at her. She was alive in a way she hadn't been for a long time, and no matter what happened with Max, she would always love him for giving her that.

A thump against the wall had her running to unlock the door as quietly as she could before bounding into her bed. She pulled the blankets up to her eyes just as the door creaked open, and she pretended to be asleep as Alice came in to add coals to the fire. If the girl thought it odd that there was ash dropped across the floor or that the room smelled of burnt rubber, she didn't mention it.

Chapter 22

If particular care and attention is not paid to the ladies we are determined to foment a rebellion.

ABIGAIL ADAMS

The whole house felt as if it existed on a powder keg waiting to go off in a marvelous explosion at the slightest provocation. Helena felt it the moment she came down for breakfast. The women present talked in low whispers while the men were suspiciously absent. She spent the entire meal wondering if someone had heard them last night or if a groundskeeper had found the charred sheath outside her window and everyone knew about it and didn't want to tell her. She was afraid to ask, so she sat in polite silence, petrified of learning the truth while nibbling on a bit of dry toast, the only food her nerves would allow her.

Toward the end she had no choice but to talk when her mother-in-law sat down next to her. "Good morning, Lady Sansbury. I hope your suite is comfortable." It wasn't until that moment that she realized Lady Sansbury had never given her leave to call her by the more familiar Clara, and that it should have occurred to her to mind all those years ago.

A footman rushed forward to offer the woman tea, but she waved him away. "As comfortable as always, dear. I have come to tell you that I . . ." She hesitated and took in a wavering breath.

"Lady Sansbury?" Helena placed her palm to the back of woman's hand. "Are you all right?"

Lady Sansbury smiled and nodded. "Yes, I simply wanted to say that I am pleased that you have found a man willing—" She broke off and looked away. "Well, someone to marry who will take proper care of you."

Helena could feel the expression of polite concern on her face freeze solid. In all these years no one had specifically mentioned her barrenness. It wasn't until she had married that she understood the phrase *monthly courses* meant that they were indeed supposed to happen monthly. Hers had always been sporadic and light. She had only understood then because she had found the maids huddled around her bed one morning in the months after her marriage giggling over her impending motherhood because of the lack of bleeding on her part. Since her younger sisters had been too young at the time to ask, Helena had swallowed her embarrassment and asked her mother why the maids would believe her pregnant. Indeed, she had even hoped that maybe she was, though she had felt no different. Only then, under duress, had her mother explained all while assuring Helena that each woman was different and there should be no concern over the fact that she only had one or two menses a year.

There had been some gossip about her lack of bearing a child in the year leading up to Arthur's illness, but no one had spoken directly to her about it. Certainly, Lady Sansbury had never even once given a glance toward her waistline. But what she had managed to stop herself from saying now said it all.

"*I am pleased that you have found a man willing to*

overlook your failures." Or perhaps she would have said "*willing to marry you regardless of your inability to provide him children.*" However the sentence ended, the meaning would be the same. Helena was a failure when it came to being a woman, according to Lady Sansbury and those of the same mind who believed a woman's main purpose was to bring children into the world. This attitude wasn't a surprise. She had spent the last few years convincing herself that it wasn't true, but hearing it still stung.

"Thank you," she forced herself to answer. Even to Helena's ears the words sounded stilted and forced.

"I do hope you will be very happy. It is what Arthur would have wanted."

Helena nodded, wondering how things would have been between her and her husband had he lived. Their first year had been near bliss but had taken a sharp turn toward coldness the second year as he became more desperate for her to conceive, until the final six months when his illness had taken over everything. Had he lived she could only assume that they would be as near to being polite strangers as a married couple could be. He wouldn't have forgiven her for failing them.

"Thank you for saying so." It was all she could muster.

Lady Sansbury smiled and squeezed her hand before rising to her feet. Helena followed her. "Lord Sansbury and I will be leaving this morning."

"Please let me know when you are in Town again. I would be honored to show you the improvements we've made at the orphanage."

The woman gave her a bland smile, still unable to move on from the loss of her son to go back to the life she had led. They both knew she would never come to the orphanage again. "Goodbye, Helena."

Helena watched her go before leaving through the opposite door, unwilling to see anyone, as her own guilt for unintentionally misleading Max wailed through her all over again. Though could it really be unintentional when she had made love to him suspecting what he wanted from her?

"Helena! There you are." Violet found her staring out the window in a little-used parlor off the breakfast room some minutes later. "Are you feeling well?" Violet asked as she closed the distance between them as fast as she was able since she was entering the final term of her pregnancy.

Helena really didn't know how to answer that. In the past twelve hours, she had gone from heights she had never imagined possible to this near despair she felt now. "I'm well. How are you?"

"You look . . . flushed." Violet cocked her head to the side as if she couldn't quite figure out the change she saw.

Suddenly very happy that she had chosen a gown with a high collar to hide all evidence of Max's kisses on her neck and chest, she said, "I am a bit tired. I didn't sleep very soundly last night."

To that Violet grinned. "Neither did I, but possibly for different reasons." If the pretty color that appeared on her cheeks was any indication, their lack of sleep was for very similar reasons.

"Quite different, I suspect," Helena said.

"Oh." Violet's face fell. "I had hoped . . ." But her voice trailed off.

"Hoped for what?" Helena faced her fully, suspicion seizing her.

"Nothing." At Helena's imploring expression, she sighed. "After Max went off alone last night, Christian went to look for him, and he wasn't in his room. I had thought . . . well, hoped . . . that perhaps he was with you?"

"I . . ." *You only have to say you don't know anything.* But the words wouldn't come. They stuck in her throat like a wad of cotton.

Violet seized on the hesitation. Her eyes went wide, and she looked around to make certain that no one could hear. "I knew it!" she whispered.

"Violet, please, it's not as you think." Even though it very much was, only they would not have the happily-ever-after Violet had already written for them in her head.

Violet frowned and pressed a gentle hand to Helena's arm. "You like him, don't you?"

"I like him very much, but there are things you don't understand, that I cannot—" She couldn't even say the words, and she closed her eyes.

Violet embraced her, almost moving her to tears. Why was she so emotional this morning? She was behaving in a very unseemly manner, unable to gather her dignity around her.

"I didn't come to talk about that at any rate," Violet said as they parted. "I came to warn you if you don't already know."

"Know what?" This had to be what the silent tension was all about.

"The men and August are ensconced in the library. The doors are firmly closed, and there have been loud voices."

"Is this about Max going missing?"

"No, it's Crenshaw business, I think."

Relief made her shoulders sag. She'd been so caught up in what had passed between them last night that she had completely forgotten what had preceded their portion of the evening. "This is about the argument after dinner?"

Violet nodded. "I believe so."

Helena had spent the morning dreading the talk she knew she must have with Max and not thinking of the very real hell he must be facing now. "I'm going to go inside. I won't have Papa browbeating him."

Her sense of pride in Max holding his ground last night, as well as her own sense of upholding what was right, held her in good stead until she stood facing the group in the library a few moments later. All the men rose when she entered, but only Max appeared happy to see her. Six pairs of eyes watched him cross over to her and take her hands.

"Good morning, Helena," he said as if the room hadn't been full of harsh discussion up until the moment they all saw her.

"I've come to make certain that Papa is treating you well." She gave a pointed look to her father, who glared back at her.

"You have no business here, Helena," Papa said. "This is about Crenshaw Iron and our railroad in India."

"Good. Then I trust you are not attempting to intimidate Maxwell by threatening to withdraw your support of our marriage. Because it *would* be my concern should you attempt to sway my betrothed."

Papa clenched his jaw as his gaze darted between the two of them. "It would be premature to call him your betrothed when there is no betrothal contract."

"Whether Maxwell and I have a contract is between us. It doesn't require your signature." One of the advantages of being a widow was that she had miraculously acquired personhood with the death of her husband. It was a benefit she was loath to give up.

"So it doesn't." Papa relented, and she felt a minor jolt of victory. "I expect to see it regardless. I am your father."

"Of course," she said, seizing on this unforeseen bargaining chip. "I will send it over the moment it has been negotiated to my satisfaction."

Papa's gaze darted to Max at the reminder that his actions here could make those negotiations more difficult.

"Well." Helena gave a casual shrug. "I am glad to see that all is satisfactory. We do possess the ability to separate business and family, do we not?"

Papa hesitated, but he eventually inclined his head. "We are civilized."

"Good."

Max hid his grin until he tucked her hand into his arm and walked with her toward the door. Leaning his head toward hers, he said, "Your interference is very timely. He was doing just that when you walked in."

"I'm happy I could help."

The simple act of being near Max made her feel lighter, and she was genuinely able to smile for the first time that morning. Leading him into the corridor outside the room, she closed the door behind her.

"We were never able to talk last night. Might you be free to take a few minutes this afternoon?"

Max shook his head, and his smile softened as he drew his thumb over her bottom lip. "I wish, but no. August has managed to cajole Papa into sharing the contracts he's written with firms in India, and we are spending the day going over them. I leave tomorrow and couldn't in good conscience abandon August to face them alone. They're horrendously skewed to the disfavor of the builders and laborers. She'll have a devil of a time getting them changed without someone here to back her up." He shook his head in disgust. "Perhaps it's because I was left in the dark over much of the negotiations before, or perhaps it's because Papa's changed for the worse, but they're so much harsher than I expected."

She took his hand, wanting to take the anxiety and grief away from him. "I'm sorry you have to face this part of your father."

"I want him to pull out of India completely. We have no business there, especially when moving in will cause so much harm."

She couldn't believe that she was going to have to give up this very good man. "I agree. You're doing the right thing."

He gave a gentle shake of his head, that half smile she loved so much returning to hover around his lips. His gaze settled on her mouth, and she knew he wanted to kiss her. Her lips tingled with the anticipation, so she dropped her head to force herself to ignore the impulse.

"See to that and we can talk tonight. We must talk, Max, before you leave."

For the first time, concern for her shone in his eyes. "I promise."

He placed a kiss to her forehead. She closed her eyes at the warm press of his lips and fought to keep herself from leaning into the reassuring comfort he offered.

The rest of the day passed in a fog. Helena moved around the estate like a corporal ghost, accomplishing small tasks but never truly present in any of them. Even dinner would remain a blur that she could hardly remember taking part of. The only portion that would stand out for her in the months ahead was that Mr. Crenshaw had made another toast to their happiness and future children. It wasn't the toast she would remember, but the way Max had looked at her after. As if she was all he had ever wanted. And now she had to break his heart.

"Helena, dear, why don't you take some time with your Maxwell before joining us in the drawing room?" Mama came up behind her and put a gentle hand on her arm as they walked from the dining room. A knowing smile touched her features.

"Are you certain?" Helena had planned to sneak away before bed like they had last time.

Mama nodded and leaned closer. "The man is leaving tomorrow. I am not so rigid that I cannot understand you might want a moment of privacy to say goodbye. Only a moment, mind you. Take a stroll through the gallery before joining us."

Max was already standing, clearly having no intention of staying to smoke and drink with the men. Mama patted Helena's hand and followed the other women out. A moment later, Max had replaced her at Helena's side.

"Is now a good time for you?" he asked.

No. She didn't want to have this discussion with him, but there was no hope for it. She put her hand on his arm and gave him a tight smile. Without realizing that she was taking them there, she led him toward the room where she had found him last night. Along the way, she asked, "How did the rest of your meeting go?"

"Not well." His jaw was tight as he studied the paintings they passed. "All this talk of legacy has made me think very hard about the reputation I want to leave behind, for myself, the Crenshaw name, and the ironworks. It doesn't involve dishonorable contracts and exploitative labor."

"What can you do about it? I assume your father still has a large stake in the company?"

He was silent for a moment as they walked, as if weighing the burden of what he meant to say. "August and I talked before dinner. We're thinking about calling for a vote if we can't make him see reason."

"A vote to unseat him?"

"Yes, potentially. I don't want any part of the India expansion if it can't be done with some sense of fairness. I believe that if we invest, we must be only that, investors. We have to allow local leaders the autonomy to manage the project; otherwise, we're simply exploiting resources, negating the good our railroad might do."

They had come to a stop as he spoke, his words weighing down their steps.

"That's . . ." She took in a breath as she considered the real impact of that. "I'm in agreement, but you could very well break your family."

He nodded, pain evident on his face as he looked at her. "I know. But it's a break that started when my parents believed marrying off my sisters to be more important than their wishes and what was truly best for them." He studied her face as if attempting to read her thoughts. "It may very well anger your father."

She knew he was asking for her agreement in light of

that fact. The weight of the betrothal ring sat heavy on her finger. "I think you must do what you feel to be right. I'll support you."

His lips twitched in a smile as the lines on his forehead relaxed. She quickly continued walking, leading them into the room. The sky was a bit clearer tonight, so pale moonlight filtered in through the leaded glass windows, casting a pleasant glow over the cozy space. It was rather romantic.

She let go of his arm and walked to the windows. The moon was high above them with only wisps of clouds floating around it. Oh, to be anywhere beneath that moon but here. She took in a deep breath and said, "I am sorry I didn't tell you this earlier, but I wanted you to know before you left."

She turned to him only to see him smiling at her. It wasn't a joyous smile. It was the smile that said he was going to eat her up and make her enjoy it. The same devious grin he had given her last night before he had done just that and buried his face between her thighs. Blushing profusely at the memory, she held a hand up between them even as heat tumbled through her stomach. "That's not why I brought you here."

"Then talk." His grin firmly in place, he proceeded to stalk her as she backed up until her skirts touched the wall.

"How am I supposed to talk with you looking at me that way?"

"Are you saying I'm a distraction? That being alone with me makes you lose your head? Forget your chaste intentions?" He leaned forward, pressing a hand into the wall next to her. His scent very nearly overwhelmed her as he leaned in. It wasn't only his cologne. It was that she could smell *him* underneath the fragrance. She could easily source his scent from the artificial now because she had tasted it on his skin and breathed him in.

"Yes, that is precisely what I'm telling you. I have to say this, and you are not helping."

He leaned forward, almost touching her but not. The heat from his body warmed her front. It was as if he'd unleashed the magnetism he kept bottled up inside him so that she had to fight to keep herself from moving into him. His breath caressed her cheek when he said, "That's because whatever you have to say will not change the way I feel about you. I want us to be more than this, Helena. I want you in my bed every night and by my side every day."

A sharp pang tightened her chest, and she covered his mouth only to have him kiss her fingers. "Max, please, you're not making this any easier."

"Good, because I believe you are about to tell me all the ways we do not suit, when you know perfectly well that we do."

"We do suit in many ways. I admit that," she said. His brown eyes were so warm and hopeful that she had to look away as she scooted past him. Her instinct was to turn up the light, but as soon as she reached the sconce, she stopped. This was a conversation best held in half-light and shadow.

He had turned to stand silently as he watched her. The grin had changed into that delightful scowl she loved so much. Looking at him as she spoke was not an option. Instead, she walked past him and back to the window.

It took her a moment to recall the words she had practiced in her head all afternoon. The only way to make him understand was to tell him about her first marriage. Then he would know why she wasn't willing to try it again. The first time had been almost too painful to bear; this time— with Max—it would be so much worse. She sensed that if she truly allowed herself to fall in love with him, then his inevitable rejection would shatter her, splintering her into too many tiny fragments to ever be put back together again.

"I was nineteen when I married Arthur. Our family's friendship stretched back for decades, so we grew up on summer holidays by the sea and winter sleigh rides through the hills. We were friends first, long before we ever even understood what marriage was. He was honorable and good, and when his older brother and mine would play pranks on me and my sisters, he never failed to step in and defend us. He wasn't like them. He was quiet and kind."

"I know you must miss him." Max had walked closer than she had realized. His voice was right behind her, close enough that he could touch her if he chose. Close enough that it vibrated through her when he spoke. "I would never presume to push him from your heart. I only ask for a small piece for myself."

She closed her eyes to fight back the burning of tears. She wanted to tell him that he would always live in her heart, that he had already taken it all, but it would only confuse things. "He was the second son of a viscount, Lord Sansbury, whom you met. He had inherited a small estate with a decent income from an uncle, but he wasn't the match my father had hoped for me. I was supposed to marry someone destined to become an earl or a viscount, an heir to a title, not a second son.

"I haven't told Violet, but Papa even considered approaching Christian to arrange a match between us. He and Mama had a great row over it, which she won because soon after it became publicly known that Christian had invested his meager inheritance in Montague Club. Suddenly, he went from prospect to scoundrel in Papa's eyes. I didn't mind because, while Christian is handsome, I had already made my choice.

"All that to say that Arthur had to prove himself to my father. He did that by proving his affection for me. He made Papa believe that he was the best choice because he would take the best care of me. I don't think I realized that that's what won Papa over until you had to do much the same. Although, Papa already liked Arthur, so his hurdle wasn't as high as yours."

"*Did* Arthur take the best care of you?" The tone of his voice suggested that the story was making him suspect that Arthur hadn't.

She nodded and crossed her arms over her chest to fight the cold coming in through the window. Almost immediately, Max's coat settled over her shoulders, and she luxuriated in both the warmth and the fact that he was so attuned to her needs. "He did. He was a good husband. The first year was everything I had hoped for in a marriage. He was patient and attentive. We spent every free moment together. He took the time to learn my favorite things: my favorite dessert, my favorite wine, my favorite play . . . he knew it all, and I was certain that we would be happy for the rest of our lives together."

"And then what happened?"

She took a deep breath. It was difficult to find the words because she had never said them out loud before and certainly never to another person. Her heartbeat was that of a rabbit being hunted.

"And then I never conceived a child."

The words were loud in the quiet between them. She couldn't look at him to see the disappointment that would start to slowly dawn across his face as she kept talking and he finally understood what this would mean for them. Instead, she kept her gaze focused on the moonlit glow of the silver birch tree outside.

"By the end of the second year, our marriage had lost the closeness I loved. There was a distance between us that I couldn't cross. It only seemed to get wider, because I could not do the one thing I was meant to do in our marriage." Fighting past the ache in her throat, she said, "Our marriage bed had become a place of desperation where there was little room for tenderness and affection."

"But it could have been him—"

"No," she said, squashing that bit of hope in his voice. "Two physicians confirmed that I will likely never bear a child. By that time, Arthur was sick with cancer. He went from healthy to on his deathbed in a period of six months, and it is my deepest regret that I was never able to give him a child before he died. He is well and truly gone with no part of him left here to carry on."

Max's hands were on her shoulders, and he placed a kiss to the top of her head. "My God, Helena," he whispered, but she couldn't determine how he felt beyond his distress for what had happened to her. She didn't dare face him, knowing she couldn't abide his disappointment, so she simply did not move. Even when he dropped his forehead to rest on her head and nuzzled his nose into her pinned-up hair, she stayed still, silently soaking up the comfort he offered. "Was he cruel to you?"

"Cruel?" It wasn't the question she had expected. An ache welled in her throat that he would be concerned for her after what she had revealed. When she could speak again, she said, "He wasn't violent or abusive. He was cold, distant . . . angry. He tried not to be angry at me. Please understand that he was a good man. He never wanted to be angry with me, but it was there. I understood it, because I had been angry with myself."

The last time they had lain together had been not long after his diagnosis. Both of them had been reeling from what it might mean, and he had come to her bed in the night. She had hoped to comfort him, but without prelude, he had shoved up her nightdress and taken her. His grunts had been less those born of pleasure than desperation. She could still hear them. She didn't know why this one night stood out in her mind, because it wasn't that different from the others that had preceded it. Perhaps it was that he had seemed colder somehow, more distant. Or perhaps it was that she had felt shamed and humiliated as she had lain there and finally accepted that what they'd once shared was lost to her forever.

"It wasn't right that he did that to you." Max was before her, taking her face between his hands. "You know that, don't you?"

She gasped and covered her mouth with a fist, unaware

until that moment that she had relayed the shameful story out loud. "He had just found out he was dying, and he wanted a child," she said when she could finally draw breath. "I never denied him myself."

"Then you gave him your consent to be so cruel?"

She shook her head and moved away, uncomfortable with this new direction of the conversation. "My consent was given when I said *I do*. What other consent does a wife have?"

"You don't believe that." Pain and horror mingled on his face. "There is a difference between what is legal and what is right."

"Of course there is, but . . ."

But had it been right?

If August had come to her and confessed that Evan had treated her in such a way, would she tell her that it was her duty to accept? No, never! Why had she been so willing to accept that treatment for herself? She knew immediately that it was because she had felt herself deserving of it. What right did she have to tenderness when she was such a failure? What right had her body to pleasure when it couldn't perform the only thing it was made to do?

Arthur must have thought the same.

She didn't realize how violently she trembled until Max's arms came around her. "Come here," he whispered and gathered her up into his arms. She buried her face in his neck as he sat them down in the chair he had vacated last night to hold her on his lap. No matter how she tried to keep in her tears, the incessant quaking only served to shake them out of her. It didn't seem to matter, because Max appeared to be in no hurry. He stroked her back and pressed his lips to her hair, content to hold her as she had her cry. She didn't even know why she was crying—this had all happened years ago—but once the tears started they wouldn't stop until every last one of them had been wrung out of her.

Finally, she lay there against him exhausted. Hours

might have passed for all she knew. He touched her face, the pad of his thumb tracing a lazy line along her jaw. "I still love you, Helena."

Let me love you.

She had heard those words last night, savored them even, as she had made them into something more than he had meant. She had allowed herself to pretend they were in love. Never once had she allowed herself to believe that he really did. Affection? Yes. But love?

She sat up, dislodging his hand. "Max, please. I know that you feel some affection for me, but love is a strong word."

"A true word."

She shook her head. "Then that is all the more reason we should end this now before that emotion has a chance to deepen."

"End this?" His brows drew together, and she ached at the pain in his eyes. "Why?"

"I cannot bear your children. Children that you want. Children your parents want you to have. You heard the many toasts your father has given in honor of us and the many children we shall have. He even gave you a very harsh ultimatum all in the effort to have grandchildren. The legacy of Crenshaw Iron must be preserved at any cost." She swallowed over the lump in her throat. "That cost is me. Us."

He was shaking his head before she had finished. "No, that's not fair. Don't hold my father against me."

She covered his mouth before he could say more, and he glared at her. "I'm not. You yourself have even said that you want children. Perhaps not now, not next year, but you want children, Max. You can't deny that having a family is something you have wanted for yourself."

Taking hold of her wrist, he moved her hand away from his mouth. "Am I not allowed any say in this?"

"No. Perhaps. I don't know." Even though his arms were the only place she wanted to be, she made herself stand, and dropped his coat onto the arm of the chair. "I don't think your feelings are honest, because I am telling you that what you want is impossible. Therefore, you change what you want so you can have me." She shook her head, aware that she was so exhausted she wasn't even making sense anymore. Taking a deep breath, she said, "I believe that you think you want me, and right now, in this moment, you are willing to say whatever will get you to that goal. You are an honorable man, so you probably even believe yourself. But it's a lie you're telling yourself. You can't so easily make yourself not want a child. Believe me, I tried for many years."

He stood. "You're right. I do want children—*did* want children—but I want you more, Helena."

"For now, yes, but one day you'll feel differently. Go home, Max. Go back to your life in Manhattan and Newport and don't think about me anymore."

"You ask the impossible."

"Please, go back to your life and I'll go back to mine."

"And what if I still want you to be my wife?"

"Then I feel sorry for both of us." She hurried from the room before he could do more than call her name. The truth was that she knew he would not want her later. Once the gravity of her inability to have children penetrated, he would be relieved that she had let him go.

"Helena!"

She whirled to see that he had followed her and was in the corridor coming toward her. Fresh tears wet her cheeks. "Don't come any closer." Desperation filled her voice. If he did, she wouldn't be able to push him away again; she knew the limits of her own strength. If they spent another night together, then her resolve might very well melt away.

He stopped abruptly, hurt and despair evident on his face.

"Please." She turned then and ran, holding the shredded pieces of her heart together as she did.

Chapter 23

❦

If you are not too long, I will wait here for you all my life.

OSCAR WILDE

Max sat on the sofa and held his face in his hands. It didn't help that they smelled like her. Lilies and the sweet salt of her body.

That conversation had not gone at all as he had anticipated. He had been prepared for Helena to assert that the physical distance between her life in London and his life in New York was too great to overcome. He'd had a list of counterarguments ready in his head.

They could compromise. He'd agree to return to London every year. Or she could reside here for three months and spend the rest of the year with him—six months if she balked at that. He'd been prepared to agree to any amount of time if it meant that he could have her.

Her next declaration would have been something about her family, and then his family. He would have argued against both, because nothing mattered except what was between them. Nothing except the fact that he loved her. That she loved him if only she would let herself acknowledge it. Then he would have kissed her and petted her until she admitted that she felt the same. They would have spent the night again in her bed, and in the morning he would have kissed her goodbye, secure in the knowledge that she would be joining him in a few months at most.

This . . . this was so much more severe than he had ever dared to imagine. He had known that her first marriage had produced no children, and he had never seriously contemplated the reason for that. Violet had mentioned once that Helena's husband had died from some sort of intestinal cancer, and Max had merely assumed that the man's illness had prevented or at least greatly interfered in their plans for children.

"Max."

August stood framed in the doorway, her smile fading as she saw the expression on his face. He could only imagine how he must look. His eyes were dry but burning. His chest felt hollow, ravaged by grief and anger and despair in a way he had never experienced.

She walked cautiously into the room as if expecting something to jump out at her. "What's happened? Where is Helena?" She looked around, searching the shadows.

"Gone. To her room maybe." His voice sounded vacant and dull.

Her hand settled on his shoulder, and he nearly shrank from the comfort. "Did you argue?"

He shook his head. "Not really, no." Taking in a shuddering breath, he said, "I told her I love her, and she told me the reason we can never marry."

"Oh, Max, I'm so sorry." She sank onto the sofa beside him and put her arms around him. "I would have sworn she would say yes to you. I know this was all pretend, but I saw the way she looked at you and you at her."

"It's not for lack of affection."

She was silent as she pulled away to study him, a crease forming between her brows. "Then why?"

He didn't mean to talk about it. Helena might not want anyone else to know, but the words came out of him of their own volition. "She's unable to bear children, and she believes that if we marry, I will eventually resent her for it."

August let out a little gasp of surprise even though she tried to stifle it. Eventually, she said, "And is she correct in her belief?"

He looked at her so sharply, she flinched. "No! How could I resent her for something she cannot control or change?"

"Then you're prepared to accept that you won't father children if you marry her?"

It was his turn to flinch. "Dammit, August." She was always pointed and honest, getting to the meat of any issue facing them.

He stood and walked to the window, his gaze locked on that damned tree that had overseen the worst heartbreak of his entire life. That was the crux of it. That was what kept him here, paralyzed with pain and rage. His instinct had been and still was to fight for Helena. She had quickly come to mean more to him than anyone he had ever met.

But what if there was a kernel of truth in her words? Not that he could ever resent her, but the part about wanting children.

He had always seen himself having children. He had always known that one day the reins of Crenshaw Iron would go to his child. And he had reveled in that. Found security and purpose in those dreams of the future. Hell, Helena had even come to feature in some of his wilder imaginings as the mother of that child.

What if he couldn't make that longing go away so easily?

He wanted to rip the thought out by its roots and tear it apart. He despised himself that he couldn't because a thread of truth kept it intact.

Even as he acknowledged that, he also accepted that it didn't matter. He wanted Helena more than anything else.

"Excuse me," he said as he made his way from the room, his need to see her and reassure her overcoming everything.

He almost went directly to her room but changed his mind. Instead, he went to his room, locked the door, and took the small oil lamp from the bedside table. With renewed purpose, he let himself into the cramped passageway and went to her room. Pausing at the door, he listened for any sounds coming from within. It would not do to walk in while a maid was helping her undress. He wouldn't mind, but the poor maid might be scandalized. Hearing nothing, he pushed open the door.

A low fire burned in the hearth, and a single sconce inside the door was lit, but the room was empty. Her bed was turned down waiting for her, but she was nowhere to be found. Cursing softly, he debated waiting but determined it would be best to return to his room to do so, lest a servant get too suspicious.

He waited an hour, thinking that perhaps she had managed to return to the drawing room despite her tears and finished the evening with the others. But when he checked, her room was still vacant. He returned twice more throughout the night, and even took a few tours of the house, but short of knocking on every bedroom door, he didn't know how to find her. The poor maid he'd come across on one of his outings had seemed frightened by his query.

Dawn came and went as he waited in her room. Finally, he had no choice but to accept that he wouldn't get to talk to her alone again before he left.

The morning was cold and gray with the promise of snow to come. Max dressed in sharp, efficient movements, eschewing the efforts of Farthington's man, who gave him a look of disapproval as he delivered a steaming jug of water.

"We should have shaved you *before* you dressed, sir." The man took a place inside Max's bedroom door like a sentry awaiting his orders.

"I'm capable of dressing myself, Howard."

"Yes, you are, sir." However, he made no move to leave.

Rolling his eyes, Max leaned forward to better see the mirror and tilted his head back. The razor trembled in his hand, and he grunted as he nicked his neck.

"Allow me, sir." Howard reached forward, divesting him of the razor. The man continued to make quick work of tidying the line of Max's beard.

Max hadn't slept at all. He was tired and cranky, near despair with the knowledge that he was losing Helena and there was nothing he could do about it because he had to return to New York and face the labor strike that was almost certainly waiting for him.

"Are you almost ready?" Papa said from the door.

Howard adeptly stepped back as Max turned his head. "Yes. Have you been down to breakfast?"

Papa frowned at the unexpected question. "Eggs and kippers. Did they not bring you a tray?"

"Was Helena there?" he asked, ignoring the question.

"No, I don't believe she was. Why?" Then his frown deepened. "Have you quarreled?"

"I wanted to see her before I left." Finished with the shave, he quickly thanked Howard, who gave a cursory bow and left. Then Max picked up the washcloth and held it to the nick to stanch the trickle of blood.

"I'm sure she'll come out with the others. They're prepared to see you off with the pomp befitting a son of the house."

"I'd like a moment alone with her." The blood flow seemed to have stopped, so he tossed the cloth aside and took his coat from the hook where Howard had left it and shrugged it on. His trunks had already been taken out of the room when his breakfast tray had arrived. It still sat untouched on the table.

Papa took his watch out of his pocket. The gold chain caught the light. "There's not much time for that. Your train leaves in a half hour. It will take nearly that long to get to the station."

"Dammit." He couldn't stop the increasing feeling of urgency that had made itself known throughout the morning. "Then I can take another one."

"Perhaps, but you'll risk missing your ship. You have to get to New York. You've already delayed enough as it is. With the threat of a strike hanging over us, it might already be too late. I only agreed to this little sojourn because I cannot overstate how important it is to have Farthington on our side. This marriage must happen, so if you quarreled—"

"We are fine, Papa." He yelled without meaning to, but he was tired of this charade. "Helena is to be my wife, and nothing will stop that." If only he could make the woman herself believe that.

Papa nodded with satisfaction. "Good to hear. You have done well, my boy." He patted him on the back. "Your mother is waiting to say goodbye."

Giving himself one last glance in the mirror, he followed Papa down the corridor outside and down the stairs. His sisters were waiting at the bottom with hugs and well-wishes. August's eyes asked the question she wouldn't put voice to: Had he made things right with Helena? He couldn't answer, so he gave a quick shake of his head and spent the next few minutes saying goodbye to Evan and Christian. His mother came downstairs when he was finished, taking up several more precious minutes of his time. It's not that he didn't want to properly say goodbye to her, but that he needed to see Helena. He needed to let her know that he wouldn't give up on them.

His desperation reached a fever pitch when the small group finally made it to the entryway only to find Lord and Lady Farthington standing there alone. He managed cordial goodbyes before he asked, "Where is Helena?"

"Outside, I believe," said Lady Farthington with a kind smile.

Max stepped through the open door to see the carriage already waiting for him and loaded with his trunks. Helena stood at the top of the steps with her sisters on either side of her. She didn't look at him, instead keeping her gaze straight ahead.

"Good morning," he said to Penelope, the sister closest to him.

"Goodbye, dear Maxwell. It was lovely to meet you," she said. Christine joined in, but Helena was suspiciously silent.

"Goodbye, Helena," he said as his family and her parents joined them on the steps.

"Goodbye, Max." She offered him her hand, the pleasant facade she often wore firmly in place. It couldn't hide the sadness she felt, however. Her eyes shimmered with it. He kissed her hand with regret as everything inside him said that this felt all wrong. She should be coming with him. They should not live an ocean apart.

But, of course, they must. There was no other way right now. Her father mumbled something about train times, and he reluctantly let her hand go.

"Goodbye," he said for what felt like the hundredth time to the group at large.

And then he turned and took the steps that would lead him farther away from her. Each one a tiny echo of the hollowness inside him. He might have been able to keep going, but at the carriage door, he turned in time to see pain cross her face.

The very wrongness of what they were doing jarred him into action. Taking the steps two at a time, he hurried back to her. Heedless of anyone else, he took her in his arms and kissed her, deeply and thoroughly as she should always be kissed. One of her sisters giggled, her mother gasped in outrage, and Christian let out a low whoop of encouragement. But then they all faded away as she kissed him back, and it was only the two of them.

He kissed her until he couldn't breathe anymore, and when he pulled back far enough to take in air, he breathed her in. She stared up at him with her wet morning glory eyes, looking more beautiful and fragile than he had ever seen her.

"I love you," he whispered, touching her sweet face. "Always."

Her lips were slightly swollen from his kiss, and she made a soft sound of regret in the back of her throat. He pressed another kiss to her mouth and then slowly let her go. Without another glance back, he hurried down to the carriage and left.

Chapter 24

❧

*There are no more thorough prudes than
those who have some little secret to hide.*
                                           GEORGE SAND

The day turned sunny and warm enough to melt the remaining snow. It was in complete opposition to the despair and misery churning inside Helena. She tried to tell herself that life would quickly return to normal, but even she didn't know what that would look like anymore. What was normal after knowing the sheer bliss a few hours in Max's arms would bring her? How was she supposed to go about her day when he had taken part of her with him? Nevertheless, she tried.

After watching in silence as his carriage had disappeared through the gates of Claremont Hall, she had skillfully dodged the concern of his sisters and escaped to the desk she used in the library. There she replied to the correspondence she hadn't been able to get to while Max had been here. She answered queries from Mr. Wilson about enlarging the residence hall's kitchen and sent instructions to the orphanage for the annual Christmas dinner. A tele-

gram had arrived from the furniture maker about the need
to substitute birch for pine in the bedroom sets because of
a supply issue, so she jotted down a response and had a
footman take it to the village. She wrote to Charlotte, who
was preparing the first set of women and children to move
into the residence hall in early January, to reassure her that
the linens were set for delivery on the first of that month.

After tea but before dinner, she spoke with August about
the skills-training program they were developing for the
women who wanted to work in the forge. August had taken
the lead in finding men willing to teach the residents and
had some promising prospects. Instruction would begin as
soon as the women moved in. Then, after a dinner of polite
conversation where everyone pretended to ignore the fact
that Max had kissed her in front of them, she joined the
group in a game of charades in the drawing room.

It wasn't until after a maid helped her dress for bed and
she crawled between the sheets that Helena allowed herself
to feel the abject misery that had been clawing at her all
day. Max was gone, and as far as she knew, she would never
see him again. Or worse. She would be forced to see him in
polite social situations when he inevitably came back to
visit his sisters.

What if one day he returned with a wife? Would she be
forced to watch him with another woman? To sit in silence
with a smile painted on her face as he gazed upon the
woman in adoration?

It was unthinkable. She tossed and turned for a while but
finally drifted off to sleep only to be awakened in the small
hours of the morning by a blood-chilling screech. She sat up
in bed certain that her own tortured mind had conjured the
sound when it happened again. Gathering her dressing gown
around her, she ran out her door. Voices raised in panicked
tones drew her down the corridor and around a corner.

"Isabelle, you must stop this. You're hysterical! Tell me
what's happened." Mama was trying to soothe her sister to

no avail. The woman took in great big gasping breaths of air but could not do more than sob and gesture vaguely toward the door of her bedroom.

Papa was the first to gather himself and approach her door. Usually so certain of himself, he hesitated, his hand hovering above the door handle. Helena hurried to his side and put a reassuring hand on his arm. Other guests filtered into the corridor, their confused voices rising in alarm.

Papa pushed the door open and whispered, "For the love of God."

Hereford was in Isabelle's bed, his eyes open and vacant as he stared at the ceiling. The blanket covered him but was low enough on his chest to imply that he was nude. Hereford and her aunt were lovers—had been lovers—and he had died in her bed! Helena covered her mouth in shock. Papa came to his senses first and turned back to the guests in the corridor, reassuring them that all was fine. His words fell on deaf ears, because Isabelle had found her voice and was saying, "He's dead. I can't believe he's dead," over and over again. Mama wisely led her away into her own bedroom. The damage had been done, however. Hereford's name was sent volleying from one person to the next in scandalized whispers as servants had joined the fray.

"We must send for a physician." Papa's voice rose above it all, directing a footman to see to the task, even though it was far too late to save the man.

Finally able to tear her gaze from Hereford, Helena turned to help direct people away from the scene, only to come face-to-face with Camille, who had pushed her way past the crowd to the doorway.

"Oh my God!" the younger woman gasped as she saw Hereford. Her face blanched, and she touched a hand to the wall to steady herself.

"I'm so sorry, Camille," Helena began, rushing over to her.

Camille dropped to her knees as if all strength had left

her body; her hands shook as she brought them up to cover her face. Helena knelt beside her and took her trembling body into her arms. "He's gone," Camille whispered. "I can't believe he's gone." Then she threw back her head and laughed.

The shock of finding her husband dead and in the bed of his lover must have been too much to bear. Helena helped her get to her feet and kept an arm around her. Thankfully, August and Violet met them in the corridor. "Send for tea," Helena said, as August took up position on Camille's other side. Together they got her back to her bedroom as Violet sent a maid for tea. By the time they brought her to the chair near the hearth in her room, she was trembling with sobs.

The rest of the day was overtaken with the aftermath of Hereford's death. Two physicians came out to the house, both confirming that he likely died from an aneurysm. That didn't stop vicious rumors from circulating belowstairs that he might have been poisoned. Most of the guests opted to leave that day, so Helena was left to fill the role of hostess as Mama tended to Isabelle. It wasn't until almost midnight that she returned to her own room alone.

She was so tired that her hands shook with fatigue, but she sat down at her desk and wrote a letter to Max to tell him what had happened. It was hardly necessary. He was on a ship now, and she was certain someone in his family would inform him of what had transpired, but she needed him now. She needed his arms around her and the comfort and security only he could bring her. Writing him was the only way to feel close to him, so she took out a sheet of parchment and relayed the entire terrible affair to him. When she was done, she curled up in bed and hugged the pillow he had slept on. Tears came seemingly without end.

She didn't cry for Hereford. She cried because life was fragile. She cried because she missed Max. She cried because she might have made the biggest mistake of her life in letting him go, but she didn't know how to live through

his eventual disdain of her. She knew that she wouldn't.
Those last months with Arthur's coldness had been the
worst of her life. She couldn't bear it from Max.

ONE MONTH LATER

The rain had turned to slush an hour ago, but Helena was
on a mission and could not go home until she had finished
it, much to the consternation of Ostler. He'd silently endured their morning at the new London Home for Young
Women with his typical grace, standing sentry as she had
directed a furniture delivery. Their first twenty-five women,
along with their children, had been settled into their flats
the previous week, with another twenty-five due in two
days. There was still much to do before they could be settled properly, but the incessant rain that had started at midday had ensured that another wagon load of furniture would
have to wait until tomorrow to be delivered.

She should have returned home, but with a couple of
hours to spare, she made a stop she had been wanting to
make for weeks. It was probably ill-advised, but here she
was stepping into the very masculine shop of Truefitt and
Hill on St. James's. The warm scents of leather and spice
greeted her as a man looked up at her from behind the
counter. Ostler paused to shake off the umbrella before following her in with a severe expression on his face.

"Good afternoon, my lady," said the man behind the
counter. "How can I help?" His surprised expression had
quickly settled into polite inquisitiveness.

"I . . ." She found herself tongue-tied. The store was a
barbershop that also traded in cologne and other grooming
products for men, so she had never found a reason to come
here before today. She was slightly out of her element and
at a loss to explain her visit without giving herself away.
Her longing for Max had brought her here. "My father,
Lord Farthington, is one of your patrons."

"Oh, why yes, his lordship is here often." The man straightened, suddenly more interested in her.

"I thought so. I hope you can help me. I am looking for a gift for him and my brother, and I hoped you knew what cologne they both prefer."

"Of course." He pulled out a leather-bound ledger from beneath the counter and flipped through some pages. "Here it is. Lord Farthington prefers a bay rum." He walked across the room to a display case and took out a green bottle. "This, my lady." He splashed a drop on a small piece of parchment and held it out for her.

The pungent scent had her wrinkling her nose. It was one she didn't like. "Yes, that's it."

He nodded and set it on the counter before moving to consult the book again. As he did, she let her gaze roam over the hundreds of small bottles in the case. One of them had to be the scent Max wore. She could kick herself for not asking him about it, but it was hardly something that came up over polite discussion. The first nights after he left, she had been able to close her eyes and remember his smell. She could feel the warmth of his skin against her and the way butterflies took flight in her stomach when she breathed him in. But that had been fading lately. She had told herself that it was a good thing, that she had to move on with her life. But she hadn't listened. So here she was in this shop desperately hoping to find him here among the bottles so that she could take him home and sleep with his scent on her pillow tonight. No, she might put it on her skin so that she could close her eyes and pretend that he had touched her.

The scandalous thought had her blushing in the middle of the store. Before she knew what she was doing, she was uncorking bottles and smelling their contents, intent on finding the one that smelled most like Max.

"My lady?" The clerk drew up short as he approached. "Lord Rivendale wears this one." He picked up a brown bottle. "It's from Grant and Company with leather base notes."

She nodded without looking at him. "Yes, I'll take that one, too." She wrinkled her nose at one that smelled like licorice and put it back on the shelf. "Do you have something richer? Something like . . ." She bit her lip as she thought of a proper description for her memory of Max's cologne. "Orange blossom, perhaps, or bergamot with a smoky tinge. Something deep and warm."

Setting the bottle for her brother beside the one for her father, he said, "You'll be looking for something in this area." He indicated a row near the top filled with green and blue bottles. "Bergamot, lemon, orange blossom with a hint of leather." He selected one and removed the lid, holding it out for her.

Too crisp. It needed more texture. "No, not that one."

They tried three more before she found it. The unassuming square bottle was made of thick blue glass. As soon as she breathed in, she recalled burying her face in Max's neck as he moved over her, breathing him in as his groan born of sheer lust filled her ears. She flushed all the way down to the tips of her toes. She was certain her eyes must be dilated with remembered pleasure, so she kept her head tilted downward as she clutched the bottle.

"Would you . . . would you like that one?" the man asked.

"Yes." Her voice was hoarse and low. "Please wrap it up with the others," she said, louder this time.

"Very good, your ladyship."

Traffic and rain made the drive home very slow. She tried not to think of the cologne or the scandalous things she planned to do with it later while sitting across from Ostler, but she wasn't successful. As soon as the carriage rolled to a stop outside her home, she bounded out. If Huxley hadn't stopped her inside, she would have run to her room.

"Telegram for you, ma'am." He held out a yellow sheet of paper. When she looked at him in question, he added, "The telegraph boy brought it round earlier this afternoon."

To: Lady Helena March, 43 Berkeley Square, London

I miss you STOP How long must I wait QUERY

From: Mr. Maxwell Crenshaw, Crenshaw Iron Works,
New York, NY

Tears wet her eyes before she could stop them. Part of her had made herself believe that he had already moved on. He'd sent a few letters since returning home. One regarding Hereford's death. One in response to her query about his Christmas plans—he'd spent the day with extended family. Another to let her know that his negotiations with his employees had resulted in avoiding a strike. His letters were so calm, friendly, and direct to the point that she hadn't believed he ached for her as she did for him.

Holding the package with the cologne tight against her chest, she let herself imagine what it would be like to end this misery for both of them. To tell him that he didn't have to wait at all. It would be as near to bliss as she would ever get.

"Will there be a reply, milady?"

Helena blinked back the ache of tears and said, "Yes, I'll write one out."

He gave an abbreviated bow. "I'll have it sent immediately."

Hurrying to her desk, she pulled out a plain sheet of paper and wrote, *One month is not enough.* When enough time had passed, he would come to his senses and realize he wanted his legacy more than he wanted her. She was certain of that.

His reply came via telegram later that night. *How long?*

She went to bed with those words in her head, imagining his impatient and gruff voice saying them against her ear as she fell asleep in a cloud of his scent.

Chapter 25

*I can live alone, if self-respect, and circum-
stances require me so to do.*

CHARLOTTE BRONTË

MARCH 1876

Today marked three months since Max had seen Helena. Three months since he had touched her skin,
tasted her kiss, and smelled her perfume. They had been
three of the longest, most hellish months of his life. Aside
from battling Crenshaw Iron's demons—convincing the
board to support his solution to dealing with the workers'
demands over his father's more authoritarian approach had
not been easy—he'd had to battle his own personal devils.
Helena had yet to choose him, and he didn't know what to do
with that. He'd managed to convince himself that if he gave
her time alone, she would come to accept that his love for her
wasn't going away. Now he wondered if perhaps she was the
one who had moved on.

His second telegram demanding a timeline had gone
unanswered. Instead, a letter had arrived several weeks
later in which she had studiously avoided addressing the

topic as she gushed about the success of the training program she and August had implemented for the female residents of her charity. He hadn't pressed her again, preferring to congratulate her on the accomplishment and resign himself to the fact that she would need more time. Now he wondered if not pushing harder had been a mistake.

Violet's child had been born a couple of weeks ago at the end of February. Christian's telegram had alerted him of the baby's arrival and assured him of the good health of both mother and child. Max had immediately thought of Helena and how she might be feeling. It had to be difficult for her to watch someone she cared about go through the birth of a child knowing it was something she would never experience for herself. He'd sent a telegram asking how she was doing. Her reply had been quick and to the point—*Good. Thank you.*

He hadn't heard from her since, but he *felt* something was changing. An ache had taken root in his chest, and he'd found no relief from it no matter how many hours he worked a day.

"What do you say, Maxwell? Another round?" Walter, the man who spoke, was one of the board members who had taken Max's side in the debate against his father. He gestured at the half-filled tumbler before Max.

Max blinked, forcing his mind back to the table in the private room at Delmonico's and the five men he'd had dinner with. They were men of industry Max had known for years, and they met every month to discuss business and current events. "Actually, I was thinking of retiring early," Max said.

Suddenly, the thought of spending another hour out was exhausting. He usually enjoyed these dinners but tonight wanted nothing more than to sit in front of his fire at home sipping a brandy and remembering the night in Helena's bed at Claremont Hall.

"Are you ill?" Walter asked, concern clouding his features.

"No, a bit tired." He pushed back from the table and stood; the others rose to wish him a good night. "Good evening, gentlemen." A waiter hurried away to retrieve his coat, hat, and gloves.

The streets were dark, and winter hadn't yet loosened its grip on the city. By the time he got home a quarter hour later, his fingers were numb and that brandy sounded even better.

"Evening, Charles," he greeted his butler after hurrying inside.

"Good evening, Mr. Crenshaw," Charles answered, helping him out of his coat. "The day's post is in your study."

"Anything interesting?"

"A letter from London."

A lump of anxiety churned in his stomach. He didn't have to ask who the letter was from. Somehow, he already knew.

"Will there be anything else, sir?" Charles asked.

"No, thank you. That's all for tonight." Max couldn't seem to look away from the open door of his study, the letter calling to him.

"Very well. Good night."

"Good night." As Charles disappeared down the hall leading to the back of the house, Max managed to get his legs to work and made his way to the study.

A pile of correspondence sat waiting on the corner of his desk. He ignored it briefly to pour himself a bit of brandy and take a swallow. It warmed him on the way down, giving him the strength to approach the stack. As he'd suspected, a letter from Helena sat on top. Her beautiful, flowing script stared back at him.

Taking another swallow, he picked it up and sat in the armchair before the fire, staring at the envelope the whole time. Judging from the date, she had written it the very night of the child's birth. This would be the letter. The one that let him know if she wanted him for her future or not. There was no sense in prolonging things. He tore through the sealed envelope and read.

My dearest Maxwell,

I am writing to convey my happiness on the birth of your niece. You will no doubt have been apprised of the particulars by the time you receive this letter. Violet was gracious enough to ask that I attend to her, along with August. The labor was as straightforward as such a thing can be and ended in the small hours of the morning. Violet was strong and brave during the entire ordeal. I confess it was Christian that I worried for near the end. I have never seen a man so distraught and agitated as he. He refused to leave your sister's side and was there when the sweet little creature made her debut. Rosalie Violet Halston is a perfectly healthy baby girl, and her mother is well.

The joy she brought to both Violet and Christian confirmed that my decision in regard to us is the right one. You deserve every happiness, and that includes children and securing your legacy. I think it's best that we do not correspond anymore.

Yours affectionately and forever,
Helena

Max's vision blurred as he stared at the letter in his hand. Helena's name swam on the page as tears filled his eyes. All this time he had allowed himself to hope that if he waited her out she would finally accept that he refused to give up on them. But here she was, telling him that she wouldn't write to him anymore. What was he to do with all contact with her severed?

Yelling in outrage, he grabbed the tumbler filled with brandy and threw it into the fire where it burst into a shower of glass. The flames raged higher for an instant before settling again. Max fell back into his chair and dropped his head into his hands.

"Is everything—" Charles hurried into the room but stopped when he noticed the state of his employer.

"Leave me," Max growled, not looking up until he heard the discreet click of the latch as the door shut.

A hundred different ideas swirled in his head. He could go to her and negotiate, he could write to her and lay out the reasons they would suit, he could proclaim that he loved her more than his legacy; but none of those would work. He knew in his heart that she wouldn't believe him. Time is the only thing that would convince her.

Leaving her letter on the floor where he'd dropped it, he walked from the armchair to his desk and pulled out a sheet of paper from the drawer.

My dearest Helena,

My feelings for you have not changed, but I have accepted that I have no choice but to respect your feelings on our relationship. August assures me that her position is secure with the dock project. I believe the best recourse now is to end our betrothal. I will leave the announcement to your discretion.

Yours,
Maxwell

The day after receiving the letter from Max, Helena sat having tea with Violet and August in the Leigh townhome in Belgravia. Christian and Evan were at their club working, and the baby was sleeping, so it was only the three of them in Violet's morning room. It was the first time since Rosie's birth nearly a month ago that they had been able to get together. Violet appeared tired but blissfully happy. August was in good spirits, having taken the afternoon away from her work to be here.

They had spent the first half hour catching up. Rosie was healthy and strong, August's dock project was moving along successfully, and the London Home for Young Women was nearing the final stage of completion with the factory almost finished. Women and children had been residing in Penhurst Hall for two months now, and despite a few minor setbacks, Helena couldn't have asked for a more successful opening.

She should be happier, but the pain of losing Max seemed to only get worse. This last letter had almost broken her, for it signaled the end. He was moving on, and once their betrothal was finished, he would be done with her and out of her life except for a peripheral presence as the brother of her dear friends. It was no less than what she had wanted, but it was still bitter medicine.

She waited for a break in the conversation before she said, "Maxwell has written that he believes it's time to put an end to our ruse."

August paused, her mouth dropping open slightly in shock as she glanced at her sister. "Well . . ." She appeared to be searching for the right words.

Helena continued, "With both of our fathers battling the objections from the board of Crenshaw Iron regarding the Indian railroad, I believe they'll be too busy to care. We shouldn't encounter any resistance." Over the past few months, Max had followed through on his word and gathered the support of the board in New York to vote against the expansion. Mr. Crenshaw had been distressed to say the least. Her own father had been unhappy as well, as it would greatly slow the railroad progress for England.

The sapphire on her finger caught the light, and she felt a stab of regret that she wouldn't be able to wear it anymore. As foolish as it was, having it on her finger was like carrying a small piece of him with her wherever she went.

Violet went quiet.

Catching Helena's line of sight, August added, "It's simply too bad you won't be able to wear it anymore. It's beautiful on you."

"But this is good," Violet said, her voice suspiciously bright. At their questioning looks, she continued, "Obviously, I'd prefer Max with Helena, but if it's not meant to be." She shrugged. "Amelia has been writing to me, absolutely horrified that her parents are planning to bring her here next month." To Helena she explained, "Amelia Van der Meer is a very dear friend from New York. Her parents hope to find her a titled husband. She's always adored Max, so I hinted that she might come to an arrangement of sorts with him to avoid coming here altogether." Mistaking Helena's expression of horror to be about potentially revealing their deception, she said, "Oh, don't worry, I didn't tell her the whole truth of things. After the first flurry of excitement in the New York newspapers, the gossip about you two seems to have fizzled. Max is very good about not talking about his personal life, so I believe many rightfully assume that with the distance between you, the attachment ran its course. I simply encouraged the thought."

Helena sat with that a moment as she imagined how she might feel knowing he was courting someone else. Fury and heartbreak churned within her. Still, she managed to keep her voice calm when she asked, "And how does your brother feel about that? Does he favor Miss Van der Meer?"

Violet shrugged one shoulder. "Max has said in the past that he admires her. I think it only natural that the two of them form an attachment."

Rising panic forced the next words out of Helena. "But he has no need for an attachment now."

"That's true," August added carefully. "But it would certainly ease the consequences of Papa's anger."

"Yes, it would," Violet agreed. "The Van der Meers are very good friends of our family. I suggested it because I know that Max has escorted her to various functions. He even wrote to me about attending a party at the Van der Meers over Christmas."

"Now that you mention it"—August waved a finger in the air—"in his last letter he mentioned having dinner at their house. That must have been earlier this month."

Violet smiled at Helena. "See, there's no need for concern. I should think Papa would be soothed by the knowledge of another engagement. Of course, we must make it appear that you dropped Max. We wouldn't want people to think anything less. They should think he is merely soothing the pain of your loss with Amelia."

But Helena didn't want him with another woman.

She had tried to be selfless and noble where he was concerned, but it turned out she wasn't very good at it. Every day and night without him had been one long, excruciating exercise in missing him. Rising, she walked to the window that overlooked the garden. She had known that he might marry, but this was too soon. She needed time, another year, maybe two, to get over him before he married.

"Well, I suppose it's for the best, then," Helena said.

The room was silent, prompting her to turn and face the sisters. They sat with identical expressions of shock and hurt. Over the lump in her throat, Helena asked, "Why are you both looking at me like that? You knew this betrothal would end."

A look passed between the sisters that Helena could not read. Before she had an opportunity to interpret it, the nanny appeared in the doorway. "Excuse the interruption, my lady, but Lady Rosalie has awakened from her nap."

"Thank you, Nora." Violet rose and said, "Please excuse me while I see to her ladyship." To Helena she said, "Don't leave before I come back."

The moment Violet was gone, August walked over to her and took her hand. "Please don't be upset by this, but in a moment of despair, Max shared with me the reason you refuse to marry him. I don't think he meant to. I simply came upon him not long after you had talked that last night at Claremont Hall."

"Why didn't you say anything?" She was relieved that someone knew besides herself and Max.

"It didn't seem like it was any of my concern, and you never mentioned it." August hesitated. "I understand why you would be wary of involving yourself in another marriage, and perhaps you are right. That is a choice that you have to make. However, I can tell you that what Max feels for you is real. In every letter he writes to me and to Violet, he asks about you, and not simply in passing. He wants to know that we are taking care of you. He wants to know that you are happy."

"That's very kind of you to tell me, but facing a future devoid of children is more serious than a temporary heartache."

"But what of your future?" August asked. "You seem prepared to sacrifice what you want without even considering that you might have it."

"I don't expect you to understand, August, and I appreciate your concern, but it would be very unfair of me to trap him into a marriage. He might change his mind in two years or ten years, and then where will we be? I won't be stuck in a lifelong marriage with a man who resents me more with every passing year. It almost happened once, and I could not bear it with Max."

August surprised her by smiling gently. "Then you can get a divorce."

"A divorce?" The word sat like an expletive on her tongue that she wasn't supposed to know. "I don't think that's possible. Very few are able to obtain a divorce. It takes an act of Parliament. I should think they wouldn't relent."

August's smile widened. "Helena, dear, I think you're forgetting one very important detail. Max is not an Englishman. When you marry him, you'll become an American. No act of Parliament will be required. Divorce will be expensive, and I'm certain there will be a scandal, but it's not unheard of in our courts."

Helena went hot all over, her skin prickling as it grew too tight. Then she became cold, a chill sweeping down her body. "I could never divorce."

But could she marry the love of her life, knowing that she could set him free if he chose it later?

"It's not ideal, I admit, but what if accepting that you have this option . . . this opportunity to free him if it comes to it, helps you take this chance?"

Helena shook her head. "It's unthinkable." Her entire life she had been taught to believe that marriage was an unbreakable union. *She* believed that. If she said the words *I do* to him, she would mean them for the rest of her life.

But this had never been about her own intention, had it? Had it been solely about her happiness, she would have proposed to him months ago on that train ride to find Violet, probably. How had she been so stupid to never consider that there might be a way? That as much as it would hurt her, she could release him from their marriage if it came to it?

Still, doubts raised their heads. "I . . . I don't know that he would agree. Perhaps he's already decided that it was right to have this distance between us. Has he been talking to Amelia Van der Meer?" She wanted to believe that Violet had invented the story to urge her to confront Max, but she wasn't entirely certain of that.

August shrugged. "I suppose you'll have to ask him. But please think on it, Helena. I know I have no right to ask you to do this; however, I've come to think of you as a sister. I want you to be happy, and I know that Max could make you happy. I know that he *wants* to make you happy." August hugged her and very softly whispered against her ear, "You deserve to be happy."

Helena squeezed her eyes closed against the tears that threatened. Could she actually do it? Could she go into a marriage with divorce on her mind? It was nearly unfathomable.

"Your parents won't like me very much when they find out the truth. Your father has been very clear about his legacy."

August smiled and met her gaze. "And when have the Crenshaw siblings ever allowed our parents control of our lives? Remember, you'll have all three of us on your side. I can't ask you to take on their displeasure, but I promise that if you do, you won't do it alone."

By the time Helena returned home an hour later, she was shaking inside with the possibility August had presented her. She should be preparing for the dinner she would be attending later that evening with a few members of the orphanage's board, but instead, she wandered aimlessly around the house, her sight turned inward on the possibility presented to her. Part of her demanded she take it, while another, possibly bigger part of her quaked in fear at what it might mean. She'd have to give up her life here. She'd have to accept that he may actually one day want to divorce. More immediately, she'd have to face the possibility that Max had already changed his mind.

Chapter 26

✤

If I had a flower for every time I thought of you . . . I could walk through my garden forever.

ALFRED LORD TENNYSON

TWO WEEKS LATER
MANHATTAN

Crenshaw House looked as if someone had taken a French chateau and placed it squarely in the midst of Fifth Avenue. Its steeply pitched roof was tiled in blue slate and featured a series of dormer windows and matching towers on each end of the house, making it appear even taller than its five floors. Its limestone and painted stucco facade made the creamy white stand out even more against the sea of brownstones around it. Helena was quite taken aback at the sight of such extravagance. She had known the Crenshaws were wealthy, but she had only known them in London. Here they lived like veritable royalty.

The doorbell was answered almost immediately by a butler who stared down his nose at her in obvious curiosity.

"How may I help you?" he asked.

"I am here to call on Mr. Maxwell Crenshaw."

Apparently deciding that she and her maid appeared refined enough to invite in off the street, he stepped back and
let them pass. The inside of the house was even more ex-
travagant than the outside. Past the marble tiled entryway,
the floor sank a few steps into an actual jungle with all sorts
of leafy green plants, most of them she couldn't even name.
A skylight soared four stories above them, shedding light
through an intricate arrangement of leaded glass in soft
colors like powder blue, rose, and amber.

The grand staircase on the far side of the display was
completely made of marble and split halfway up to curve
both left and right to the first floor. A near life-size family
portrait of the five-member family held a prominent space
on the wall at the split, directly opposite the front door. It
must have been painted a few years back. Violet was obviously younger, and Max did not have the beard she loved so
much. But she was taken aback by how handsome he was
even without it. He had a strong jawline and a hint of that
serious scowl she loved so much, and his eyes seemed to
find her across the distance.

The butler cleared his throat in an obvious bid to garner
her attention. "I am afraid the family is not at home."

She nodded, ashamed to have forgotten her manners.
"Yes, I know. I am Lady Helena March." His eyes widened
the tiniest bit in recognition. "I have arrived from London
only this morning." She had taken long enough to get rooms
at the Fifth Avenue Hotel secured for herself and her maid
before hurrying over. "I came directly to see Maxwell, only
it occurs to me that he is probably at Crenshaw Iron."

"Yes, he spends most days there, but I'm afraid he does
not reside here . . . your ladyship," he added belatedly.

This wasn't entirely a surprise to her. She hadn't considered that he might have moved out of his parents' home, but
it seemed likely that he'd want to have his own space.

"Would you mind writing down his address so that I
may convey it to my driver?" She pulled out one of her call-

ing cards and offered it to him. She had hired a carriage for the day at her hotel.

He stared at her before hesitantly taking it from her. "I am happy to send someone to fetch him. I am certain that he—"

"No, please. I have a carriage waiting, and I would prefer to surprise him. He doesn't know we docked this morning." He didn't know she was coming at all, actually. She had left notes for both Violet and August but had begged them not to tell him. She wanted to see his reaction for herself when he saw her. It would tell her everything she needed to know in a way that his letters and telegrams could not. If he showed one inkling of doubt, then she would leave on the next ship bound for England.

Thankfully, the man smiled, his bearing easing to be involved in the tiny bit of subterfuge. "Very well, your ladyship. Your secret is safe with me, and please accept my congratulations on your betrothal. The entire staff here wishes you well."

Helena swallowed. Even though she had accepted similar felicitations over the past several months, it never got easier. "Thank you."

He nodded and hurried away, returning not a moment later with the address written on the back of her card. "Mr. Maxwell will be happy to see you."

Thanking him again, she hurried back out to the carriage, her stomach roiling with nerves as she told the driver to take them back to the hotel.

"Will we not be going to Mr. Crenshaw's home, my lady?" her maid asked.

"Not yet, Owen. He won't be home for some time, so there's no use in waiting there."

The young woman nodded and let her gaze take in Central Park as they traveled along Fifth Avenue. Even though Helena had suspected Max would not be home, her heart beat as if she had narrowly missed a collision. Now that she was here, she was almost certain this was a mistake. There was a difference between not knowing and merely suspecting, and she was certain she would prefer to exist in the realm of the latter.

Three hours later when the sun was setting, Helena ventured out from her hotel room to finally face Max. She arrived at his home off a pretty little square known as Gramercy Park at approximately seven in the evening. It was a neat and tidy neighborhood full of tasteful brownstones with a beautiful park in the middle. It suited him far better than the chateau on Fifth Avenue. After the driver helped her down, she asked him to wait for her. He agreed, and she stood to watch him pull the carriage off to a little side street. Only when he turned the corner did she gather the nerve to ascend the steps to the modest four-floor brownstone. She had left her maid back at the hotel, so she would have to face her fate alone.

It took a moment before a middle-aged man answered the doorbell. He was dressed well, but he had the look of someone who had hurriedly donned his coat. A white linen napkin was clasped in his hand, giving her the impression that she had pulled him away from his dinner.

"My apologies for interrupting. I was hoping to speak to Mr. Maxwell Crenshaw."

He stared at her as if he'd never seen a woman before, his mouth partially open in what could only be shock. She had taken pains with her clothing, selecting her most elegant frock in deep blue because it matched her eyes and her ring. The gown was just short of formal evening attire but could have passed for an elegant dinner gown.

"I am Lady Helena March," she added.

The man blinked and seemed to come to his senses. "Apologies, Lady Helena, I wasn't expecting you."

"No, I suspect not. I had hoped to surprise Maxwell."

"Oh . . . oh well, then . . . Would you like to come in? It's Thursday, and he has dinner out on Thursday, but you are welcome to wait for him."

The interior of the brownstone was decidedly masculine in dark woods and blue tones, but the furniture was light colored and the lines clean and uncluttered. It made her think of him and his many contradictions: firm but soft when he needed to be, severe but yielding.

She followed the butler to a drawing room facing the street and declined his offer of refreshments. She had eaten a light supper back at the hotel and could not imagine forcing more food down past the nerves swirling in her stomach. As she waited, she took a tour of the room, admiring the paintings, mostly landscapes, and the few pieces of decoration he had out on the shelves, marble miniatures of great works of art. She forgot what they were almost as soon as she inspected them. A steady rain began to fall, trickling against the front windows. A carriage clattered down the cobblestone street, setting her heart racing, but it continued past. She found a book on a low table on the far side of the comfortable-looking chair by the fireplace. A bookmarker stuck out the top as if he had been reading it only last night before retiring for bed. She sat in the chair and reverently ran her fingers over the title: *The Gilded Age: A Tale of Today*. With nothing to do but wait, she picked up the book and began to read.

Some time later, the butler poked his head into the room. "I believe Mr. Crenshaw has arrived."

She hurried to her feet and placed the book back on the table. The front door opened, and she could hear the man greet his employer and Max's reply, something about the rain—she could hardly make out the words over the buzzing in her ears. Straightening her shoulders, she hurried to the door of the drawing room, wanting Max to see her before the man could announce her presence. She made it there just as Max was taking off his rain-soaked coat, having already handed his hat and gloves to the man. He reminded her of the night he had come to her drawing room in the rainstorm. Rain dripped from the ends of his hair. Greedy for the sight of him, she let her gaze take in his wide shoulders, emphasized so beautifully in the frock coat.

The butler made to speak, but then cleared his throat and nodded in her direction. "You have a visitor, sir."

Max turned, his brow furrowed in surprise and not a little displeasure that someone would come calling so late, but the moment he saw her, his expression changed completely. His face went slack in surprise, and then joy lit his eyes. "Helena," he whispered as if afraid that she might disappear if he said her name too loud. Then he smiled, and her heart seemed to swell two sizes in her chest.

"I came to . . ."

"Could I bring refreshments for you and the lady, sir?" the butler asked.

"No, thank you, Charles. That will be all for the night," Max said without taking his eyes from her.

"Very well, sir." The man disappeared down the hallway carrying Max's drenched outerwear.

Once they were alone, she said, "Sir Phineas has made it known that he would be interested in a courtship." Why she chose to begin with that she didn't know.

His eyes immediately clouded. "You came all the way here to tell me that?"

"No . . ." She wrung her hands together before her. "I simply want you to understand that there are options."

His frown deepened. "Options for what, Helena? I don't understand."

Why would he? She hadn't actually said what she meant to say yet. "I told him that I was flattered by his affection, but that my heart belonged to another."

He let out a breath.

"I saw your letter before I left home." She rushed ahead. "I know that you might not feel the way that I feel anymore, which is why I wanted you to understand that I will be fine if you no longer . . ." She couldn't bring herself to say it. If Max refused her, she would not choose Sir Phineas, but he didn't need to know that.

He walked slowly over to her, but she held her hands up between them to stay him about a foot away from her.

"I wondered why I didn't hear from you," he said. "Thank you for coming to tell me in person. However, while I admire Sir Phineas, I would be obliged to track him to the ends of the earth if he laid one hand on you." He grinned.

She smiled, hardly able to believe what she was hearing. While relief flooded her, she had to ask, "You still want to marry me, even knowing there will be no children?"

His eyes, solemn and earnest, stroked her face. "I have thought of little else. I admit that at first there was sadness, knowing that we will never have children born of our love, but it doesn't stop me from wanting you. From loving you. I even made myself consider the children I might have with some other woman, and Helena, I cannot even imagine it. Those children are not mine because their mother is not you."

A sob lodged in her throat at how perfect his words were. She never expected him to not feel sadness. Indeed, if he did not, she would have to wonder if he had sufficiently pondered the prospect. She managed to stifle the sob, but not before a tiny sound slipped out. He moved to embrace her, but she stepped back against the doorjamb and kept her hand on his chest. He obliged her but only barely kept his distance.

"What about Amelia Van der Meer?"

"Amelia?" He frowned as if he hadn't heard the name for ages. "Violet's friend?"

"Yes, Violet said that you had begun escorting her. That she had advised her to come to an arrangement with you similar to ours to avoid going to London next month. If you truly wish her, then I will not stand in your way."

"Violet is making mischief. I haven't talked to Miss Van der Meer since she chased me around the ballroom at her parents' Christmas party."

"Are you saying Violet invented the story?"

He nodded. "I am saying that my sister has envisioned our marriage since June. I think she would say whatever it took to make it happen."

She couldn't help but feel relief. "And what of your . . ." She couldn't say the words, but she had no choice. "Your . . . mistresses?" When he looked at her as if she had lost her mind, she said, "I'm certain you must have women—"

"You little fool." He grinned and pulled her against him, his arms going around her so tightly she thought she might meld into him and that she might like it very much. "I haven't seen any woman since I returned. I keep telling you and you keep not believing that I only want you." He kissed her before she could respond to that, and her knees very nearly fell out from under her. His taste and smell were so familiar that she wanted to curl up in his arms for days. No, weeks.

"Then where were you?"

"At my club. Stupidly and regretfully at my club while you were here." He kissed his way down her neck before burying his face there, his breath coming in short, erratic pants. "I can't believe you're here." Finally, he pulled away enough to look down at her while still holding her against him. "You've come to marry me. Tell me you have?"

"I have, but I have a condition."

"God, anything." He smiled.

She stared into his eyes, hoping to convey the gravity of her meaning. "You will divorce me if you ever feel the need for a child."

His smile fell. "Never. It will never happen."

"But it might, Max. You have to promise that you won't let me stand in your way."

Taking her face gently between his hands, he said, "Don't you understand that you will always be in my way? Wherever I go, you will always be there. Whatever I do, you will always be there. You are a part of me, Helena, for good and for bad. And I am yours. I will never abandon you, and I will protect you always." She could get lost in the depths of his eyes. "For this to work, you have to feel that way, too. You have to be willing to fight for us. To fight for yourself."

All at once everything inside her cracked open. The walls and the fortress of cool civility came crumbling down, along with her every reservation. He was hers. He would be hers until her dying breath. She nodded through the sudden blur of tears. "I love you, Max. I don't think I was ready to acknowledge how madly I've fallen for you, but I am now. I want to be your wife. I don't want to live another day without you."

"Then there will be no more talk of divorce." It wasn't a question, but he raised a brow as he looked down at her.

Shaking her head, she said, "No, there will be no discussion of divorce."

He growled in triumph and swung her up into his arms and over his shoulder. She let out a shock of laughter. "Where are you taking me?" Though it was fairly obvious they were going upstairs because he was already on the second step by the time she found her voice.

"To my bed," he said, taking the stairs two at a time.

"But I have to go back to the hotel. My maid is waiting. Everyone will know if I don't return."

"Let them know." He smacked her bottom, and she let out a yelp at the same time a tremor of anticipation moved through her. "I'm keeping you captive here until I make you my wife."

Epilogue

Grow old along with me! The best is yet to be, the last of life, for which the first was made.

ROBERT BROWNING

TWO YEARS LATER

Y ou look as handsome as always," Helena said, rising on her toes and sliding her hands into Max's hair to pull him down for a kiss. Brushing her lips against his, she marveled at the way her stomach still tumbled pleasantly whenever she kissed him. "Don't be nervous."

He grinned down at her and brushed his thumb over her cheek. "I'm not nervous. Maybe slightly anxious, but not nervous." He glanced past her into the looking glass of their guest suite at Charrington Manor, Evan's ancestral estate, and adjusted his tie.

They had married a week after her arrival in New York two years ago and had never spent a night apart since. The wedding had been a small gathering of Max's friends and the Crenshaw extended family. Obviously, August, Violet, and their parents had been unable to attend, but all had sent their well-wishes. This was their first trip back to England, when the family would gather in a couple of hours for the christening of William Alexander David Sterling, August and Evan's firstborn and heir to the dukedom. While she and Max had exchanged frequent letters and telegrams with his sisters, his parents had been noticeably absent in their communication. When Max had succeeded in withdrawing Crenshaw interest from India, his father had raged and then took his wife on an extended tour of Europe.

The couple had only returned to London a few months ago, weeks after the birth of August's son. In that time they had taken pains to reach out to each of their children. The progress to repair the relationships was slow, but the gesture had garnered them an invitation to Charrington Manor for the christening. Max and his sisters were understandably wary of their parents, but Helena hoped this could be the beginning of their reconciliation. She didn't believe any of the siblings would have a particularly close relationship with them, but she didn't think it was a good idea for excessive animosity to linger.

"It's the first time seeing your parents in over two years. I think some nerves are appropriate." She ran her palms over his coat, smoothing out invisible lines.

He sighed. "I don't know why they have to be so damned difficult."

"They want to make amends." The letter that had arrived before she and Max had left New York had stated as much. "Perhaps their difficult days are behind them."

"This is my parents you're talking about."

She laughed and took his hand, lacing her fingers with his. "You're right. We can only hope for slightly less exasperating. But Crenshaw Iron is fully in yours and August's hands now, and we're wed. There's hardly any mischief they can get up to."

"We can hope." He brought her hand to his mouth and pressed a kiss to the back as he led her out of their room and toward the stairs where his parents waited in the drawing room below. The idea was to meet with them and his sisters briefly before setting out for the chapel.

The old manor house had been extensively refurbished since August had married into the family. The walls had been replastered and covered with fresh papering, the rugs were new and plush, and the hardwood flooring gleamed with fresh varnish and wax. Helena could hardly take the time to admire the work because her heart was like a wild thing in her chest. As the one who had advocated for this meeting, she felt responsible if it didn't go well.

Please let it go well.

The family was already assembled in the drawing room. Little Rosie's giggles bubbled out to greet them as a footman opened the door for them. The little girl was dressed in her finest pink gown and sitting on the knee of her grandmother playing with a colorful paper pinwheel the woman had obviously given her. Millie showed her how to blow it just so to get it to spin, and the girl tried then giggled again at her failed attempt. Violet and Christian sat on the sofa opposite them watching, Violet with a smile on her face, and Christian with a slightly more guarded expression. Mr. Crenshaw stood next to his wife and granddaughter, looking on fondly at the scene.

"Max. Helena." Millie was the first to catch sight of them, her smile widening.

Mr. Crenshaw sobered and straightened. Christian moved to take Rosie into his arms, tossing the girl up in the air and catching her to distract her and drawing more giggles from her. Millie stood and hurried over to them. "I am so happy to see you both." Tears shimmered in her eyes as she took Helena's hands and kissed her cheek before she moved on to embrace her son.

Max hugged her back. "Mother, it's good to see you."

She appeared overcome and reached up to cup his cheek. "You haven't changed a bit."

"Neither have you," he said.

It was true. The couple appeared virtually the same as the last time Helena had seen them. The only difference was Mr. Crenshaw had obviously made a complete recovery, having replaced the weight he had lost due to his illness. They both seemed to be in good health.

Evan and August had been standing near the window that looked out over the garden, but they approached now. August gave them a soft smile, but strain was visible around her mouth. She and Helena had stayed up late the night before ruminating over how the morning might go. Evan kept a hand on her lower back in silent support.

"Now that you're all here, I have something I'd like to say before we head over to the chapel," Mr. Crenshaw said. "Millie and I would like to thank you for including us in this special day."

Evan had moved to stand behind August, his hands on her shoulders and his expression somber. "You've always been welcome here," he said.

Mr. Crenshaw gave a nod of acknowledgment. "That may be true, but I think we can all agree things have been strained, to say the least. We bear responsibility for that. Our travels over the past year have made me reevaluate things." His wife walked over and took his hand. He squeezed it gratefully, and one corner of his mouth quirked upward. "Millie helped me see that I've been too narrow-minded these past several years. My drive to expand Crenshaw Iron . . . to see you girls settled . . . well, it made me lose focus on what matters. Family is more important than business. We raised you three with that principle and then forgot ourselves."

"Papa—" August began, but he held up his hand to stop her.

"No, it's important that I say this. I don't always agree with your decisions—in fact, I think it's clear that we have different philosophies about many things—but I should have listened to you. I raised each of you to know your own minds and to voice your opinions, and then I charged ahead with what I wanted.

"I know I don't deserve it, but I'd like a chance to get to know my grandchildren. To play some part in their lives before . . ." His lip quivered and he noticeably swallowed.

"Oh, Griswold . . ." Millie wrapped her arms around him and then looked at each of her children in turn. "He had another attack when we were in Lucerne last summer." August and Violet gasped, and Max stiffened at Helena's side, prompting her to take his hand again and tuck herself against him. "I didn't tell you because there was no point in worrying you. It wasn't as severe as the first one in London, but it helped us reconsider how we'd like to live the next few years. He has agreed that it's best to put his remaining stock in trust for the grandchildren and leave the business."

"But what will you do?" Violet asked her father.

"Before returning to London, we spent the winter along the Mediterranean. We thought we might buy a home in Monte Carlo and split our time between there and London," he answered.

"Have you truly recovered, Papa?" August was the first to move forward, reaching out to cover her father's hand.

He nodded and gave her fingers a squeeze. "I have a few years left as long as I get plenty of rest." Drawing himself up to his full height, he cleared his throat in a rare show of nerves and said, "The point is that I would like another chance, if you would grant me one. Another chance to be part of your lives."

"Oh, Papa." August hugged him, and Violet followed suit.

Max extended his hand, and his father grasped it. "I believe we can muddle through as long as we avoid the subject of Crenshaw Iron." Not only had Max pulled their company out of India, but he'd also created an employee relief fund that paid death and injury pensions among other benefits, which his father had seen as a step too far in conceding to worker demands.

Mr. Crenshaw smiled. "Perhaps we can."

Helena wasn't gullible enough to think there wouldn't be bumps in the road, but the relief that came over Max's face convinced her that this was the correct path forward. She didn't know if the parents could ever make things right again, but at least there could be a resolution to the fracture within the family. Admittedly, it was made easier for her by the fact that the older couple would be staying in Europe, while she and Max would return to New York where they had moved into Crenshaw House on Fifth Avenue. It had seemed wasteful to allow the home to stay empty. Now they used it to host the many fundraisers they held every year for the newly created Crenshaw Foundation.

Conversation continued for a few minutes, and then Evan's mother, Margaret, his sisters, and Camille joined them. Helena hurried over to greet them both, staying behind to spend a moment alone with Camille to discuss the London Home for Young Women. The widow had had a tough go of things after the death of her husband and the suspicion rumors had cast her way. To her credit, she hadn't appeared to let the rumors bother her and had held her head high since she'd been out of mourning. Not only did she attend social functions despite the whispers, but she also volunteered with the home, an endeavor Hereford most definitely would have forbidden. The home itself was thriving, and Helena had managed to open homes in Brooklyn and Queens based on the model.

"I'm so glad to see you," Helena said. "I hope you'll be able to join me for tea next week. I'd like to talk to you more regarding the vegetable garden idea you wrote me about. I think it could be a great addition to the school." Helena still sat on the board, though her role was more advisory.

"Of course. I'm excited to talk more with you." Camille's voice was light, but she glanced behind her at the closed door of the drawing room as she spoke, visibly distracted. "I . . . um . . ." She turned to face Helena again. "I'd love to speak with you. I thought a garden would give the children—"

"Camille." Violet hurried over to join them. "How are you?"

"Did I see Jacob Thorne out there?" Camille whispered, taking Violet's hands in what appeared to be apprehension.

Violet's brow rose in question. "Probably."

"He was invited?" Though she still whispered, Camille's voice sharpened in agitation.

"Of course he was. You know he and Evan are very close." Concern turning to amused inquiry, Violet asked, "Why? Don't you like him? I thought you were a member of Montague Club."

"No, it's not that." But Camille couldn't seem to stop herself from glancing toward the door again.

"Then what is it?" Violet leaned in.

Seeming to realize she had said too much, Camille released Violet's hands and straightened, pushing a strand of a hair from her brow. "Nothing, I was simply surprised. Excuse me, I must go say hello to August."

Helena stifled a laugh as Violet watched her friend cross the room through narrowed eyes. "That was odd," Violet said. "That *was* odd, right?"

"Very odd," Helena said. Just then the door opened and two gentlemen walked in, one of them Jacob Thorne. "Oh, this will be interesting."

Violet disguised her giggle by covering her mouth with her hand. Thorne's gaze kept going back to Camille as he made his way through the room, greeting everyone in turn. Camille, for her part, was very careful not to look his way even once.

"Well, it looks as if there is another couple in need of nudging."

"Violet! You will not interfere. That was very ill of you to taunt me with Amelia Van der Meer."

Violet laughed. "It worked, didn't it? Sometimes people are stubborn when it comes to what they want, and they need a little nudge." Wagging her eyebrows, she wandered off to commit mischief.

"Spoken like a true Crenshaw," Helena muttered.

Max quickly took Violet's place at her side and pulled Helena against him. "What is Violet off to do?" he whispered as he kissed her brow.

"After her success with us, she fancies herself a matchmaker now."

He chuckled. "Lord help them."

ACKNOWLEDGMENTS

My heartfelt thanks to all of the readers and reviewers who have loved this series from the very beginning. I love each and every one of your posts, tweets, and emails about my heiresses. Thank you so much for reading their stories and sharing them. A big thank-you to my author friends who have taken time out of their busy schedules to read my books. I appreciate all of your kind words and your shares. The book community is one of the most open and welcoming, and I'm so lucky to be a part of it.

Thank you to my agent, Nicole Resciniti, for your enthusiastic encouragement from the very first phone call when I said I might have an idea for a series about American heiresses. Thank you to Sarah Blumenstock, aka the best editor ever. You always bring out the best in my writing and your instinct for a good story is incredible. Thank you for championing my work and loving this series as much as I do. Thank you to the entire Berkley team for making my books sparkle and getting them in front of readers.

Tara, you have been there since my very first submission. I appreciate all the hours you have put into reading my work and offering the best feedback and, especially, the many hours of complaining and commiserating you've endured. You're the best. Laurie, you are an amazing cheerleader and friend. I wish I liked my writing half as much as you do. You help me see the bigger picture of the story when I get lost in the weeds and always have encouraging words. Thank you for being you. Nathan and Erin, this ride wouldn't be the same without you. You have been with me since that very first Saturday morning at Starbucks. Elisabeth, Janice, Jenni, Lara, Nicole, Seána, and Virginia, every writer needs a support system and I'm so grateful you are mine.

Finally, a big thank-you to my family. To my parents, you always encouraged me and made me feel like I could achieve anything I wanted. Every girl should have that in her life. To my husband and daughters, I appreciate all the ways you help me write and even some of the ways you interrupt me. Thank you for being exactly who you are.

Don't miss

THE DUCHESS TAKES A HUSBAND,

coming soon from Berkley Jove!

BLOOMSBURY, LONDON
WINTER 1878

Smile, but not too wide. Smiles in public are meant to be mysterious, not expressions of joy. Keep your shoulders squared at all times but always, always, remain demure. Chin tilted downward the slightest bit, darling. It wouldn't do to appear too confident. A wise woman knows her place is one of support and encouragement. When a suitor gazes upon her, he should see a prospective helpmate, someone who will assist in his life instead of forcing her own will. No one likes a headstrong woman.

Camille, Dowager Duchess of Hereford, closed her eyes, trying to block out the words. No matter how she tried to ignore them, her mother's advice always seemed to play in the back of her mind when she least wanted to heed it. As the only child of Samuel and Martha Bridwell, she had been raised to the most exacting standards from birth. Her mother had been fastidious when it came to her grooming, comportment, and even her friends. Her education had centered around the intricacies of both running a large household and navigating the treacherous waters of Society. Nothing had been more important to her parents than seeing her married well, and Camille had all these speeches memorized, having heard them relentlessly.

Unfortunately, her parents' ideas of married well had been vastly different from Camille's. She had valued kindness and affection, while her parents had valued social status. That was it. That seemed to be their sole requirement.

She opened her eyes and smiled at her reflection in the mirror before her, the muscles in her face responding from memory, curving her lips upward in a cold imitation of happiness. She hated this practiced smile. It made her feel aloof and untouchable. While it had its uses in London ballrooms, it was not what she needed now. She was at Montague Club not a mansion in Mayfair. The gaming club was for entertainment not social climbing. Something a bit more sincere would probably be better for her purposes this evening, though she honestly didn't know. She'd never tried to seduce a man before. Her stomach fluttered in nerves and perhaps a tiny bit of anticipation as an image of Jacob Thorne came to mind.

She let the smile drop and leaned forward to get a better look as she rubbed her fingertips along the bracket lines left behind in the fair skin on either side of her mouth, hoping to make them disappear. At twenty-three she wasn't old, but recent years had given her face a maturity that her mother had warned her against when Camille had last visited her in New York.

Haven't you been wearing the night cream I sent you?

Camille had lied and answered yes, but when she'd returned home to London, she had found another case of the fancy French jars waiting for her. At the time she'd been annoyed. She'd been in mourning for a dead husband whose loss she did not grieve, and her mother was already stressing the importance of marrying again. Well, Camille did not want to marry again. *Ever.* But now she rather wished she had started applying the night cream. Men liked women who looked young and fresh. The cream might help that, but there was nothing she could do about her eyes.

You poor girl, I know you say you don't miss him, but deep down I think you do. Your eyes are so terribly sad.

Camille hadn't bothered to correct her mother. Her eyes *were* sad, and she didn't really understand why. Hereford was dead and not around to control her life anymore. She did not miss him or his high-handedness. She was a wealthy widow with all the freedoms inherent in the position. Though the bulk of the money her father had transferred to Hereford upon their marriage had gone to his heir on his death, she had been provided a small pension and a London residence. Then, completely unprompted, her father had bought her an estate situated not far outside of London. She suspected he had been motivated by guilt but had never questioned him. So given that, she should be very happy, but there were her eyes, staring back at her and calling her a liar.

She smiled again, this time wider and with joy, revealing a row of mostly straight, white teeth, but her brown eyes did not brighten at all. Sighing, she sat back, thinking of all the women she had seen Thorne escort about the club and their easy smiles. It reaffirmed her instinct that he would like her better if she could smile more naturally, and she would have tried again, but the door to the ladies' dressing room swung open and a beautiful woman came sweeping in. She paused in surprise as soon as she set eyes on Camille. She appeared to be only a few years older than Camille with dark eyes and hair and a golden complexion.

"Well, well, well, you do exist." The newcomer smiled and took a seat beside Camille on the elongated ottoman that was set before the mirror and vanity. "Lilian Green," she introduced herself.

"Camille—" she began but the woman took over.

"Duchess of Hereford, yes, I know." Lilian Green's smile had no trouble lighting her eyes as she turned toward the mirror and leaned forward to adjust a hairpin hiding near her temple in her raven tresses. She was elegantly dressed in a modestly cut chocolate-colored gown.

"Dowager now," Camille clarified.

"Of course, Dowager." She paused, her sympathetic eyes catching Camille's in the mirror. "I am sorry for your loss, Your Grace."

Camille gave a nod of acknowledgement. "Please call me Camille. I'd prefer to have one place where my title doesn't matter." She hated the title, actually. It had brought her nothing but pain and frustration.

"Then you must call me Lilian. When Jacob told me another woman had joined the club, I was happy, of course, but then I never saw you here and I wondered if he'd made you up simply to placate me. I am always at him to bring on more female members and stop referring to it as a gentlemen's club." She chattered easily as she arranged other pins in her hair.

"You know Mr. Thorne well then?" There was no reasonable explanation for why the fact that Lilian had called him by his first name made her feel so heavy inside. Lilian seemed unaware of this fact as she pulled out a small cosmetic tin from the handbag dangling on a strap looped around her wrist and dabbed a bit of scarlet rouge on the apples of each cheek and her lips.

"Would you like some?" she asked instead of answering the question, holding the little pot out to Camille.

"Oh, thank you." Perhaps a little color would brighten her face. She put a dab of the cream on her fingertip and slicked it across her bottom lip. It was brighter against her lighter skin and blond hair, but she loved the effect. Usually she only wore neutral shades meant to subtly enhance her peaches-and-cream coloring, but the scarlet was arresting, drawing the eye immediately to her lips. She couldn't help wondering if Thorne would like it. Another swirl of anticipation swooped through her, prompting her other hand to press against her stomach.

"That color works well on you. And to answer your question, yes, Jacob and I know each other well. I'm a long-time member." Lilian winked and rose, adjusting her skirts.

It was absolutely none of her business, but she couldn't help but wonder if Lilian and Jacob were lovers. He had lovers. Camille knew that. She had been a member of the club for approximately three months and in that time she had seen any number of women arrive by the ladies-only entrance and greet him very warmly. Sometimes he'd offer his arm, other times he'd slide his hand around their waist and disappear with them into parts unknown and she wouldn't see him again that night. She couldn't say with reasonable certainty that he slept with *all* of them, but it was a fair bet that he'd bedded a few.

"How many women members are there?" Camille hadn't thought to ask when she'd filled out her registration form and paid the rather expensive dues. She'd joined because Hereford would have been appalled, not because she'd been trying to prove a larger point about equality of the sexes.

"A dozen, give or take, not nearly enough. I have to hurry off, but I would love to chat more. Will you be here another evening this week?"

Camille opened and closed her mouth when she realized she didn't know what to say. If Thorne rejected her proposition, then she couldn't imagine showing her face here again, but she didn't want to miss the chance of making a new friend. She didn't have many of those. Since coming to London over three years ago, she'd become *that American* because she could never seem to live up to the expectations of being Hereford's duchess. It had become the done thing to invite her to events only to sneer at her behind her back. Fellow American heiresses, the Crenshaw sisters August and Violet, were her friends but they were both happily married now and starting families of their own.

"Perhaps we could have tea one afternoon?" she offered.

Lilian's smile was genuine when she said, "I would like that very much."

They exchanged goodbyes and Camille was left alone. She didn't bother practicing her smile again, because it could quickly become a procrastination tactic. Either he was attracted to her and he said yes, or he wasn't and he said no. Taking a deep breath and letting it out slowly, she rose and brushed out invisible wrinkles on her skirts. She wore an emerald-green gown cut the slightest bit lower than modest and in the natural shape that emphasized the flare of her hips.

Pushing open the paneled mahogany door, she made her way down the wide corridor to the gaming room. It was nearly ten o'clock in the evening, which meant Thorne was probably there talking with patrons or dealing cards. He owned Montague Club along with his half-brother Christian Halston, Earl of Leigh, and their friend Evan Sterling, Duke of Rothschild. Both men were married to the Crenshaw sisters, so Camille had met him socially a handful of times. While she had always been charmed by his handsomeness in those social settings, it wasn't until she had joined Montague Club a few months ago that she'd found herself viewing him differently . . . as someone she might want to get to know in an entirely more intimate way.

The double doors that led to the main gaming room were thrown wide open, revealing a dimly lit but richly appointed space. Gilded sconces were set at intervals giving off flickering gaslight that was immediately absorbed by the dark wood paneling, creating playful shadows and an aura of intimacy. Aubusson rugs in dark red and gold matched the sofas and overstuffed chairs set in small groupings near the fireplaces on either end of the room. Rosewood gaming tables topped with green baize were scattered throughout the middle of the room. It was a slow night so only a few had men playing at them, while the rest sat empty.

As usual, the table where Jacob Thorne stood dealing cards was busy. He was well-liked and the club members seemed to gravitate toward him. He was as sinfully handsome as his half-brother, Christian, but not nearly as forbidding. They were both tall and filled out a frock coat nicely, but where Christian's smile seemed to hold an edge of cynicism, Thorne's was more open and friendly. That was partly why she had decided to approach him with her indecent proposition. He was kind and trustworthy. She didn't think he would laugh at her or brag to his friends, but even more than that, he was the only man who had turned her head in a long time. Since before her parents had introduced her to Hereford. Once she had met her future husband and reluctantly agreed to the marriage, she hadn't looked at men the same way. She'd begun to despair that she ever would again, but something about Thorne had her looking twice.

She studied him as she made her way around the tables to reach him. He was dressed as well as the men he entertained with nothing about him to indicate he owned the club and they were customers. His clothing was bespoke like theirs and had probably come from the same tailor. He was the son of an earl after all, though born outside of wedlock. He had been raised by his father and that aristocratic arrogance shown on his face and in his mannerisms, except he wore it more naturally than many. It wasn't conceit with him, so much as grace and charm.

His well-formed lips parted in a smile as he dealt another hand of Vingt-Un and made a joke she couldn't hear. The men at the table laughed as they added to their bets. Thorne picked up the deck of cards with a skill born from years of practice and tossed another card onto each stack. His hands were strong but graceful with long fingers and clipped nails. If all went to plan, he could be touching her with those very hands soon. She paused as a flush warmed her face, but it was too late. He'd caught sight of her.

"Your Grace." He smiled as the other three men greeted her in turn. "Have you come to join us?" he asked, his voice rich and smooth.

She swallowed and willed the butterflies in her stomach to cease their antics. She'd talked to him many times since joining his club, and tonight didn't have to be any different. Only it was. Fighting past her nerves, she took the chair at the end of the crescent-shaped table. "Yes, but I'm afraid I've never played the game before."

"Not to worry, Your Grace. We'll teach you, won't we, gentlemen?"

They murmured their agreement. A footman came forward almost immediately, bearing a small tumbler of her favorite whisky on ice. The service here was remarkable. Accepting it with a smile, she spent the next several minutes watching the men play. The game seemed easy enough, one simply tried to get the sum of their cards to add up to twenty-one without going over. It wasn't complicated. Finally, Thorne dealt her in, and she promptly lost the first two hands.

"Too aggressive," he warned her with a shake of his head when she asked for another card on the third round. The gaslight played in his thick black hair, and she wondered if it would be as soft as it looked.

"I'm not aggressive," she said.

"Stand on anything higher than fifteen," he instructed. "The risk is too high otherwise."

"Good God, Thorne, don't help her. You already win most hands; if you teach her to best us, there will no use in any of us playing."

She recognized the man who spoke as a young lord who had inherited his title a few years ago. Most men at the club had been a bit reticent about her presence; they accepted it but didn't embrace it. Their clubs had long been a refuge from female companionship. He'd been one of the few who had not been bothered by her.

"Come now, Verick, you can't be upset that a mere woman might best you?" she teased.

Verick grinned and said, "My male pride can only take so much, Your Grace, before it needs soothing."

She didn't miss the inuendo, but Verick wasn't who she wanted. She also didn't miss the way Thorne's eyes cut to him at the comment. A little whisp of pleasure flickered to life in her belly that Thorne would care.

"All right, I'll stand." Her cards added up to sixteen. The other men went over and she won by default. She smiled in satisfaction.

The game continued for a little while with her winning a few more hands before the men drifted away, leaving her alone at the table with Thorne. He handled the cards easily as he shuffled, his gaze flicking up to her from beneath a thick fringe of lashes. "Another hand?"

"Actually, I hoped we might talk a bit." She cleared her throat as it threatened to close. "In private," she forced the words out.

"Intriguing." He shuffled the cards and set them in the small tray on the table before placing his palms on the green baize and leaning toward her a bit. "It almost sounds as if you have a proposition for me."

She swallowed under the force of his gaze, letting her eyes take in the strong lines of his face to avoid meeting it. He had high cheekbones that any woman would kill for, and his nose was blade straight. "Of sorts."

"Shall we go to my office?" The inky slash of one brow rose in question.

No! That would be too intimate. What if he refused her and she was forced to sit there beneath the intensity of his stare? What if he said yes and expected to follow through tonight? It couldn't be tonight. She'd only concocted the

scheme over the last week. If he agreed, she would need a
couple of days to prepare herself.

"Perhaps semi-private would be best. One of the lounges."

He nodded. "Follow me."

Taking one last fortifying sip of her drink, she left it
there as she walked with him. He led her through the larger
rooms where a few groups of men congregated on leather
chairs talking politics to a smaller room in the back corner
of the club. A small fire roared in the hearth and bookshelves lined one wall. It faced a side street that was quiet
at this time of night and, though it was adequately lit, the
moonlight that came through the windows made it seem
more intimate than she would have liked. The door was
open to the nearby lounge, however, so they weren't completely alone.

"Will this do?" he asked, indicating she should take one
of the chairs before the fire.

"This is fine." She had to walk by him to sit and caught
the scent of his cologne, a very pleasing mix of sandalwood
and vetiver. She had admired it before but this time it made
her thoughts swirl in her head, or maybe it was because she
had to move so close to him. He was tall and broad, and the
very indecent question she meant to ask him made her
aware of how very large and solid he actually was. Her
breath hitched in a strange mix of fear and anticipation.

He waited for her to settle herself before he sat down
opposite her, his long legs stretching out before him as easily as if they were old friends convening for a visit. His
gaze searched her face, the firelight casting a sable tint to
his deep brown eyes.

"A drink for you, sir?" A footman materialized in the
doorway.

"No, thank you, Frederick."

The footman gave an abbreviated bow and left them
alone.

"So what is this proposition, Your Grace?" he asked.

"Camille," she said, but he didn't reply. He simply watched her with the corners of his mouth turned up in that easy way he had about him. That expression always seemed to say that he knew far more about you than you knew about him. "I've been having an issue . . ."

God, is that how she meant to ask him? To come to him as some sort of charity case in need of his help? To admit that something was wrong with her? Had she not once practiced what she might say in this moment? No, she'd been too focused on the goal to actually plot out a persuasive argument. Her heart pounded as her mind went blank.

How could she properly explain to him that she didn't understand why she never enjoyed sex? She was starting to believe that something was wrong with her and he was her last hope. But she couldn't say that. Of course, she couldn't.

He shifted back in a languid pose and clasped his hands across his stomach as he waited patiently. She had to say it now before she lost her courage. With tact not an option for her at the moment, she decided to be as straightforward as her pride would let her. Squaring her shoulders and raising her chin a notch for confidence, she met his gaze and said, "I would very much like to go to bed with you."

Ready to find
your next great read?

Let us help.

Visit prh.com/nextread

Penguin
Random
House